Berkley books by Thomas H. Block

FORCED LANDING
MAYDAY
ORBIT

FORCED LANDING

THOMAS H. BLOCK

BERKLEY BOOKS, NEW YORK

This Berkley book contains the complete
text of the original hardcover edition.
It has been completely reset in a typeface
designed for easy reading, and was printed
from new film.

FORCED LANDING

A Berkley Book / published by arrangement with
Coward-McCann, Inc.

PRINTING HISTORY
Coward-McCann edition / June 1983
Berkley edition / April 1984

ISBN 0-425-06830-7

A BERKLEY BOOK ® TM 757,375
Berkley Books are published by The Berkley Publishing Group,
200 Madison Avenue, New York, New York 10016.
The name "BERKLEY" and the stylized "B" with design are
trademarks belonging to Berkley Publishing Corporation.
PRINTED IN THE UNITED STATES OF AMERICA

Acknowledgments

I'd like to thank the men and women at Patriot's Point, South Carolina, and also the dedicated personnel of the United States Department of the Navy for their gracious cooperation with my endless requests. The following Naval groups deserve an additional salute: the staff of VP-8 at Brunswick, Maine, the captain and crew of the aircraft carrier U.S.S. *Dwight D. Eisenhower* (CVN-69) and, especially, to the captain and crew members of the submarine U.S.S. *Barbel* (SS-580). Thanks again for taking me aboard.

*To all those great people who work at
the world's greatest airline
and, of course, to EFB.*

The airplane has unveiled for us the true face of earth.
SAINT-EXUPÉRY

No matter how many miles a man may travel, he will never get ahead of himself.
GEORGE ADE

1

THE IRANIAN SUBMARINE *Sharaf* cruised nineteen meters below the dark surface of the Gulf of Oman as it maintained a southeasterly heading toward the Arabian Sea. With the Straits of Hormuz well behind them, the crew had settled into their normal routine. They were, at that moment, sixteen hours out of their home port of Abbas on a routine patrol scheduled to last twenty-seven days.

Hamed Ammar lay quietly in his bunk, his head propped by a pillow, his face slightly turned from the other man who sat at the writing desk a few feet away. Rather than face him directly, Ammar allowed his gaze to fix on the maze of pipes and wires that ran along the ceiling of the small box-shaped officers' cabin as he listened to the sounds that traveled through the old diesel-electric submarine.

The mild whir of the twin motors, the creaks and groans of the hull fittings, the low murmur of voices had been friendly sounds once. Now they seemed ominous, foreboding. Each voice had a cutting edge to it that penetrated Ammar's consciousness. The young Iranian lieutenant turned back toward the other man in the cabin.

"What you told me earlier is true," Mohamed Abu-Zeid said after he had regained his roommate's attention. "I also hear," he continued casually, "that the *komiteh* have begun to enforce the ban on public swimming." Abu-Zeid leaned forward, picked up a piece of baklava from the plate on the desk, then popped it into his mouth. "I have seen for myself, firsthand, the young girls being arrested for immoral behavior. They had done nothing more than laugh while they walked down the street."

"Unquestionably enough of an offense," Ammar answered bitterly as he raised himself from his reclining position. "The Khuzistan madmen," he hissed angrily. "They will bleed us like leeches. They intend for not even a small degree of happiness to remain. They will not be satisfied until we are a country completely without joy."

Abu-Zeid held up his hand nervously, then glanced toward the closed door of their tiny cabin as he listened for footsteps in the corridor. To their good fortune, there seemed to be none. Abu-Zeid sighed with relief, then turned to Ammar. "You should know enough to keep your voice low," he said in a barely audible whisper. "Captain Jaffar still makes his home in Abadan. He is well favored by the uppermost authorities in the *Pasdaran*. If Jaffar overhears, the council will have your name—and mine," he quickly added with a frown, "at the head of its next list."

"I only pray that Allah can spare us from the elite councils," Ammar seethed, although this time he had taken the precaution to lower his voice. "The cockroach eaters seem to have absolute control over every last one of the crucial meetings."

Abu-Zeid shrugged. Although he was half Arab himself, he agreed with Ammar in principle, that the Arab influence in Iranian culture had gotten out of hand. Unlike most of the remainder of the Middle East, Iran was predominantly Moslem without being Arab. The Iranian culture and roots were unique, the people different. But that had become an academic point. The Arab influence was now an unalterable and pervasive factor in modern Iranian life. "Nothing will be resolved by name-calling," Abu-Zeid finally answered.

Ammar swung his tanned, muscular body out of the bunk and leaned closer to the fellow officer who shared the cabin with him. "The *Pasdaran* is intent not on saving Persia, but on destroying it instead." The sound of that historic, archaic name for their country hung between the two men. It was, Ammar knew, the closest thing to an overt signal he could give to Abu-Zeid, who was the only one of the seventy-three men aboard the *Sharaf* he dared to approach, even cautiously. The decision on whether to tell him more—regardless of what the American had insisted on—would rest on his friend's next response. Ammar continued to look at Abu-Zeid expectantly, all the while attempting not to give away his actual concerns and intentions. No matter how good a friend he had been, too much hung in the balance for Ammar to say more until he could firmly gauge the man's true feelings and allegiances.

Abu-Zeid shifted in his seat, took another bite of baklava, then scowled at Ammar. "Exaggerations are very dangerous. Things are not so bad. This is simply another period of change, a time of turmoil. The passions on both sides will fade. The extremists will mellow. I know for a fact that the farmers in Azerbaijan have once again been given a free hand to make their own planting and harvesting decisions. Progress is slow but definite." Abu-Zeid then smiled broadly, as if to show by example that events in their country were not so bleak. It was, he was certain, too dangerous to believe otherwise.

"Perhaps." Ammar lay back in his bunk. He allowed his eyes to drift away from his friend's face and looked up instead at the curve of the ceiling where it conformed to the shape of the submarine's bulkhead. That was, he knew, the last chance for Abu-Zeid. It had come and gone. Ammar now had to work very hard to keep his true feelings deeply buried if he were not to have a problem in those crucial moments that lay ahead. He also knew that there had been a recognizable note of despair in his reply to Abu-Zeid, and he hoped that it had not been noticed. No matter how painful it was, the original resolution had to be followed to the letter. "Perhaps you are right," he lied. "Things are getting better. Slowly but surely."

"Slowly but surely," Abu-Zeid repeated as he nodded and smiled. He was happy to have this unnecessary turn in the conversation behind them. He rose from his chair. "And since we speak of getting better, what shall I say to Captain Jaffar? Has your stomach settled enough to allow you to join us in the control room—or shall I say that you require several extra days of rest and relaxation?" Abu-Zeid added good-naturedly. "We are somehow limping along without your talents, but I'm certain the crew would welcome a visit from you."

Ammar forced himself to smile. His eyes drifted away from his friend and toward the ceiling again. He stared at one of the paint-encrusted nameplates that announced, in English, what the source and purpose of that particular set of pipes were. Ammar felt that there was justice in the fact that this obsolete American submarine—purchased by the Shah barely one year before the revolution had deposed him—would be the key element in overthrowing the madmen and gangsters who had done so much to ruin Iran. Fate and irony—the plan had the handprint of God on it. "Yes. I feel better," Ammar said as he looked back at Abu-Zeid. "It must have been no more than severe indigestion. Tell Captain Jaffar that I'll be fit to resume my post in the control room shortly."

"Very well."

Ammar glanced at his wristwatch. "Are we still precisely on schedule?" he asked as nonchalantly as he could. "Do we expect to pass abeam the point off Masqat within the half hour?"

"Yes. Our progress is textbook accurate. The *Sharaf* runs as if Allah himself was in command." Abu-Zeid yawned, stretched his arms above his head, then reached for the door handle. "I'll pass on your information," he said as he began to step out of the cabin.

"Thank you."

"See you soon." Abu-Zeid stepped into the corridor that led through the center of the old submarine, then began to make his way aft.

Hamed Ammar watched as the door to his cabin closed, then sat himself upright. He looked down at his watch and allowed his eyes to be mesmerized by the smooth arc created by the sweep-second hand. *Allah is in command,* Ammar said to himself. *Allah is in command.* He believed that Allah would guide him because he so desperately needed to believe it. In less than five minutes, Hamed Ammar would begin the action that he had planned so carefully for during every waking moment of the last several months.

· · ·

Clifton Harrison's newly grown beard had begun to itch, and he scratched at it vigorously as he continued his rapid walk in the damp night air. He rounded the corner of a dilapidated warehouse, stepped down a rotting staircase and onto one of the numerous docks along the northern edge of the seaport town of Masqat in the Sultanate of Oman. After a few additional steps, Harrison could make out in the distance the man he had left stationed at the entrance to the pier. "Are they all aboard?" Harrison called out as soon as he was within voice range. Ned Pierce was known to be trigger-happy, and Harrison had no intention of being mistaken for someone else and winding up with a bullet in his chest.

"That's right," Pierce answered back in a low growl. He waited until Harrison stepped up beside him before he put down the .38 pistol. "That guy Moss was the last," Pierce added. "He went to get some extra radio parts, or something like that."

"Fine. What about the captain?"

"He went onboard a half hour ago."

"Give yourself ten minutes, then come down. We'll be ready to cast off by then. Be certain you give the captain back his pistol as soon as you get onboard." Without waiting for a reply, Harrison turned and began to trot quickly toward the darkened outline of the boat tied to the end of the dock. The aroma of salt air and rotting fish drifted over him, and he could hear the rhythmic lapping of the water against the wooden pilings beneath his feet.

As Harrison approached, he could see Zindell on the flying bridge of the fiber glass cabin cruiser. His big, bulky body was hunched over the chart table the two men had set up earlier, the pinpoint of light from its desk lamp bright enough to silhouette the stump where Zindell's left arm had once been. "Captain. The news is good," Harrison called out as he stopped at the edge of the pier and looked up at the one-armed man on the flying bridge. "I finally got through. The telephone message was waiting."

Jerome Zindell laid down the calipers on the chart and turned to face the man on the pier below him, a dozen feet away. "Was it exactly as it was supposed to be? No variations?"

"That's correct, sir. Exactly. The sub's right on schedule."

Harrison peeked at his watch. "We should shove off in ten minutes to keep ourselves within the limits of the mission profile."

"Very good." Zindell fumbled with the chart in front of him with his one hand for a few seconds, then glanced back down at the man on the dock. "Come aboard. Prepare to get underway."

"Yessir." Harrison could feel his heart pound with excitement. He climbed down the plank that led to the deck of the motorboat. As he stepped aboard, the lower cabin door opened. Olga stepped out.

"I thought it would be you," she said. "Is everything okay?"

"It's perfect. We'll be underway in ten minutes." Harrison smiled at her. "How are the men holding up?"

"They're restless. Anxious to get going."

"I don't blame them."

"Me neither." Olga Rodriguez laid her hand on her right hip where the leather bolas coiled into the loop of her belt. She turned to face Harrison more directly, her legs slightly parted. The light from the open cabin door poured out from between her thighs and cast two long shadows across the deck. "It's going to be one hell of a night," she said in a throaty whisper, the hint of a Spanish accent in many of her words. She was almost panting with anticipation.

"Yes." Harrison stared at her. Even with the light from behind, he could see that her shoulder-length red hair had been pushed back and tied with a scarf. It made her look different— but still as sensual as ever. She was not particularly beautiful, just incredibly sexy. The physical powers she possessed were a raw, vigorous gift that Harrison accepted gratefully. He knew that he could hardly control himself whenever she was around. He had given up trying.

Olga sidled up to him, a smirk on her face. "Better keep your hands off," she said tauntingly as she pressed her swelling breasts against his chest and pressed her left hip against his groin. "You know the captain's rule."

"Screw the captain," Harrison answered as he ran his hand down the front of her blouse. But he had the good sense to make his comment quietly, in a voice that no one beyond the two of them could have possibly heard. Harrison had no intention of violating any of Zindell's rules, not now, not ever. As soon as Harrison's hands had descended low enough to reach the top of Olga's pants, he dropped them suddenly to his sides as if they had been yanked away by invisible ropes.

"We'll have time tonight. After things calm down," Olga whispered as she nodded toward Zindell on the bridge.

"Right." But Harrison knew that Olga was wrong on at least one point. Things would never, for him, calm down again. He would never allow them to. The sensations of living life to its maximum—the dangers, the passions—were too exciting to allow them to fade for even a moment. As he glanced away from the piers and toward the blackness that he knew was the Gulf of Oman—the place where they would begin the incredible journey that Zindell was taking them on—Clifton Harrison wondered why he had wasted so many of his thirty-three years and why he had thrown away the last five in a Connecticut suburb and a New York office. No matter what Zindell had planned for them, it was one hell of a lot better than what would have happened if that imbecile of a Greenwich detective had figured out the truth any sooner. Being a married man, being a municipal bond trader in Manhattan seemed so far in his past that Clifton Harrison found it difficult to believe that he had ever done more than dream it.

Without needing to look again at his wristwatch, Hamed Ammar knew that it was time. He took a deep breath, then rose from his bunk and stepped toward the wall locker at the rear of his small cabin. Ammar fumbled with the key, his trembling hand making it difficult to fit it into the lock. He finally opened the locker and stuck his hand in, all the while listening carefully for footsteps in the corridor. There were none.

Concealed behind a stack of clothes were two metal bottles. Ammar took out the larger of the two, a green-colored cylinder with an oxygen mask attached. He slipped the bottle's holding strap over his shoulder, put on the oxygen mask and checked it carefully. Satisfied that the fit of the rubber mask against his face was airtight, Ammar reached into his locker for the second bottle.

The young Iranian lieutenant grasped the blue, spherical

bottle gingerly, as if it might be a volatile explosive. He knew quite well that no amount of physical roughness could make any difference to the bottle's contents, but that didn't matter: it was still too dangerous to be handled any other way. Ammar stepped up to the door of his cabin, paused for another moment to be certain that no one walked the narrow corridor, then opened the door and moved outside.

The narrow corridor was deserted, although ten meters away through the opened hatch, Ammar could see several of the crewmen in the forward torpedo room. Some were asleep in their bunks while others moved about in silence. Ammar's body was shaking so badly that he was sure his shipmates must hear his bones rattling. Surely they must hear the roaring that filled his ears. *Allah be with me!* Light reflected brightly off a row of brass fittings and valves at the forward end of the compartment, and Ammar could see one of the enlisted men in animated conversation as he leaned casually against the stack of torpedoes on the port side. He heard someone in that compartment begin to laugh, and several others joined in.

Ammar turned his attention to the tiny officers' wardroom, which was no more than three meters from the door of his own quarters. That was, if any place, where trouble would come from. It seemed quiet. Ammar glanced over his shoulder. No one was coming down the corridor from the other direction either, and the door to Captain Jaffar's stateroom—four meters from where he stood—was closed. That was as it should be. The Captain was undoubtedly still in the control room.

Ammar bent down and laid the blue spherical bottle on the linoleum floor. As he did, the oxygen bottle on his shoulder swayed to the right, and clanked noisily against the steel bulkhead. Ammar ignored the sound and, with sweaty hands, began to twist open the valve on the pressurized canister he had laid on the floor.

"What are you doing?!"

Ammar looked up. A figure stood at the entrance to the officers' wardroom. It was Mohamed Abu-Zeid, a plate of baklava in his one hand, a sheaf of papers in the other. His eyes had opened wide with astonishment when he saw the crouching man in the corridor, an oxygen mask strapped to his face.

Ammar felt a mixture of fear and dread pass through him as he watched his friend take a tentative step in his direction. He attempted to ignore Abu-Zeid and concentrate instead on the bottle at his feet.

"Hamed, is that you? What are you doing?" Abu-Zeid asked. "Is there trouble?"

Ammar blocked out the words. The valve on the bottle was tight, and it took a great deal of strength to turn it. As quickly as he could he twisted the valve on the blue canister several more times until, finally, he heard the audible hiss of the escaping gas.

"Stop!" Abu-Zeid suddenly lunged forward, uncertain of what was happening, but sure that it was something that must be prevented. The plate of baklava fell out of his hand and crashed to the floor, pieces of the shattered plate scattering up and down the corridor. Ammar stood bolt-upright, tripping over his own feet as he backed toward the wall. The hissing bottle of toxic gas lay on the floor between him and Abu-Zeid.

Abu-Zeid reached for the blue canister, but by the time he touched it his eyes were bulging and his mouth had opened wide. A progressive shiver ran through his body as he began to stumble forward, his hand pushing against the hissing bottle of lethal gas but doing no more than shoving it harmlessly across the floor. The invisible, odorless poison continued to pour out of its pressurized container.

Abu-Zeid fell facedown at Ammar's feet, his hands groping at his friend's pants leg several times before his fingers clutched enough of the cloth to hang on. For the next few seconds Abu-Zeid clawed his way to his knees, using the other man's leg as support. But he got no further than picking his head up and looking at Ammar's face, half hidden by the oxygen mask, before he fell heavily back to the corridor floor, his head banging hard against the linoleum. Abu-Zeid's eyes remained opened but lifeless; his tongue hung grotesquely out the side of his mouth.

Ammar stood rigidly with his back against the wall, Abu-Zeid at his feet. Rather than face the body that lay no more than inches in front of him, Ammar looked down the length of the narrow corridor. In the forward torpedo room, several of the men had already fallen to the floor. As Ammar watched, one of them—it appeared to be Chief Ardabeli—staggered past the opened hatchway, his hands clutched to his throat in a futile gesture against the inevitable. The man passed out of sight to the starboard side of the cluttered, steel-encased room. An obscene array of sounds—gasps, choked-off shouts, feeble cries—filtered back from the compartment. There were more than a dozen men in that area and, Ammar knew, every one of them would be dead within moments. There was no escape from the invisible demon that he had let out of the blue canister. Ammar closed his eyes and prayed to Allah as he waited for the lethal gas to finish its journey throughout the submarine.

Carried on the current of air propelled by the ship's ventilation system, the deadly gas drifted its way aft.

In the control room at the center of the ship, Captain Jaffar huddled over the navigation table. Jaffar heard a strange muffled noise and glanced up. To his amazement, he watched both Kani at the bowplanes and Rafsanjani at the hydraulic manifold collapse simultaneously, as if their legs had been suddenly cut from beneath them. Before Jaffar could respond, three more men on the far side of the control room also fell to the floor. None of them had shouted any kind of warning, and only one of them, Mellat, the electrician's mate, had managed to utter so much as a sound—a brief, strangulated gasp that sounded more animal than human.

Jaffar spun around and lunged for the panel on the corner bulkhead. He hit the emergency alarm button with his fist. The submarine filled with the noise of a loud and pulsating Klaxon horn. "Toxic gas!" Jaffar shouted as he pressed his hand against the All-Compartments transmitting switch on the ship's intercom. "Battery gas! Secure all compartments! Shut down the ventilators!" Jaffar felt a spasm of dizziness. His vision had blurred and his arms had weakened. *Chlorine gas. From the batteries.* Yet even as that thought registered in his mind, he knew that it was wrong. Chlorine gas was deadly, but it had an odor to it. It was visible. It was an unwanted but predictable by-product of the batteries they used to power the ship while underwater. Yet it was a condition they almost never experienced, and one they carefully monitored against. It was not possible for the chlorine gas . . . to have gotten this far . . .

undetected...this gas...was too toxic...was something...
something else...

Captain Jaffar sank to his knees, then crumpled to the floor.
He was the last man in the control room to fall unconscious.

In the crew's mess behind the control room, most of the
men were not able to pick themselves up from their seats when
the Klaxon alarm sounded—and those that did dropped immediately to the floor. In the crew's quarters, men fell from
their bunks as they attempted to move in response to the shrill
alarm. Those who remained mobile for a short while stumbled
over the bodies of those who were not, as they scrambled to
get away from the unseen enemy that was tearing out the insides
of their throats and lungs.

In the forward and aft engine rooms, men ran to their battle
stations only to succumb to the gas as quickly as they arrived.
Mohamed Mehdevis staggered along the guardrail between the
twin banks of diesel engines that had powered the ship on the
surface less than one hour before, his hands pressed against
his face in a futile attempt to stop the suffocating pains that
consumed him. Mehdevis lost control of the muscles in his
legs and, though he was still conscious, stumbled and fell
against the row of aluminum-colored cylinders. Within an instant, Mehdevis' face and arms were being seared by the re-
sidual heat in the metalwork of the engines. The smell of his
own burning flesh was the last sensation to register in his brain.

Abol Khanoum was at the electrical controls in the maneuvering room when the alarm began. He had heard Captain
Jaffar's orders over the intercom and had followed them to the
letter. He slammed shut the hatchway between the maneuvering
room and the aft torpedo room—the rearmost compartment in
the ship—and then had the presence of mind to pull out an
oxygen bottle and mask from beneath his seat.

Khanoum twisted the valve on the portable oxygen bottle,
then slid the mask over his face. Nothing. No oxygen. He
ripped the mask away and looked down at the pressure gauge.
Two thousand pounds. Full. Yet the bottle seemed empty. He
frantically rapped on the valve, then put the mask on again.

Still nothing. He was growing dizzy, light-headed.

Khanoum sank back into his seat and gazed blankly at the rows of dials, meters and maneuvering levers in front of him. Then he looked at the useless oxygen bottle in his hands. Full . . . yet empty. Suddenly he saw what should have been obvious all along: the gauge's pressure needle had been carefully bent clockwise so that a zero reading would keep the needle pointed to its full mark. Full *was* empty. Someone had depleted the ship's emergency oxygen bottles, then had tampered with the gauges on them so no one would notice. Someone . . .

Khanoum slumped forward and died. His body sagged listlessly and settled at the foot of the quadrant of levers that controlled the ship's motors.

In the aft torpedo room, the eleven men at that station had gotten the least amount of the lethal gas in their compartment before the hatch had been closed and the ventilators shut down. Aram Bactar pressed his face against the small glass porthole in the closed hatchway and peered forward into the maneuvering room.

Bactar saw Khanoum in the maneuvering room put on his emergency oxygen mask, and he then ordered the men in his torpedo compartment to do the same. Yet to his amazement, he saw that Khanoum had taken his mask off again and had begun to work frantically with the valve on the bottle. After several more seconds, the oxygen bottle slipped out of Khanoum's hands and the man fell unconscious.

"The bottles are empty! They indicate full, but they have no oxygen inside!" one of the men from the rear of the torpedo compartment shouted.

Bactar spun around. His face was covered with sweat. "Wait. Whatever has caused the toxic condition, it has been sealed outside our airtight hatch," he answered. His voice had been barely loud enough to carry over the incessant howl of the Klaxon horn. Bactar gestured toward the oblong steel doorway, the handle fully turned, the locking pins all in place. "We are safe."

At that moment, the submarine pitched forward, the deck beneath their feet inclined steeply toward the ocean floor. "The diving planes!" one of the young torpedomen shouted. "There is no one alive in the control room to work them!"

"The water is shallow—we are in no danger!" Bactar knew he needed to prevent the spread of panic among his men. "Once the ship has reached the bottom, we can utilize the emergency escape hatch." Bactar gestured toward the hatch in the ceiling. "It will not be difficult," he said as he prayed that no one would point out any of the hundreds of complications that could make their escape impossible. "At least we are safe from the toxic condition that has spread through the ship."

As if on cue, one of the men in the rear of the room fell to his knees and began to gag. Even while the others watched in horror, two more men collapsed. One started to claw at his face, the other emitted a shrill and hideous scream.

"Impossible—we are airtight!" Bactar shouted in defiance of what he now knew was the truth. Some of the poisoned air had gotten into the compartment before the hatch had been closed. Their fate would be the same as that of the rest of the men on the ship. "Get out, quickly!" Bactar ran toward the center of the compartment where the roof-mounted escape hatch was. He knew a hurried escape would be riskier, but there were no other options left to them. "There is no time for the safety procedures! Get out!"

Even as he moved the six-meter distance farther aft to get beneath the escape hatch, more of his men continued to collapse to the floor. Several of them writhed in pain as they tried to breathe in the chemically saturated air, the insides of their bodies seemingly on fire—yet numb as ice. Bactar reached the base of the ladder and began to push a young technician, Salar Fadl, up ahead of him. "Go! Quickly! Up to the hatch!"

Salar Fadl was halfway up the ladder when his arms gave out. He screamed a short howl of pain and fear as he tumbled backward.

Bactar tried to prevent Fadl's fall, but his attempt to grab the young man's body nearly cost him his own position on the ladder. The young technician fell past Bactar and then crashed onto the compartment floor below. Bactar looked down at Fadl's motionless body, then around the remainder of the aft torpedo room. No one stood. Most were motionless, except for a few men whose arms and legs twitched in obscene spasms. There was no one left to worry about. There was no one left but himself.

"Get out! Keep climbing!" Bactar spoke to himself aloud as he prodded himself farther up the ladder toward the escape hatch and away from the nightmare below. His foot slipped once, but he managed to grab hold of a section of tubing to prevent himself from falling. "Be careful. Not too quickly." The circular hatch was only an arm's length away.

Bactar felt the motion of the ship change. Perhaps someone had taken over control, perhaps the situation onboard the *Sharaf* was not hopeless after all. He paused for a moment as he tried to determine in which direction the ship was now pitched. But being inside the bowels of the submarine, without the help of the reference gauges in the control room, there was no reliable way to tell. Senses of motion were fraught with deception. Illusions were more real than reality. The loud Klaxon horn continued without interruption.

Bactar decided that there had been no change at all in the ship's motion, that he had simply deluded himself into thinking so. Even if there had been a change, more than likely the out-of-control submarine had simply been caught in a swirling sea current. The ship could be pointed anywhere from straight up to straight down, for all that he could tell.

Bactar pulled himself up the next step and into the escape chamber. He then turned around and reached for the lower hatch so he could lock himself inside the seven-foot steel tube that would serve as his escape route. Once inside that small chamber, he would flood it by opening the hand valve on the wall, then pop open the exterior hatch. By holding his breath, Bactar might be able to reach the surface—as long as the submarine had not gone much deeper than forty meters. Any lower, and he would drown before reaching the surface.

As Bactar bent over to close the lower hatch, the choking sensation he had seen in the others suddenly forced itself on him. With one breath of air, his insides had turned to pure fire.

A wave of intense pain washed over him and caused Aram Bactar to lose his strength. His arms sagged out of control and his legs buckled. He tumbled forward and fell past the lower ledge of the escape hatch. As he did, his left arm swung outward and hooked itself between the rungs of the aluminum ladder. Bactar's falling body, arrested by his left arm, snapped violently around and smashed into the frame of the ladder. The impact broke his shoulder and neck and caused Bactar to hang from the ladder like a bird with a grotesquely broken wing might hang from a fence. Yet for the few seconds that still remained to his life, he felt nothing beyond the horrid, unrelenting pain of chemical suffocation.

When Hamed Ammar had moved from the narrow corridor outside his cabin to the control room, he had done it carefully. Ammar knew that if the oxygen mask he wore were to be ripped away from his face—either by accident, or forcibly by one of the crew who had not yet fallen unconscious—then he, too, would die.

As Ammar entered the control room, the ship had begun to pitch forward violently enough to cause him to be thrown off his feet and against the bulkhead where the Fathometer and standby helm were located. The bodies of the officers and crew were strewn everywhere, but Ammar paid no attention to them; instead, he focused on the bow and stern planes and the large gauges in front of them. Fifty meters of depth were indicated for the rear of the ship, while fifty-six meters were shown at the front. They were being driven on a downward path that might cause them to crash, bow-first, into the ocean floor.

Ammar staggered to his feet and headed for the diving controls. As he moved forward, the hose from his oxygen mask became entangled in one of the wall-mounted trimming levers. It would have yanked the mask off Ammar's face if it were not for a sudden change of motion in the ship at that moment that forced him to stagger backward. Ammar grabbed onto the trimming levers, untangled his oxygen hose, then started toward the diving controls again.

Allah is in command. Inside his mask, perspiration dripped down Ammar's face. He tripped over the body of Kani, then stepped on Rafsanjani's outstretched hand. Death was everywhere. The carnage in the control room was far worse than Ammar had imagined it would be. *Allah stay with me, I beg you.*

Ammar grabbed the large brass wheel of the bowplane and

turned it quickly. Satisfied that the front end of the submarine was responding, he reached for the wheel that controlled the direction of the stern diving fins. When the gauges showed that the *Sharaf* had reversed its descent and had started up again, Ammar stepped around the bodies that littered the floor and began to work the trim and ballast levers. The Klaxon horn continued to bellow in his ears.

With the changes created by each successive valve he yanked open or shut, the submarine was jolted farther and more rapidly toward the surface. Ammar stumbled backward, then grabbed on and held fast to the ladder that led up to the conning tower, the oxygen bottle nestled to his chest, his face pressed against the ladder's rails so there was no chance that his mask might be taken off by the random motions of the wildly bucking ship. No more than an arm's length above him, a dangling hand— the dead helmsman's—swayed back and forth out of the opened hatch between the control room and conning tower on the deck above. Ammar fixed his eyes on the man's fingers—long, nicotine-stained, motionless except for the swaying of the ship— as he waited for an indication that the submarine had broken through to the surface.

There was no doubt when that moment came. The *Sharaf*'s extreme pitch-up angle caused the bow to break through the top of the waves like a rocket. As fast as the front end came out, it crashed back to the surface of the sea just as quickly. The force of that impact caused the lights inside the ship to blink on and off several times, but they finally remained on. Ammar was thrown to the floor, even though his hands still gripped the rails of the conning tower ladder.

When the gyrations stopped, Ammar picked himself up carefully, then looked around. The gauges on the panel told him that the ship was buoyant, seaworthy and riding on the surface. He could see that his oxygen hose was still intact, his face mask firmly on. Ammar attempted to gather his thoughts and recall the next step in the plan, but the loud Klaxon alarm seemed to drive his memory away. He stepped toward the rear of the control room, across Captain Jaffar's body, and pressed his shaking hand against the switch that silenced the alarm.

Except for the distant humming of the twin electic motors

from the rear of the ship, the interior of the *Sharaf* became deadly quiet. Ammar could hear the loud echoes of his own labored breathing in the oxygen mask as he positioned several more switches and levers in the control room. Satisfied that all the necessary work had been accomplished, he climbed the ladder into the conning tower, then farther up another set of rungs to a hatch at the top of the roofline. After working the bolts and catches, Ammar gingerly pushed against the circular steel plate above his head.

The night sky was above him. Some of it was masked by the superstructure of the bridge, but other sections were brilliantly studded with stars. There was a half-moon on the horizon, and Ammar knew it would provide enough illumination for what was still to come. He propped open the hatch and paused for a moment, his body half inside the conning tower and half out in the night air on the bridge. As much as he wanted to go topside, Ammar knew that it was not yet time. Reluctantly, he checked his oxygen bottle again, then descended the ladder to finish the jobs that remained.

Ammar moved through the conning tower, down into the control room, then turned and worked his way aft. He kept the oxygen bottle and hose pulled tightly against his chest as he maneuvered around the bodies that lay in the compartments. The enlisted men's galley, the mess and crew's quarters were nearly impassable, and Ammar worked his way slowly around each knot of bodies, some piled one on top of the next, others scattered side to side. He was glad that he had taken the precaution to remain aloof from most of the crew, that he had hardly gotten to know any of them except in their official, technical capacities.

Ammar hustled through the forward and aft engine rooms and into the maneuvering room. When he reached the end of that compartment, Ammar leaned over the body of Abol Khanoum and yanked back on the large silver maneuvering handles. The sound of the twin electic motors that propelled the ship began to slow down and die. Ammar stood quietly for a moment, until he felt the gentle rocking that told him that the submarine had come to a complete stop and was now dead in the water.

Ammar opened the hatch that led to the aft torpedo room. He took several steps toward the center of the compartment before he became aware of the body that dangled from the ladder beneath the emergency escape hatch. Aram Bactar. Ammar winced.

Other than Abu-Zeid—his roommate and a fellow junior officer—Aram Bactar was the only enlisted man he had felt close to. They had been raised in the same section of northern Tehran and had discovered, through conversation, that they had several friends in common. Ammar was suddenly flooded with guilt at the thought that he should have approached Bactar, that he should have given him a chance to be part of the plan. *Allah, I pray to you, do not desert me.* Ammar grabbed Bactar's arm and removed him from where he had been pinned. The skin on Bactar's arm was still warm and, as he touched it, Ammar shivered. He laid the body gently on the floor, silently spoke the first few words of the prayer for the dead, then opened his eyes and climbed the ladder. He raised the exterior hatch to allow the cool night air to blow in.

Ammar retraced his steps back to the control room, but this time continued straight ahead down the corridor to the forward torpedo compartment. He opened the emergency escape hatch on that end of the ship, then headed back to the conning tower where he picked up a battery-operated searchlight and clipped it to his belt. He climbed above-decks to the bridge.

After checking the compass, Ammar aimed the portable light and flashed it several times utilizing the designated code. As he waited, he glanced around the dark silhouette of the ship. The *Sharaf* rode well, with no apparent lean. That meant that all the proper ballast tanks had blown dry, as they should have. Ammar looked down the deck to where the forward hatch stood raised. With three exterior hatches opened, the poisoned air would soon be drawn out. That was good, although Ammar had no intention of taking off his mask until the American had shown up with his test equipment and verified that the air inside the submarine was no longer dangerous.

Ammar flashed the light several more times. He was about to repeat the process when a light on the horizon blinked back the recognition code he had been waiting for.

* * *

"There it is. Steer ten degrees to port. Have the men put on their masks." Zindell then began the clumsy task of fastening his gas mask with one arm.

"Yessir." Clifton Harrison spun the cabin cruiser's steering wheel, then turned back to where Olga stood behind him on the bridge. "Have the men put on their masks."

"Right." She moved rapidly down the ladder and disappeared below.

Harrison waited for Zindell to finish fastening his mask before putting on his own. It would be difficult to communicate with each other with the masks on, but no verbal communications would be necessary from that point on—not unless something had gone terribly wrong. The script for the next few moments had been carefully rehearsed dozens of times. Harrison felt a clump of tense excitement in the pit of his stomach; he could hardly wait until they pulled up alongside.

They were within a few hundred yards of the submarine before its dark shape was clear enough to be unmistakable in the dull glow of the moonlight. For a brief moment Harrison was totally awed by the immense vessel that lay in the water ahead of him. He had never seen a submarine up close, not even an old diesel boat like this one. Harrison knew from his homework that the sub was nearly 300 feet long and weighed 2,700 tons. Lying dead in the water, its black-painted hull riding high in the light, choppy sea, the submarine seemed even larger and more threatening. Harrison reminded himself once again how this entire experience was literally a world removed from what he had learned as a navigator in the Air Force five years before. He hoped to God that he wouldn't screw up any of his assignments.

Several of the men had come from below and stationed themselves along the smaller boat's rail. As the cabin cruiser maneuvered in close, the men threw out their lines. The sole figure on the deck of the submarine—one man wearing an oxygen mask, the portable bottle draped over his shoulder— grabbed the lines and tied them fast. Without a word being spoken, the men jumped quickly aboard the deck of the submarine.

Jerome Zindell was one of the first to go aboard. He stood on the teakwood decking of the old submarine, just forward of the dark superstructure of the bridge. His portable oxygen tank was strapped to his back and his one arm rested casually against his hip as he slowly surveyed his new command. He took a few seconds to allow the old memories—his days on the *Trout*, the *Wahoo*, the *Harder*—to play back in his mind. It was the better part of a lifetime that he had spent inside those old sewer pipes.

Even in the washed-out light from the half-moon, Zindell could see that the boat had fared well after its years in dry dock and its eventual sale to the Iranians. That was another testimonial to the strength of the old hulls, another vote of support in his decision to use this particular ship. Zindell turned and motioned toward two of his crew.

Olga Rodriguez and Ed Wieckowski came forward, each of them holding a small metal cage in one hand, a portable oxygen bottle in the other. Zindell carefully examined the cages they held. Inside each were two gray pigeons, and all four birds fluttered nervously. Zindell glanced at his wristwatch, nodded his approval, then pointed toward each of the hatches he wanted Olga and Wieckowski to go to. The two crew members held the cages at arm's length in front of them as they moved rapidly toward opposite ends of the ship.

Hamed Ammar stepped out of the shadows and moved next to Zindell. Even beneath his oxygen mask, it was easy to see the sheepish, anxious look on the Iranian's face.

Zindell smiled, patted Ammar on the shoulder, then held up one finger to indicate that they'd need to wait another minute before they could speak. Ammar nodded eagerly to show his understanding.

After what seemed an interminable delay, Olga and Wieckowski finally came out of the hatchway in the bridge, she a few seconds ahead of him. They carried the cages down to Zindell.

Zindell looked at his watch, then examined the birds again. All four were still alive and continued to jump nervously in their cages. Zindell removed the oxygen mask from his face, and the others in the crew did likewise.

"Carry aboard the supplies. Remove the bodies." At his command, the eight seamen in his crew started into action to unload several wooden boxes from the cabin cruiser. "Prepare the boat," Zindell said to Harrison, who had remained on the flying bridge.

"Yessir." Harrison disappeared below.

Zindell turned to Olga. "Take care of the birds."

"Certainly." Olga smiled, reached into her birdcage and grabbed for the first pigeon. The bird fluttered away from her groping hand several times, but Olga persisted. Finally, she caught the gray pigeon and wrapped her fingers tightly around it.

Olga withdrew the bird slowly from its cage and held the frightened animal at arm's length. She then carefully reached out with her other hand and took hold of the pigeon's head. With a slow and continuous motion, Olga snapped the bird's neck until it cracked, then casually pitched the carcass overboard. Olga repeated the action with the other three birds. The glaze in her eyes and her short, quick breaths gave away the pleasure she took in her task.

"I expected a more scientific testing of the air," the Iranian said as he turned away from the woman and toward the one-armed American. He smiled meekly to indicate that there was no malice in his statement.

"The old methods are sometimes best. Test life with life. It's a good technique."

"I see." But the Iranian didn't understand. He knew from past experience that Westerners were always difficult to talk to—and his previous conversations with this man during those meetings in the back alleys of Tehran and Abbas had confirmed that he would be no exception. "The gas performed exactly as you predicted," Ammar said after a brief silence.

"That's good to know. I'll tell my supplier."

The two men lapsed into silence again, the rhythmic slapping of water against the hull and the movement of the men below-decks the only sounds to fill the empty night air. "Were there any problems?" Zindell asked to pass the time as he began to walk slowly aft.

"None," Ammar answered as he followed in the American's footsteps. "It went as you had planned." Ammar left no doubt from his tone that he would prefer not to discuss the horror that had taken place just a few minutes before. "At least now the madmen in Khuzistan will get a taste of their own medicine," he volunteered as he steered the conversation to a subject he was more comfortable with. "Soon we will be able to sink their patrol boats. Then we can block all shipping from entering Iranian ports." Ammar's voice had grown loud and firm again; it carried boldly on the warm night breeze. "That will bring the cockroach eaters to their knees."

"Right." Zindell watched as the first of the bodies were brought above-decks. With Olga supervising, the crew began to pitch the dead Iranians overboard. Their bodies sank immediately, but pieces of their clothing—caps, shoes, torn segments of shirts, pants and jackets—floated on the surface. Zindell was glad to see it because that was what he had expected—the floating scraps of clothing would add a nice touch to the display, an appropriate amount of evidence to support the obvious conclusion to anyone snooping around that the submarine had, for unknown reasons, torn itself apart.

"But I must be truthful," Ammar said. "I am surprised at two things; first, that your crew is so small in number. Second, that you have allowed a woman aboard the *Sharaf*." Ammar pointed to where Olga stood.

"This is only half the crew. We pick up the rest very soon." Zindell had given the Iranian what he knew he would want to hear. "As far as the woman is concerned, she is our nurse."

"A nurse? Then what in Allah's name is that device she wears on her belt?" Ammar pointed to the leather implement that hung from the woman's hip, next to the pearl-handled knife that also dangled from her garrison belt.

"A bolas."

"I have never heard of it." Ammar looked again at the device that the woman wore. Three strands of rawhide equal in length hung from its central core, each strand attached to a metal ball that would fit into the palm of a person's hand.

"The bolas is from South America."

"I see." Ammar had no idea what its specific use was, but he could tell that it must be a weapon of some sort. "What is its purpose?"

"It's part of her equipment." Zindell glanced toward the cabin cruiser and saw that Harrison had climbed off. That meant that the next step in the plan was about to begin. "Our nurse carries the bolas at my request. It's good for back problems— it gets people off mine."

"What does that mean?" Ammar forced his voice to become firmer as he attempted to sound more like the officer that he was. He would not take insults from any man—especially a foreigner—and the American's words had a mocking tone to them. "Is this some sort of joke?"

"Yes." Zindell flashed a friendly smile. "A small joke." He shrugged. "The fact is," he whispered as he leaned toward Ammar, "that the lady is the third in command. She uses the bolas to enforce discipline. Other than my own pistol, we have no small-arms weapons aboard. For obvious reasons." Zindell knew that in a pickup crew like this one, tempers could easily flare. He had no intention of allowing an underwater gun battle to occur.

"Can she control the men?" Ammar asked incredulously. No Iranian woman would have dared to even try.

"No question about it." Zindell had several times seen Olga use both the bolas and the pearl-handled knife while he was with her in Cuba, and he knew for a fact that it would be more than enough.

"Very well. If you say so." Ammar turned his attention away from the woman and toward the problem that was much more of an immediate concern to him. Technically, as far as he was concerned, Ammar felt that he should be in full command of the *Sharaf*. That would make the one-armed man second in command, and the woman as third. Perhaps, he hoped, there would be no problem with the American after all, that they had all come to realize that the problems in Persia must be left under the direction and control of a Persian. Ammar could not imagine that the American CIA could have expected any other arrangement.

Zindell turned away from the Iranian and faced Harrison. "Go ahead with the scuttling," he ordered.

"Yessir." Harrison cast off the lines. With the cabin cruiser's throttle set and the rudder prepositioned, the unmanned fiber glass boat pulled slowly away from the submarine. When it had gone no more than fifty yards, it was evident that the cabin cruiser was already riding measurably lower in the water. By the time the small boat had traveled another hundred yards, its deck was awash. Soon the fiber glass boat began to heel to one side, then toward its stern. Sixty seconds after that, it had disappeared completely and silently below the dark waves of the sea.

"That was very fast," Ammar said. He pointed to where the cabin cruiser had gone down, where now only bubbles remained. "No debris."

"That was the plan." Out of the corner of his eye, Zindell saw the gesture from Harrison. The supplies were already onboard and in another five minutes all the bodies would be removed. "We installed a large sea vent on the bottom of the hull so it could be opened and flooded quickly. We didn't want any wreckage—pieces of fiber glass that hadn't come from a submarine—left for people to get suspicious over."

"What difference would it make? The world will know soon enough that the *Sharaf* has become part of the action to liberate Persia."

"Soon enough does not necessarily mean this very moment. We may need a few extra hours or even days to get ourselves ready for the first attack," Zindell answered patiently, his rehearsed lines coming out easily and convincingly. "By the way," he continued, simply to fill the remaining time, "what does *Sharaf* mean?"

"Honor." Ammar averted his eyes from the American's stare and toward the dark sea. An officer's cap—Abu-Zeid's perhaps—floated on the crest of a swell several meters in the distance, its bright metal emblem making it easy to see in the reflected moonlight. Ammar shifted his weight restlessly as the pangs of guilt returned. He pushed the gnawing thoughts aside with the knowledge that Allah had been behind the plan, that the death of his friends on the *Sharaf* was indeed a small price to pay for the liberation of Persia. Allah would explain it to them and they would understand. They would commend Hamed for his brave fight to free their beloved Persia.

"This boat was originally S.S. 566," Zindell announced. He looked at the dark outlines of the bridge—a place where he had stood many times before. "I served as engineering officer on her between the summer of sixty-six and the fall of sixty-seven."

"Really? I was not aware of that." Ammar knew the ship had been American, but it never occurred to him that the one-armed man might have served aboard it. That was good news, since his knowledge of the ship might be useful.

"She was named the *Trout*. We spent most of our patrols in the North Atlantic. From that assignment I went to the *Wahoo* as executive officer." Zindell glanced down at his wristwatch; he gave himself a few more moments to wallow in this harmless nostalgia. "My first command was S.S. 568. The *Harder*. One hell of a boat."

Ammar fidgeted. In spite of the one-armed man's assurances, any discussions concerning command were still too delicate to be dealt with directly. He needed to wait for a more opportune moment to bring up the subject. "The *Sharaf* is a fine ship also."

"Yes. The *Trout* is a fine boat." Zindell bit into his lower lip at his slip of the tongue that the submarine they stood on was, for him, still the *Trout*. Yet as far as he was concerned, ships were more like men than women; the name you began with was the one you finished with. Continuity. Historical ties. The Navy usually felt the same way, because when a sub was lost they would build a new one with the same name. Usually. But not for the *Thresher*. It was as if nothing had happened to that nuclear boat, as if his father and the other 129 men aboard on that April day in '63 had not died a horrible death below.

"Which ship did you say was your first command?" Ammar asked. He decided that the more often he brought up the subject, the easier it would be to create a discussion of that sensitive point later on.

"S.S. 568. The *Harder*." Zindell would have preferred that particular boat for this job, but since the *Harder* had been sold to Italy he was left with little choice. With Iran officially on the outs with most every nation, no one would listen if they complained about a missing submarine. More than likely, the Iranians would admit nothing so as not to lose face. That was a little extra insurance.

"When will the additional men be along?" Ammar asked as he looked out toward the black horizon. "Will McClure also be with them?" He thought back to his meetings with the strange man from the CIA he knew only as McClure. Ammar shuddered. There was something hideous about McClure's smile and the way his eyes moved so coldly, so slowly across whatever he watched. Ammar hoped that McClure would not show up.

"Yes, he'll be on board with the second group," Zindell said, even though he knew it wasn't true. He glanced at his wristwatch. "They'll be here very soon." *McClure*. Zindell wondered what the hell that madman was doing at that very moment. Probably sitting by himself in the corner of some dingy New York bar and emptying one tumbler of straight bourbon after the next. He was a real psycho by anyone's standards—and the only one who could've come up with a scheme as crazy as this one. If McClure hadn't volunteered to take the most hazardous part for himself, Zindell never would have joined up with him. "Do you still have your signal light with you?"

"Yes." Ammar pointed to where it hung from his belt.

"Fine. Aim it in that direction." Zindell indicated starboard with his hand.

Ammar frowned and opened his mouth to protest, but then quickly decided against it. He would tolerate the American's orders a short while longer, until all the men were aboard and the submarine was safely beneath the surface. Then he would make it very clear who was in charge and who would give the orders. "In this direction?" he asked through clenched teeth.

"Yes. Use the same recognition code. We should be seeing them shortly. I'll check with my radio man to be sure that he hasn't picked up any signals from other ships in the area. We don't want any surprises."

"I'll let you know as soon as the signal light is acknowledged." Ammar aimed the searchlight and turned it on. The narrow beam of artificial light shone out across the gentle swells of the dark sea and mixed in with the silvery cast from the half-moon on the horizon. "The sooner we get them aboard, the sooner we can begin our attack against the criminals who control Persia."

"My sentiments exactly." Zindell pressed the palm of his hand against the .38-caliber pistol in his pocket. "I'll be right back."

"Very well."

Zindell stepped rapidly around the conning tower, then up metal rungs and onto the bridge. Satisfied that everyone else had gone below, Captain Zindell descended into the conning tower and quietly closed the hatch above his head.

Ammar flashed the light across the dark sea several times before a loud metallic banging filled the night air, followed shortly by a second, similar sound. He turned and pointed his light toward where the first sound had come from. Nothing was there, the deck remained deserted, all was well—except...

Ammar spun around and shined his light aft to verify what his pounding heart now told him: both the forward and aft escape hatches had been slammed shut. He had been locked above-decks.

Impossible! Ammar dropped the searchlight and bounded up the rungs that led to the bridge. As he jumped onto the upper level, he saw in the moonlight that even that hatch had also been closed. As Ammar raced toward it, he heard the familiar gurgling noises from the *Sharaf's* ballast tanks. The tanks were being flooded with water; the submarine was about to dive.

"Stop! Open the hatch!" Ammar yanked senselessly against the locked steel plate that had been intentionally closed to him. "Please! In the name of Allah! Open the hatch!"

Ammar saw the first waves break over the bow. The submarine had begun to settle slowly into the sea, its forward motion almost nil so the ship would remain at nearly the same spot it had been for the last thirty minutes. Ammar tugged twice more on the locked hatch, then scurried toward the aft area of the bridge. The American had tricked him—but Ammar saw no reason why. None of it made sense. Without him, any attack against Iranian ship movements would be more complicated, not less. Ammar knew that he was a necessary element in the struggle to liberate Persia. The American's action was unexplainable, insane—unless there had never been a plan to attack Iranian shipping, unless it had all been a trick, unless...

The water had completely covered the teakwood deck and had begun to slap farther up the sides of the bridge. Ammar climbed another set of rungs and then another, until he was perched atop the highest structure of the submarine, the lookout's platform. Ammar could see some of the bodies of the dead crew of the *Sharaf* as they began to float up from the cold water below. The sea itself, a flat plate of unrippled silver when viewed toward the glow from the half-moon on the horizon, seemed to be churned up by isolated movements in several spots. It took Ammar a few seconds to realize that the eerie forms that sliced through the calm of the silvery surface were dark, triangular fins. The numerous fins from an encircling school of sharks cut closer and closer to where Ammar would soon be in the water.

"Allah! Save me! Help me!" Ammar screamed as the last of the *Sharaf*'s superstructure slid into the water. The young Iranian officer let out a long, night-splitting howl as he found himself treading water. He thrashed around wildly in the cold, becalmed sea as he twisted first one way and then the other in a senseless, futile attempt to save himself.

Ammar felt something bump into his left shoulder. It caused him to scream long and hard again as he desperately paddled forward as fast as he could from whatever was behind him. When he finally looked over his shoulder, Ammar saw that what he had bumped into was the body of one of the dead crewmen that had been borne up from below by the buoyancy of the cold seawater. But at the same time, something else in the distance caught Ammar's attention—something that caused him to begin to scream irrationally again, this time without any way to stop himself, without any hope for a pause. Less than twenty meters from where he was treading water, Hamed Ammar could make out through the phosphorescent glow of the water the hungry sharks that were coming toward him.

2

VICE ADMIRAL E. G. HASTINGS turned around slowly as he took in the view from the center of the flight deck of the aircraft carrier *Yorktown*. "You've done a hell of a job," he said. "Even the deck surfaces look perfect. I noticed on my last inspection that some spots had begun to erode badly."

"That's correct, sir," Paul Talbot answered as he nodded in agreement. "In this case, the restoration wasn't purely cosmetic. An irregular deck surface is dangerous to the visitors." Talbot gestured toward a group of schoolchildren who marched across the deck a dozen feet in front of them.

"Yes. Of course." Admiral Hastings tilted his head back and took another look at the Island's superstructure. Satisfied that nothing had been added to the old warship to diminish its dignity—that was the official purpose of his periodic visits—he began to walk slowly toward the string of yellow arrows painted on the deck that marked the route of the *Yorktown*'s self-guided tour. "I have to give you high marks for your attention to detail. Of all the vessels under my jurisdiction, the *Yorktown* is the best."

"Thank you. I've got good people." Talbot squirmed slightly, then changed the subject. "With the State behind the project, it makes this a great deal easier."

"The radio station, too." Hastings pointed toward the glass-enclosed area thirty feet above them on the aft side of the bridge. "Placing the State-owned public broadcasting station up there was a good utilization of space. I've recommended similar cross-functioning for other members of the association, but none of them have yet to act on the idea."

"It's worked well for us." Talbot glanced up at the row of angled windows above him. He could see the reflection of the station's panel lights and the dark silhouette of the announcer as he hunched forward in his chair.

"The arrangement has worked well because you've made it work. I can see that your personal efforts were behind it," Hastings added with a smile. He enjoyed complimenting Talbot. Of all the directors of technical standards of the exhibit ships, Paul Talbot was the best. He was a tall, thin man in his early sixties who had managed to blend the caution and intelligence of his many years with the innovations of someone far younger. Talbot was the most courteous, most cooperative, most technically competent technical director that Hastings dealt with. He was also ex-Navy, a retired chief, as the admiral recalled. "These periodic trips to Charleston have become my favorite duty."

"It's nice of you to say that."

"But don't quote me," Hastings added with a laugh. "I'm not supposed to show any favoritism."

"I understand completely." Talbot forced a smile.

"You'd be surprised," Hastings continued as he began to walk ahead slowly, "how many stupid requests we get from the other members of the Historic Ships Association." He reached the hatchway in the Island's superstructure and stepped inside. "Too many of the governing boards want to turn these exhibits into nothing but circus sideshows. We can't permit that."

"Of course not." Talbot lingered at the hatchway for an instant before he stepped inside. He turned and glanced once more at the group of schoolchildren on the deck as they swarmed around the display aircraft on the port side. A young boy standing by the empty tail hole where the jet fighter's engine had once been caught Talbot's attention. The young boy had a certain quality about him that made him look like his grandson Keith. It wasn't so much any physical resemblance as it was the way he stood, the way he moved his head and poked quizzically at the rusting hulk that once was an airplane. Talbot sighed, shook his head imperceptibly, then turned and followed Vice Admiral Hastings inside.

"How is the engine room renovation going?" Hastings maneuvered himself behind a group of elderly visitors bunched at the throat of the passageway that led below-decks. The two men edged forward slowly.

"It's going very well." Talbot could hear the growing tightness in his own voice. *Relax. Stay calm.* The last thing he needed was for the Department of Navy representative to poke around in the engine room. Everything would probably appear ordinary enough, but there was no sense taking any chances. Hastings was sharp and he might spot the subtle differences. "It's one hell of a mess right now. Paint and grease. Puddles of oil."

"I can imagine." Admiral Hastings followed an overweight woman in a faded yellow dress as they began to descend the passageway steps. "We'll need to inspect that section before you put it on the official tour. If it's not far enough along right now, I'll have to come back."

"That would be best." Talbot's stomach muscles relaxed and he wiped a thin bead of perspiration off his pale, drawn face. "I'll notify you within the next thirty days."

"That'll be fine." Hastings reached the bottom of the passageway, turned toward the hatch that led to the hangar deck and stepped through it. "Be certain to give me plenty of advance notice. My schedule's pretty tight."

"I'll do that, sir." Talbot stepped behind the admiral and the two men looked up and down the hangar deck. The brightly colored pennants and flags draped from the overhead beams swung rhythmically in the slight draft that blew through the 800-foot length of the *Yorktown*'s below-decks work area. A group of teenage boys huddled over the three brightly painted green torpedoes that surrounded the old Navy prop airplane parked on this end of the hangar deck. Several teenage girls stood a dozen feet behind the boys and giggled among themselves. Talbot strummed his fingers against the flashlight that dangled from his belt, then cleared his throat. "It there anything else you'd like to see?" He wanted, very badly, to have the admiral satisfied with the technical end of his tour. Then he'd be able to deliver him back to the big shots upstairs. It was ironic that the admiral had selected this particular week to do an inspection of the *Yorktown*. Deep down, Talbot knew it was an ominous sign, a mystical signal of some sort. Yet there was nothing he could do about it. It was too late.

"There is one more thing," the admiral said as he turned around. "A personal thing."

"Sure." Talbot's heart began to beat rapidly again. "Whatever you'd like."

"That's very nice of you." Admiral Hastings took Talbot's arm and guided him gently toward a far bulkhead on the starboard side of the hangar deck. They walked around the bulkhead, then stepped over a security chain with a sign on it that said visitors were not allowed beyond that point. "Did I ever mention to you that I once served on this ship?"

"Yessir, I believe you did mention it once." Talbot could see from the gleam in Hastings' eye that he was about to hear that story again. But that would be okay, a welcomed diversion. Talbot wondered for a brief instant if Hastings remembered their discussion a year before when he had mentioned his own career in the Navy. Probably not. Officers—especially the high-ranking ones—had little recall of what the enlisted men had done, retired or otherwise. "What year did you first begin your tour of duty on the *Yorktown?*" Talbot asked politely, even though he thought he remembered the date.

"Nineteen fifty-six. I was a junior officer. I bunked in boys' town." Hastings steered Talbot through a restricted hatchway and out to the catwalk on the starboard side. The afternoon sun had ducked behind a growing layer of clouds to the west and the sky was bathed in a bright but one-dimensional glow. The two men edged forward along the narrow catwalk. "We called the junior officers' quarters boys' town. We were all kids, fresh out of the academy."

"Really?"

"Yes."

Talbot stepped around a puddle of water that lay in their path, then continued down the catwalk behind Hastings. He glanced up at the sky. The weather forecast seemed accurate so far. The cloud layers had increased rapidly since noon and, hopefully, it would begin—as predicted—to rain by nightfall. "Those bunks are up here somewhere, aren't they?" Talbot asked, even though he knew exactly where they were and what the nickname for the area had been. Although he had never served on the *Yorktown* before she was decommissioned and given to the State of South Carolina in 1975, his first shipboard combat duty had been on a sister-carrier, the *Essex,* during the fall of '44.

"That's right. My old bunk isn't far. I'd like to see it again."

"Certainly." Talbot ran his hand along the deck edging plates as they moved forward along the catwalk. During his thirty years in the Navy he had served on a great many ships, first as an enlisted man and then as a chief. But none of those years evoked as many memories as did those early days on the carrier *Essex*. He had served on the *Essex* during the Battle of the Philippine Sea when he was barely twenty-three years old— long before he had met Charlotte, years before they would have Amy. Talbot shivered at the rush of discomfiting associations those memories evoked. He quickly pushed them out of his mind.

"Boys' town was in here." Admiral Hastings stepped up to the heavy gray metal door, yanked on the lever to retract its latches, then pushed against it. The door creaked noisily as it slowly swung open. "This is the spot." The admiral stepped inside.

"Do you want my flashlight?" Talbot asked as he followed through the hatch.

"Yes." Hastings took the flashlight and clicked it on. "The forecastle deck, forward of the elevator trunk," he said, as if he were repeating a set of road instructions. Yet his voice had acquired a hushed, almost sepulchral tone. The admiral led the way through the chipping gray-painted passageways which, with every passing step, became darker and darker. Soon they were totally dependent on the narrow white beam from the flashlight.

"I'm sorry we don't have the interior lights working in this section, Admiral. I think there's a wiring problem."

"Quite all right." They turned a corner, stepped over a

doorsill and stood inside an enclosed area. Hastings swept the beam from the flashlight around in a slow arc several times before he finally turned back to Talbot. "This is it. No question about it." He reached out and touched the frame of the bunk that leaned against the wall. "This was mine. Fleming was to my right, Anderson below." Hastings allowed his gaze to wander around the cramped room. "It seems even smaller than I remember it."

"It always does."

"Right." Admiral Hastings cleared his throat, more out of embarrassment than for any other reason. "If you'd do me a favor..." he said, his voice trailing off as he reached into his pocket. He pulled out a small Japanese camera and handed it to Talbot. "It's for my grandson. He's studying World War II in school. When I told him that I once served on this ship— it's a ship he's read about—he begged me to get a picture of myself standing next to where I slept." Hastings shrugged his shoulders; there was a sheepish grin on his face. "I know it's foolish, I hope you understand..."

Without replying, Paul Talbot took the camera and stepped back across the room. He was out of range of the flashlight's beam and well into the darkness.

"Take a few of them," Hastings said as he leaned awkwardly against his old bunk. "The automatic flash will adjust for the bad light."

Talbot nodded, again without answering, even though he knew that the admiral couldn't see him where he stood. Talbot put the camera to his eye and looked through the viewfinder. *My grandson begged me.* He clicked off one, two, then three pictures in rapid succession, hardly realizing whether or not he had aimed the camera properly.

"Take a few more. If you don't mind." Hastings changed his pose.

Talbot did not bother to respond at all this time. He kept the camera up to his eye and continued to work with the viewfinder. But no matter how hard he tried to clear it, the image remained blurred and indistinct. *My beloved grandsons. God help them. God help me.* Paul Talbot raised his hand and wiped at his eyes, but as soon as he did they would blur again. His eyes overflowed their heavy load of tears.

• • •

Dominick Trombetta glanced up at the wall clock, then out the window. The night sky was crystal clear, and beyond the group of floodlights that covered the terminal buildings, he could see the bright half-moon as it began to rise. It was a nice evening in New York, but according to McClure it was raining like hell in Charleston. Good. That was the condition they needed before they could go ahead with the plan. Trombetta thanked God that it was almost over for him—he hadn't slept worth a damn for the last week, and hadn't slept soundly for the past six months, not since he had agreed to go along with McClure.

"Here's the rundown on what we've got packed in the security section."

"Thanks." Trombetta reached for the stack of papers that Tom Baizley had brought in and, shuffling through them quickly, saw that none of them affected the things he had already planned for or the steps that still remained to be done.

"Are we going to move the security-class material tonight?" Baizley ran his fingers along the worn edge of Trombetta's desk as he shifted his weight. Normally, he wouldn't have questioned the boss about how and when they intended to transport valuable material, but he was getting too much heat from the men on the floor. "The security room is packed to the rafters. The guys say they can't fit another single thing in there." Baizley pointed his thumb toward the closed door that led to the main floor of Trans-American's airfreight warehouse. "They say we haven't moved a piece of that crap for the last three days."

Without looking up, Trombetta leaned back in his seat and slowly removed the half-rimmed reading glasses from where they had hung low on his nose. "Is that so?" he asked, in a tone that made it obvious he wasn't asking a question. He ran his hand through the small tufts of white hair that remained as a frame to his aged face and bald skull. Once he had turned sixty, Dominick Trombetta had grown increasingly weary and older looking almost daily, and he could sense that he didn't have too many years left. If he stayed with this job until he was sixty-five—three long years away—he didn't think he'd live much past his retirement. But he couldn't afford to retire early and take the cut in benefits. That was why he had listened to McClure that first time six months before, why he had done what he already had—and why he would tonight do the things that still remained.

Baizley cleared his throat. "They tell me," he repeated, not knowing what else he could say, "that we haven't moved a piece of that security-class material this week. Not since last Friday." Baizley had been off Tuesday and Wednesday, and he had been amazed that the security room was even more stuffed with valuable cargo when he came back for the Thursday shift. "When the boys suggested that I look into the security room, I was surprised to see as much as I did."

Trombetta turned and frowned, as much from the nervous rumblings in his stomach as the need to appear annoyed at any intrusions into his private domain. The scheduling of the movements of security-class cargo was solely the responsibility of the department supervisor. That was Trombetta, as it had been for the last dozen years. "Do the boys on the floor have any other suggestions? Have they been opening those crates and peeking inside? Have they been taking free samples again?"

"No. Of course not." Baizley was visibly agitated, and he held his hands up to indicate that he didn't want to pursue that matter any further. There had been too many security violations in airline cargo operations in the past, particularly there at Kennedy Airport in New York. Not more than one year before, the FBI had caught a Trans-American employee dipping into a few of the shipments of gold coins. The shit had really hit the fan over that one. "My men know better than that. It's just . . ."

"I sure as hell hope they do." Trombetta rose from his desk and walked over to the window. He ran his hand along a film of dirt along the sash, then looked outside again at the tarmac before he turned back to Baizley. "For your information," he began, his tone as cold and abrupt as he could force it to be, "we're shipping it in the morning. All of it. On Flight 255."

"All of it?" Baizley glanced down at the paper in his hand, confirming what he already knew. "That flight goes from here to Chicago, then Denver and Seattle. What about the Los Angeles consignment? What about the stuff for 'Frisco?"

"That, too." Trombetta paused for the effect. Even though

what he was doing was highly irregular, as the supervisor of Trans-American's airfreight it was well within his authority to route valuable cargo any way he chose. "The Los Angeles freight will connect to Flight 944 in Chicago. San Francisco can connect to 88."

"Why?" Baizley looked down at his paperwork again, then back at Trombetta. "I don't understand," he said, genuinely puzzled. "It doesn't make any sense, not when we've got non-stops to the coast. They leave within an hour of the same departure time as 255 does."

Trombetta forced himself to smile. "Here. Let me show you. You'll learn something." He stepped back to his desk and flipped open a large black book. He hoped to hell that Baizley didn't notice how his hand had begun to shake. Everything would depend on how convincing this explanation was—an explanation he knew would need to be given to the police more than once during the next few days. "You know the policy on moving valuable material. We need armed guards for every phase of the operation. But here, you can see," Trombetta continued as he pointed down the columns of the work chart that he had opened to, "that we're too thin on personnel. Barrett's on vacation. Gordon's out sick. Fogarty, Weber and Brewster are on compensation days." Trombetta paused to see how Baizley was taking it.

"I wondered why you gave so many men time off this week," Baizley said with a shrug. "The coverage looked too thin to me. I think I even told you so," he added in a neutral voice.

"You were right. I'd forgotten that I had promised all three of them. I didn't realize that we'd be getting in so many security shipments." Trombetta had known about this batch of gold shipments for weeks, but he could easily cover up his early knowledge of them. The bottom line was that he could be faulted for the bad scheduling of his guards, but that should be as far as any investigation into his involvement would go. At least he hoped so. "With everyone off, we can only cover one outbound security-class departure. I picked Flight 255 because a great deal of the cargo is going to Chicago and Denver anyway, and our Chicago station has enough staffing to cover the transfer flights for the material that goes on to the West Coast."

Baizley nodded. "I see. Okay. Have you notified Chicago yet, or do you want me to do it?"

"I was going to do it myself, but you go ahead." Trombetta patted his young assistant on the shoulder. "I want Chicago to be prepared." *But none of that cargo will ever get that far. Not if McClure is half as smart as he says he is.* Trombetta broke into a big, artificial smile. "I'll be real glad to finally get that security room emptied. I probably shouldn't have waited this long." If Baizley had brought the explanations for shipping everything on 255 so easily, Trombetta felt certain that he wouldn't have a bit of trouble with the police. "We've had too much of that valuable crap around here for too long. It's begging for a problem."

"I know. I'll be glad to get rid of it too." Baizley glanced down at his work sheet. "I'll have the boys load the security carts—it'll probably take two carts to carry it all—around five in the morning." Baizley peeked up at the clock. It was almost midnight, which meant that it was almost time for a coffee break. He would brief the men when their break was over.

"Fine." Trombetta nodded his agreement, then cautiously added the last point he still needed to cover. "I'll supervise the loading myself. I'll go over to the aircraft when our crews and the guards do. With a shipment this large, I want to be damn sure it gets on the right airplane."

Baizley laughed. "Sure. Be my guest, I don't blame you. I'd hate to be in your shoes if we somehow screwed up and sent three thousand pounds of gold off in the wrong direction."

"Right." Trombetta glanced down at his desk drawer, where he had hidden the two small satchels that McClure had given him. He needed to place one of the satchels—the bigger one—inside one of the boxes of gold, but that would be easy enough to do when he went into the security room to check the shipping manifest. The second satchel, the smaller one with the bands of double-sided tape around it, would be placed inside the upper corner of the airplane's galley. He could do that unnoticed while the cargo men loaded the hold below. Then he would meet McClure, get paid the rest of the money he had earned and finally be done with it. Trombetta glanced at the clock, then out across the wet airport ramp and, finally, back at

Baizley. "Once we get that security room emptied, we'll be back to business as usual. That should be one hell of a relief."

Paul Talbot stood at the edge of the deck and watched the fog that surrounded the pier. It continued to thicken slowly. He shifted his weight, exhaled nervously, then glanced at his wristwatch again. It was five minutes past midnight. The evening-shift radio announcer would be on his way down from the bridge. Very soon after that, the operation would begin.

Talbot ran his fingers along the gray-painted steel of the *Yorktown*'s hangar deck. He silently prayed that everything would go according to schedule. His resolve had slipped drastically during the last few days, and one more postponement would put him in the impossible position of needing to tell Yang that he didn't want to go through with it. The whole thing had become an insane nightmare—but one that he had no way out of. He knew that neither his wife, Charlotte, nor their daughter, Amy, would understand. But it was something he had to do anyway. There was no other way to begin to make up for the past—even this wouldn't be anywhere near enough. Nothing ever would. But at least after tomorrow, he might be able to look at himself in the mirror again.

"Has he left?"

Talbot whirled around toward the sound of the man's voice. From out of the darkness of the hangar deck he could make out a silhouetted figure coming toward him. "Keep your voice down," he whispered angrily. Yet even as he said it, Talbot knew it was an unnecessary precaution. It was already too late for any one person to stop them, even if that person figured out what was about to happen and why.

"Sure thing," Richard Yang answered nonchalantly as he swaggered up to where Talbot stood on the starboard elevator platform. "Stay cool. Everything's cool."

"Sure." Talbot's skin crawled as he watched that ever-present insolent smirk grow at the corners of Yang's mouth. If he were thirty years younger, Talbot knew that he would take a swing at this young Oriental half-breed bastard. Yang couldn't be more than twenty-eight years old, yet he acted as if he had already been around a lifetime. Two lifetimes. "How are things below?" Talbot asked to change the subject. He had to face the facts; he was sixty-three years old. Too old to have any options left.

"Like I said, everything's cool."

"Does that mean that we're on schedule? No problems?" Talbot had allowed his exasperation to surface, and he worked very hard to try to keep control of his voice.

"Sure does, pop." Yang smiled maliciously. "Everything's cool."

"Fine." Talbot knew that his dislike for them—Yang and his group of madmen—was too strong to keep buried. He never should have dealt with them to start with. This crew of theirs— no, wrong word, it was no more than an undisciplined mob of misfits and lunatics—was impossible to work with. He was glad that, except for Yang, they all avoided him whenever they could. Yang's orders, probably. Just as well. Talbot turned to ask Yang a technical question about the progress below-decks when he heard footsteps echo through the empty hangar deck. "Someone's coming."

The two men turned and faced the growing, rhythmic sound as it vibrated off the cavernous hangar deck of the deserted aircraft carrier. It came from somewhere toward the bow, near where most of the exhibit aircraft and the movie theater were.

"Don't be worried," Yang said in a low but bored voice. "It's very normal that we should be here. He won't suspect a thing." Yang removed his eyeglasses, rubbed his eyes, then carefully hooked the wire half-circles around one ear then the other. The old-fashioned round silver frames glistened brightly where they poked through the tangled strands of his black and curly hair. Yang turned to face Talbot squarely. "Try not to look so nervous, pop. It's not fitting for a man in your position."

"Go to hell." Talbot watched as a solitary figure in the distance approached out of the shadows where the torpedo exhibit stood.

"Hello," the young radio announcer called as he noticed the two men standing ahead of him near the gangplank. "Working late, huh?"

"We've got final cleanups to finish before our new engine room parts are delivered at the end of the week," Talbot answered, using precisely the words that Yang had told him to use. "We want to have that engine room opened to the public within the next few weeks."

"Good. When it's open, I'd like to see it."

"Certainly."

The young man gave a friendly nod as he stepped around the two men. There was a stack of records under one of his arms, a raincoat under the other. "Looks like I'll need this," he said. He tried to put his raincoat on with one arm and after two records slipped from under his other arm he dropped the rest of the stack on a nearby table, put the slicker on correctly and then piled the records back under his arm. "Crummy night."

"Been raining steadily for the past few hours," Yang added. "Fog, too. Going to be a bitch driving home."

"Sure will be." The young man gave a polite wave with his free hand as he stepped quickly out from under the protective overhang of the *Yorktown*'s flight deck and into the wind and rain. In a few seconds he was across the gangplank, down the wooden stairs and onto the expansive concrete pier that led to the parking lot.

Talbot and Yang stood silently as they watched the young man disappear into the bleakness of the rain-swollen night. Yang cleared his throat. "Perfect so far," he said. Even Yang had found it hard to believe that the moment had finally arrived. "Thirty more minutes should do it. We'll buzz the bridge when everything is ready."

"Okay." There was nothing else for Talbot to say, it had all been gone over a thousand times. He looked out into the night sky and wondered, for the millionth time since it had begun, if he were doing the right thing.

"Please," Yang said, his arm extended in an exaggerated gesture of politeness, "after you—Captain." He had over-emphasized the last word enough to make it sound as sarcastic as he had intended.

Without saying a word, Paul Talbot turned and walked briskly into the overlapping shadows of the bow section of the hangar deck, the sound of his footsteps amplified by the acoustics of the metal ceiling and walls. By the time he had gone past the entrance to the ammunition elevator, he heard Yang's footsteps fade in the distance toward the stern of the ship.

Talbot stopped where he was. He took a deep breath. He

knew he was the only person in the forward end of the *York-town*, that the other six were down in the engine and boiler rooms. Seven people onboard a ship large enough to accommodate 4,000 men. Talbot shivered, then glanced at his wristwatch. There would be at least twenty-five more minutes before he had anything else to do. The last thing he wanted now was free time—time to think, time to reconsider, time to feel another surge of the guilt that had become so much a part of him. Instead, Talbot turned slowly around to look at what lay before him on the hangar deck, at sights he knew so well that he could have seen them with his eyes closed.

The white paint on the ceiling's big iron crossbeams had begun to flake slightly, but the paint on the corrugated wall panels still looked fresh. The colorful pennants that hung from above—signal flags, actually—gave the hangar deck too much of a carnival appearance, at least for Talbot's taste. The two airplanes on his left—World War II vintage—shone in their new coats of deep-blue paint, their engines sprayed a bright silver, their propellers handsomely polished. Talbot began to walk forward slowly, past the arrow of the visitor's sign that pointed toward the right, for those who wanted to go topside to tour the flight deck and the bridge. Ahead of him, where the elevator trunk once was, were the curved panels of masonry he had helped erect a few years before in order to set aside that area as the visitor's movie theater.

Talbot stopped. He let his gaze roam among the groups of plaques and photographs that lined the outside wall, a collection of *Yorktown* memorabilia that parents would read to their bored children while everyone waited for the next movie to start. Although the fathers might sometimes find the plaques interesting, the kids couldn't be pacified so easily. The kids wanted to get inside to see the actual combat movies of World War II—movies that were taken from the deck of the *Yorktown*.

Action newsreels of the old fighter airplanes—aircraft just like the two parked on the hangar deck behind Talbot—were shown launching in droves to go out on their missions. Pictures of the landings, too, with some of the aircraft torn up so badly by combat damage that the touchdown on the carrier's deck was hardly more than a controlled crash. Pictures of the pilots—those whose aircraft hadn't flipped over and burned on the landing, or skidded off the deck and into the water—being hauled out of their mangled airplanes, their life vests covered with blood, their young faces contorted in pain. The lucky ones.

There were also pictures of the Japanese. A wave of kamikaze aircraft—looking at first like no more than specks of dirt on the film, but growing rapidly with every passing moment—plunged headlong through the surrealist curtain of anti-aircraft flack being sent up by the *Yorktown* and its escorts. In one remarkable sequence, a kamikaze pilot got so close to the *Yorktown* that you could make out the pilot's face in the cockpit. But the Japanese pilot had aimed slightly too far aft and high and, instead of crashing into the carrier's deck, he had passed harmlessly over the fantail and then crashed into the sea. All for honor and glory—all for nothing.

Talbot closed his eyes. Suddenly he could see Keith and Thomas sitting beside him, watching that same combat movie for the third or fourth time in succession, saying almost the identical things during each showing. That had been as recently as a year ago last summer, which was only a month or two before.... Talbot forced his eyes open, then turned and walked hastily toward where the arrow pointed to the steps that led to the bridge. He moved through the deserted passageways quickly, and soon found himself on the catwalk along the port side of the Island. He continued forward and entered the bridge.

Talbot made a cursory check to see that everything was exactly as he had left it. His coffee cup, empty for the moment, was in its holder beside the captain's chair in the forward left corner of the bridge. In the center of the room the control panel beside the helmsman's wheel still appeared to be functioning normally—and he could see that the interphone to the engine room was still turned on. The portable electronic devices Yang had brought aboard that night—the small radar set, the voice transmitter, the depth gauge—were lined up on the ledge beneath the row of windows that surrounded him. Talbot lifted his head and glanced outside. The weather, if anything, had gotten worse. There was nothing to see outside but fog and rain. Even the flight deck, no more than thirty feet below him, was nearly invisible through the dense swirls of gray mist.

Talbot turned and peeked into the captain's sea cabin, another spot he had allocated for himself so he wouldn't need to leave the bridge for any reason. Everything in that tiny cabin—the supply of food and water, the pillow and blanket, his toilet articles, the portable tape player that Amy had given him on his sixtieth birthday—were in place.

The interphone from the engine room buzzed once. Talbot took a step toward it, then stopped. He allowed it to buzz a second time before he finally picked it up. "Bridge."

"We're ready down here, pop."

"Good." Talbot looked around the bridge one more time, as if there was something else he needed to check, as if there was one more thing to do before he could go ahead. Yang's voice had sounded hollow and scratchy in the interphone, but there was no mistaking his arrogance. "Are both the boilers on line?" he asked. "Are the generators putting out okay? We can't take time later for electrical problems."

"Listen, pop," Yang answered. There was marked annoyance in his voice. "When I say that everything's ready, I mean everything's ready."

"Very well. Have Davis blow the ballast tanks. In the sequence we discussed. We may do some damage to the pier pilings, but it shouldn't be very much."

"I don't give a shit about the pier pilings. How's the radar working?"

"It seems to work fine." Talbot peered at the tiny ten-inch screen, a unit from a small airplane, he had been told. "I don't see any targets. It looks clear."

"Great." The sound of Yang's laughter filled the interphone line. "Then it sure sounds to me—you'll pardon me for the pun, pop—but it sure sounds to me as if we're going to be in for some clear sailing."

Lee Burdick chugged ahead in his old Ford, the engine laboring under the need to keep itself throttled down because of his slow forward speed. The drive from his apartment in downtown Charleston to Patriot's Point seldom took more than fifteen minutes, especially at these early morning hours. Because of the weather, Burdick had allowed himself an extra ten—and he realized now that ten minutes might prove to be too little. As the old Ford climbed the incline of the Silas

Pearman Bridge, he repeatedly rode both the gas pedal and the brake to keep his speed below twenty miles an hour. Someday he would need to get the engine and transmission adjusted or, better yet, buy a new car.

Although the rain had tapered off to no more than a misty drizzle, the fog was so thick that Burdick couldn't see much farther ahead than a few of the roadway's white strips. It was quarter to six already, and he still hadn't opened the station, hadn't warmed up his equipment, hadn't made his morning coffee. Okay, he would need to readjust his schedule. He decided he would play the Haydn symphony first, so then he'd have time to at least get the coffee made before he did much talking. He mulled over a few witty remarks about the morning fog to use on the show.

Burdick drove down the exit ramp, then steered carefully through the back streets. Within a few minutes he had entered the deserted Patriot's Point parking lot. The wide expanse of unmarked blacktop made it even harder for him to keep his bearings, and twice he almost ran off into the grass before he realized what part of the lot he was in. Burdick parked the Ford across from the entrance turnstile. The red, white and blue markings of the admission booth were no more than dimly visible through the fog, although the booth was hardly thirty feet away. He turned off the car's ignition, scooped up his notepad and records, then hustled out of the car and toward the pier.

Haydn number 93. A Chopin Polonaise. Two of the Beethoven sonatas by Perlman and Ashkenazy. Burdick splashed through the puddles on the concrete pier as he walked rapidly, the remainder of the first hour's show running through his thoughts. *Read the piece from* The New York Times *about Horowitz.* Burdick's eyes were straight ahead. The fog by the water's edge was even thicker, and it swirled around him with a consistency that gave the feeling he could almost pull it apart with his hands. *Do the fund drive promo at least once every hour.*

Lee Burdick was half the way through his next step when his thoughts started to focus on what his eyes had begun to see. He took that last step, then stopped. His mouth opened. The records in his left hand fell out of his fingers and dropped noisily onto the concrete pier. Ahead of him, where the dock turned at a right angle to provide for the entrance to the wooden stairs that led to the gangplank, there was . . .

Nothing. The gray vapors of fog rested on the surface of the glass-smooth sea. "What in God's name . . ." Burdick spun around and looked down the pier he had just walked, thinking that he must have somehow come down the wrong one. But he knew better. Impossible. There was only one pier at Patriot's Point. *This is the only pier. Christ Almighty*.

He vaulted to the edge of the dock and, in amazement, looked up and down its length. "Oh, my God." The sound of his excited, strained voice contrasted sharply with the placid quiet of the early morning and the soft lapping of the tide against the pilings. *The* Yorktown *is gone*.

Burdick rubbed his eyes. He couldn't believe it. Yet the evidence was unmistakable. The wooden steps were still there, but their edging had been torn away. Splinters of the shattered wood lay on the surface of the water below. A dozen severed cables—telephone lines, the electric service—dangled incongruously from the adjacent poles. *The* Yorktown *is missing*.

Lee Burdick stumbled backward. He moved once, then twice, in a random, spastic motion before he finally got his wits together enough to turn himself around. "God." He walked across the stack of records that had fallen out of his hand and onto the pier, but he didn't feel them beneath his feet or notice the noise they made as they cracked.

Burdick took one more glance over his shoulder before he began to run. He ran back down the pier. He needed to reach a telephone, someone, anyone, to report the most insane thing he had ever witnessed in his entire life. *Gone*. He couldn't imagine what he would say to whomever was the first person he spoke with. An ancient relic of an aircraft carrier—900 feet long, 27,000 tons in weight, a permanent exhibit owned by the State of South Carolina—was gone. Missing. Vanished. Even though he had seen it with his own eyes, Lee Burdick wondered how in hell he would ever get even himself to believe it.

3

THE MORNING SUN lay just barely above the horizon, and it glimmered off the side of the DC-9 jetliner that sat at gate 23 of Trans-American's terminal at Kennedy International Airport. Dominick Trombetta looked down the clean lines of the airliner and along the two horizontal stripes of rich-toned red that contrasted nicely with the brilliant white of the fuselage. He turned to his men. "Let's move it," he said as he peeked down at his wristwatch for the fifth time in as many minutes. Six-ten A.M. As usual, his crews were running late. "What's going on here, a damn work slowdown or something?" *No wonder this job is making me old.*

"Sure thing, boss." The lead man in the cargo crew smiled to show he was only kidding—he knew enough not to take Trombetta too seriously, and also not to push him too far. "This one first?" he asked as he pointed at one of the crates on the security cart.

"Yes. Be careful. Get good leverage before you push against it."

The man nodded, then gestured to where he wanted the other three men to grab hold. They began to shove the first of the heavy cases of gold into the belly cargo compartment of the airplane.

"Careful. Easy, now." If one of those cases slipped backward and gouged a hole in the skin of the airliner, Trombetta knew that maintenance would delay the flight or, worse, ask for a substitute airplane. Any delay at this stage might mean trouble.

Trombetta looked at the most senior of the two armed guards stationed on either side of the security cart. "Evans, nothing goes in this compartment but our shipment. Don't let any of those assholes from the ramp bullshit you otherwise. Got that?"

"Yessir."

"I'll be right back. Nature calls." Satisfied, Trombetta ducked around the nose of the jetliner and climbed up the stairs that led to the jetway connected to the airplane. The briefcase he held in his hand began to tilt backward awkwardly because of the weight inside it. Trombetta worked on keeping the briefcase as straight as he could while he climbed the staircase slowly and carefully. McClure had told him that the package wasn't dangerous to handle, but Trombetta wasn't going to take any chances.

He opened the door to the jetway. To his left, the narrow tube that led to the terminal and the men's room—the tube the passengers would eventually walk down—remained relatively dark and completely deserted. But instead of turning left, Trombetta turned toward the airliner.

The door to the DC-9 jet was open. The aircraft door lay back against the fuselage, its massive bulk covering a portion of the cockpit side window. Just inside the airplane was the galley—in full view of everyone who entered the jetway. Trombetta cursed himself again for not convincing McClure to use a Boeing 727 instead, where at least the ship's galley was out of sight in the center of the cabin. For some reason, McClure had insisted on the smallest airliner they owned, the DC-9.

Trombetta examined the jetway's loading canopy. It was snugly in position so that no more than a few feet of the aircraft's exterior were visible to him. At least that part was good. If he couldn't see outside, then no one out there could see him as he went aboard.

Trombetta stepped into the cool, darkened interior of the

DC-9. With its electrical system still shut down, the only light in the cabin came from outside where the morning sun crept through the long rows of cabin windows. *The forward upper corner of the galley. Make it fast.*

Trombetta's hand had begun to shake again. He laid his briefcase on the galley counter, then snapped open its latches. Inside sat the square black package that McClure had provided him with, its exterior covered with long strands of double-sided adhesive tape.

"Damn." Trombetta's perspiration-soaked fingers fumbled repeatedly with the tape as he tried to peel off its outside covering. Finally, he managed to get the tape started. Soon it was completely exposed. He took out the plastic package, then shoved the peelings from the tape back into his briefcase.

Forward upper corner of the galley. Trombetta unlatched the top cabinet and stuck in his hand. The area was tall and deep, and he needed to push himself onto the galley counter ledge in order to reach in all the way.

There was a sudden loud noise from outside the airplane. Trombetta froze in position. He knew full well that there was no way he could explain what he was doing, why he was fooling around in the galley, why he hadn't gone into the terminal building. Trombetta turned his head slowly to look up the jetway.

Dark, no one there. Trombetta closed his eyes and said a silent prayer of thanks. The noise had evidently come from below—from his own men, probably. For an instant, Trombetta wondered if one of the morons who worked for him had dropped a crate and broken it open. Maybe the crate that he had put McClure's other package in. Trombetta pushed that thought out of his mind—he could only handle one nightmare at a time.

He wiped his face with his free hand, to push away some of his sweat. Then he began to position the plastic package farther back into the upper compartment of the galley. *Phoenix, Arizona. Two more months. Make this quick.* Trombetta's probing fingers found the corner. He pushed hard to get the package to stick against the aluminum. *Please stick. Don't fall behind the cabinet.* He removed his hand from the package tentatively. To his surprise, the package remained firmly against the upper corner. *Great. McClure knows what he's doing after all.*

Trombetta tested the strength of the tape a few times by pushing against the package. It remained securely in place against the dark aluminum corner of the upper galley compartment.

Trombetta's heart pounded so loudly he could hardly hear himself think. *Two more months. Arizona. Warm and dry air. Clear blue skies. No more cold weather. No more bullshit.* Trombetta pulled his arm out of the cabinet, then eased himself off the ledge of the galley counter. He looked around once more to be certain that he hadn't left anything that could be traced back to him, then snapped his briefcase shut. He grabbed the briefcase and stepped out of the airplane, then out of the jetway and onto the steps that led to the ramp.

Dominick Trombetta tried to let out a sigh of relief, but found that he couldn't because of the continued pounding of his heart and the shaking of his hands. But none of that mattered now. His job was done. *Arizona in two months.* Now all he had to do was make the final telephone call to McClure, then pick up his money.

It was 6:20 A.M., eastern standard time, when Paul Talbot decided that they had sailed far enough eastbound—they had gone nearly two hundred miles already—to execute the next step in the plan. He turned himself around in the captain's chair of the *Yorktown* and looked toward the stern of the ship.

The visibility had picked up somewhat during the last few hours, but so had the wind and the seas—both just as predicted. Rain showers surrounded the ship on all sides and the base of the heavy clouds remained ragged and low, but it looked to Talbot as if they had enough for their operational purposes. He took one more sip of coffee from his mug, put it back in the holder, then spun himself around. He lay his hand against the interphone switch. "Engine room from bridge. Our position and conditions are correct for dumping."

There was a long pause before a reply came out from the speaker in the bridge. "Sure thing, pop. I'll leave one man in each engine room to monitor. The rest of us will be topside in a few minutes."

"Understand," Talbot answered. He gazed out ahead of the

Yorktown, where small whitecaps had just begun to form ahead of the bow. The giant ship rolled slowly but continually in the growing swells. "Has the number two bearing temperature remained within limits?"

"It's a little warm, but your idea worked fine. I'll have Davis repeat the oiling procedure if and when it reaches its limits again."

"Okay." Talbot held his finger on the transmit switch, but he couldn't find anything else to say to them below. If this were a normal crew, there would have been something else to add, some expression of feeling, satisfaction, camaraderie. But if this were a normal crew, they wouldn't be about to do what was ahead. "Attempt to complete the dumping as quickly as possible. When I see you on the deck, I'll ring for dead slow."

"Okay, pop."

Talbot turned away from the interphone. It would be several minutes before they came up to the flight deck and got themselves into position for the dumping. Until then, he had nothing to do but continue to steer the eastbound course and monitor the radar set for targets.

Talbot stepped up to the small screen and huddled over it. An electronic line swept back and forth like a metronome across the radar's green-colored tube. It kept time with the motions of its antenna, which Yang had clamped to the outside ledge of the bridge the night before.

Talbot watched as the electronic sweep line went from the port to the starboard quarter, then back again. A few of the heavier rain showers were displayed on the scope as fuzzy areas of off-colored white, but no other targets of substance were within the radar's range of twenty miles. That meant no ships and, of course, no masses of land or shorelines.

Talbot marveled for a moment at how well the portable radar had worked for him as he had steered the *Yorktown* out of the fogshrouded mouth of Charleston harbor. He had made continual adjustments at the helm to avoid what the radar had depicted as the shorelines, and it was an easier job than he had thought it would be. Once out on the open sea—only fifteen minutes of careful sailing after they had swung away from the dock at Patriot's Point—the radar gave enough advance notice of conflicting ships that Talbot easily altered course to avoid

them by a wide margin. They didn't want to run the risk of
being spotted by some other vessel, even though the darkness
and the fog were a perfect cover to prevent any visual sightings.
Their avoidance of other sea traffic, the low clouds and the
heavy weather, plus the action they were about to take, would
give them the time and distance they needed from any Coast
Guard pursuit, if one were eventually launched. McClure had
been right so far, none of this had been a problem.

A problem. You could have a serious problem. Talbot let
out a deep sigh. The words of his son-in-law—his ex-son-in-
law, now that the divorce papers had arrived—ran through his
thoughts. It was one year ago this month. September seven-
teenth. If only he had listened to Russ about the crack, if only
it hadn't been Keith's birthday, if only he hadn't been so damn
pigheaded. Talbot walked to the window behind the captain's
chair and looked out. The carrier's flight deck was still empty,
none of them had yet to come up from below. He ran his hand
along the metal framework of the bridge windows, his fingers
pushing through the rivulets of water that had leaked around
the old and dried weather stripping. Talbot gazed absently
across the angled flight deck and into the bleakness of the
rolling sea.

"Grandpa! Look!"

Talbot turned, but he knew from the sickening sound
what he would see. The small crack he had noticed months
before in the sailboat's mast—the one Russ had told him
about repeatedly—had let go in the sudden gust that had
swept down on them out of the afternoon thunderstorm.
"Hold on! Keith, grab Thomas!" The mast had splintered
in the center, then tumbled. Shards of wood flew in all
directions. The boat itself, only twenty-two feet long and
already working hard at remaining seaworthy in the suddenly churning sea beneath the afternoon storm that had
caught them more than a mile from shore, began to roll
uncontrollably toward starboard. "Hang on!"

Talbot threw his body to the port rail in a desperate
attempt to keep the boat upright, but it was too late. They
began to roll over, slowly at first, then more rapidly as

the boat broached from the incessant walls of water that pounded against them.

"Grandpa! Help me!"

It was Thomas' voice, and Talbot turned in time to see the eight-year-old boy lose his grip on the rail and slide into the ocean. "Hang on! Hang on! Don't let go!" Talbot screamed irrationally, even though he could plainly see that the boy had nothing within reach to grab. "Hang on! I'm coming!" He dove into the water near the boy, but the downed mast of the sailboat had come between them. "Grab the sail! Thomas! The sail!"

"Help! Help! My life jacket!"

Though he could only glimpse the boy every few seconds because the tangled sail and splintered pole rose and fell between them as it was carried on the violent waves and swells, he could see that the boy's life jacket had unsnapped or been cut by one of the roughened pieces of wood. The jacket had partially come off. It hung half off his shoulders . . . was in his arms . . . pulled against his chest . . . "Hold the jacket! Don't let it go!" Talbot pushed frantically against the downed sail and, finally, clawed his way around it toward where he had last seen the boy.

But Thomas was gone. The torn life jacket floated on the water a few feet away, but the boy was nowhere in sight. Talbot thrashed around in the water in all directions and screamed Thomas' name as long and as loud as he could, until he finally swallowed so much water he nearly could not catch his own breath. *God. Help me, God.*

"Grandpa!"

Talbot turned toward the new voice. It was Keith, eleven years old that very day, a good swimmer, a strong boy. "Keith! Where are you! Hang on!" He finally saw the boy as he bobbed up and down in the depression of a swell, at least twenty feet from the overturned sailboat. Thirty feet from where Talbot was. "I'm coming!"

But Talbot had to fight his way back through the debris, past the overturned boat, before he got himself on the clear side. He began to swim into the face of the waves. They splashed over his head repeatedly, until the taste of salt water was etched so deeply into his lungs that he couldn't stop himself from gagging. "Keith!" he yelled loudly, the one time he inhaled a full enough breath to get a word out.

There was no answer. He thought once that he heard a faint cry from the distance, but he couldn't be sure. Keith, too, had disappeared. He was somewhere beyond the crest of the next series of waves, or the next one after that. Or the next.

When Paul Talbot glanced down from the motion of the distant sea and back to the *Yorktown*'s deck, he saw Yang and the others below. They waved indignantly at him. Evidently, they had been on the deck and signaling him for some time. Talbot acknowledged their wave, turned to the interphone and, after clearing his throat, called below for the ship's engines to be slowed. The *Yorktown* came to a near standstill in the water.

"Asshole," Richard Yang said to no one in particular as he jerked his thumb toward the bridge. He walked to where his three men stood on the open flight deck. "Okay," he said to the younger two, "you cut the cables. John will drive the tug."

John Solenko mounted the small yellow tug and put it in gear. He drove it ahead slowly, to where the first of the five display aircraft were moored to the deck of the *Yorktown*. "It'll go off that way," Solenko shouted over the wind and noise from the chugging of the tug's engine.

"Give them another minute to clear that last cable."

"Right." Solenko sat back and watched the two younger men finish their work. When the last cable had been cut, he put the tug into gear and steered it straight ahead. Pushing the aircraft from nose to tail, he quickly had the old, engineless jet fighter teetering on the edge of the flight deck as if it were no more than a plastic model about to fall off a boy's bedroom shelf.

"Careful," Yang shouted above the noise. "That's the only tug we've got."

"Screw you." Solenko backed a few inches off, then jerked the tug forward. The momentum of the collision caused the old fighter airplane to bounce rearwards. It tilted on its main wheels, rolled over the edge, then fell tail first off the carrier and into the sea. The two younger men cheered, and Solenko gave an exaggerated bow from his sitting position on the tug. "Tell Mary what a good job I did," Solenko shouted.

"Wonderful performance," Yang said loudly. "Your wife will be proud. But not until we finish with the other four." Yang gestured across the flight deck, to where the remaining aircraft—rusty old relics from one war or another—were positioned. "Once they're in the water, Davis will release the oil slick from below. That should make it look like this is the spot where this tub of shit," Yang said as he stomped his foot against the *Yorktown*'s deck, "went under. They'll figure the boilers blew or something like that, and we went straight down."

"With all hands."

"That's right." Yang began to move toward the next display aircraft, the three other men behind him. "Let's get this done quickly, so we can get back to full speed. We've still got another hundred miles before we reach the rendezvous point."

"Don't forget the net," one of the younger men added.

"Of course not." Yang smiled indulgently. "You'll get a chance to erect the net very soon. As soon as we get these four pieces of aeronautical crap into the water."

A light morning breeze blew across Long Island Sound from the south and it carried a refreshing smell of salt water with it, even as far north as Westchester County Airport. Edward McClure stood a few feet from the door of the white Learjet. The sunlight played off his tanned skin while the breeze added just enough airflow to make the experience exhilarating. He enjoyed most any physical sensation, and this one was quite pleasant.

"Almost done," the copilot called out as he walked around the tip of the left wing.

"Take your time." McClure tugged at the vest of his brown suit to straighten it, then adjusted the fall of his jacket. Through his dark sunglasses he watched as the Learjet's copilot finished the preflight inspection of the airplane he had just chartered, all the while casually stroking the neatly trimmed corners of his dark mustache.

"We're all set," the copilot said as he approached the door. It was company policy to use the customer's name whenever possible, but the name they had gotten from this particular gentleman—John Smith—was too far afield to be taken very seriously. Still, his money was good—and he had paid in cash. "After you, sir."

"Thank you." McClure jumped into the small cabin and sat in the back. He watched the copilot close the entrance door, then climb into the cockpit with the pilot. "Incidentally," McClure called out before the two of them began their cockpit routines, "how long will it take to get to Kennedy Airport? My friend should be there shortly."

"On a nice day like this," the pilot answered as he pointed to the cloudless sky above them, "not very long. It's only forty miles. Fifteen minutes at the most, by eight o'clock."

"Very good."

"The flight from Kennedy Airport to West Palm Beach will be a little over two hours."

"Fine." McClure sat back. While the engines were started and the Learjet taxied out, he ran the schedule of events— those already past, those still to come—through his mind again. Trombetta was due to show at 8:15. The Trans-American flight was scheduled to depart at 9:00. Everything had worked perfectly so far. There would even be a few extra minutes to kill. McClure decided that the next time he did something like this— not that there would ever be a need for a next time, not after this score—he would time it so precisely that there wouldn't be an extra minute in it anywhere. Just like he had done in Vietnam. Loose schedules made for loose operations.

The Learjet took off on the southeast runway and headed straight for Kennedy Airport. McClure split his attention between the view out the window—the flat blue waters of Long Island Sound, then Oyster Bay, Roosevelt Raceway and Belmont Park as they began the final approach for landing—and a peek at what the pilots were doing. He quickly sized them up as two technocrats who made a big deal out of nothing; two amateurs, basically. McClure smiled to himself. He wondered how either of those hotshots would've been in 'Nam, a helicopter gunship strapped to their asses, tracer bullets flying inches from their heads. Not well, he was sure. He laughed out loud.

"On the ground in three minutes," the copilot called back.

"Thank you." McClure reached for his briefcase, pulled it onto his lap and opened it. There were two metal cylinders inside, each with a pressure gauge mounted near its valve stem. He checked both pressure gauges. Both were okay.

The Learjet swept in low over a highway, then the airport boundary, the runway, and finally made its touchdown. It maneuvered off the runway and began the circuitous taxi route to the general aviation parking area on the west side of the field. McClure sat upright in his seat—it was almost time to start the next phase of his plan. He slipped off his sunglasses, took the oxygen bottle out of his briefcase, turned the valve, then pulled the mask over his face. He waited until the pilot brought the Lear to a stop at a crossing intersection to allow an opposite-direction jumbo jet to taxi by. McClure took the second bottle, the blue spherical one, out of his briefcase and opened its valve. The hiss of escaping gas melded in with the noise from the Lear's engines.

The copilot was the first to grab for his throat. He rose up in his seat, as far as his cinched seatbelt and shoulder harness would allow. He was gasping, but with an odd, frightened sound mixed in—a combination of a cough, a wheeze and a cry.

"What's wrong?" The pilot had begun to unfasten his seatbelt and reach across to his copilot before the toxic fumes finally hit him. He let out a short, curdled scream before he threw back his head and began to claw irrationally at his face. His fingernails cut long red gashes into his cheeks. After a few seconds of frenzied motions, his hands fell heavily to his sides and his head dropped.

McClure watched in fascination. *Incredible.* He looked down at the blue bottle he held in his lap. *Very effective. Well worth the cost.* He closed the bottle's valve, laid it back in the briefcase, then rose from his seat. He knew he had to act quickly to avoid becoming conspicuous to the control tower.

McClure moved carefully, well aware that if the oxygen mask on his face slipped off then he, too, would die. Death itself didn't frighten him—he had long ago grown accustomed to the prospect of it while he was in Vietnam—but he couldn't jeopardize the project because of a silly physical error. Life had become too exciting again, too much worth whatever efforts it required. He would not allow it to slip away too carelessly. The exhilaration he felt at that moment was worth more than any price he might ever have to pay.

McClure held the oxygen bottle closely against his chest as he reached for the Learjet's door handle. When the door popped open, the loud whine of the jet engines filled the small cabin. But so did the breeze from outside. In just a few seconds, McClure was certain that the toxic gas had been dispelled from the airplane and had been carried harmlessly away. He took off his mask and let the oxygen bottle drop to the floor, then took a deep breath and waited.

The corner of his lips curled into a smile. All was well, he felt fine. McClure exhaled slowly, then turned toward the cockpit.

The pilot had unfastened his seat belt before he died, but the copilot had not, so McClure reached across his body and unlatched the buckle. He then dragged each of them out of their cockpit seats slowly, careful not to have their arms or legs come in contact with any of the controls. He placed the bodies of both men into seats in the cabin, then slipped back to the cockpit and into the pilot's seat.

"Lear twenty-four Bravo," the cockpit speaker blared. "I repeat, continue along the outer taxiway. Cleared to the general aviation ramp."

McClure grabbed the radio microphone. "Roger. Understand. Lear twenty-four Bravo is cleared to continue along the outer taxiway." He released the parking brake, pushed the twin throttles a few inches forward, then wheeled the Learjet to the left and down the long strip of blacktop that led to the assigned parking area. As he entered the ramp, he parked toward the rear where he would be less easily seen from the operations building. McClure set the aircraft's parking brake and shut down the engines. It was 8:05. Trombetta was due any minute. Yet there was still one more job in the cabin for him to accomplish.

McClure moved back to where the pilots were. He strapped

their bodies into the passenger seats, then maneuvered their heads, arms and shoulders to make it appear as if they were asleep. That would satisfy any casual onlooker from the outside. Then McClure reached around to the hip pocket of the dead pilot and pulled out the man's wallet. "Sorry," he said as he opened the wallet and pulled out the wad of bills, "but if I'm going to fly the trip, then I'm the one who should be paid." He closed the empty wallet and shoved it back into the dead man's pocket, then placed the stack of bills inside his own jacket pocket. McClure was about to return to the cockpit when he spotted Trombetta. The old man walked directly toward the Learjet from across the ramp. McClure waited until Trombetta approached, then swung open the aircraft's door. "Come in," he said. "Come in and we'll conclude our business."

"Just give me my money." Trombetta was slightly out of breath, and there was the glow of perspiration across his forehead and the top of his balding skull—the combination of physical exertion, general nervousness, plus apprehension about dealing with McClure. Trombetta knew he had no choice, that he had come too far already to not try to collect his money. He prayed that McClure would give him no trouble—yet he now realized that there was little he would be able to do if McClure simply refused to pay any more than the token down payment he had already made. Trombetta climbed aboard the jet. "Who are these people?" Trombetta asked suddenly when he saw the inert bodies of the two pilots strapped in the passenger seats. He took a half step backward, away from McClure.

"The pilots I stole the Learjet from. I drugged them. They'll be sleeping for a long time." *A hell of a long time.* McClure managed a friendly smile. "Listen, I'm running on a tight schedule—let's get this over with. I've got your money."

"Fine." Trombetta couldn't take his eyes off the two men strapped in the seats a few feet from him.

"Let me close the door," McClure announced matter-of-factly as he maneuvered around Trombetta and toward the left sidewall of the Lear.

"No. Leave the door open."

"I need to close it. I have your money here and I don't want anyone outside seeing me pay it to you. That would be no good for either of us." Without waiting for his answer, McClure swung the Lear's door closed. "You do the counting," McClure added as he pushed down on the door's locking handle. "I don't want any bitching later on that I cheated you." He reached into his inside jacket pocket as if he were going to retrieve his billfold. Instead, he pulled out a small black pistol.

"What the hell's going on?" Trombetta visibly squirmed. "I did everything you asked. What's the matter?"

"Nothing." McClure shrugged his shoulders, as if his behavior were as much a mystery to him as anyone else. "Loose ends. I hate loose ends. You might become one."

"Don't be ridiculous."

"It's perfectly obvious to me. Sit down." McClure produced a set of silver handcuffs out of his other jacket pocket.

"What are you doing?" Trombetta couldn't take his eyes off the barrel of the pistol as he sat himself in the right rear seat. The gun was pointed directly at his chest.

"Don't worry, you'll get paid. Here's the money." With his free hand McClure reached into his coat pocket and pulled out the wad of bills he had taken from the pilot. He waved them in front of Trombetta's nose before he put them back into his coat pocket. "But not yet. Not until this job is finished. Then I'll land and you can take your money. Then you can leave."

"No." Trombetta didn't know what else to say. "There's no need for this. There's no need to handcuff me," he stammered. "I'm with you." He was sorry as hell he had ever dealt with McClure in the first place. He should have known better than to trust a madman.

"It's only until takeoff. I don't want you to change your mind. You might try to get away."

"I won't."

McClure smiled. "True. Especially if you're cuffed to the airplane." He laughed loudly, then reached forward and snapped one end of the cuff to Trombetta's right wrist, the other end to the metal brace that ran beneath the seat. With the small pistol pointed directly at Trombetta, McClure removed the key from the handcuffs and put it in his coat pocket. "It won't be uncomfortable for you, although you might get bored. If one of my two drugged pilots wakes up early," McClure said as he pointed at the two dead men in the forward passenger seats, "you can strike up a conversation. Now, if you'll excuse me, I've got work to do." Without waiting for Trombetta to lodge another protest, McClure stepped back into the cockpit.

He adjusted the pilot's seat so he would be comfortable, then pulled up his briefcase and laid it open on the copilot's chair. Satisfied that the cockpit was ready, he dialed in the proper radio frequency, canceled their flight plan to West Palm Beach and substituted in its place a nine o'clock departure directly out of the area and to the North. Those jobs done, McClure began to monitor the appropriate frequency for the first call-up from Trans-American Flight 255. "By the way," he called over his shoulder, "if any of you three gentlemen want a cup of coffee, just let me know." McClure glanced toward the back of the plane in time to see the expression of horror register on Trombetta's face. The old man had obviously figured out the actual condition of the two pilots in the cabin. Equally obvious now was the fact that Trombetta didn't know what to make of McClure, what would happen next.

McClure laughed again, then turned his attention back to the radio. Once Flight 255 had begun to taxi out, he would start up the Learjet's engines and leave. That would put him a few minutes ahead of the Trans-American flight—a few minutes ahead of the airliner that was now the total focus of his attention.

4

JEROME ZINDELL STOOD near the navigation table in the control room of the submarine. He had scrawled the original name for the old boat—*Trout*—on a sheet of paper and taped it over the metal nameplate where the Iranians had the word *Sharaf* etched. Zindell looked up at the new paper nameplate for several seconds before he hunched over his navigation chart. "I expect a visual contact any moment," he said without looking at the man he spoke with. "We'll stay at periscope depth from now until the sighting."

"Yessir." Clifton Harrison peeked over the captain's shoulder and at the chart on the desk. "Olga and I will take turns at the scope."

"Very well." Zindell nodded to indicate that the conversation was ended. He watched as Harrison scrambled up the ladder that led to the conning tower and the periscope. Satisfied, he looked around the rest of the control room.

Since they had submerged at dawn, the mood aboard the boat had changed markedly. It always did. The red lights that had bathed the control room and conning tower in an eerie, surrealist glow were gone, replaced by the normal white lighting they used during daylight conditions. The surface of the sea was choppy but since they were submerged—even to a relatively shallow depth so the periscope could be used—there remained only a slight fore-and-aft rocking motion in the boat, gentle enough to go unnoticed. Being beneath the sea was the most pleasant location for a submarine.

Unless something goes wrong. Zindell took a deep breath, laid the calipers down on the navigation chart, then leaned against the table. He allowed his gaze to wander aimlessly across the score of gauges that dotted the port bulkhead. *U.S.S. Thresher lost at sea. One hundred and twenty-nine dead.* That's what the headlines had said. But Zindell knew that the actual figure was 130. His father had been aboard. Yet no one, other than a handful of military people, would ever know what happened to retired Admiral Alex Zindell.

The decision had come down quickly from the Pentagon. Don't admit Admiral Zindell's presence. It might tip off the Soviets about the actual mission the *Thresher* was on when it went down, since it was well known that the retired admiral worked for years on techniques to make nuclear subs more silent during deep dives. The decision to cover up his presence on the *Thresher* had been made offhandedly somewhere within the bowels of the Pentagon, probably as nothing more than an overreaction by a junior aide. But it had turned his father into a nonentity. No official eulogy, no official mention. Nothing.

Zindell stood upright and stretched his legs. "I'm stiff as hell," he said to no one in particular.

"Me, too, Captain," the man a few feet away at the bow plane controls answered. "Stiff. Dead tired, too. When we finish, I'm going to rent a plush hotel room for a week. I'm not going to get out of bed."

"Good idea." Zindell felt the tension travel in knots along the muscles of his calves and thighs. He knew it was partly because of the slight swaying of the boat that demanded constant compensation—getting your sea legs, it was called—and partly because of the level of their work and tension of the situation.

"It's no wonder I see myself coming and going," the bow planesman continued. "We've got twelve people doing the work of seventy-five. We've got one hell of a small crew."

"True."

"But I'm not complaining," the man added quickly. He didn't want to appear like a crybaby, especially to the captain. There were rumors of a possible bonus, on top of the generous guarantees they had already received for these few weeks of work. "For what we're getting, it's worth it."

"Right." But even Zindell could sympathize with the complaints. They had been operating the boat continuously for eight days with less than one-fifth the normal crew. They needed to work double shifts to cover two and three stations simultaneously, with just a few hours break here and there for eating and sleeping. The strain had begun to show. Zindell turned away from the bow planesman, rocked his head back and forth to ease the tension in his neck, then began to rub his right hand against the stub of his shoulder where his left arm had once been.

Bastards. Look what they've done to me. Even after seven years, he still found it difficult to believe that his arm was gone. It had been sliced off in a pigpen of a Turkish hospital after his accident—an injury that should have ended with his arm being saved, had there been a decent medical facility around. Zindell remembered vividly the moment when the Turkish lieutenant tugged on exactly the wrong handles at the wrong time during the demonstration of how to release the emergency underwater flares.

The flares had exploded backward toward them. It killed the Turk instantly and injured several of the others gathered in the aft torpedo room. It took most of the flesh off Zindell's left arm. The sight of the exposed bone beneath the charred skin and shattered muscles was still the theme of many of his nightmares.

Zindell picked up the navigation calipers and bent down over the chart again. He thought about how ironic it was that he had lost his arm while trying to train the Turks in the use of the old sub they had bought from the U.S. Navy. He wondered idly if any Americans had suffered injuries during the initial training on the *Trout*. Probably not, but you could never tell. Iranians. Turks. They were all the same. They were all idiots.

Because of his injury, the Navy had forcibly retired Zindell.

Sent him packing. The monthly disability checks came on time, but they were far from enough to cover what he had lost. No one had asked him how he felt about being medically retired. His whole life—since he was a young boy being led around the base by his father—had been involved with the Navy, with the submarine service. Jerome Zindell knew that he had become a nonentity, just like his father. He hadn't lost just an arm in the submarine service, he had lost two lives. His father's. His own.

Zindell was deep in thought when the first sounds—a muttered voice, followed by a loud shout, then a thud—reached him. He spun around and stepped quickly into the companionway that led aft, just in time to see the man on the other side of the bulkhead crash back onto the deck. "Stop it!"

But the man paid no attention. He scrambled to his feet. His face was red with rage, his eyes wide. The man—Carlos Sánchez, one of the control system personnel—fumbled with the pocket flap of his dirty windbreaker, then pulled out a knife. *"Cerdo!"* He had spit out the word contemptuously as he glared across the compartment at someone on the far side. "You pig! I will kill you!"

"Sánchez! Stop! I order you!" Zindell took a half step forward. He couldn't see who the other man involved in the fight was, but it didn't matter. Right or wrong made no difference, they had no men to spare anyway. Zindell thought for a moment about his pistol, which was locked in the combination safe in the captain's cabin. That was thirty feet forward of where he stood.

The sound of the bolas as it whirled through the air filled the room. An instant later there was a yelp of pain from Sánchez. He dropped his knife to the floor and turned.

Olga stood at the aft entrance to the crew's mess, her legs straddling the ledge of the watertight door, the pearl-handled knife held in her outstretched hand. She had caught Sánchez around the forearm, the leather strands of the bolas cinched tightly down around the fabric of his windbreaker.

"Leave it on the floor." Olga stepped over to him and, with one flick of her right hand, unwound the bolas from Sánchez's arm as if it were an obedient snake. "If you make a move for your knife, I will wrap these leather strands around your balls.

I would be willing to bet, *señor,* that the pressure from the metal balls of the bolas would be enough to make your own balls fall off." It was obvious from Olga's smile that she would welcome the chance to make good her threat, to show off her skill.

Sánchez eyed her for several seconds. Finally, he turned to Zindell. *"Comandante,"* he said in a strained voice. "This man has insulted me. I cannot work with him. Not any longer." Sánchez pointed toward the corner of the compartment.

"Leave your knife where it is. Go to the forward torpedo room. Immediately. I'll be there shortly." Zindell stepped aside to allow Sánchez to pass. The only advantage of having a small crew was that it was easier to figure out who was doing what and who wasn't, easier to separate the men. That last part was a requirement in dealing with personnel problems in such a confined area. Sánchez would be taken aside and reasoned with. But Zindell also knew that he had to deal with the other man in the fight, whoever he was. He stepped into the compartment.

Ned Pierce smiled arrogantly, the gold fillings in his teeth contrasting conspicuously against his dark-brown skin. "Sorry, captain," he said, both of them knowing full well that he wasn't sorry in the least. "A little joke. A misunderstanding. Nothing to get worked up over."

Zindell walked directly up to him. He knew that any hesitation would be interpreted as personal weakness on his part— a condition he couldn't tolerate, not now, not ever. "Second time for you. You're more than half the way to court martial," Zindell said in a low, threatening voice, his face only inches from Pierce. "Aboard the *Trout*—especially on this cruise— there is only one possible outcome, one possible sentence for a court martial." Zindell stood his ground. He waited a full ten seconds without adding another word. Finally, he spoke. "Take a guess what the punishment for a court martial will be," he said in nearly a whisper. He turned slowly around and began to walk away. He gestured for Olga to pick up Sánchez's knife and follow him.

As Zindell walked past the radio room, the technician inside called to him. "Captain, I've had a sonar contact for the last several minutes. Heavy screws, closing fast. Sounds like what we're looking for."

"Very good. Relay the bearing and distance to the conning tower. Harrison is there with the periscope."

"I know. I've already done that. I know you were occupied," the technician said as he motioned to the aft wall with his thumb.

"Fine." Zindell nodded his approval. He was glad that at least a few of his pickup crew were worth a damn. Moss was the radioman's name. Frank Moss, as he recalled.

"Also," Moss continued, "the teletype checks okay on the frequency and code you gave me." He patted his hand along the side of the gray teletype machine that stood near the entrance to the electronics room. "I sent a general query message to the Pentagon, and we received an automatic reply."

"Is there any chance they know we're out here? Could your message have alerted them?" Just the word *Pentagon* was enough to cause Zindell's skin to crawl.

"No, sir. The message I sent was a test that gets answered automatically by their equipment. It verifies that the line is open and functional, that's all."

"Good." Zindell was pleased with the radioman. Even though he was an absolute loner—he preferred to take even his meals by himself—he certainly knew his business. Moss was a good man to have aboard on this trip. Zindell headed back to the control room. "By the way," he said as he turned back to Olga. "You did a good job back there."

"Thank you." She fondled the bolas in her hand for a few moments, then placed it back on its spot on her belt. "Always a pleasure to serve my captain in any way I can. Would you like me to go forward and talk to Sánchez?"

"No. I'll do that myself. Go to maneuvering and see if they need help back there. I expect to have contact with the target shortly."

"Certainly." She inhaled deeply, allowing her ample cleavage to surface above the jungle camouflage blouse that was cinched in at the waist with a four-inch garrison belt. She stood in front of him a moment longer than was necessary, then turned and walked away.

Zindell watched as she left the control room. Of all his choices, she had so far proven herself to be one of the best. He wondered for an instant what would make a woman behave as she did, but he quickly dismissed the thought. She followed every order to the letter, and that was his first priority. His only priority.

"Captain. A visual contact. Bear one-six-zero."

"I'm coming up." Zindell grabbed a rung of the ladder and edged himself up as rapidly as he could with his one arm. Harrison moved aside from the periscope as Zindell stepped up to it. "Our target?"

"Can't tell. Still too far."

Zindell adjusted the focus knob and squinted into the sight glass. "I have the target. Indistinct but visible. Bearing, mark," Zindell called out as Harrison took the readings off the calibration rings of the scope. The sea was moderate, and the swells broke often enough to churn up the water visibly. "We're riding too low. Bring the boat up another six feet."

"Planesmen, bring the boat to thirty feet," Harrison called into the mouthpiece of the communications interphone he wore. "Then steady as she goes."

"I've got her now." Zindell picked his head up from the periscope eyepiece and smiled. "It's the *Yorktown*. Definitely." He bent over and looked into the periscope again. The huge gray-painted warship had begun to cross slowly from right to left. Zindell had an excellent view of the vessel, the bow and port beam three-quarters visible as she plowed gracefully through the heavy seas. "She's riding well. Definitely seaworthy. Apparently in excellent condition for our purposes. Have the radioman begin to transmit on the lowpowered set. Use the special code."

"Yessir." Harrison relayed the order below.

"When she comes within a thousand yards we should have radio contact." As always, whenever he looked through a periscope things seemed clearer, sharper than they did at any other time. The telemetry divisions and crosshair marks made everything extra orderly and predictable—far more so than they appeared above the surface, in real life. When viewed through the periscope the world became a place he could manage, a world he could deal with. "Take a look," Zindell said to Harrison as he stepped back from the center of the conning tower.

Harrison grabbed the periscope and turned it slowly to keep

the *Yorktown* in view. "She's beautiful . . . enormous . . . riding high . . . the flight deck has been cleared . . . the net erected . . ."

"Right." Jerome Zindell stood in the aft section of the conning tower and nervously strummed his fingers along the edge of the railing. His mind was occupied with the only element that remained unresolved, the only part of the plan he had no way of knowing about until it either happened or it didn't. If it did occur, it would happen sometime in the very near future. Zindell hoped to hell that McClure wasn't having any problems, that he would be able to accomplish his end of their bargain.

Steven Harris sat at a window seat on the left side of the DC-9 jet, but instead of looking out he concentrated on the electronic game in his lap. "Almost . . . wait . . . just a few more. . . ." But then the screen on the game began to fill with alternating streaks of white. A short musical tone began to play.

"Oh, oh. You told me that you had this game aced. You're not as good as you think you are," the teenage boy beside him said.

"Wanna bet?" Steven waved the game in his friend's face. "Let's go, Straka. Put your money where your mouth is."

"Sure thing." Gene Straka took the game and turned it back on. He studied the images in the green scope for several seconds before he waved his hand. "I'm gonna take some practice first. You do it all the time."

"No way!" Steven reached for his game, but Gene pulled it farther away, out of reach and toward the aisle.

"Give it back."

"No."

"Straka, if you don't give it back to me *right now,* I'll bust your face."

"You and what army?"

"You're the one that's gonna need the army." The two teenage boys began to wrestle within what the confines of the narrow airline seats would allow.

The arms of an attractive female seated behind them reached across the seatbacks. She grabbed both boys by the hair, then stood up behind them. "I'd bang your heads together, except that the hollow sound might disturb the other passengers."

Marion Miller smiled at the three giggling teenage girls across the aisle who had turned to watch. "What do you think, Emma?" she asked the black girl who sat between her two friends across the aisle from the boys. "Should I crack these two walnuts?"

"Sure thing, Miss Miller." Emma's full, rich voice was laced with laughter.

"The rest of the senior class would be in your debt. Probably forever," one of the other girls chimed in, also with a laugh.

"I know I'd be," Frank Cobb said from his seat beside the teacher. He turned back to the playbills he had been reading.

"You're killing me," Steven announced in a choked-off, falsetto voice. He began to pant like an overexercised dog. "You're choking me," he continued, suddenly switching to soprano. "My hair follicles are tangled around my eye teeth. I can't see if I'm breathing. Everything is growing dark, dim, black . . . it hurts when I laugh . . . I'll never dance again. . . ."

"Very good, Steven. Very original," Marion said sarcastically. She released the two boys and patted them both on the head. "Be good little boys, now. Promise me you'll be good. I'll buy you lollipops when we get to Chicago."

"Yes, Miss Miller." The boys had answered in unison. Then Gene suddenly snapped into a rigid military salute, held it for several seconds and, with a flourish, pretended to fall over unconscious.

Steven immediately took the cue. He reached for his friend's limp body, pulled it upright, then placed his ear against Gene's chest. After a few solemn moments he turned to the three teenage girls across the aisle. "My diagnosis," he said, his voice now in a deep and measured baritone, "is that either this gentleman has passed away or, possibly, that my wristwatch has stopped."

"Okay, Groucho. Be a good boy now. Please."

"Sure thing, Miss Miller."

"When Harpo comes around," she added as she ruffled Gene's hair, "tell him to calm down, too. Spend a few minutes thinking about your play reports," she announced as she glanced at each of the six of them. Satisfied, she sat back in her seat and closed her eyes. Her teaching job was still so new to her that any of the three high school boys with her, each seventeen years old and 175 or so pounds of pure energy, could easily ignore whatever she said and there was very little she could do. At twenty-two, she was hardly much older than them herself, and at five feet four inches and 115 pounds she was certainly no physical threat. Even the three girls on the trip were as big as she was. But the official authority was hers, so she used it. A first-year teacher was still the teacher, and a senior in high school was still the student. The marvelous thing was that, at the better schools at least, the system still worked. It worked best in those areas the students enjoyed the most—like drama—and for those teachers they enjoyed to study with.

Marion Miller ran her hand along the strands of her long blond hair, then glanced around the cabin. The airliner they traveled on was three-quarters full. There were a few empty seats scattered here and there among the passengers, but not too many. Half of the people onboard were businessmen, but there were a number of women and also several families. Marion adjusted her seat belt and reached for a magazine in the seat pocket in front of her when something out the window caught her eye. She looked out. "Frank. Look." She nudged the boy who sat beside her.

"What?" Frank Cobb put down his theater playbills and turned to the window.

"It's an airplane. See? It's coming closer." Even as she spoke, the small jet grew in relative size as it maneuvered nearer to the airliner's left wing.

"It's getting pretty close. I wonder if our pilot sees it."

"He must."

Captain Drew O'Brien slowly scanned the center instrument panel of the DC-9 jet as was his custom, and each of the dozens of needles and countless lights indicated precisely what they should. Everything was, as usual, perfectly routine.

"Trans-American 255," the cockpit speaker blared, "the traffic I mentioned earlier is at two o'clock and ten miles, a thousand feet above you. A USAir Boeing, also westbound. Once you've cleared USAir, I'll have a higher altitude for you."

"Roger. Understand," the copilot answered as he pressed his microphone button. "We're standing by for the higher altitude as soon as you can get it for us."

"I also have additional traffic for you," the air traffic controller continued. "Unknown, at your seven o'clock position, three miles, fast moving."

"What altitude?" the copilot asked on the radio.

"Altitude is not being reported. Probably down low."

"Roger."

O'Brien nodded, then turned to his left and looked below and behind them. In the distance was the Hudson River, which they had crossed several minutes before. O'Brien could easily make out the ribbon of water as it reflected the bright morning sun. But he saw no aircraft low, although he knew that a solitary aircraft would be easy to miss against the changing pattern of browns, grays and greens that comprised the northern New Jersey terrain. "I don't see anyone." O'Brien turned and scanned out ahead of the airliner. In the distance he could see what he knew was eastern Pennsylvania through the clear skies.

"The traffic is still in radar contact," air traffic control reported. "Eight o'clock, two miles, closing fast."

O'Brien shifted his eyes rearward again, but now at a more level angle and toward the horizon line. "Wait. There's something." He peered out the port window at the silhouette that he had spotted. "Someone . . . he's coming out of the sun . . . hard to see. . . ." The object grew in size rapidly. Visually, it soon sprouted wings, then a tail.

"Nine o'clock, one mile."

"Yes. A small jet." The other airplane was distinctive now. Even the make and color were easily recognizable. "A Learjet. White. No other markings."

"What the hell's he doing?" the copilot said, more as a comment than a question. He pressed the microphone button and passed on the information to air traffic control.

"Roger," the man on the ground answered. "Understand, a Learjet." The traffic controller paused for a moment while he checked further. "Definitely no flight plan on file for a Lear, not for anywhere near this area during the next two hours."

"Okay, we'll watch him." O'Brien straightened himself in the pilot's seat. He took the control wheel in his hands, hit the thumb switch to release the autopilot and began to fly the DC-9 jet manually. "He's probably flying visually. Maybe a training flight out of Westchester or Stewart."

"Then what the hell's he doing?" the copilot said again, this

time as a question. He leaned to his left and craned over to
see. The Lear continued to hover motionless off their left wing,
which meant that it was flying at the same speed and on a
parallel course with the airliner. "Do you want to change our
heading?"

"No." O'Brien took one more look at the Lear to gauge the
path that the aircraft was taking. The distance was no more
than half a mile. It was an annoying situation, but not an overtly
dangerous one. The Lear was holding steady to its parallel
course, although it seemed to be edging slightly nearer to them.

"The traffic is now at nine o'clock and less than half a
mile," air traffic control confirmed. "Your radar targets are
beginning to merge on my scope. Verify that you still have
that traffic in sight?" the air traffic controller asked. There was
a nervous edge to his voice.

"Yes," O'Brien answered to his copilot while he kept his
eyes fixed on the white Lear. "Tell him I intend to hold this
heading. I want that clown in the Lear to make the first move.
He's obviously playing games. I'll try to get his registration
number as he crosses over." O'Brien played gently with the
airliner's controls, his left hand on the wheel, his right hand
on the two throttles that controlled engine speed. It was obvious
that the Lear pilot had seen them from the slight changes in
course that he had made. The Lear was playing it much closer
than normal; it was still nothing to be alarmed about, although
O'Brien intended to report this incident to the FAA when they
landed in Chicago. There was no real danger, as long as that
jerk . . .

"Flight 255, this is the Lear," a loud voice suddenly boomed
out of O'Brien's cockpit speaker. "Do you read me?"

O'Brien reached for his microphone and snatched it off the
side panel. "We sure do, Lear. What are you trying to do?"
There was a great deal more anger in his voice than he had
intended to display, but the anger was sincere. He felt every
bit of it. O'Brien had no patience for pilots who cut margins
too close, who fooled around with situations that were potentially dangerous. "You'd better break off and get out of here.
Right now."

"Listen to me," the voice from the Lear began again as soon
as O'Brien had ended his transmission. "Don't touch your

microphone. I've got some information for you. It's important. Very important." There was a pause for several seconds before the Lear pilot spoke again, although his transmitter continued to put out its signal—a low, steady hum—the entire time. "No one on the ground can hear me because I'm using a special radio. Very low powered. I'm also monitoring your transmitters with a broad-band receiver, so don't try to call anyone from this point on. What I'm going to tell you is for your ears only." There was another pause, and this time there seemed to be the faint sound of sneering laughter in the background. Finally, the voice resumed. "Listen closely. Follow my instructions. Each to the letter. If you don't, every one of you will be dead in sixty seconds."

Edward McClure glanced backward, out of the cockpit and into the Learjet's tiny but elegant cabin. The rich tones of real leather, the polished woods, the attractive wall panels of carefully colored fiber glass made a ludicrous statement when contrasted with the condition of the people who occupied the cabin.

The bodies of the two dead pilots were hunched over, still strapped in the pair of rearward-facing seats. Their outstretched arms lay at odd angles on the plush carpeted floor. Their legs stuck awkwardly into the small aisle that ran the length of the cabin. Behind them, still handcuffed to the right rear seat and facing forward was Trombetta, the airline's cargo supervisor. His jacket and tie were askew and the front of his shirt hung out from beneath his belt.

When Dominick Trombetta saw that McClure had turned toward him, he began the same plea that he had used nearly continuously since they left the ground at Kennedy Airport twenty minutes before. "Please. I'm in this thing with you. Totally. There's no reason to do this to me. Let me go."

"Good view, huh?" McClure replied as he ignored what Trombetta had said. He gestured toward the DC-9 airliner that flew no more than 400 yards to their right. "Nice color scheme your airline has. I like the two-tone red. Classy, but not overstated. Do you agree?"

Trombetta did not answer. Instead, he pulled senselessly for the thousandth time against where the handcuffs were fastened to the chair rail. It was to no avail. All he managed to do was rub his wrist raw. The blood oozed out of the cuts on his reddened skin, along the metal chain of the handcuffs and onto the floor. It had turned a large spot on the beige carpet into a patch of dirty brown. "Please," Trombetta said again, "let me go."

McClure smiled. "Don't be foolish." He turned his attention away from the cabin and back to the Lear's flight controls. Satisfied that everything was well, he turned to the portable electronics box that he had earlier placed on the empty copilot's seat. McClure reached across and carefully adjusted the box's five-inch antenna, then once more checked the voltage of its storage batteries. Everything checked perfectly. He glanced at the panel clock. Nine twenty-four. A full minute had gone by since he had last looked. It was time to go on to the next step, now that the airliner's crew had been given enough time to stew in their own juices, stew in their mounting fears.

McClure reached for his microphone and pressed the button. "Okay, Flight 255, I'm glad to see that you haven't used your transmitter," he began. It was always good technique to remind everyone what the specific ground rules for the day were. "That was very smart. Very cooperative. Now I'm going to lay it all out for you." McClure ran his tongue across his lips—this was the part that he relished the most. Unfortunately, on this occasion he would not be able to see the changes in their facial expressions—that slow transformation from general fear coupled with a tinge of natural human curiosity to the more specific, more intense blends of agonized desperation and total panic. Just like he had seen so many times in Vietnam—even among the 'Cong officers, who were supposed to be so damn inscrutable—that visual change to total desperation was always easy to read. Predictable. And necessary. It was the required prerequisite for eventual and total obedience.

"Thanks to the earlier cooperation of one of your loyal employees," McClure began his next transmission, "there is a radioactivated bomb planted onboard your aircraft." He resisted the temptation to peek back at Trombetta. "It contains enough explosive to blow you out of the sky. It is, of course, located in a spot that you can't get at while in flight." McClure glanced again at the portable control panel on the copilot's seat, then back at the airliner. "I'm going to lead you somewhere. You will follow me. Closely. The flight will be conducted at a very low altitude. We will begin a rapid descent shortly. But before we do," McClure continued, his words slowed measurably so there would be no chance for any misunderstanding, "I'll make the assumption that you'll need proof. Proof of my intentions. Proof of my ability to destroy you. I know that, under similar circumstances, I'd want some sort of proof myself."

McClure reached across to the portable electronics panel. He snapped off the safety switch, then poised his finger above the button labeled Number One. He hesitated for a few moments while he gave some thought to adding one more sentence to his transmission, a few more words to give the crew of Flight 255 at least a general warning so they would know what would occur next. McClure decided against it. While the next act was enough to acquire their undivided attention, the element of total surprise added to it would guarantee cooperation, guarantee the deal.

Edward McClure pushed down on button Number One.

Stewardess Carol Fey carefully stacked the cans and bottles she had taken from the cabinet below as she prepared the forward galley area for the morning drink service. "Take out a few extra tea bags," she said over her shoulder to Lucy. "The Japanese group in row eleven will probably want tea."

"Probably."

"I'm glad we don't serve a meal until we leave Chicago," Carol continued as she fiddled with a pack of plastic spoons. "I'm not up for it."

"Not feeling well?" Lucy Kellogg asked. She took out the tea bags, then gathered up napkins from the lower cabinet on the galley's rear side.

"Not exactly."

"Oh." Lucy turned and smiled knowingly. "Late date?"

"Matter of fact, yes." Carol made it obvious from her gesture that she didn't mind talking about it. She wanted to, actually. She didn't know Lucy very well, but this sort of news was too exciting not to share with someone. "A new boyfriend."

"Anyone I know?"

"No. He's not with the airline." The night before had been Carol's fourth date with Pete and it had been their best yet.

Pete was a real gentleman. He was good looking, interesting and talented. Better yet, he was single. "We're getting sort of serious," Carol added. Even though he hadn't pushed for it, Carol had decided that last night the timing would be right for them to make love for the first time. The dinner at The Emporium had been very good, the wine excellent. They had strolled through the closed mall for an hour afterward, window-shopping, holding hands and chatting about nothing in particular. They then went to her apartment for after-dinner drinks. The lovemaking that followed was natural and easy. But it had gone on until three in the morning. She had set the alarm for 6:00 A.M. to give herself time enough to wash and dry her hair. "I should have called in sick today," Carol said as she silently counted the bottles that she had laid along the galley edge.

"I know the feeling." Lucy smiled sympathetically, then stepped forward to help her friend. "Looks like we can use more napkins," she added as she stretched up to reach the door of the upper forward compartment. She swung the small aluminum door open.

The electronic signal that had been sent by the portable panel in the Learjet had traveled the open span between the two aircraft at the speed of light. It had been picked up by the self-contained antenna of the unit taped to the upper corner of the galley compartment and, being of the proper frequency, was gathered in by its receiving set. The radio signal routed itself through the circuits of the device, through a miniaturized amplifier and, finally, along its output channel. From that point the surge of voltage traveled into a wire that brought it to the electric blasting cap that was an integral part of the package.

Lucy Kellogg had been looking straight into the dark confines of the upper galley compartment when the blasting cap exploded. For the briefest time the sudden explosive glare of light reached her eyes before the effects of the blast did. Her eyes registered the visual effects—a pinpoint of soundless brilliance that expanded outward at a speed her senses could not measure, the intensity of the light increasing as its size grew. But before any of that light-induced message could travel the short distance to the cognizant sections of her brain, the heat and pressure effects of the blast traveled beyond the lip of the galley shelf. Because she had opened that particular cabinet at that particular moment, the explosion slammed full force against her face.

Her scream was short. It mixed with the flat, dull roar of an intense explosion heard too close to its source. Before her muscles had reacted enough to allow her body to fall backward, both her eyes had been charred unmercifully and were pushed far back in their sockets. Slivers of shattered aluminum rammed into her skin. Blood suddenly gushed from her cheeks, forehead and neck, and clumps of hair were torn backward from her scalp and ripped away. Several of the dangling strands of her silky blond hair began to smolder from the wave of intense heat that overran her as easily as a locomotive could run over a small animal.

Yet in spite of its intense power at that short range, the blasting cap was not forceful enough to carry on its destruction for very far or very long. Carol Fey, who had been knocked down by the force of the concussion and whose left arm had been slightly singed by the peripheral effects of the searing heat, had not lost consciousness. "My God! Oh, my God!" she wailed repeatedly as she attempted to stand up. Her hand groped for the galley ledge, slipped off once, twice, then finally took hold. She pulled her upright, slowly, shakily. "Lucy!" Carol reached down to her friend. Lucy had fallen on her stomach. Carol began to turn Lucy's body over.

Carol's terrorized scream filled the entire length of the DC-9. The sound of her shrill voice carried above the noise, shouts and commotion that came from the startled, frightened passengers. Carol saw suddenly, in one horrible moment of total revulsion, how badly mutilated her friend's face had become, how unrecognizable, monstrous.

Even as the few passengers who were brave enough to come forward in those first few moments piled into the galley area, the stewardess continued to scream without interruption. Her eyes remained fixed on the pulpy mass of charred and blood-soaked flesh that lay at her feet—the remains that were, not fifteen seconds before, the person who had been speaking gently and softly with her.

"Give me a hand. God Almighty. Let's get her outa' here." Dwight Tobey pushed around several gawking passengers and stepped into the galley area. He reached across and pulled the hysterical stewardess toward him, past the dead body, then into the crowd that had gathered in a knot behind the galley entrance. "Get her outa' here. Put her in a seat. Someone help her. Getta doctor." Then Dwight turned back to the body that lay on the galley floor. Even though the contents of his stomach had begun to churn up into this throat, he managed to keep himself from gagging long enough to turn the body back over. He could see that there was no chance whatsoever that the stewardess could be alive. *It's just like the farm. There's no difference. Flesh and bone, that's all.* By talking himself into it, Tobey found the courage to push the damaged body back against the galley wall where it would be less conspicuous to the people in the cabin. "Get me a blanket. Hurry." Someone from behind handed him a bright red airline blanket and Tobey quickly draped it over the mangled remains of the stewardess.

"What about the pilot?"

"Yes! The pilots!" Several others in the cabin began to shout the same concern about the fate of the pilots that the two older men in the second row had just voiced. Their alarm spread through the cabin as if it were a high wind blowing across an open field. "God help us! The pilots! The pilots are dead!"

"Wait. I'm a pilot."

Tobey looked at the person who had made that statement. A woman, mid-thirties, slender, attractive. She stood a few feet from him, although she had turned to face the cabin. Her voice was loud enough to carry throughout the cabin's length and it had served to instantly quell the mounting panic.

"I'm a pilot," she said again, her voice still strong and clear, although there was a great deal of nervousness in it.

Tobey wondered if she really was a pilot and, even if she were, how long her meaningless announcement would keep the people in the cabin from total hysteria. At least for the moment her words had worked to calm them slightly. Besides, the airplane was obviously still under control. At the instant of the explosion the airliner had jerked wildly to the right and dipped its wings, but it had quickly straightened itself out. Tobey wondered if that meant that the autopilot alone was flying the aircraft. He didn't know enough about airplanes, one way or the other, to decide.

The third stewardess was coming forward from the rear of the cabin, and Tobey watched as she pushed and shoved her way around the standing, milling crowd in the aisle. He decided not to wait for her. "We might not need another pilot," he said loudly, mostly for his own benefit. *The autopilot is on, but both pilots are dead*. That, he now realized, could easily account for the stable flight condition they were in. If it were true, he suspected that he and his family would be dead very soon, also—along with everyone else onboard. He spun around and yanked hard on the cockpit door handle. At first the door would not budge, but then he felt the lock release. Someone inside had released it. The cockpit door swung open.

The man in the right seat—the copilot—lay slumped forward against the control wheel. He was motionless. There was a jagged piece of aluminum trimwork sticking out of his neck at the base of his skull. A steady river of red ran down his skin and disappeared beneath his shirt collar. Tobey turned to the other man in the cockpit.

"Help me. Get his body off the wheel," the captain said in a strained, hollowed voice. "Hurry."

"Are you okay?" Tobey reached for the copilot's body and pulled it backward. He held the man against the seatback so his inert body and dangling arms would not interfere with the flight controls. "Are you all right?" Tobey asked the captain again as he looked at him closely. The man's right shirt sleeve was torn in several places and there were spots of blood soaking through the white cloth. Other than that, he seemed to have no other visible injuries.

"Yes. I'm okay." Drew O'Brien trimmed out the aircraft's controls, then scanned the instruments. Both engines ran normally, the electical system was okay, the pressurization and air conditioning continued to put out what they should. Everything was apparently in working order. "What's happened in the cabin?"

"One stewardess is dead. Another is injured, but only slightly. She's hysterical. The third stewardess is trying to calm the passengers. What happened up here? Can we land okay?"

The fear on O'Brien's face was replaced by the flush of anger as he glanced at the white Learjet that continued to fly

a steady formation off their left wing. He grabbed his microphone off the side panel. "Bastard! Murderer! You've killed
some of our people."

"Don't touch that microphone again!" the cockpit speaker
blared in response. "Not unless you want to die. I'm serious.
You won't get any more chances." There was a pause in the
transmission from the Lear while, evidently, the man who
spoke gathered in his thoughts. "It wasn't supposed to be much
of an explosion...just enough to show you...I guess I put
in too much...." The man's voice sounded less self-assured
than it had any time earlier. He paused again. Finally, after
several long seconds, he resumed speaking. "It doesn't make
any difference. Not everything can work out exactly as I
planned." The voice from the Lear had grown more cold, more
firm with every passing word. "We will begin the descent very
soon. Idle power and full speed brakes. I'm going to cross
under you first, then you stay off my left rear on the way down.
Rock your wings once if you understand."

O'Brien moved the DC-9's control wheel to comply. He
didn't know what else he could do. "What's the condition of
the copilot?" he asked over his shoulder.

"No pulse, no heartbeat. It looks like his neck is broken."
Tobey touched the jagged piece of aluminum that was still
stuck in the dead copilot's neck, then looked at the section of
wall behind the copilot's head that had exploded outward. Contorted pieces of metal and fiber glass hung loosely around the
small hole in the bulkhead wall—the wall which divided the
cockpit from the galley. The explosion had blown out the piece
of trimwork, and that was what had killed the copilot.

"Unfasten his seat belt. Get him out of the seat." O'Brien
didn't want to run the risk of the copilot's body becoming
entangled in the flight controls, although at the moment that
possibility seemed the least of his problems.

"What about that small airplane?" Tobey asked as he unlatched the copilot's seat belt and began to carefully drag his
body backward out of the seat. "What does he mean?"

"Sabotage. Hijacking. He's a terrorist of some kind. There
are radio-controlled bombs onboard our flight. We have to
follow him. I don't know where we're headed."

"Christ!"

The radio speaker crackled again. "Don't get any bright ideas about outrunning me. This radio-controlled detonator is good for ten miles. If I lose sight of you for more than a few seconds, I'll press the button."

O'Brien gestured out the window, toward the Lear. "Explain the situation to the third stewardess. Have her brief the passengers. Get everyone in their seats."

"Okay." Tobey opened his mouth to add more, but he couldn't think of anything else to say. *Terrorists. Hijacking. Radio-controlled bombs.* It was too insane to believe, yet it had happened. It was happening to him, happening to his family. The thought of Ann and the kids in the cabin crossed his mind, but he pushed that thought aside for the moment so he could concentrate on the job the captain had given him. Tobey turned to leave, but then stopped and turned back to the captain. "There's a woman onboard who said she's a pilot. Do you want her in the copilot's seat?" Tobey pointed to the empty flight chair on the captain's right.

"No." But O'Brien knew that he had answered too abruptly, reacted negatively for no real reason. "Wait." The woman might be a professional corporate pilot or even an airline pilot. She might be a great deal of help. "Tell her to come up."

"Right."

O'Brien sat further upright in his flight chair and was engrossed in the sight of the Lear as it passed beneath them to position itself on his right side, just as the hijacker had said it would. When O'Brien turned to his right, the woman was already there. She was attractive and competent looking. She appeared to be no more than thirty years old. "Are you with an airline?" he asked, although as he continued to watch her he began to doubt that possibility even before she answered. Her actions showed that she was uncomfortable, uncertain of how to even sit in the airliner's cockpit.

"No. Nothing like that. A private pilot. Single engine only." The woman brushed back her short cropped hair, more out of nervousness than for any real purpose. "This sort of airplane is beyond me." "She waved her hand at the flight panel crowded with endless rows of gauges, dials and lights. "But I'd be able to work the radios for you. Show me where they are. I can dial in the frequencies."

"Sit still. Don't touch anything. First I've got to explain the situation to you." *Explain this nightmare.* O'Brien let out a deep sigh, then glanced back out the window at the Learjet. It had begun its descent. O'Brien shook his head in disgust, then pulled back on the airliner's throttles and yanked out the speed brakes. He had no choice but to obey. O'Brien began a high-speed descent to follow the Lear as he explained the situation to the unknown, frightened woman who sat on his right.

5

JOE ELDERMAN'S FACE was bathed in the macabre green light from the radarscope. It magnified the mounting panic he was experiencing as he pointed his fingers to the spot on the electronic tube where the target had last been seen. "Right here. Twelve miles southwest of Huguenot, on a bearing of two-four-two. The last altitude I saw from the airliner was thirty-six hundred feet." Elderman wiped the perspiration off his forehead, then looked at the radar screen several more seconds as if he expected Flight 255 to suddenly reappear. Finally, he looked back up at his supervisor.

"On a two-four-two bearing," the older man who stood beside him repeated. He leaned forward and unfolded a chart. He quickly found the proper coordinates and laid his index finger on the area that Elderman had described. "Somewhere around here, you say?"

"Yes."

"The New Jersey-Pennsylvania border," the supervisor announced as he read the names and symbols on the chart. "A few miles west of the Delaware River, around Dingman's Ferry."

"Or even farther west than that," Elderman volunteered.

"The airliner was still headed westbound when he disappeared from the scope. He could have gone another five miles. Maybe ten." Elderman couldn't believe that this had happened on his shift, on his scope. In his eight years as an air traffic controller, he had never witnessed an actual crash.

"Hand me your telephone. I need to give the coordinator an update."

"Sure." Elderman passed over the telephone. While the supervisor talked, Elderman glanced up and down the long rows of radarscopes in the dimly lit air traffic control center. The rest of the controllers were hunched over their screens, their attentions on their individual tasks. But Elderman caught a few of the quick glances in his direction as each of them tried to learn more of what had happened in sector five. Each controller said his own silent prayer of thanks that it was Joe Elderman and not them in his chair this particular September morning.

"Here." The supervisor gave the telephone back. "Anything else you can think of?"

"I wish I could. I do know that the country around there— the Poconos—is pretty desolate. Heavily wooded, lots of lakes, from what I remember."

"You're right." The supervisor studied the chart for a short while longer, then peeked at the radarscope. There were still no targets displayed anywhere near the area in question, although he really didn't expect any. The airliner had gone down, period.

"It's weird," Elderman said as he followed the supervisor's eyes to the blank radar screen. "Everything was normal until this unknown Learjet came toward them. The first time I noticed the conflicting target, it was five or six miles from Trans-American and heading straight toward it."

"And you gave the crew immediate notice of the conflicting traffic?"

Elderman could tell from the change in the supervisor's tone that this was an official question. "That's right," he said as he tried to remember exactly how far away he had first called the conflicting, unknown target. The taped radio conversations would have that information, but he didn't want to wait until they played the tapes back to know for sure. "The crew saw the traffic. They identified it as a Lear."

"Go on."

Elderman squirmed in his seat. Another man, also an FAA supervisor, walked up alongside the radarscope, but he stood a few feet away, in the shadows. He had taken out a pencil and pad and had begun to take notes. "I did everything by the book," Elderman continued, hesitantly. "Once the Trans-American crew confirmed that they had visual sighting with the Learjet, I turned my attention to other traffic I was working to the north." Elderman waved his hand toward the top edge of his radarscope to indicate where that other air traffic had been.

"Did you notice anything else about the Trans-American flight or the Learjet target?" the second supervisor asked as he stepped closer. He scribbled on his pad. "Anything from that point on?"

"Yes. Sort of." Elderman bit into his lower lip. He hoped to hell that he hadn't said too much already and that nothing he was about to say would reflect badly on him. You could never be too careful when it came to the legal types. They were nothing but Monday-morning quarterbacks. Still, his role in this accident seemed pretty clear-cut. Nothing he did had any bearing on it. At least he hoped not. "The unknown target—the Learjet—seemed to edge in slowly toward the airliner, as if it were flying an intentional formation."

"Intentional?"

"Maybe. That's what it seemed like. It took a minute or more to happen. When they finally got less than half a mile apart, the two radar targets merged together."

"Did the radar targets ever separate any time after that?"

"No. Never."

"Not even after the rapid descent had begun?"

"No."

"Were there any radio transmissions from the Lear? Any further transmissions from the airliner?"

"None from the Lear." Elderman thought about the background noise—a low-level humming—that had begun on the frequency about then, but he decided not to mention it. It probably meant nothing—general interference of some sort—and would only complicate his side of the story for no reason. But he did decide to say something about the chopped-off sentence that he had gotten from what he presumed was Flight

255. "Something did come across, but it was very garbled. You might be able to make more out of it on the tape."

"What was it?"

"Just a few words. Hard to tell. But one of the words sounded like *murdered,* another *killed."*

"I see." The second supervisor closed his notebook. "We'll pull the tapes, but it's probably one of those irrational last transmissions from a flight that knows it's going down."

"That's what it sounded like to me." Elderman was pleased that no one had focused on anything he had done or had hinted that his actions were suspect. "This is one hell of a shame. A real tragedy."

"It sure is." The second supervisor shook his head in disgust, then turned and walked away.

The first supervisor began to fold up his chart. "We'll add this data to what we've already sent to search-and-rescue. Write all you can remember in your report. When you're done, you can go home." The supervisor motioned for another controller across the room who began to walk toward them. "Henderson will relieve you. Go home and have a drink. Relax." The supervisor smiled. He was happy that for now it appeared that this accident had nothing to do with any of his boys or any of his equipment. "By the way," he said as Elderman stood up and began to walk toward the administration area with him, "do you have any thoughts on what could have happened? Strictly off the record, of course."

Elderman nodded. "Off the record, sure. The Lear was playing games with the airliner. An intentional game of tag. He must have cut it too close. They must have collided. The two of them came down together."

"That's what I figure," the supervisor agreed. He opened the door that led into his office and gestured toward the desk that he wanted the controller to use to write his report. "It's a real crime. Some moron on a lark killed lots of innocent people." The supervisor looked at his wristwatch. It was 9:35. "At least the weather out there is good. They've got eleven hours of daylight to conduct a search. Unless someone living in that area saw that airliner go down, it might take every bit of those eleven hours for a search to cover all that territory. I used to camp up there and I know for a fact how right you were. The

Poconos are one hell of a big, remote area to find a wrecked airplane in."

Even through the raindrops that rolled rapidly down the windows of the bridge of the *Yorktown*, Paul Talbot had spotted the submarine's periscope a minute before the radio had begun to crackle with the first message. He reached for the microphone and replied with the authorized response that told the submarine that all was well on the carrier's end.

"Continue your southeast heading," the speaker blared again, the man's voice somewhat garbled by the very low level of power the portable transmitters put out. "We will maintain our relative position off your port bow. Slow to half speed so we can keep up."

"Roger. Ahead half." Talbot reached for the signal lever to the engine room. He pulled the handle back to the halfway mark. Within a few seconds the answering bells on the bridge rang and Talbot felt the vibrations of the huge ship's engines as they began to slow.

"Verify that the landing net has been erected." There was a few seconds' pause in the transmission from the submarine before the man spoke again. "The captain wants to be certain that the net has been properly secured."

"Stand by." Talbot leaned over to the intercom and pressed the appropriate switch. "Engine room, I have the submarine in radio contact." Talbot peeked out the bridge window, but was now unable to visually pick out the trail created by the periscope against the choppy, whitecapped sea. "I had visual contact a moment ago, but not right now." Talbot knew that visual contact meant nothing, but his old Navy training caused him to report all the facts as he saw them, without interpretation. Deciding what details were important and what weren't was an exclusive domain of the officers—a responsibility he had never experienced before this trip.

"Hey, pop, get your bifocals checked." Yang's voice had a lilting, teasing laugh to it. "I've got a man leaning on the port side rail who just called me to say that the sub is plain as day. Directly off our midsection, a few hundred yards."

Talbot forced his eyes to scan the spot Yang mentioned. In a few seconds he again found the periscope, its black mast sticking up even higher out of the waves. "Negative sighting from the bridge. No visual contact with the submarine," Talbot lied. He had no intention of allowing Yang to correct him again, even though he had been right about the sub's location. "They want verification that the deck net has been secured properly," Talbot continued as he passed on the submarine's last message.

"Hell, yes. Tell that underwater skeptic that we guarantee our work." The background sound of laughing came across the intercom. "Tell him that we're offically off the clock, that our part of the job is finished—at least until McClure's Air Force arrives." More laughter came out of the wall speaker before the engine room switched off their end of the intercom.

Talbot passed on the message, word for word. To his surprise, the man on the receiving end acknowledged with no comment. Perhaps he, too, understood too well what a childish bastard Richard Yang was. Talbot dismissed the thought as he concentrated on relaying a few minor but necessary items to the sub. Satisfied that all was finally taken care of, he terminated his transmission. The portable radio lapsed into silence.

Paul Talbot stood with his hands against the old and cracked leather of the captain's chair. His body swayed back and forth in rhythm with the rolling sea that the giant warship wallowed through. Out of a sense of duty, Talbot glanced once more around the bridge. All was well. The ship's autopilot held the steering controls within a degree or two of the on-course heading and the engines continued to run smoothly.

Talbot glanced below at the flight deck. The net that Yang and his men had erected—a weave of steel cabling that stretched across the width of the flight deck—made the scene below appear as if a badminton game for giants was about to be played. The knitted cable stood tall enough to be nearly on eye level with the bridge. Talbot had never seen a steel net of this sort in actual use, although he had heard of it. If a landing aircraft broke its normal tail hook and time and fuel allowed, the men on the carrier would erect the net of steel webbing and the airplane would be snared by it during its runout on landing. Without it, there was no way to get an airplane with a broken tail hook stopped on the short and pitching deck of an aircraft carrier.

Talbot reached for his coffee cup and put it to his lips. The brown liquid in it was tepid at best, but he didn't want to leave the spot where he stood. A fresh pot of hot coffee sat on the hot plate in the captain's sea cabin, a dozen feet behind him. He didn't have the energy to get it. Even though there was nothing left to do, somehow there was still too much to do, too much ahead of them. Talbot stood physically inert, but his mind raced ahead to what was expected to happen on the *Yorktown* within the next few hours.

The man that McClure said he had hired—Talbot hadn't asked for a name, and McClure hadn't volunteered one—would have already stolen the aircraft with the gold on it. If plans were going according to schedule, that aircraft would be headed out to rendezvous with the carrier at that moment. Once landed, the gold would then be unloaded and everyone would head for the submarine. Talbot would be dropped off in Spain. He would work his way to Switzerland to deposit his share. Then he would get word to Charlotte and Amy that the money was theirs but that it should be withdrawn slowly so as not to alert the U.S. government. A half million dollars in a numbered Swiss account was not enough to pay for the deaths of Keith and Thomas, but it was the only thing Talbot could do for his wife and daughter. Once he had gotten word to Charlotte and Amy, Talbot would disappear. To Africa or South America, probably. Charlotte and Amy would be set for the rest of their lives—and Talbot would no longer have to look into their eyes, listen to their sobs late at night. There was no way to get his grandsons back, but at least this was something. It was the only thing he could do.

Talbot cleared his throat, then looked out the window. The sea was frothy white. The bow of the carrier bobbed up and down in the increasing swells. The surface wind had also picked up. That, at least, was a good sign. When the proper moment arrived, Talbot would turn the ship directly into the wind and that would allow the pilot to touch down on the *Yorktown* at an even slower speed. The more wind they had across the deck, the easier the landing would be for that unknown pilot.

Talbot wondered for a moment about that man, a person he had never met, never spoken with. Stealing the airplane was dangerous enough, but landing on this heaving deck in foul weather was unquestionably a great risk. What made a man do a thing like that? Was it the money alone, or could there be more to it? "Damn," Talbot said out loud, the sound of his voice echoing off the emptiness of the vast ship's bridge where he stood alone.

Just like me . . . No choice. There was more to every event than most people could ever imagine. Life was very involved, very complex. Too complex. Talbot said a silent prayer for that unknown pilot. For some reason he felt an empathy with him, felt that the pilot would be different from Yang and the hoodlums in the engine room. Talbot prayed that the pilot wouldn't get hurt, that no one would get hurt. Money was one thing, but life was another. McClure had assured him that this mission—barring an unforeseen accident—would be free of risk, that no one would get hurt. Without that assurance, Paul Talbot knew that he never would have gone along with this crazy idea, no matter what the financial reward. No amount of money was worth a life.

Talbot sighed heavily, then edged himself onto the captain's chair. He picked up a pair of binoculars and began to scan the horizon, port to starboard. Other than the submarine's periscope cutting through the waves abeam the *Yorktown,* there were no targets in sight. Everything was quiet. Too quiet. Talbot laid down the binoculars and reached across for the cassette player that Amy had given to him as a birthday present. Talbot slid in the new Willie Nelson tape that he had bought the day before but had yet to play. He pressed the machine's start button.

After a few seconds of silence, a melancholy piano began. The carefully fingered notes resonated with a haunting clarity off the flat metal walls of the bridge. The introduction to the song ran very slowly, as if the musicians themselves were reluctant to get on with it. Finally, the plaintive voice of Willie Nelson began, his words formed carefully, the tone of his phrases full yet as vulnerable and fragile as a thin piece of elegant crystal.

> *Oh, it's a long, long while*
> *From May to December*
> *But the days grow short*

When you reach September
When the autumn weather
takes the leaves to flame
One doesn't have time
for the waiting game.

Paul Talbot reached for the cassette player to shut it off, but his fingers would not respond to instructions from his rational mind. Something else—nostalgia, pain, suffering, guilt—was in control. He did not want to hear any more, but he could not stop himself. The lyrics continued to assault him, the notes of the solo piano played so forlornly that Talbot felt himself slipping between them and falling toward the hollow end of a bottomless pit.

The days dwindle down
to a precious few
September
November
And these few precious days
I'll spend with you
These precious days
I'll spend with you.

6

THE AIR CONDITIONING and ventilating system continued to work properly as it purged the airliner of the last traces of smoke, floating dust and odors from the explosion ten minutes earlier. Without taking his eyes off the flight panel, Captain Drew O'Brien spoke to the woman who occupied the copilot's seat. "Get the next chart out. From the case on your right."

"This black case?"

"Yes."

"Okay." Janet Holbrook fumbled with the leather cover, opened it, then took out a stack of charts. She rifled through them silently, once, then twice, before she finally located the next chart in the series. *Calm yourself down. Do things slowly, step by step. You won't be any help if you make mistakes.* "I found it. I'll tune the next frequency."

O'Brien did not answer. Instead, he moved his eyes from his flight instruments to the white Lear that flew a short distance ahead. "We're too damn low," O'Brien mumbled as he wrestled with the airliner's flight controls to stay lined up with the more maneuverable smaller aircraft. "That insane maniac is going to kill us."

"Watch those hills ahead!" Janet sat up higher in the co-pilot's seat, her eyes wide as she watched the tree-lined rise in the terrain loom in front of them. She shot a quick glance at the radio altimeter, which showed their height above the ground. A bare 200 feet. She would not have flown anywhere near this low, not even in her single-engine Piper.

"I see the hill." O'Brien began to ease the airliner slightly higher. "Maybe he'll hit the ridge," the captain said hopefully. But even as he spoke the Lear began to rise also, until it, too, was slightly higher than the elevated terrain. The ridge line flashed beneath them at over 400 miles an hour, which changed the visual images of the trees, the open grassy fields, the dusty country roads into nothing but indistinct blurs of motion and color. "This guy is getting more daring as time goes on. Every-time we cross a hill, he crosses it a little lower." O'Brien glanced at his panel clock. Nine forty-one. They had been at this low-altitude madness for nearly fifteen minutes.

"Maybe someone on the ground will spot us."

"I doubt it." As O'Brien spoke, a truck popped into view as they sped across the next line of trees. "Look." It was a milk truck, its polished stainless-steel body glistening in the mid-morning sun, its blue cab shining brightly. At least it looked like a milk truck. But at this altitude and speed, it came and went too quickly for either of them to be certain. "No one will see us long enough to be sure of what they saw. They'll guess we're a military jet on maneuvers, if they bother to guess at all." O'Brien nodded toward the Lear ahead of them. "This guy has obviously picked this route for a very good reason. It's very rural, there's very little chance of us being spotted. I doubt that he'll take us over any populated areas."

Just then the Lear banked sharply to the left, held its steep angle for a brief moment, then quickly rolled level on a new heading. "Son-of-a-bitch." O'Brien wrestled with the DC-9's control wheel to follow as best he could. He could hear the shouts and squeals from the passengers in the cabin as he frightened them even more with the abrupt maneuvers. "See what I mean?" O'Brien said once the airliner had been leveled and put back in formation behind the Lear again. "Now we're headed south. He's avoiding some area to our right."

"I understand." Janet looked at the horizon, where a slight

haziness in the otherwise clear sky showed that a populated area lay off the right wing tip. "Lancaster," she said as she tapped the radio gauge in front of her. The radio she had tuned a few minutes before had come to life. "We're due east of the Lancaster station right now."

"Okay. Mark the bearing and time on your chart. At this altitude we'll lose radio reception very soon. Try to figure where the next station will be if we hold this course. Tune in stations on either side of where you think we're going. That's the only way we can verify where he's taking us."

"Right." Janet picked up a pencil and made a mark on the chart. She resisted the temptation to ask the captain what good that information would do them. Knowing where they were was not their problem—getting away from a homicidal madman was.

"Captain."

"What?" O'Brien glanced over his shoulder at the man who had entered the cockpit.

"My name is James Westcott. I'm a New York attorney. A group of people in the cabin have asked me to come up. They want to know what, exactly, is going on. They have a right to know."

"They sure do," O'Brien replied, his voice rising. "We all have a damn right to know. *I* have a right to know!" His reply had ended at nearly a shout. He paused for a moment to calm himself. O'Brien knew it was the man in the Learjet he was angry at, not this passenger. "Didn't the stewardess brief everyone? I passed on the information that . . ."

"Don't be ridiculous. None of this is acceptable. We've bought a ticket on your airline and we expect to be protected. There must be other alternatives."

"I'm open to suggestions." O'Brien fed continuous inputs into the airliner's control wheel, to keep them in proper formation behind the Lear.

"How can we be sure this terrorist, as you've called him, is telling the truth? How can we be sure there's a bomb onboard? He might be bluffing."

"I've got two dead crew members who'd swear that he isn't." O'Brien regretted his choice of words but he, too, could hardly control his mounting tension. He could imagine how bad things must be in the cabin. At least in the cockpit there were details to be attended with and a general sense—no matter how inaccurate—that control of the flight was still his. In the cabin, the passengers could only sit and wait. "I'm sorry. I didn't mean that like it sounded. But we have no real alternatives. We've got to assume that if he's managed to plant one bomb, then he's managed to plant two."

"I agree with the captain," Janet added. She looked with obvious dislike at the passenger standing between her and the captain.

"Thank you," O'Brien answered sincerely. He was glad that his reasoning made sense to at least one other person besides himself. He wondered if he should also mention the other thought that occurred to him. He decided that he should, that this lawyer was right—the passengers did have a right to know every alternative, no matter how remote or ludicrous. "As I see it, the only chance to escape is to try to land before the Lear pilot realizes what we've done. A fast landing—a crash landing, actually. I've been looking for an airport, even a small one, to see if there was enough time to put it down on a runway before the Lear pilot realized I did. But this guy must be keeping us away from airports on purpose. I imagine that's one of the reasons we've done so many turns."

"I see." The attorney paused, wrinkled his nose, then peeked out the windshield. "What about an open field, a meadow?" he asked. He gestured down at the plush green pasture that loomed ahead. Within a few seconds that meadow had passed beneath them.

"Isn't crash-landing an airplane of this size very risky?" Janet asked. From the tone of her voice both men could tell that she already knew that it was.

"Sure is. We might get away with it, but the odds are low."

"Then I don't think it's an acceptable idea," Westcott said. He spoke as if the idea had not been his originally. "You're saying that if the bomb didn't get us, then the crash landing might."

"Exactly." O'Brien nodded in agreement. He took one hand off the control wheel to wipe away the growing bead of perspiration from his forehead.

"What about air traffic control? Aren't they aware of what's happened to us? Aren't they tracking us on radar?"

"No." O'Brien did not want to take the time to provide this man with a short course in airline flying, but he felt that he had little choice. "Air traffic control called us continuously during the descent, but I had been instructed by the Lear not to answer—the Lear pilot said he was monitoring our frequencies. I couldn't take the chance."

"I see." Westcott made a mental note of that fact. It might come in handy for the eventual lawsuit against the airline. "How about radar?"

"We're too low. Below radar coverage. Air traffic control must think that we've crashed. A collision with the Lear, most likely."

"And they'll conduct a search in the area where we were last seen on radar?" Westcott steadied himself with his hand against the cockpit bulkhead to help ride out the bumps that had begun to bounce the airliner around.

"Yes, that would be my guess."

"By the way," Westcott said. "There are no doctors onboard. None that will admit to it at least. The body of that dead pilot was put in the rear."

"How is that stewardess?"

"The hysterical one? She's calmed down, from what I can tell. The other stewardess is attending to her." Westcott decided to say no more since the behavior of the crew could be a focal point in his lawsuit.

"Okay. Good." O'Brien hadn't known any of the crew on this trip, not even the copilot. That, in itself, wasn't unusual— Trans-American had grown so large in the last several years that it was routine for members of a crew to be total strangers. That, perhaps, had made the death of his copilot Frank and the stewardess slightly easier for him. O'Brien couldn't recall the copilot's last name, and he hadn't remembered the names of any of the three stewardesses after they had first met during check-in for the flight.

But the facts surrounding their hijacking were not so easy to take. All of them were negative. Trans-American Flight 255 would soon be more than a hundred miles from where the search for them would be conducted. It might take days before anyone realized that they hadn't crashed at all. The Lear pilot had done his homework well on this one. "We're out of options," O'Brien said in a low voice. "Wherever the Lear leads us, we've got to follow. Maybe we'll be able to do something to escape after we land."

"Maybe." James Westcott sounded even less convinced than O'Brien had. "I'll give the stewardess the information you've given me." He wrinkled his nose again, then looked back at the captain. The bouncing from the turbulence had increased measurably and Westcott swayed from side to side in the narrow cockpit passageway as the airliner yawed continuously back and forth. "I only hope that your airline plans to pay the ransom demand very quickly, so we can get out of this mess."

O'Brien ignored the lawyer's statement. He took a deep breath, then spoke to Westcott without looking back. "Have the stewardess brief the rest of the passengers with the information I've just given you." O'Brien waved his hand to indicate that he no longer wanted to talk. The man behind him had become an unnecessary irritation and, besides, talk itself had become a monumental waste of time. All they could do was follow that madman in the Lear to whatever landing site he had picked out.

"How do you feel?" Takeo Kusaka asked his wife.

"Fine," she responded. "The motion does not upset me."

"Good." Kusaka's own stomach lurched repeatedly from the constant jarring motion the high-speed flight at such a low altitude had inflicted on the airliner. He was glad that his wife, who generally did not enjoy travel of any sort, was taking the discomfort so well. Kusaka turned and glanced again at the young boy across the aisle. He sat hunched forward in his seat and continued to cry softly, his big tears rolling slowly down his cheeks. "This is a very difficult situation," Kusaka said to his wife. "For all of us."

"What does he cry over?" Iva Kusaka asked in a whisper as she noticed the young boy across the aisle.

Kusaka shook his head in sympathy. "He cries with concern for his dog." Kusaka had switched back to Japanese again, in violation of his own rule that the three of them would speak only English on this trip across the United States. "The animal is below, in one of those cages in the cargo area." Kusaka tapped his foot on the floor to indicate where he meant. "He is concerned that the dog will be met with harm."

"I understand."

"The dog has an unusual name. Aquarius. I do not know the meaning of the word."

"I do not know the meaning either." Iva spoke solely in English, to honor the initial request of her husband. "Perhaps it is simply a name."

"No. When I asked the boy, he told me that he, too, was an Aquarius."

"Then it must mean something."

"Yes." Kusaka had slipped back into English. "Remind me to ask again later. To clarify."

"I will."

Kusaka looked beyond his wife and toward his assistant, who occupied the window seat of the row they sat in. "Think how bad this must be for our pilot," he said, in order to acquire his assistant's attention. "It is a most difficult time for him. He must make decisions that will affect us all, yet it is a routine very far from the ordinary."

"Our situation is more difficult," Shojiro Ichiki responded. His voice was slightly too sharp to be in reply to the president of their company. But Ichiki had been gripped by a fear so intense that he hardly knew what he had said. "We must sit and wait. Yet we have no idea what we wait for."

"We wait for a ransom demand," Iva Kusaka answered before her husband could speak. She purposely paused for a moment to methodically adjust the brim of the black hat she wore over her silver-gray hair, then she faced Ichiki again. "But regardless of the demands that the hijackers insist on, we will undoubtedly be the pawns." Iva Kusaka gestured broadly around the cabin of the airliner. "We will be kept safe because, without us, all this is pointless."

"How can you be so certain?"

"She is right," Kusaka answered. He looked closely at Ichiki's thin, owlish face—his fears seemed to have tightened the muscles around his neck and jaw and that made him appear even more gaunt, haggard, drawn. Ichiki's eyes—eyes which darted back and forth in even the best of times—were in continuous motion as he attempted to look everywhere and at everyone simultaneously. "How are you feeling?"

"Not well," Ichiki fondled the airsickness bag in the pouch in front of him. He expected that quite soon he might have to use it. "I am not accustomed to the turbulence." The slight sickly-sweet, pungent odor of vomit permeated the cabin. Others had already succumbed to the unrelenting jolts, and the smell made Ichiki's condition worse.

"Do not fight the sense of motion, attempt to flow with it. Remain relaxed." Kusaka paused to allow his advice to be heeded. "There is nothing for us to do but remain in a tranquil state. There is no use in producing anxiety. It will serve no purpose."

"Others seem not to feel that way." Ichiki gestured to a young man who had gotten up from his seat at the front of the cabin. Kusaka and his wife looked toward where Ichiki pointed.

"Damn it!" the young man shouted. "We can't just sit here! We've got to do something!" The young man stood awkwardly in the aisle, his body swaying from side to side. He turned to face the people in the cabin, but his eyes were aimed high over their heads toward some random spot at the rear of the airliner. "We can't just wait! We've got to do something! We'll die if we don't."

A barrage of responses erupted from the passengers. Some shouted in agreement, others yelled at him to sit down. Several began to cry loudly, or make irrational, angry sounds that were an odd mixture produced by the tidal wave of conflicting emotions that flooded over them.

"Sir! Please sit down!" Stewardess Laura Lingren rushed up from where she had been comforting airsick passengers at the rear of the cabin. She grabbed the young man by the arm. He seemed not to notice her. "Sit down, please! That's what the captain said we should do." She was nearly in tears herself, and the absurd actions of this man weren't helping her to keep her self-control. "Sit down!" She tried to tug him back toward his seat, but the man would not move.

"Let me handle this."

Laura turned. An elderly man stood in the aisle behind her. His thinning hair was pushed sidewards across his head. His face was round and puffy. He wore a blue-checkered sports jacket and a bow tie. "Sir, you too. Please sit down."

The old man smiled graciously, as if the stewardess had said nothing. "Allow me." He then gently nudged her aside. The old man stepped forward to be next to the young man. A steady stream of words continued to pour out of the young man, but few of the phrases made any sense. The young man appeared to be on the verge of either violence or tears. "Wait. Hold on, buddy. I've got a question for you. Can you hear me? Can you help me out?"

The younger man stopped his ranting. He looked puzzled. "I . . . didn't hear . . . who are . . ."

"You hear me? That's great. What sort of business are you in?"

The younger man slowly shook his head, bewildered. "I don't see . . ." He paused, ran his hand through his hair, then moistened his lips. "I don't understand. I don't see what difference that can make."

The older man smiled broadly. "Trust me." He patted the young man on the shoulder in a friendly gesture. "Now, what sort of business are you in?"

The young man didn't know what to say. "Real estate," he he stammered.

"Where?"

"Chicago."

"You sell homes?"

"No. Very few homes. Mostly commercial things. Factories, office buildings."

"I see."

"Listen," the young man said, his voice now lower than it had been, "I still don't see what difference this makes. None of this is important."

"My name is Benny Randolf. I'm a musician." Randolf stuck out his hand. He kept it out in front of him until, finally, the real estate man had no choice but to shake hands with him.

"Bishop," the young man replied automatically. He shuffled his feet and began to appear self-conscious as he realized for the first time that all eyes were on him. "Roy Bishop."

"Fine, Roy." Benny Randolf turned his body so both he and Bishop faced the greatest portion of the occupied seats in the cabin. Each of the men held one hand tightly to the aircraft's overhead luggage rail to steady themselves in the jolting, bouncing turbulence. "Roy Bishop here is in real estate," Randolf announced loudly. "Commercial real estate. He says it's not important." Randolf made an exaggerated gesture, a combination of a shrug and a wince. A man sitting in the middle of the cabin laughed. "Is there much of a market for unimportant buildings in Chicago, Roy?" Benny Randolf asked, a look of astonishment on his face. Several others in the cabin began to laugh. "Wait. I'm serious. This is something I've been wanting to know for quite some time." Benny's voice was high-pitched but it carried well through the airliner's cabin, and its tone and timbre added to the effect he attempted to create. "Are these unimportant buildings that you sell—are they old buildings or just short buildings?"

An expectant silence fell over the people in the cabins. Some were quiet because they waited for Benny Randolf to make more of his nonsensical question, while others waited to see what Bishop's response would be. After what seemed an eternity, Bishop raised his hands in front of him. His demeanor had changed completely. His face was bright red. He was self-conscious and embarrassed. "Okay," he said meekly. "I get the point. You're right. I've calmed myself down." He paused for a second, then added softly. "I'm sorry. I shouldn't have gotten carried away."

"Nothing to be sorry about." Benny slapped him on the back. "We're all in this together. Each of us is frightened. I bet that's what these hijackers are betting on. Let's fool them. Let's keep our wits. It's bound to help, no matter what they have in mind." A few of the people in the cabin quickly shouted their loud and vocal support of what Benny Randolf had said. Others joined in. Soon nearly every one of the seventy-eight passengers on Flight 255 became part of the jubilant, expressive display of their new-found fortitude and courage.

"Great, wonderful!" Benny waved his hands in time with the mounting shouts of support, as if he were the leader of an assembled choir. He added a little dance step as he turned back and forth so he could make eye contact with as many passengers as possible. "Let's keep our wits!" Benny shouted. It had suddenly become the unofficial battle cry of the unwanted war that they were conscripted participants in.

"Let's keep our wits!" a big man with a beard shouted along with the rest. He stood up from his seat in row two, but a big jolt of turbulence nearly knocked him back down again. He managed to grab a seatback to steady himself. "What we need now is a drink!" He began to step cautiously toward the galley.

"Sir! You must sit down!" Laura began to move toward him.

"Wait." Benny grabbed the stewardess by the elbow. "Let me handle this," he whispered.

"But he shouldn't be out of his seat. Not with this turbulence."

"He'll be all right. Trust me." Benny turned from her without waiting for her reply. He waved at the big man. "What's your name?"

"Nat Grisby." With his free hand he rubbed his beard, a gesture that had obviously been designed to show it off. "I'm a photographer. I'm just like your friend. I take unimportant pictures!" He laughed loudly at his own feeble joke. A number of people in the cabin joined in to laugh with him.

"Fine. I think you're right. We should all have a drink," Benny said. There was unmasked authority in his voice. Somehow, Benny Randolf had become the person in charge of the cabin. He stepped forward gingerly. "Let me help you. We'll pass drinks out." Benny glanced back at the stewardess, who nodded her reluctant approval before she turned to go back to the rear of the cabin to attend to her other duties. "But we've got to make the liquor last," Benny said to Grisby, in the tone of another joke. "Not too much to any one person."

"Of course not." Grisby led the way to the galley. As soon as they had stepped around the corner and were out of sight of the passengers, he turned to Benny. His expression had turned serious. "That was one hell of a fine job you did with that young guy. I couldn't think of anything to do with him, except maybe punch him. That would've been a mistake."

"Yes." Benny nodded in agreement. "A definite mistake. We could have had a real panic back there. I was lucky."

"Where'd you learn how to do that?" Grisby stepped up to

the galley area. Most of the galley was in shambles, but he quickly found the liquor cabinet below. It had remained untouched by the explosion.

"From being a second-rate musician. I play in lots of less-than-elite clubs. You've got to come up with some way to handle the drunks."

"It also seems to work on people who are drunk with fear."

"I guess." Benny looked over the galley area. The body of the stewardess who had been killed in the explosion lay against the far wall. She was completely covered with the airline blanket. A tiny stream of blood flowed from beneath the corner of the blanket and it ran along the edge of the galley until it disappeared beneath the aluminum trimwork. "Careful of the body," Benny whispered to Grisby.

"Yes. I know." Grisby stepped carefully around the galley. He kept an even greater distance from the body than was necessary. "We were lucky there wasn't more damage."

"We were lucky. She wasn't." Benny pointed at the bulge beneath the airline blanket.

"Maybe." Grisby rubbed his beard, then bent over to lift up the aircraft's liquor box. There was a defeated, anguished look on his face. "We might be the lucky ones," he said in a hoarse whisper. "But only time will tell."

The ground beneath them had flattened considerably. Compared to what they had flown over in Pennsylvania, the terrain below looked no worse than a badly wrinkled shirt. There were small undulations everywhere, but none of them gave more than a brief hint of a rise in the elevation of the ground. Even before Janet confirmed it by her radio crosschecks, Drew O'Brien knew from the features of the land that the area they skimmed over was the Maryland-Delaware peninsula.

"I'm beginning to pick up Salisbury," Janet said. "The radio reception is much better here."

"Sure. Look how flat everything is." O'Brien took a few seconds to eye the terrain on either side of them. Even though they had remained less than 200 feet above the ground, the task of flying the airliner was slightly easier now because there were no hills to contend with, no terrain-induced variable wind patterns. O'Brien was thankful for that. His arms ached and his back was sore from the constant demands of the tension-filled manual flying he had done for the last half hour. He was also glad that the turbulence, too, had lessened. But now he had another consideration to think about, another discomforting thought to reckon with.

"Back to the left, buddy," the radio speaker crackled. "Don't press your luck."

"Bastard." O'Brien gripped the DC-9's control wheel tightly as he fought to keep his anger down. Every time he heard the voice of that madman in the Lear, every muscle in his body automatically became rigid. O'Brien decided to try to keep the airliner in the same relative position it had been, if he could get away with it.

"This is your last chance, hero. If I don't see your wing tip by the count of five, I'm going to press the button. Ready? One, two, three . . ."

O'Brien wheeled the airliner abruptly to the left as he pushed forward on the throttles. Within seconds he had reestablished himself in the proper position.

"Very good," the radio blared. "I'll see that you get the Distinguished Flying Cross for your cooperative attitude." The man in the Lear laughed across the open microphone. "But I'm getting tired of calling your attention to your sloppy formation technique. Next time, I might get your attention with the proverbial big bang."

O'Brien shook his head in disgust. "I think he's serious. I can't take that chance again."

"Were you doing that on purpose?" Janet motioned with her hands to show what she meant. "I thought you had fallen directly behind the tail of the Learjet by accident."

"No." O'Brien took a deep breath. He didn't want to share the next piece of information with her because it probably meant nothing. But she had been a good copilot so far, and it was probably best to keep her totally informed. "Since we crossed the Chesapeake and the terrain flattened, we no longer had the constant problem of hitting the hills."

"That's true."

"But another possibility occurred to me." O'Brien tapped his finger on the radio altimeter. It read incredibly low, no more than 160 feet. Their height was equal to no more than the 15th floor of an office building—not very high by any standards. Worse, they were traveling forward at nearly two-thirds the speed of sound. "At this altitude, we're below the radio antennas in the area."

"Oh, God. I never thought of that." Janet shot a quick glance out ahead but could see nothing except the endless expanse of the flat farmland crisscrossed by ribbons of fenceline, blacktop and dirt.

"When we came across that big highway ten minutes ago, all I could think of was the sight of a State Police barracks you see on the Interstate—with their antennas sticking up. We'd be shishkebab on a stick."

"And that's why you tried to stay directly behind the Learjet?" Janet had suddenly seen his reasoning.

"Exactly. I wanted that bastard to run interference for us. If we were lucky, he'd hit the tower head and I'd have enough time to veer out of the way."

"Maybe I should sit up closer. Keep looking directly ahead."

"No need. It's a waste of time. At this speed, we'd never see the tower soon enough to avoid it. Probably wouldn't even know what hit us." O'Brien wouldn't have normally spoken so openly—especially with a woman passenger—but from the little time he had spent with Janet he had come away with the impression that she could take whatever was necessary, whatever was the truth. She wasn't like most of the women he had known in his life. "Besides," O'Brien added, "I think our crazy man up ahead has planned this entire affair far too well to have us unintentionally speared out of the sky. He's probably surveyed the route quite thoroughly. He's determined that there are no towers along here. At least I hope so."

"Me, too." Janet gestured toward the Lear, which bobbed and swayed in the mid-morning air current no more than a quarter mile ahead. "For the first time, I hope this guy knows what he's doing."

O'Brien allowed himself a small smile. This unknown woman had remained calm enough to even see the irony of the situation. They had become dependent on this murderer for their salvation. O'Brien remembered reading somewhere that terrorists and kidnappers were known for turning themselves into indispensable allies to their victims, or at least what seemed that way. The Patty Hearst story all over again—except that Drew O'Brien knew damn well what he would do if that madman in the Lear handed him an automatic rifle.

"I guess we're out of options," Janet said.

"Yes." O'Brien realized now how glad he was that he wasn't alone in the cockpit, how happy he was that she had joined him. There was nothing more for them to do from there on but fly the airliner and follow the orders from the Lear. "You say you're a private pilot. Tell me more about that," he asked to pass the time as he continued to wrestle with the airliner's flight controls to stay in the prescribed formation.

"Not much to say." Janet turned in the copilot's seat to face him more directly. She pushed a few loose strands of her short-cropped hair back in place. "I was always interested in flying. I figured I could use it in my work."

"What work?"

"I'm an investment broker. I had delusions of grandeur about winging hither and yon to close important deals. Then, after I started flying lessons, I discovered that there was a world of difference between driving a small airplane around the sky strictly for pleasure and using it for all-weather transportation."

"Right." Something had caught O'Brien's eye out the left side of the windshield. He leaned forward and strained to make it out.

"I found out it would take me years—not to mention the expense—to get an instrument rating and then . . ."

"Damn!" O'Brien slapped his free hand down against the pedestal between the pilots' seats. "I should've realized. How damn stupid could I be!"

"What?" Janet also leaned forward, but to her everything ahead still appeared the same.

"The coastline!" The indistinct line on the far horizon began to develop shape and substance as it materialized out of the haze. O'Brien peeked at the compass. "On this heading we're going out to sea! Christ!"

Janet looked down at her chart, then at the radio she had tuned. "We're south of Ocean City, Maryland." She looked back up. "Where could he be taking us?" She sounded more frightened now than she had any time before.

"I don't know." A sudden idea flashed into O'Brien's mind

and it caused him to wince visibly. "Maybe we should take the chance," he said as he thought out loud, his words tumbling out rapidly. "The beach. I could crash-land at the edge of the water." Out ahead, O'Brien could see the line that separated the land from the sea. "The sand is smooth. If I put us down at the edge of the water, there wouldn't be too much chance of fire."

"It still sounds very dangerous." Janet sat bolt upright and looked along the coastline. "We've got to decide. *You've* got to decide. Hurry." The beach was nearly beneath them. The expanse of white sand ran perpendicular to their path of flight. "It would take a big turn," she said. She indicated with her hand how far the airliner would have to maneuver to line up with the beach.

"I know." O'Brien bit into his lower lip. He rocked the control column in his hands once, then twice, as he began the motions to turn the DC-9 along the beach. Each time he hesitated, then rolled the wings level before he had changed the airliner's heading by more than a few degrees. He remained in formation with the Lear. *Crash landing. Soft sand. Might flip over. Might explode.* "No good." O'Brien let the last of the beach slide beneath them. "Too risky." Yet he knew what had nearly compelled him to try, regardless of the risk. The prospect of what lay ahead was unnerving. The view of the boundless Atlantic Ocean in the windshield added another impossible element to the nightmare. He couldn't imagine what the Learjet pilot was up to.

"Where is he taking us?" Janet had also arrived at the same point in her mind. "There's nothing out here. Nothing but water." Her eyes were wide with fear. She looked at O'Brien for the answer.

"Maybe not." O'Brien played with the airplane's controls, more as an excuse for not needing to answer her immediately. "I think he just wants to keep us away from land," he finally said. "To do away with any possibility of us being seen. He'll have us swing back to shore someplace farther south."

"I see. That makes sense."

"You better go back and tell one of the stewardesses. Tell her to make an announcement. The passengers are going to notice the water pretty soon." O'Brien motioned over his shoulder toward the rear, where even now he could make out the increased commotion as the people in the back began to realize that the airliner had headed out to sea. "Hurry. Before they come unglued again."

"Right." Janet maneuvered carefully out of the copilot seat. On her way by she touched O'Brien gently on the shoulder, then turned and left the cockpit.

O'Brien continued to steer the airliner, but his mind began to review other things. The fuel situation. At their very low altitude they burned fuel at an enormous rate. For the moment they had enough, but sometime soon it would present a problem. The second additional factor might become the weather— the farther south they traveled, the worse it would be. O'Brien glanced ahead of them, toward where they flew. The clouds there had gathered together to form a continuous, thick overcast. Soon the overcast would lower and rain would begin. If they continued much farther south before they turned inland, low clouds, wind and heavy rain would become part of the picture.

"They took it pretty well." Janet climbed back into the copilot's seat. "Except for a few people, most seem to have their spirits up. People are moving around the cabin, talking to each other."

"That's good news." O'Brien wondered how long their bravado would last.

"Yes." Janet nodded absently, then gazed out the window.

The two of them lapsed into silence. The minutes passed until, finally, another half hour had gone by. O'Brien turned on the aircraft's radar. He watched as the rain activity ahead of them increased. The first big raindrops splattered on the DC-9's windshield. Shortly, a continuous rain began. Flight visibility dropped steadily until all that could be seen was the water directly below and the white Learjet ahead. The turbulence, which had decreased after they had left the coast, had increased again in the mounting wind and rain.

One hour passed. Each time O'Brien attempted to talk to the Lear pilot on the radio, he was quickly cut off by the man's incessant threats to use the hidden bomb and blow them out of the sky. O'Brien finally gave up and decided to leave the radio transmitter alone. Another thirty minutes dragged by. "I should've put us on the beach," O'Brien mumbled. He was sorry that he hadn't put the airliner down while he had the chance.

"Don't be ridiculous. You had no choice. You did the only thing you could."

"Maybe." O'Brien looked again at the airliner's fuel gauges, as he had every minute or so for the last half hour. The gauges were approaching the bottom of their scales. That meant they could fly for another forty-five minutes, no more. Without overwater navigation equipment there was no way to tell with any certainty how far they were from land, but O'Brien felt he could take an educated guess: they were very far, too far.

O'Brien cleared his parched throat. He had put off using the next sentence as long as he could, but now he knew that there was no choice. "We've only got forty-five minutes of fuel left. We'll have to ditch in the ocean."

"God help us." Janet's voice was hollow, shaken. The view out the cockpit window was obscured by the heavy rain, but she could still see how much turmoil the seas were in. At their altitude of 300 feet, the details of the frothy whitecaps, the boiling, churning water were the most terrifying things she had ever looked at. She could see the face of death in the sea below. "Is there a chance? Can we ditch and get life rafts in the water?"

"Sure." O'Brien looked directly into her eyes, as a sort of antidote to the lie he had just spoken, the first outright lie he had made since the hijacking began. The DC-9 carried life jackets but no life rafts. In the type of sea beneath them, life jackets alone would keep them alive a short time at most. But they had no choice but to try it, no matter how futile. Ditching while they were still under control was better than falling out of the sky after the engines had failed from fuel exhaustion. "Have the stewardesses get everyone ready. Life jackets on. Everyone briefed on which exit to use."

"Okay." Janet began to pick herself out of her seat, but she heard a click in the radio speaker. She stopped. It was an indication that the Learjet pilot was about to transmit.

"Wake up, folks," the voice on the radio said. "It's time we wrapped this up."

"What does he mean?" She faced O'Brien.

"I don't know. Wait. There's something . . ." O'Brien leaned forward in his seat. He strained his eyes to see ahead, beyond the white Lear. A dark shadow had appeared on the horizon through the shroud of rain. It was a large mass on the surface of the sea, and it rode slightly to the left of where the Lear was headed. A ship. It grew in size and distinction, like a movie picture being rapidly adjusted into focus. "Look!" There was nothing else O'Brien could say about the startling gray-painted giant that took form in front of the airliner.

He and Janet remained speechless, dumbfounded as the silhouette of an aircraft carrier filled their view from the cockpit of Trans-American Flight 255.

7

THE AIRCRAFT CARRIER *Yorktown* was directly off the left wing when Edward McClure wheeled the Learjet into a tight left turn to circle it. He reached for the microphone and began to transmit to the airliner again. "There's your airport, ace. I want you to set up a left-hand circle around the carrier. Be careful not to drift too far away."

"Don't be insane!" the pilot from the airliner snapped back as soon as the radio channel had been cleared by McClure. "It's too small! I can't get an airliner on the deck of a pitching aircraft carrier!"

"Calm down, captain," McClure transmitted. He watched as the airliner followed him around in a wide circle of the ship below. The clouds were low and ragged and the wind continued to whip up the high waves and the churning whitecaps, but the rain had stopped. Conditions were perfect for what remained to be done. "Let me explain how this will work. It's been calculated, there's nothing to worry about." McClure nearly laughed out loud at his own ludicrous statement. Even from an altitude of only 300 feet, the aircraft carrier seemed an absurdly small target to put any airplane on, never mind one as large as the DC-9. Still, his calculations had clearly shown that it would work.

"Hurry up. I'm almost out of fuel," the airliner replied.

"I know how much fuel you have. Thirty more minutes would be my guess. Am I correct?"

There was a long pause before the airliner answered. "Yes," O'Brien finally admitted. "Thirty minutes—at the most. Make this fast."

"That's more than enough." McClure wrestled with the Lear's flight controls to stay in position in spite of the constant buffeting from the wind. The airliner stayed right behind him, and McClure had to grudgingly admire the skill of its pilot as he managed to maneuver that big ship so gracefully and accurately through such poor conditions. "You're doing a fine job," McClure transmitted. "I can see that you're talented enough to pull this off. But I want you to first observe two additional things. There's a net stretched across the middle of the carrier's deck. Also," he continued as the Lear passed adjacent to the *Yorktown* again, "there's a submarine abeam the carrier on its port side, approximately five hundred yards away. You can see its periscope sticking out of the water."

"Stand by."

McClure waited as the airline captain inspected the scene below. While he did, he glanced over his shoulder toward the airline freight supervisor who was still handcuffed to the rear seat in the Lear. "How's it going back there?"

Dominick Trombetta did not answer. He lay slumped in the seat, his head tilted back, his mouth partially opened. His face was ghostly pale, his breath came in shallow, rapid gasps.

"You still awake?" McClure shouted.

Trombetta opened his eyes, then slowly sat himself up. "Let me go," he pleaded again as he pulled his right arm up as far as the handcuffs would allow.

"Very soon." McClure pointed at the aircraft carrier out their left side as if he were conducting a sightseeing tour. "That's the *Yorktown.*"

Trombetta ignored him. Instead, he looked at the two dead pilots in the seats in front of him. *God help me. Get me away from this madman.* He began to pull on the handcuffs again, but all that his effort managed to accomplish was to rub raw the cuts along his wrists. The blood began to drip slowly down his fingers and onto the beige carpet.

"Okay, 255. Listen to me closely and I'll explain how this works," McClure said as he began to transmit again. "The submarine has an identical panel to the one I've got," he continued as he glanced over at the portable electronics box on the copilot's seat. "They have the ability to detonate the bomb, so I recommend that you stay within visual sight of that periscope at all times if you don't want him to hit the trigger. Now, as far as the landing goes, this is how you'll accomplish it."

As McClure watched, the *Yorktown* began to turn to port just as he expected it would. "The ship is beginning to line up into the wind. That will give you forty miles an hour of wind, plus the ship's speed of thirty miles an hour. Effectively, you'll be touching down with seventy miles an hour less speed than normal because of the head wind across the deck."

"That's not enough!" the airline pilot shouted into his radio as soon as McClure had taken his finger off his transmit button. "Let us go to shore. I can put us on a deserted beach. Any place you say. But not here. It's not possible!"

"Sure it is." McClure frowned. The pilot was being more trouble than he had imagined. "We're too far from shore, so put that crap out of your mind. This is your only choice—the carrier or the sharks." McClure paused to let his words sink in.

"What is the net for?" the airline pilot asked.

"Good question. Glad to see that you're being cooperative." McClure glanced back at Trombetta to nod his approval, as if the ariline cargo supervisor had been part of the conversation. McClure pressed the transmit button again. "First I want to point out a few facts that I think you'll be interested in. I calculate that the weight of your aircraft on landing will be approximately eighty thousand pounds. Do you agree?"

"Yes. Approximately."

"Are you aware that the current fleet of U.S. aircraft carriers have basically the same deck size as the carrier below us, and that a modern F-14 fighter has a maximum weight of seventy-two thousand pounds?" McClure stopped talking for a moment, but kept control of the frequency. "As far as relative size goes, the wingspan of a Grumman F-14 is sixty-four feet, while your aircraft is only twenty-eight feet wider. But the most interesting news is something historical." McClure took his finger off the transmit button.

"Stop this insanity! I can't get this airliner to stop on the deck of that carrier!"

Insanity. "Listen, asshole, you're getting me pissed off." McClure looked back at the airliner as it swooped around to begin another turn to circle the 900-foot-long bobbing deck below them. McClure took a deep breath to calm himself. *Insanity*. That's what they called anything that pushed normal limits, that challenged the usual way of doing things. That was what they had called his battle techniques in Vietnam. "You better start watching your mouth," McClure transmitted in a cold fury. He didn't intend to take any more verbal abuse from that airline pilot, gold shipment aboard or not. Another outburst and he'd be tempted to push the button and blow that smart-ass into a million pieces.

"Go ahead with your message," the airline pilot replied in a forced neutral tone. "I'm listening."

"Okay, this is interesting," McClure transmitted. "In nineteen sixty-three the U.S. Navy experimented with landing a C-130 *Hercules* transport on the carrier *Forrestal*. One touchdown was made at over one hundred thousand pounds of total weight." McClure was excited now, and his voice showed it. "The *Hercules* has four turbo-prop engines and a forty-foot bigger wing-span than you do! It can be done! You can get that piece of iron of yours on the deck!" McClure was totally convinced that the DC-9 could be landed successfully on the *Yorktown*.

"But, damn it, I don't have a tail hook!" the airline pilot said. His voice was strained and angry, but he was obviously now being careful with his choice of words. "I can't grab the deck cables with no tail hook! My wheel brakes won't stop me in time!"

"That's what the net is for!" McClure laughed on the open frequency. "That's our insurance."

"I don't understand."

"Easy." McClure was enjoying himself again. He played gingerly with the Lear's flight controls to keep it tracking around the *Yorktown* in a continuous circle, in spite of the effects of the howling wind and the jarring turbulence. "On aircraft carriers they have an alternate system for stopping aircraft in case a tail hook is broken. That's what the steel-webbed badminton net is for. Land into the net. It'll stop you from rolling overboard."

"Are you sure it's strong enough?"

"Hell, yes. That's what it's been designed for." McClure wondered if it really was strong enough. The net should, theoretically, be able to stop the DC-9—especially when the airliner touched down at such a low speed because of the headwind. But you could never tell, not until you tried. The net itself might be old and frayed, its attachment points weakened, the installation itself screwed up by the people below. There was nothing to do but watch and see. If the airliner rolled through the steel net and off the end of the deck, that would be the end of the entire program, period. But there was no sense dwelling on negative factors. "That's all I've got to say," McClure transmitted. "I'm signing off now. Remember that the submarine can detonate the bomb if you fly out of sight of his periscope. I'll be coming down to meet you. See you on the *Yorktown*."

"Wait."

McClure switched off his radio before the airline pilot could get in another word. There was nothing left to be said, and only one more thing left to be done. McClure snapped on the Learjet's autopilot, put the aircraft back into its continuous turn to the left, then unbuckled his seatbelt and climbed out of the cockpit.

"What's going to happen?" Trombetta asked. He sat as far forward as his handcuffs would allow. His forehead and bald skull glistened with perspiration. "Let me go."

McClure did not answer. Instead, he reached behind the liquor cabinet and pulled out a battered old suitcase. "Excuse me," he said to the dead pilot strapped into the left passenger seat. "Do you mind holding this for me? Thanks." McClure placed the suitcase on the dead copilot's lap. He unlatched it. Out of the corner of his eye he watched Trombetta stare wideeyed at the contents in the suitcase.

"What are you doing?" Trombetta asked nervously. He knew instinctively that none of the possible answers would be what he wanted to hear.

"I'm afraid it doesn't concern you." McClure took off his

brown suit jacket and laid it carefully on the lap of the other dead pilot. "Hold this for me, sport," he said with a smile. He then turned back to the suitcase and took out a bright yellow life jacket. He put the life jacket on, then reached in the suitcase for the next item.

"What's that?" Trombetta asked. He knew very well what it was.

"A parachute." McClure put on the straps and tightened them. "I've got a lunch engagement." He reached for his suit jacket, took out the wad of money from one pocket, his revolver from the other, then laid the brown jacket back neatly on the dead pilot's lap.

"Don't shoot me. Please." Trombetta had backed away as far as the handcuffs and the Lear's curved sidewall would allow. His eyes were fixed on the dark tip of the pistol's barrel.

"I'm not going to shoot you." McClure shook his head sympathetically. He pointed the pistol in the other direction, toward the front of the aircraft. "But I do have to get going. To the submarine, for lunch."

"No!"

"Yes." McClure grabbed the Lear's door handle, twisted it, then pushed the lever down.

The door popped open. The noise that filled the cabin was deafening. The wind and the shrill scream of the engines blended together to erect what seemed like a solid wall of sound. The damp, cold outside air instantly swept away the carefully controlled climate in the tiny elegant cabin and replaced it with an uncomfortable chill. McClure ignored the physical discomfort from the raw wind as he secured the Lear's door in the opened position. He then turned and faced Trombetta.

Trombetta began to shout senselessly, but his words were unintelligible. He yanked repeatedly against the handcuffs, but they remained firmly anchored to the seat rail. Trombetta staggered to his feet as best he could and stretched his free arm toward where McClure stood in the opened doorway. But the distance between them was too great and Dominick Trombetta could not reach the man he groped toward.

McClure had turned his back to the cabin. He peered out the opened doorway and shielded his eyes against the biting wind as he watched the path that the Lear took in its continuous pattern around the *Yorktown*. When they had come around full-circle again to the proper side, McClure turned toward the Lear's cockpit. He carefully aimed his pistol.

McClure fired three shots in rapid succession at the Lear's lower cockpit panel. The shots were loud enough to make themselves heard above the intolerable noise in the cabin and Trombetta jumped back at the sudden explosive sounds. McClure threw the pistol out the opened door. Then, without looking back at the cabin, he stepped into the archway. When he verified that the Lear was over the correct spot, Edward McClure pushed himself out the doorway without hesitation. He was gone from sight before Trombetta realized that the man was about to jump.

Trombetta let out a gasped, curdled scream when he realized that he was now alone in the Lear. But when the aircraft began to change its direction of flight, Trombetta was faced by a new fear so enormous that it caused him to get a grip of himself. *God no!* The aircraft's autopilot had disconnected. *Autopilot! McClure shot out the autopilot!*

The Lear wobbled from side to side as the turbulence tossed it from one wind pattern to the next. The nose of the aircraft began to pitch down and to the left, but before it had gone very far in that direction a sudden gust brought it abruptly up and toward the right. The Lear, now out of control, slewed back and forth in random, spastic motions.

Get free. Trombetta saw the nightmarish details of the scene in front of him in what seemed like slow motion, but his mind began to work at lightning speed. *Get free. Any cost.* Trombetta flung his body around the cabin of the Lear, to the limits the cuffs would allow. He felt a bone in his wrist snap under the strain of the unyielding metal strap he was imprisoned in, but he paid no attention to the pain. *Get free. Any cost.* The small cabin of the Lear was closing in on him like a coffin. *Do anything. God help me!* Trombetta did not know for sure if he could fly the airplane, but he knew for certain that he would die if he didn't try. First he had to get to the cockpit, then he would steer the aircraft well enough to keep it upright, then head it toward the beach. He would, somehow, manage to crash-land the Lear. He would walk away from this. But none of it was possible unless he got his right hand free.

Trombetta stretched out as far as he could. His right wrist
burned with searing pain, but he continued to ignore it as he
stretched each muscle in his body to its maximum. He was
trying to reach the liquor cabinet, trying to locate a knife. *Cut
my right hand. Cut it off. Only way.*

But no matter how hard he tried, he was still several inches
away from the closed wooden cabinet. The Lear bucked wildly,
and Trombetta was thrown against the sidewall. His head
slammed hard against the fiber glass panel and it almost caused
him to lose consciousness.

Trombetta shook his head to clear it, then looked around
him. *The pilots.* He stretched forward again. The pain from
the broken bones in his wrist was now so severe that it caused
him to scream in agony, yet he continued to lean as near as
he could to the closest of the dead pilots.

Trombetta grabbed the dead man's lapel and pulled the
lifeless body toward him, to the limits that the fastened seat
belt would allow. Trombetta then tore through the dead man's
pockets. In one of the inside coat pockets he found a small
penknife.

Trombetta opened the tiny blade of the small knife. Without
hesitation he began to hack away at his own wrist. His screams
of incredible, unbearable pain were muffled by the enormous
roar from the Lear's open door. Trombetta managed to cut into
his wrist deeply, and his frantic motions caused the blood and
fragmented sections of skin and bone to splatter in all directions.
But before he had gotten deep enough to cut the nerve endings,
the blade of the tiny penknife broke away and flew toward the
rear of the cabin.

Trombetta fell to his knees—a combination of the searing,
unearthly pain he had inflicted upon himself, plus the continuous wild gyrations of the Learjet. *No chance, no chance left.*
Trombetta picked up his head and looked at the seat in front
of him. *McClure's jacket.* The brown coat lay on the dead
copilot's lap. Trombetta reached forward again and pulled the
jacket toward him. With his one free hand he searched desperately for another knife, for something, anything to continue
to cut his hand free with. *God. Please. Let me find something.*
Trombetta rifled through every pocket, but he found nothing,

nothing but papers. Just before he was about to throw the jacket aside, he pressed his hand against the coat's side pocket.

There was something inside. Something small, something metal. It was a key.

Trombetta could hardly control his hand enough to reach in and pull the key out. *Careful.* The gyrations of the Learjet had increased again, and it almost caused him to drop the key out of his bloodied fingers. *Slow. Steady.* Trombetta glanced out the side window and saw the ocean below, at an odd angle. *No time left.* He fumbled with the key until he finally managed to force it into the lock of the silver cuffs. He turned the key.

The handcuffs sprung open. Trombetta's wrist popped free. He sat on the floor for a second longer than necessary before he realized that he had managed to get himself out of the handcuffs. What focused his attention again was the sudden rise in noise and the increase in the pressure from the wind through the opened door. Trombetta spun around, jumped to his feet and stumbled toward the cockpit.

The view straight ahead through the cockpit windshield was terrifying. Nothing but water lay in front of the Lear. Trombetta was nearly paralyzed with fear. *Quick. Take the controls. Pull out of the dive.* He forced his frozen muscles into action. He reached over the empty pilot's seat and grabbed for the control column. *Pull out of the dive!*

With every beat of his heart, the top of the angry sea grew larger and more frightening to look at—yet he could not take his eyes off it. The details of the ocean multiplied rapidly as the Lear continued its unguided descent. Dark, off-colored splotches developed between the major swells, the overlapping waves came into focus, the eddying currents grew, the churning, frothing bubbles appeared where the waves began to break one over the other. *Pull out! Now!* Trombetta yanked backward on the control column as hard as he could.

The white Lear began to change its direction of flight. But the downward momentum had gone too far for too long as the jet edged lower. The front half of the Lear cleared the water, but the tail of the sleek jet brushed the crest of a swell by a few inches. That was enough of a negative influence to cause the airplane to hesitate in mid-flight for an instant, as if the

Learjet itself were unable to decide where to go next. The swell of high water at the next crest slammed harder against the white fuselage, and that additional influence was the vote that broke the deadlock. The Lear started down.

The nose of the aircraft pitched lower until it finally caught the edge of a wave. With the front of the aircraft being dragged under, the Lear cartwheeled onto its back and began to break up. The left wing cracked off first, followed by the right wing and then the tail. The fuselage—its rear-mounted twin jet engines long snuffed out by the ingestion of the unrelenting quantities of salt water—continued to burrow itself farther beneath the sea. The battered body of Dominick Trombetta and the bodies of the two Lear pilots were taken quickly below, still inside the white fuselage, where they would rest together forever on the dark and peaceful depths of the ocean floor.

Captain Drew O'Brien could hardly believe his eyes when he saw the man tumble out of the opened door of the Learjet. "Look!"

"Where?" Janet sat higher in her seat and followed his pointing hand.

"A parachute," O'Brien said as they watched the white-colored silk canopy blossom above the rapidly falling silhouette.

"I understand now. It was part of his plan all along."

"It sure was." O'Brien shook his head in disgust as he wheeled the airliner into another circle around the carrier below. "That bastard. I should run him down."

"Don't forget about the submarine."

"Right." O'Brien knew he could kill that madman easily enough by ramming the DC-9's wing into him as he floated by, but nothing would be gained by it. A senseless act, maybe even a counterproductive one. If the submarine could detonate the bomb—and they had to assume that the sub really could—then the homicidal maniac in the parachute could land in the water and swim the short distance to the submarine without any fear of retaliation from them. Once again, the saboteur had covered all bases, planned for all contingencies. "What happened to the Lear?"

"I think it must've crashed. It was headed due east and

going down fast, but it disappeared from sight before I actually saw it hit the water."

"Okay." O'Brien glanced around his flight panel, then looked back at the scene below. The man from the Lear had landed in the water, released his parachute and had begun to swim toward the raised periscope. "It looks like the sub is coming up to get him."

"Yes." Janet watched as the submarine rose to the surface, its black hull emerging slowly through the top of the waves. The man in the yellow life jacket clambered aboard and quickly disappeared into the recesses of the sub's superstructure. A few moments later a large release of bubbles from along the sides of the dark, rounded hull confirmed that the submarine was again on its way down. She turned back to O'Brien. "What do we do next?"

He pointed to the fuel gauges. "In twenty minutes the tanks will be bone-dry." O'Brien began another turn around the carrier. He gestured toward the ship. "That small deck is the only habitable spot within our fuel range. We have no choice."

"Wait!" James Westcott rushed up to the cockpit. "I've been talking to the passengers." Westcott stood panting, his face flushed. "We don't think you should try to put an airplane as big as this one on the deck of a carrier. We should run for it. That's the consensus." Westcott braced himself against the bulkhead at the rear of the cockpit so he wouldn't be thrown around by the turbulence.

"Bullshit," O'Brien said in a low voice. He glanced at the man for an instant before his eyes returned to the flight instruments. "You mean that you and one or two others have bullied everyone into believing there was some other way."

"Now, wait a minute, captain. Everyone I spoke with..."

"You obviously didn't listen to my last P.A. announcement. You don't have the facts." O'Brien pointed his finger at the fuel gauge. "Look at this needle. In fifteen minutes we're completely out of action."

"And what about the bomb?" Janet asked. She attempted to keep her voice as calm as possible, even though she wanted to shout at this idiot who was wasting their precious time. "The submarine will detonate the bomb if we leave sight of the periscope."

Westcott wrinkled his nose, inhaled deeply, then grabbed a cross-member to steady himself. "A good many of the passengers think that it must be a bluff." He had begun to use the type of indirect, evasive speech patterns he was most comfortable with.

"Bullshit," O'Brien said, louder than before. "It's not that you *think* those people below are bluffing, you only *wish* they were bluffing!" His voice had risen steadily, although his attention remained fixed on the view out the window. "I sure as hell don't intend to make decisions based on fantasies. Those people below are murderers. That may be a hard fact for you to face, but it's true. That leaves us no choice."

"Then you intend to take full responsibility for the outcome of this landing?" Westcott asked in a firm, threatening voice. "I just want that point to be perfectly clear."

"It's perfectly clear." O'Brien wiped the perspiration off his forehead. "This will be the most difficult landing of my life, but at least we've got a chance if I can pull it off."

"You can do it. I know you can," Janet said.

O'Brien ignored her. "But trying to run is suicide. Even if that madman in the Lear was bluffing and there is no second bomb, we don't have enough fuel to get anyplace. We'd go down at sea. No one knows where we are, they wouldn't know where to look."

"Those things are your fault," Westcott shot back angrily. "You should have put us down while you had the chance. You should have found a way to call someone on the radio." Westcott wanted to point toward the dials and knobs on the center panel that he assumed were the radios, but because of the jolting turbulence he was unable to let go of the bulkhead.

"Why don't you get out of here?" Janet stared at Westcott for several seconds before she looked back at O'Brien. "Captain, do you want him to carry any other messages to the stewardesses?"

"I'll tell them myself." O'Brien banked the airliner into another turn, then engaged the autopilot. He turned to Westcott. "You heard the lady. Get the hell out of here. Strap your ass into a seat. I'm sure that's the ass you'll take care of first, no matter what."

"I resent that."

"Get out." O'Brien turned away and snatched up the public address system microphone. He cleared his throat, put the P.A. microphone to his lips and pressed the button. "This is the captain again. You've probably seen the Lear pilot bail out and get aboard the submarine. Nothing has changed for us. We have no choice but to follow his orders. I'm going to land on the carrier. The landing itself will be firm, but I think it should work out okay." O'Brien clicked off the P.A button and closed his eyes for a second.

"You should say more," Janet whispered.

"I know." He had lied so much already, a little more would make no difference. He pressed the P.A. button again. "When I stop talking I want everyone to assume the brace position. Once we've come to a complete stop, evacuate the aircraft in a quick but orderly fashion." O'Brien decided not to say anything about the possibility of careening off the deck and into the water—if the aircraft slid into the sea, nothing he could say would make any difference. Chances are they'd all go straight to the bottom. O'Brien continued to press his thumb against the P.A. button, but he couldn't think of anything further to say. "Good luck," he finally added, although he winced slightly at the sound of those two disquieting words.

"It won't be luck," Janet said, as if she had read his mind. "It'll be skill. It has to be." She looked at O'Brien and attempted to smile, but her facial muscles would not respond. "You can do it," she said, but with measurably less conviction than she had intended.

"Sure. No problem." O'Brien looked around the cockpit, then back at Janet. "Being up front isn't the best place during an accident."

"We're not going to have an accident. You're going to land it."

"Right." O'Brien ran his tongue over his dry, parched lips. "You'll be better off in the cabin." He pointed to the rear.

"No. I'm staying here. You might need help."

"It's up to you." He shrugged his shoulders, but he was glad that she had decided to stay. This landing would be the most exacting thing he had ever done, and being alone in the cockpit would have, somehow, made it more difficult. O'Brien disconnected the autopilot, then reached up to activate the controls that extended the flaps and the landing gear. He began a turn to line the airliner up with the pitching, bobbing aircraft carrier and the long white wake of churned water that trailed behind it. "Here we go," O'Brien said, in a voice almost too low to be heard.

Paul Talbot kicked aside the jagged pieces of shattered coffee cup and stepped closer to the ledge of windows on the bridge of the *Yorktown*. He craned his neck to watch the red-and-white airliner begin another orbit of the carrier, then picked up his binoculars and focused on the submarine. The man in the yellow life jacket—McClure, more than likely—had already been taken aboard and the sub had begun to dive again. While he watched, the water washed over the black hull until all that remained visible of the submarine was its periscope mast.

An airliner. God Almighty. When Talbot had first seen the airliner as it flew over in formation with the smaller jet, the sight of it was so startling that the coffee cup he held had slipped out of his hands and crashed to the floor. Even though he had watched the two aircraft continuously for the last several minutes, he still found it hard to believe that it was actually happening, hard to believe that there were two aircraft—and that one of them was an airliner!

Talbot picked up the binoculars and scanned the horizon to the starboard quarter until he located the jet on its way around. Even this far away, the airplane seemed too enormous to be landed on the deck of the *Yorktown*. Talbot adjusted the focus on the glasses until he could clearly read the lettering along the side of the fuselage as the aircraft passed directly abeam. Trans-American Airways. It was incredible. Somehow, McClure had found a way to get a pilot to steal an airliner and attempt to land it on the carrier's deck. Talbot lowered the binoculars and shook his head in disbelief. He wondered how much McClure could have paid that pilot to attempt this. Now he understood why the steel-webbed net strung across the *Yorktown*'s deck was necessary. Without it, there was no chance at all of stopping the airliner before it rolled overboard. Even with it, the odds of success seemed low.

Parachutes. Two airplanes. McClure didn't tell me. Talbot

ran his hand nervously along the gray-painted edge of the window. McClure hadn't said anything, one way or the other, about what sort of airplane they had intended to steal to transport the gold to the ship. He hadn't said anything about parachuting out of a second aircraft, or about allowing that aircraft to crash at sea. All of those facts should have been mentioned. Talbot wondered what else he hadn't been told, what other details of this crazy operation had been omitted or distorted by McClure and his gang of thieves. Talbot shook his head in disgust. *I shouldn't be part of this. I shouldn't be in with these maniacs.*

Talbot picked up the binoculars again. The airliner had flown a mile or so past the stern of the ship and had begun to come toward him again. But this time the aircraft flew a different pattern. Instead of swinging wide for another circle, the huge red-and-white airliner had rolled out earlier and aligned itself with the wake of the ship. Through the binoculars Talbot could see that the airliner's landing gear was down, and so were its flaps. He guessed that the pilot intended to come in for a landing this time.

Talbot stepped forward to the engine controls and rang for full speed. In a few seconds the answering bells responded, and he could feel the surge of additional power as the *Yorktown*'s engines increased their output to provide every ounce of power they could. Talbot checked the gauge that displayed the surface wind—it was still straight down the carrier's deck. He was satisfied that he had done everything he could to help that pilot get the airplane down and stopped. From that point on, it was totally up to him.

"Good luck," Talbot said out loud. His voice reverberated through the empty compartments of the ship's bridge. He reached for the binoculars again, but instead of raising them he held them at his side. The airliner was so near that the details were easily visible without them.

Steady. Talbot's stomach was in knots. He stood immobile at the aft end of the deserted bridge, his eyes locked onto the jolting, bouncing motions of the airliner as it swept closer to the fantail of the *Yorktown*. "Hold up the wing. Keep it steady." Talbot began to twist his body in a senseless attempt to keep the aircraft's wings level. He didn't know much about landing an aircraft on a carrier, but he knew damn well that the pilot had to keep his ship level and tracking steadily in order to pull it off. "Hold it. Hold it steady." The turbulence had increased and the silver wings of the airliner rocked vigorously from side to side. "Careful. Watch the fantail. Pick it up."

Talbot's jaw dropped. He let out a startled gasp as he realized that the aircraft had dipped too low. It was *below* the level of the edge of the deck. "Pull up!" Talbot shouted. "Pull it up!"

As if the pilot had heard him, the airliner's two rear-mounted jet engines began to put out an elongated plume of billowy black smoke. Talbot could see that the pilot had increased his engine power—but it seemed too late. *God help him.* Talbot wanted to close his eyes to avoid watching the disaster, but he found that he couldn't. He watched in horrid fascination as the aircraft's main landing gear—they reached down like two groping hands—seemed intent on smacking into the rear edge of the *Yorktown*'s deck. "No!"

Somehow, the tires missed the carrier's curled deck lip by inches. The airliner then rose abruptly as it accelerated. It flashed past the *Yorktown*'s bridge no more than a dozen yards away, its silhouette a blur of details and colors, the roar of its enormous engines jarring everything in the bridge that was not fastened down, the smell of the kerosene exhaust mingling with the aroma of the sea and the chill of the wind.

Faces in the cabin windows! People inside the airliner! Talbot picked up his binoculars and focused them quickly, but the aircraft had gone too far and was at too much of an angle to the carrier for anything inside to be visible. Still, Talbot was sure of what he had already seen. People in the cabin—where there were supposed to be none!

"Stay calm—remain in the brace position!" Flight Attendant Carol Fey had made her announcement into the rear P.A. microphone as steadily as she could. "We will be lining up again for another landing very soon—please remain in the brace position!" Carol put the P.A. handset back into its holder, her hand shaking so badly that she found it nearly impossible to fasten the restraining clip for it. Somehow, she managed.

Carol looked down the aisle of the airliner from her seat at the rear of the cabin. Everyone had quieted down again, and most had already put their heads back down. That was a welcomed relief from the outburst of terrorized screams that had filled the cabin a few moments before—a spontaneous, infectious wave of fear that had swept over all of them when the airliner's engines had suddenly increased to full power and they veered sharply away from the carrier's deck. The ship itself had been so near that it had appeared as nothing but a blur, nothing but a surrealist canvas painted out of pure motion.

Lucy, please help us. As she laid her head on her lap to resume the brace position, Carol Fey began to pray to the dead stewardess. The girl's mutilated body remained on the floor of the forward galley, but Carol knew in her heart that Lucy would be watching over them—that she would be in sympathy and would give assistance from the world of the dead. *Lucy, stay with us. Help us to live.*

Paul Talbot watched, mesmerized, as the DC-9 flew clear of the carrier and began to circle for another approach. *McClure.* As that one word filled his thoughts, Talbot flung the binoculars across the length of the ship's bridge. The binoculars crashed noisily into a panel near the helm. "You son-of-a-bitch," Talbot said aloud as he began to fully realize how much he had been lied to, how much he had been used. McClure had told him only what was convenient in order to get him to go along with this insane plan. McClure had sworn that no one would be hurt, that no one would be involved other than the people who had voluntarily signed on. All of it had been a damn lie. The airplane that circled the *Yorktown* was a passenger aircraft! It had been hijacked!

Talbot leaned against the captain's seat on the *Yorktown's* bridge. He buried his face in his hands and moaned. His head spun with a hundred questions, a thousand conflicts, a million accusations. Paul Talbot finally pulled his hands away from his face, just in time to see the airliner as it began to line up for another approach.

"God help them." Talbot stumbled to the aft end of the bridge to be as near the touchdown spot as possible. "Keep it steady. Keep the wings level!" Talbot pleaded. The airliner was less than one mile out, lined up with the deck, its gear and flaps down, its nose pitched high. It seemed to be flying slower now than it had been the first time although, remarkably, it somehow appeared to be more under control, more prepared for the touchdown. *Steady. Keep going.*

Half mile out. A gust of wind rocked the airliner's wings, but the pilot quickly dampened the oscillations and returned to an even keel. Quarter mile. The engines began to pour out more smoke, more raw power.

A few hundred yards astern. Talbot took a deep breath and held it as he watched the red-and-white airliner streak toward the edge of the *Yorktown*'s deck. The nose gear, then the main wheels cleared the lip by three feet. The main gear tires smashed down hard on the *Yorktown*.

As Talbot watched, the airliner's landing gear on its right side crumbled away as if it had been made of nothing more than plastic. The steel strut snapped off and, with its wheels still attached, bounded from the aircraft and toward the starboard side of the ship. The airliner's wing tip fell to the deck and began to slide against the blacktop. In slow motion the airliner's fuselage started to twist sideways. It was headed directly toward the carrier's superstructure.

"Keep it straight!" Talbot shouted at the top of his lungs.

But just before the aircraft careened against the *Yorktown*'s massive deck building, the left gear also splintered away. That caused the airliner to begin to veer toward port. "Straighten out!" Talbot shouted above the shrill cry from the jet engines. Sparks and smoke poured out from beneath where the fuselage slid against the flight deck. But the surface friction had slowed the aircraft measurably. When the nose of the airliner reached the steel-webbed deck netting, its forward motion had greatly diminished.

Don't break. Please. The airliner punched itself into the net. It continued slowly forward. Just before it appeared as if the aircraft would go too far and fall over the edge, the net began to spring back. The airliner ground to a sudden, jarring halt, its wings scraping against the flight deck, its flaps and landing gear torn away, its nose wrapped in the steel webbing of the safety net.

It stopped! The first few feet of the Trans-American airliner were perched precariously over the edge of the canted deck, but the rest of the aircraft was safely stopped on the blacktop. The jet engines had fallen silent, and even the smoke that had previously come from beneath the sliding fuselage had ended. *No fire. Thank God.* Paul Talbot leaned against the sidewall of the bridge in total exhaustion. He breathed deeply to calm himself. Before he had gotten back enough strength to move, he saw Richard Yang and his group of misfits run out on the deck, guns in hand, and rush toward the airliner. They quickly surrounded the cabin and began to herd together the passengers as they clambered out of the emergency exits and onto the carrier deck.

Paul Talbot closed his eyes. He had been totally shocked by the turn of events, by the realization of what he had actually become a part of. *McClure. That lying bastard.* Nothing Talbot had been told had been true. This was not just an involved scheme to get their hands on a gold shipment, it was something far more hideous. Paul Talbot had no idea what it all meant, no idea what would happen next.

8

THE OPTICAL ORANGE golf ball rolled slowly across the paperwork on the desk as Captain Dwight Martin pushed it back and forth between his outstretched fingers. After a few moments he stopped and examined the ball again, his thumb brushing gently against the dimpled texture of its hardened finish. He was anxious to get on the golf course to try out the new high-visibility balls Gloria had bought for him. Something told him that this orange-colored ball would shave at least two points off his handicap, maybe even more. Martin looked up from his desk and across the room. "Is the prognosis off yet?"

"Here it comes," Lieutenant Ted Nash hunched over the teletype machine and waited for the last paragraph to finish printing. When it was done he reached in and retrieved it, then turned and strolled casually across the room. He knew damn well what the updated weather report was for, and he had no intention of rushing himself for something so nonsensical.

"Thank you." Martin took the report and quickly scanned the pertinent paragraphs. "Damn," he swore softly. He had, evidently, picked the wrong day to make a shift swap with

Rittenhouse. "It's going to rain tomorrow. That low in the Carolinas will be here by midnight."

"Right." Ted Nash kept his expression a blank. As Captain Martin's aide, he was expected to do whatever the man asked. But he saw no need to waste time when his desk was piled high with work. "Is there anything else, sir?"

"No." Martin picked up the brightly colored golf ball and tossed it up and down casually. "No golf tomorrow, I guess. A wasted day off."

"Yessir." Nash couldn't help but frown again. He touched his fingers against his prematurely receding hairline. He was barely thirty-one years old, yet he looked at least ten years older. He had gaunt features and dark, ominous circles under his eyes. It was, he was sure, this damn job of his that had done it. Being a lieutenant in the Pentagon, in a building packed with commodores and admirals, was an experience guaranteed to make anyone feel insignificant. If Nash didn't get a transfer back to a front-line operating unit very soon, he intended to resign.

"You don't play golf, do you?" Martin asked in a friendly tone. He had, several times, considered inviting Nash out to the driving range after work, but something in the lieutenant's attitude had kept him from doing it. Nash had the personality of sour grapefruit. Martin hoped that the lieutenant would snap out of it, before it became necessary to make an official comment in the man's fitness report.

"No, sir. I don't play golf."

"It's a fine game. You should try it."

"Yessir." Nash had again answered without enthusiasm. "Is that all, sir?"

"Yes." Martin watched as Nash turned and walked across the room to his desk. He shook his head slowly, then looked to the front wall. Martin peeked around the half-dozen enlisted men who worked there and scanned the big status board. The wall-mounted map of the world—ten feet high and twenty feet across—held the magnetic symbols of U.S. Navy ships at their current locations, and it showed that all was strictly routine. Martin looked at the wall clock. Ten minutes after one. He sat back in his chair and began to toss the golf ball up and down again. He juggled numbers in his mind as he tried to decide if there was enough time left in the afternoon to get in a few holes when his shift ended. He failed to notice that Lieutenant Nash had come back across the room toward him.

"Here's a strange one for you." Nash laid down the scroll of teletype paper. "It just came through on channel 01. It must be some asshole's idea of a joke."

"A joke?" Martin put the golf ball at the corner of his desk and scanned the paper.

TO NAVAL COMMAND CENTER, PENTAGON. FROM U.S.S. *TROUT*. HAVE URGENT MESSAGE FOR SECRETARY OF THE NAVY, HIS EYES ONLY. REPLY CHANNEL 01 WITHIN FIFTEEN MINUTES. THIS IS LIFE OR DEATH MATTER.

"Some asshole's idea of a joke," Nash repeated when he saw that Martin was finished reading.

Martin looked up, annoyed and puzzled. "This is certainly not a joke. Why would you say that?"

"Look at the identification." Nash tapped his finger against the paper. "We don't have a U.S.S. *Trout*. Not anymore. That's the name of the old diesel sub we sold to Iran in nineteen seventy-nine."

"Christ. That's right. I was thinking of a different ship." Martin fidgeted in his chair. "I don't understand." *A joke*. Perhaps there was a possibility that Lieutenant Nash was correct, that the message would signify nothing beyond the need for more communications discipline on board one of their ships. But something told Martin that there was more to this than that. It was the tone of the message, not the words, that he responded to. "I'm just not comfortable with this thing."

"Neither am I. We should attempt to track the message backward. Burn the ass of whoever sent it."

"That's not what I mean." Martin scanned the teletype address along the top of the message. "Whoever did this understands the switching codes." He pointed to the string of initials and numbers at the top, the code which allowed the teletype signal to be routed along discreet military frequencies directly to Washington and then into the NCC network.

"Any radioman knows how to do that much. Channel 01 is

for routine data, it isn't classified." Nash pointed to the status board in front of them, where several enlisted men were busy adjusting the positions of the magnetic ship symbols. "One of our shipboard radiomen is bored shitless, it's as simple as that. He figures we can't trace the message back to his ship, back to him."

"No." Martin shook his head slowly. "This isn't a joke-type message. It isn't the slightest bit funny."

"We haven't seen the punch line yet." Nash pointed back at the message. "Maybe he's got something funnier to tell the Secretary of the Navy. Maybe he's got a lousy sense of humor."

"We can't dismiss this out of hand. I'm not going to do that. It could mean something."

"That's your decision, sir." Nash frowned.

"Ask for a verification. That'll tell us more." Martin picked up a pencil and pad and scribbled out the message he wanted sent. He handed it to Nash.

"I doubt that we'll get any verification. Whoever did this won't have the balls to send a phony message twice." Nash walked to one of the teletype operators and handed over the message. In a few seconds it had been sent. Less than a minute after that the teletype came alive and began to print out a reply.

"What does it say?" Martin moved quickly toward the machine.

Nash had scanned the words as they printed. "More bullshit," he said as he tore off the message and handed it over.

WE CONFIRM OUR IDENTITY AS U.S.S. *TROUT*, IN RENDEZVOUS WITH U.S.S. *YORKTOWN*. KEYNOTE PHRASE IS TRANS-AMERICAN. IRREFUTABLE EVIDENCE WILL BE SENT WHEN SECRETARY OF THE NAVY PERSONALLY ACKNOWLEDGES OUR MESSAGE. PLAY NO TRICKS OR MANY WILL DIE.

The further he had read down the message, the more Captain Martin's face turned bloodless white, his eyes widened, his jaw dropped. "God Almighty. This is incredible."

Nash shook his head in disbelief. But before he said anything he looked over Martin's shoulder to read the message again, to be certain of what he had seen the first time. It was exactly what he had thought, and it was all perfectly clear to him. "In all due respect, sir, I still think it's pure bullshit. The *Yorktown* was decommissioned years ago. None of this can be true." Nash could see from the expression on Martin's face that the captain felt differently.

"We've got to get the Secretary in here."

"That might be a mistake, sir." Nash bit into his lower lip. He didn't know how to bring the next point up tactfully enough. He decided that he had nothing to lose, one way or the other. "Bothering the Secretary of the Navy with a minor discipline problem is not a good idea, sir."

"Come over here." Martin motioned for Nash to follow him toward his desk, until they were both out of earshot of the enlisted men at the banks of the teletypes. "You obviously haven't heard a newscast this morning, have you?" Martin whispered, although he kept his eyes fixed on the teletype message he held in his hands.

"I read the morning paper."

"It happened too late for the newspapers."

"I'm afraid I don't follow you."

"Let me brief you." Martin glanced up at the status board, then back to Nash. "The old carrier *Yorktown* broke away from its moorings in Charleston harbor last night. It's one of those historic ship exhibits. It floated out to sea. At least that's what the radio news said."

"But then how can this message be true?"

"Give me a chance," Martin answered. He walked up to the status board and Nash followed him. Martin pointed to a spot not far from Charleston harbor. "The Coast Guard launched a search after the morning fog lifted. This is the spot where they say they found the wreckage. They presume the *Yorktown* sank."

"That's in line with everything I'm saying. This is nothing but a bad joke!" Nash began to smile, but on seeing Martin's reaction he allowed his smile to quickly fade. He decided to try a different tack. "If I had to guess, I'd say that some shipboard clown heard the *Yorktown* situation on the morning news. He decided to play a joke. He put two ghost ships together in a cock-and-bull message. The *Trout* is in Iran. The

Yorktown is at the bottom of the ocean." Nash tapped his finger against the teletype message. "The only thing that's missing from that message is mention of the Flying Dutchman."

"All the Coast Guard reported finding were a few scattered pieces of wreckage—display aircraft from the *Yorktown,* mostly. That's hardly enough to tell anything for sure."

"We've lost entire convoys with less wreckage to show for it than that."

"No." Martin took a deep breath, then began to shake his head. But even he had begun to doubt his reasoning. "I don't know why, but I believe this thing." He held the teletype papers carefully, as if they were a volatile combination of ingredients. "It's the Trans-American phrase, I think. Or the entire tone."

"It's your decision, sir," Nash said coldly.

"I know." Captain Dwight Martin closed his eyes and rubbed his temples. He knew that the next line he said might well be responsible for either making or breaking his naval career. He waited a few more seconds to be sure, but his mind was made up. Martin looked back at his aide. "Go get the Secretary. Tell him we need him in here."

"I could call him, if you'd like." Nash gestured toward the closed-circuit telephone on the command console across the room.

"No. I'd rather you tell him face to face."

"Yessir. If that's your decision."

"It is." Martin swallowed hard. Sending the lieutenant in person might be more diplomatic, but he knew that if he made the Secretary of the Navy the butt of a joke, that would be the end of his chance for a flag promotion. Yet he felt that he had no choice. "Tell the Secretary that I'll attempt to make contact with the *Trout* again. I'll advise whoever is sending these messages that the Secretary will be in the NCC shortly."

"Yessir." Lieutenant Nash turned around and ambled slowly toward the door of the NCC. He stepped into the corridor and turned in the direction of the office of the Secretary of the Navy.

Dwight Martin stepped over to the coat rack behind his desk and retrieved his jacket and cap. He put them on, then carefully adjusted the knot of his tie. He then neatly folded the two teletype messages and put them into his inside jacket pocket.

Martin went back to the teletype machine and instructed the technician to send one additional message—utilizing the identical channel and access code that the incoming message had—to advise the *Trout* that their requirements would soon be met. *The keynote phrase is Trans-American. Many will die.* As he watched the technician type out the short message, Captain Dwight Martin noticed that his hand had begun to tremble. *I believe this thing.* He had a hunch that it would be one hell of a long time before he'd get to the country club to hit one of his new optic orange golf balls.

"Ted. Hold up a second."

"Hurry up." Lieutenant Ted Nash slowed his pace so the man who had called out to him could catch up.

"How about lunch?" Skip Locker asked as he scurried up alongside. "My treat today."

"Don't have time. I'm too busy saving the country." Nash shrugged as he continued to walk, his pace even slower now than it had been.

"Something tells me you aren't pleased with your current assignment. Another emergency report on shipboard latrine conditions?"

"Exactly." Nash smiled, for the first time that day. "You reporters sure have a nose for the news."

"That's how we get our scoops. Intuition coupled with judicious bribery."

"I'd take you up on the lunch offer, but I'm on my way to pour bullshit into the Secretary of the Navy's ear."

"Really?" Locker pushed his hand against the loose strands of hair above his left ear and smiled, a broad grin spreading across his young face. "Sometimes I wonder how you take this military crap."

"Sometimes I wonder, too." Nash stopped, then turned toward his friend. "You and I are both outside the norm for our jobs."

"Not me. API Syndicates makes it a practice to hire smart-ass young men. That's what gives the news such a pungent aroma."

"Right." Nash laughed for a few seconds, then stood silently. He was obviously deep in thought. "Listen," he finally added, "you've been buying me lunch for a long time. You've been trying to pry something out of me..."

"Don't take it personal. Free lunch is a tool of the trade, it comes with the pencil and notebook. But I buy for you because we're friends. You and I are basically the same."

"No. I'm taller." Nash grinned as he picked up his sloped shoulders to accent the small but noticeable difference between them.

"That's not what I meant." Locker shuffled his feet nervously.

"You're also gaining weight," Nash continued, uninterrupted, as he goaded Locker in the usual manner. "That spare tire around your middle comes from those expense account lunches."

"You're barely taller than I am. My weight is correct for my height." Locker allowed himself that much of a rebuttal, but would say no more. If there was anything he disliked, it was openly discussing his stature. He had told people for so many years that he was five feet ten inches tall that he had almost begun to believe it himself. The slight increase in weight over the summer was something he intended to take care of shortly. "We've got the same mental attitude toward this place," Locker said to change the subject. He waved his hand around the empty corridor.

"That's right. What was it you called it the other day?"

"Optical rectitus." Locker smiled. "That translates into shitty outlook."

"Of course." Nash paused. A deep frown had begun to etch itself on his face. "Maybe it's time I gave you something. You know, one of those famous scoops." He lowered his voice even more. "You know I wouldn't give you anything that was really crucial to the country's defense."

"Of course not." Locker edged closer. He wanted to reach for his notepad, but he knew that would be the wrong thing to do. The first rule of journalism was never to frighten an informant by showing too much attention to what he was saying. It was best to treat everything casually. "Go ahead."

"It's that damn Captain Martin. He likes to play hunches."

"Really?" Locker knew that the information, whatever it was, was still several sentences away.

"Yes." Nash sighed. He still couldn't believe that he had been ordered to waste his time on a fool's errand. "We get an obvious crank message in the Command Center, and Martin wants the Secretary of the Navy called in. I wouldn't be surprised if he's already on the telephone to the White House."

"That's the way those guys are," Locker said sympathetically. "Bureaucrats take everything at face value." Locker stopped and waited for Nash to continue. There was no pushing a man in a top secret position, even someone as far from the usual gung-ho military mold as Nash was.

Nash glanced at his wristwatch. "I've got to get going. Martin will be on my ass for taking too long. I'll give this to you quickly. One of our ships sent out a phony message on the teletype circuit that included the *Yorktown* and the *Trout*. The message demanded that the Secretary of the Navy personally respond within fifteen minutes."

"The *Yorktown?* Isn't that the exhibit ship that drifted out of Charleston harbor this morning?"

"Yes."

"I heard that it sank."

"It did. That's what the Coast Guard said. Captain Martin is convinced otherwise."

"What does he think?" Nash casually rubbed his hand against his coat pocket, but the miniature tape recorder was not inside. He silently cursed himself for forgetting to carry it with him.

"He believes what the message says, literally. The *Trout*— a submarine we sold to Iran in early 1979—and the *Yorktown* have rendezvoused somewhere. Many will be killed unless the Secretary personally acknowledges the message. That's what the teletype printed."

"Very interesting." Locker didn't know what to make of it. "What do you think?"

"It's all bullshit!" Nash had raised his voice more than he had intended. He looked quickly up and down the corridor, but, fortunately, it remained empty. "It's a dumb joke," he whispered, "but you're right. No one in this damn place has the slightest sense of humor."

"Maybe it comes from working with the bomb."

"Maybe." Nash shook his head in disgust. "Some jokester on a ship farts on a teletype, and we spend the next few hours in flag-level conferences trying to figure out what it really means. Pure bullshit."

"That's an interesting story angle." Locker's eyes lit up at the possibilities. It was the sort of story that might make the wire. Every newspaper in the country would carry it. People liked to make fun of the Pentagon—and very few of the reporters assigned to this place had the stomach to pursue something like that. But not Skip Locker. He didn't care because, unlike most of them, he intended to use this assignment strictly as a ladder to better things. "I'll put together background material. You keep me informed. We can have great fun with this one."

"Sure." Nash frowned. "Be careful not to mention where you got this."

"Of course not." Locker would make an attempt to cover his source, but his first priority was—as always—the story. The public had a right to know what really went on in this place. The career of any one particular lieutenant made little difference. "This is good for more than lunch. Dinner, at least. Maybe a weekend at some fancy resort, if things pan out."

"That's what I like about you. You call it straight."

"A bribe is a bribe, any way you color it."

"Right." Nash nodded, then began to walk away. "I'll get back to you later."

"I'm looking forward to it." Locker watched Nash walk down the length of the corridor, then disappear around the corner. He turned and began to walk rapidly in the opposite direction, toward the staircase that led to the reporters' office. He intended to dig out background material on both the *Yorktown* and *Trout*, then get the facts straight on what actually happened in Charleston that morning. He also intended to put his miniature tape recorder back into his pocket. The next time he spoke to Lieutenant Ted Nash, Skip Locker intended to be well prepared.

The first sensation that Drew O'Brien was aware of was warmth from the hand that had gently lifted his head back from where it rested against the ledge of the airliner's instrument panel. He heard a voice, but it was too far, too hollowed and too distant to make out what had been said.

"Don't try to move. Sit quietly." Janet Holbrook pulled O'Brien back from where he had slammed into the instrument panel during the deceleration. "Are you all right? Can you hear me?"

O'Brien opened his mouth to speak, but no words would come. He managed to nod his head once, but the growing pain caused him to close his eyes again. When he opened them, Janet continued to hover over him. She had begun to unbuckle his seat belt. He attempted to speak, but all that he managed was a low groan.

"Steady. I'm helping you." Janet removed the straps from around the captain and laid them behind him. "That was an incredible landing," she said, using the first words that came to her mind to fill the quiet of the cockpit. She worked quickly but carefully to free the injured pilot. Behind her, Janet heard noises from the cabin—a few sobs, some crying, an occasional loud voice. "I'll get you out of here. Just another few seconds."

"Is he okay? Can he get up?"

Janet looked behind her. A man had entered the cockpit. "There's blood on your forehead," she said as her eyes focused on the horizontal red smear across the man's head. The blood trickled down both sides of his face and disappeared among the tangled strands of his full, burly beard.

"It serves me right." Nat Grisby brushed his fingers against the opened cut. "My mother always told me I'd get hurt if I didn't follow instructions. I picked up my damn fool head during the landing. I wanted to see what was going on. When we hit the deck, I smacked into the seatback in front of me." While he spoke, Grisby had positioned himself behind the injured captain and had draped his arms around the man.

"Be careful. I don't know if he's broken anything." Janet ran her hands over O'Brien's arms, legs and chest, in an attempt to locate swelling or badly broken bones. "I don't see any blood. No apparent injuries."

"Maybe he's just dazed."

"I hope so."

O'Brien tried to speak again, but all he managed was a wheezing cough. The pain had increased, but it was general enough in nature to tell him that it was strictly from bangs and bruises. "I'm...okay." He took several more deep breaths.

After each breath his strength seemed to increase markedly. He sat himself up in his flight chair slowly, with the help of the bearded man behind him. "Any fires?" he asked, as soon as he could get out another few words.

"No. But we probably should get out of here. No sense pressing our luck." Without waiting for an answer, Grisby began to maneuver the captain out of his chair.

O'Brien turned his head slowly from side to side as he allowed the bearded man behind him to help him up and out of the seat. The view through the cockpit window was startling—twisted strands of tangled steel cables lay stretched across the airliner's nose as if the DC-9 jet were nothing but an insect trapped in a gigantic spider-web. A few feet beyond the nose of the airliner was the edge of the carrier's deck. The top of the dark, frothing sea continued to churn forty feet below. Each random pattern of waves was quickly enveloped and then replaced by the next set of swells behind it. From where O'Brien stood, the view was a disarming reminder of how close they had come to being killed.

"If you hadn't gotten us stopped, we'd be dead." Janet had seen what O'Brien had been watching.

"It was the net. That's what stopped us." O'Brien was out of his seat. With the bearded man's help, he stood up.

"Can you stand? Are you okay?"

"Yes. I think so." O'Brien steadied himself by bracing his arms against the cockpit sidewalls. His legs were wobbly, but they seemed to respond properly. "What's the situation?" he asked as he gestured toward the gray wall of the carrier's superstructure.

"I don't know."

The three of them watched the scene outside. Dozens of the passengers had already assembled against the gray wall, and many others continued to join them. A number of passengers had sat down on the carrier's deck, either from injuries or exhaustion from their ordeal. The others milled around in a tight, anxious knot.

"Look!" Janet was the first to point to the man with the hand-held submachine gun. He stood at the forward edge of the superstructure, the barrel of his weapon pointed directly at the core of frightened passengers who hovered against the gray-painted wall.

O'Brien felt a wave of anger rise up in him. "Bastards," he muttered in a low, threatening voice through his clenched teeth.

"Are you referring to me, captain?"

The three of them in the cockpit spun around. A short man with wire-rimmed glasses and black, curly hair—he was partly Oriental, partly of some indistinguishable heritage—stood in the forward galley area. He held a black submachine gun in his hands. It was aimed directly toward them.

"Don't make any sudden moves," Richard Yang announced in a mild, unemotional voice. "I hate loud noises."

"What do you want from us?" The idea of attempting to make a grab for the gun crossed O'Brien's mind, but there was no obvious way for him to do it without great risk—risk both to himself and to the other two in the cockpit.

"Very simple. I want cooperation. If we get it, no one will get hurt." Yang peeked over his shoulder, into the cabin. The aircraft evacuation was nearly complete. "Incidentally," he continued as he turned back toward the cockpit, "I want to congratulate you on the landing, captain. It was a superb job of airmanship—or so my technical people have advised me."

"Get to your point," O'Brien said. "What do you want?"

"I'll lay it all out for you. There's no need for secrets at this point." Yang leaned against the galley wall to give himself a better angle in case he needed to fire—he could tell from the pilot's eyes that he was the sort of man who had to be watched carefully. "As you've already been informed, there's a gold shipment in the cargo compartment. That, primarily, is what we're after. I'll be honest with you. I don't have a great many men with me. But before you get any foolish ideas, let me also inform you that the ones I do have are ready and able to pull the trigger." Yang smiled. "Without the slightest hesitation, I assure you. I suggest that you tell your people not to do anything rash."

"I'll tell them." O'Brien agreed with that point—he didn't want anyone endangering innocent lives with an impetuous display of heroics, no matter how well intentioned. If there was any attempt in the future to overpower these madmen, it would come through a well-thought-out and coordinated effort.

"Once we've assembled you folks against that wall," Yang said as he pointed toward the group gathered at the superstructure, "we'll march everyone to the hangar deck. The rear half of the hangar deck has been sealed off. It's quite large, so you'll be very comfortable. Keep in mind that I'll have an armed guard stationed at the only workable hatchway in or out. You'll sit tight until the next part of our plan unfolds."

"What does that mean?" Janet asked.

"Very simple, madam. Once we've taken off the gold— we'll be hauling it to the submarine in a small boat—there is one additional asset that is still worth trading for." Yang paused to give the next word the proper impact. "You." He waited while the implications sank in. "It occurred to us that you people—there are nearly one hundred of you—are worth a tidy sum if we return you in one piece."

"You people are something." O'Brien bit into his lip so he wouldn't say more.

"Thank you, Captain. I take that as a compliment. Some of my people think the ransom angle is gilding the lily, but I disagree. It's an easy way to add a few million more." Yang motioned with the barrel of the submachine gun to indicate that he wanted the three of them to move out of the cockpit. "Walk slowly. No sudden movements. You'll regret it if you do." Yang stepped aside and allowed the three of them to pass, then fell in behind as they walked toward the rear of the airliner. "The ransom angle might, at first blush, make this project seem a little greedy," Yang continued as if he were lecturing a class. "But there's nothing wrong with greed. Isn't that the basis of the capitalist system? Greed is a founding principle in our society."

The cabin was already empty as the four of them walked to the rear of the airliner. The aft emergency exit was open and they maneuvered carefully through the half-opened staircase—with the aircraft's landing gear torn away during the landing, the DC-9 sat considerably lower against the deck than it normally would. The four of them stepped outside into the brisk, damp air.

O'Brien looked down the deck of the aircraft carrier. Even

here, it seemed absurdly small. He shivered, a combination of the biting wind and the thought of how close they had come to death. He turned around. A short, ugly woman walked toward them, her body oscillating in rigid, nearly drunken steps. In her hands she held a submachine gun, and it was raised and pointed at a small boy. The boy was ten years old, at the most, and he marched stiffly ahead, petrified with fear. "Put that thing down!" O'Brien shouted.

The woman ignored him. "I just caught this kid. He was running back to the airplane."

"Is that so?" Yang stepped up to the boy. "Where were you going?" he asked, in what might in other circumstances have passed for a friendly question.

The boy stood trembling, his face covered with tears. "My dog...is...in there." He gestured meekly toward the airliner's cargo hold. "Please. Let me get her out."

"I'll take him below," the woman said curtly. She pushed the steel barrel of the gun into the boy's back.

"Wait." Yang shook his head at the Solenko woman, then smiled. "There's no need for us to be cruel." He turned to the pilot. "If you people cooperate with our requests, then we'll cooperate with yours." Yang turned back to the boy. "I'll tell you what. You go below with these people, and I'll have the dog brought to you as soon as we open the cargo hold. Is that a deal?"

"Yessir." The boy rubbed his hands across his face to wipe away the tears. "Her name is Aquarius."

"Fine." Yang turned back to the pilot. "There's one more thing. I want your wallet."

"Why?" To O'Brien, the demand had made no sense.

"Let's just say I'm a little low on cash. Hand it over." Yang reached carefully for the wallet, the barrel of his submachine gun aimed directly at the pilot's chest. "Very good. Now, your wallet too, mister bearded wonder."

"The name's Grisby." The big, bearded man glared down at the terrorist who had threatened him. "Why don't you try to take it from me?"

"My pleasure." Yang took half a step forward. He began to swing the barrel of his weapon around.

"Wait." O'Brien stepped in front of Grisby. He kept his back turned toward the terrorist. "Don't be a damn fool. Give him the wallet."

Grisby said nothing. A few seconds passed before he finally and reluctantly reached around to his back pocket to extract his wallet. He tossed the wallet on the deck near where the terrorist stood. "Spend those dollars in good health," he said with a tone that made his actual meaning quite plain.

"I've got to save every penny I can. I'm planning for my retirement." Yang scooped up the wallet and shoved it into his pocket. "Now," he said as he turned to face the pilot, "get your people to walk slowly and orderly through that hatch on the superstructure." He pointed to indicate where he wanted them to go. "When you get to the hangar deck, a guard there will show you where we want you. From this point on, there's nothing for you to do. You might as well relax. There are toilets on the hangar deck. Food and water, too, I think. You'll hear activity above as we unload the gold and transport it to the submarine."

O'Brien looked at the man with undisguised hatred, but he said nothing. Finally, he nodded slowly to indicate that he would comply with the instructions he had been given. He motioned toward the others in his group, then began to walk toward the gray-painted superstructure. O'Brien watched as Janet moved over to the young boy, put her arm around his shoulder and began to walk with him toward the hatchway. "How long will we be captives?" O'Brien asked in a loud voice.

"Hard to say. Depends on how cooperative the United States government decides to be. I suggest you put those thoughts out of your mind."

O'Brien did not reply. He continued to walk toward the hatchway, to fall in line behind the group of passengers from his flight who were now lined up to go below as they had been directed. But Drew O'Brien's thoughts had focused on something else, on something that the half-bred Oriental with the submachine gun had failed to mention. O'Brien, too, was reluctant to raise the point of what their fate might be if the United States government failed to pay the ransom.

9

THE DULL WHITE light from the reflection of the periscope spread across Jerome Zindell's face as he turned away from the eyepiece. "The skiff is being lowered," he said to the others in the conning tower of the U.S.S. *Trout*. "It should be in the water in a few minutes."

"How are the seas? Not too rough?" Edward McClure asked. He continued to lean casually against the rail of the ladder that led to the control room below, a toothpick stuck between his teeth.

Zindell leaned forward and peered into the scope again. "The chop is down significantly. He should have no problem."

"Good. Yang isn't much of a seaman." McClure stretched his arms above his head and yawned. He had been bored since the first minute he had stepped aboard the submarine, and he wondered for a moment how anyone—Zindell included—could stomach this sort of duty. It was high-technology combat, nothing more. The enemy was never more than an inane image on a radar tube, a spectrum of noise in an earpiece, an innocuous shape through a periscope. It was too vague to be exciting.

"We should begin to get to the surface, so we'll be ready for him."

Zindell shook his head and frowned. "Not yet. It's too early." He disliked having to explain his decisions to anyone on the boat, but felt a grudging obligation to be moderately tactful with McClure. He was too much of a madman to treat otherwise. "You don't seem to remember that we've already agreed to keep ourselves submerged as long as possible during daylight conditions. There's no sense in begging for a problem."

"Right." McClure shrugged to show that he didn't care to pursue the conversation. He stepped across the small conning tower, toward where Olga and Harrison stood. "Do you smell something?" he asked in mock seriousness as he approached them. He made an exaggerated gesture of sniffing the air.

"What sort of smell?" Olga had asked quickly, before Harrison could turn and join in on the conversation. She looked directly at McClure as she allowed a compliant smile to spread across her face. McClure was slightly shorter than Harrison, but far more compact and muscular. His eyes—which had a penetrating quality to them—somehow conveyed the message that he had seen it all, experienced just about everything. Olga felt a sudden impulse to lay her hands against his stomach muscles—they were flat, rigid—and press in. She expected to find them unyielding.

"There's no way I could describe this sort of smell to a lady." McClure laughed loudly. He reached up and brushed his fingers against Olga's face. "I think you've been on this sewer pipe too long. Everything on this tub is damp and foul. What you need is fresh air. Clean living."

"Fresh air, certainly." Olga joined in on his laughter. She stepped closer to McClure. She had not met this man before he had come aboard the submarine a few hours before, but the brief time they had spent together had confirmed his reputation. He seemed to be quite a man, in every way she could think of. "The odor is nothing to be offended by. Mildew. Brass polish. Coffee."

"Don't forget sweat. And one additional thing." McClure cast a sideways glance at Harrison, who remained occupied with his duties. "The smell of fear."

Harrison spun around. "What the hell did you say?"

"You heard me."

"Let's keep the chatter down." Zindell stared at the two men a few seconds to show that he wouldn't allow this to go any further. This was his boat, period. Finally, he turned back to the periscope. It was clear to him that McClure intended to push himself on Olga—and that she intended to respond too willingly. Actually, the Cuban whore was begging for it. McClure was also going to rub Harrison's nose in it. If it wasn't for Harrison, Zindell wouldn't have given a damn what Olga and McClure did. They could screw their brains out for all he cared—a job that obviously wouldn't take either of them very much time. But the last thing Zindell needed now was a lovers' triangle to add to his problems. "Let's stick to business. This could be a crucial time."

"Sure thing." McClure stepped back across the conning tower, spit the remnants of his chewed toothpick onto the steel decking, then reached into his pocket for another. He shoved the new toothpick between his teeth, then waited until Harrison turned back to his duties on the far side of the conning tower. "I'll lay you five to one odds," McClure finally continued, "that when we get those wallets there won't be a penny left in them. Yang comes from a long line of pickpockets."

"Just so he hasn't pocketed any of the gold," Zindell answered. He kept his attention focused on the view through the periscope.

"He won't do that, it's too risky. He's got guts, but no balls—if you know what I mean."

Zindell didn't reply. Instead, he stepped a few feet back from the scope and rubbed his eyes. *Get rid of men that you can't control. Get rid of men who make you feel uncomfortable.* His father's words flashed through his mind, and Zindell wished that he was back in the Navy again. That way, McClure would have been transferred off the *Trout* so fast he wouldn't have any recollection of ever having served aboard her. But this was not the U.S. Navy. Zindell had to act differently now. "Mr. Harrison," he said in a weary voice, "get me an update on the status of the torpedoes."

"Yessir." Clifton Harrison reached across for the interphone switch that connected his headset directly with the forward torpedo room. As he did, he allowed himself another peek at McClure. That arrogant bastard continued to gaze blankly ahead toward the wall crammed with pipes, valves and instruments on the starboard side of the conning tower. Harrison felt a sudden urge to take the fire ax out of the holder on the bulkhead and smash it into McClure's head. Olga's too, maybe. "Forward torpedo room," Harrison said sharply into the mouthpiece. "The captain needs a status report." Harrison listened for several seconds before he turned back to Zindell. "Tubes number one through three are ready to fire. They've begun to load tube number four."

"Tell them to stand down. Have the men return to their maneuvering stations. I intend to surface the boat shortly."

"It's about time," McClure interrupted.

"For chrissake, pipe down," Zindell blurted out. He took half a step around the periscope and toward McClure. Zindell could see that the man had picked himself up and now stood rigidly alert, his every muscle tensed, his eyes darting from side to side in the small conning tower. He looked more like a wild animal preparing to go into a fierce battle to the death, rather than a human being about to be chastised. "Why the hell don't you butt out of things that aren't your business," Zindell found himself saying, even though his common sense told him that he shouldn't.

"This is my business. Every bit of it."

"Bullshit." But Zindell had managed to cool himself down enough to realize that if he didn't control this situation very soon, then it would collapse under its own weight. "Remember our deal, dammit. You're in charge of everything but the *Trout*. When you're here, you're under my command."

"But I'm not under your boot. Don't you forget it."

Zindell's face flushed red, but he somehow managed to hold his tongue. He exchanged a quick glance with Harrison, who was looking to him for a signal. Harrison had taken a step toward where McClure stood in the center of the conning tower, obviously prepared to join in if there was going to be a battle. *Harrison is loyal. He'll take McClure from behind. I'll take out Olga.* Zindell was mildly surprised that he had already decided on Olga's lack of loyalty simply from the way she had stood next to McClure. That seemed to be enough of a signal. "There's no need to get upset. We're nervous, that's all."

"Yes. We're just excited. Tired." Olga stepped nearer to the center of the room. She put her arm on McClure's shoulder, in what had been intended as a calming gesture.

"Speak for yourself. Both of you," McClure snarled. But something in his voice said that his tidal wave of temper had also ebbed.

"Excited. Tired. She's right. That's what we are." Zindell shot another quick glance at Harrison, who had edged even nearer to the fire ax, his hand lying inconspicuously on the bulkhead only inches away from it. Zindell knew that it would take only a brief nod from him to transform McClure into a dead man. "We've got to keep control of ourselves. We're too close now to blow this thing."

McClure stood his ground silently as he stared directly at Zindell. Finally he turned to Olga. Her hand continued to lie gently on his shoulder. "I think the captain is right. We're just tired."

"Yes." Olga sighed in relief, then backed away. As her hand slid away she became acutely aware that she had shown everyone—herself included—where her allegiance was. She avoided Zindell's stare and began to curse herself silently for being so malleable. But then she looked up at McClure, and within a few seconds her doubts were washed away by a new flood of passion and desire.

"Get an update from the radioman," Zindell said as if nothing had happened. "Verify that there are no conflicting targets on the sonar, that the area remains clear of ships. Tell Moss to prepare to operate the antiaircraft radar as soon as our mast is above the waterline."

"Yessir." Harrison looked disappointed, but he quickly stepped back to his console and passed the orders on.

"Come on. Let's get up already," McClure announced to break the silence. There was enough of an edge of nervousness in his voice to turn the remark into a request. *I hate this fucking sardine can.* McClure pointed to the ceiling of the gray-painted steel hull inches above his head. "I want to get some fresh air into this tub."

"Be patient. You'll be thankful that the *Trout* can stay underwater as long as it does when people start chasing us. Then you'll be glad as hell that we're down here."

"Maybe." McClure shifted his weight. There was nothing about this submarine that he liked, nothing about Zindell except that he knew how to operate this tub of shit. "Running from a fight isn't my style."

"I'll be happy to leave you on the surface, if you prefer." Zindell watched the quick change in McClure's expression again. Clearly, he had again said too much, made the comment sound too much like a threat. "You can take two rubber rafts—one for you, one for your share of the gold," Zindell quickly added.

"No." McClure paused. "Thanks anyway," he added in a conciliatory tone. *I'll get this son-of-a-bitch later. I'll make him sorry he was ever born.*

"Your choice." Zindell forced a weak grin, to match the enigmatic smile that had developed on McClure's face. Zindell wondered for a moment what in God's name could be going on in the man's head. "Everyone relax. We've got a few more minutes."

"Okay."

Zindell turned away and, for lack of anything else to occupy himself with, began to carefully examine the periscope in front of him. The shiny shaft of stainless steel rose vertically from floor to ceiling, held in position by two black cables that dragged it up from out of the dark hole near his feet. Tiny rivulets of water trickled slowly through the periscope's seawater seal where it penetrated the roof of the hull. The water broke into a procession of drops, which flowed lazily across the brass body of the periscope, the section that housed the eyepiece and focus adjustments. The water drops then dripped off the bottom, one by one, and fell silently into the cavity below. As he had done so many times in the past, Zindell was mesmerized by the sight of each drop of water as it progressed from the top to the bottom of the periscope. He would have continued to watch them if McClure hadn't spoken out.

"Where's the boat now? Even Yang couldn't be this slow."

Zindell leaned on the periscope, his one arm draped around the focus control to steady himself, his face pressed against

the eyepiece. He peered out. "The skiff's in the water, away from the carrier. Here it comes." Zindell stood back from the scope, hit the lever to lower it, and stood silently while the stainless-steel tube traveled by. When the periscope was completely retracted, he turned to the others. "Surface the boat."

"Yessir."

Harrison had no sooner spoken when the first noises began to float up from the control room below. Muffled voices were followed quickly by the clicking and clunking sounds of levers and valves being repositioned. A few seconds later the hissing of compressed air began. Like the building of a symphonic score, the noise from the air being forced into the submarine's ballast tanks grew louder, more patterned, more resonant with each passing moment.

"Here we go," Zindell said to no one in particular. He knew from his years of experience that the sounds meant that the boat had begun to pick itself out of the water. But as far as he could tell from the physical sensations, nothing had changed. *Innuendo*. That's what his father had called the job of maneuvering a submarine. There was never any direct evidence of anything, no reliable way to determine depth, course or speed, except by consulting the gauges. Without a reading from those essential instruments—scores of needles that pointed to countless stenciled numbers mounted inside glass-enclosed cases—there was no way to determine whether the submarine was near the surface or rapidly approaching its crush depth. For the one millionth time since he had heard the news about the *Thresher*, Zindell imagined for a moment what it must have been like for his father. Until the instant that the steel walls of that nuclear submarine crushed in like an eggshell, the only precursor to their inescapable fate came from those silent needles and the random popping of rivets which were propelled across the width of the boat's interior with lightning speed, taking with them any piece of arm, leg or head in their path. Zindell whispered, almost loud enough to be heard, the well-worn prayer that his father's death had been swift.

"Captain. We're on the surface," Harrison announced.

"Stand by." Zindell grabbed the periscope, put his eye up to it and walked around in a slow circle. "All clear." Satisfied that the area was still free of unknown ships and aircraft, he slapped the control handle back. The periscope lowered into its recess. "Open the hatch. Lookouts to their stations. Loading party to the aft torpedo room."

"Yessir." Harrison barked the orders into the communications microphone, then motioned for Olga to climb the short ladder that led to the hatch in the conning tower's roofline.

Olga scurried up the ladder. "I'm opening the hatch." She spun the locking lever, then pushed upward.

The whiff of salt air blew down through the opened hatchway. "Officers to the bridge," Zindell said. He inhaled deeply, the fresh sea air a welcomed relief from the stale odors of the boat. Zindell waited while McClure followed Olga, then Harrison followed McClure. Satisfied that the three of them were at their stations above-decks and that everything onboard the *Trout* was in good order, Zindell edged himself upward slowly and carefully, his one arm maneuvering awkwardly from rung to rung on the metal ladder.

"Here comes the skiff."

Zindell followed Harrison's outstretched arm until he, too, saw the small boat as it bobbed up and down on the slightly choppy sea. Behind it, appearing even more of a behemoth than in reality it was, was the *Yorktown*. The aircraft carrier sat motionless, the slight movements of the ocean barely able to sway it. On its flight deck sat the damaged airliner, its red-painted sides reflecting incongruously against the gray warship it rode on, its nose perched precariously over the edge of the flight deck by several feet. "I hope that airliner doesn't fall overboard," Zindell commented aloud.

"What difference would it make?"

"None, I guess." Zindell turned from McClure and faced the skiff. The small boat had begun to approach the submarine from the starboard quarter. "Make ready with the lines."

Zindell watched as the men from the loading party climbed out through the aft torpedo room hatch and onto the submarine's deck. As the skiff approached, the lone man in the small boat uncoiled a rope and held it in his hands. "Prepare to grab that line," Zindell shouted. The men on the deck began to move toward the appropriate spot on the submarine's fantail before the captain's words had died away in the brisk wind. "Thank

God the sea is down. This would have been one hell of a job if it were still rough out here."

"Right." McClure edged toward the aft of the submarine's bridge and watched anxiously. If Yang screwed up, he could easily send the gold to the bottom of the ocean. Then all their efforts would have been for nothing. McClure vowed that any errors from that half-breed bastard would turn him into instant shark bait.

"He's coming in too fast."

"He's a fucking moron," McClure shouted. The skiff bobbed and heaved on the swells as it plowed toward the stern of the *Trout*. But just before it would have been too late to avoid a disaster, the man in the skiff maneuvered hard to starboard. The skiff rubbed noisily but harmlessly along the stern of the *Trout* as it came to a dead stop in the water.

"That was too close." Zindell had turned slightly pale.

"He's an asshole." McClure was glad that he had spent those long practice mooring sessions with Yang in Charleston the month before. "The line's secure." With the gold safely alongside, McClure managed a sigh of relief. "I hope that clown remembered to bring the wallets."

"He better have."

As the people on the bridge watched, Richard Yang picked out a small box from the stack inside the skiff. He began to maneuver himself carefully onto the submarine. Once he had stepped aboard, he hurried in the direction of the bridge.

"We're right on schedule," Yang shouted. He was slightly out of breath and he needed to pause for a moment before he began to climb the short ladder that led to where McClure and the others stood. Yang was surprised to see that one of the four people on the bridge was a woman—she was Spanish-looking, with frizzy hair and a big leather belt with a pearl-handled knife and an odd coil of leather hanging from it. He made no comment about her, one way or the other.

"Was all the gold there?" McClure pointed toward the skiff, where the loading party had already begun the task of removing the wooden crates and taking them below. "Did it seem to be the right amount?"

"Yes." Yang was now sorry that he hadn't squirreled away

some gold for himself. It was too late for that now. "If anything, there seems to be a little more gold than we expected."

"My airline man was very thorough." McClure smiled out of satisfaction with himself, then glanced in the direction the Lear had gone down. He wondered for an instant if he might spot any fragments of the small jet, but he couldn't see any pieces of wreckage floating on the endless waves and swells.

Zindell cleared his throat to get everyone's attention. "Are these the identifications I asked for?" He pointed to the box that Yang held.

"Yes. I took wallets from the men, and whatever the women still had with them. I've got a couple dozen at least." Yang peered into the box, then back up at the one-armed man who stood in front of him. McClure had already cautioned him that the submarine captain was not a man to be trifled with, so Yang had decided to be as accommodating as he could. "I can get more, if you like."

"No. This is fine. We'll take them below." Zindell motioned to Harrison. Harrison stepped forward and took the box. Zindell noticed that Harrison's eyes had darted back and forth between Olga and McClure, as if he were about to say something to both of them. Zindell prayed that he wouldn't. After a few seconds Harrison turned abruptly and strode toward the hatch that led below, the box of wallets and identifications in his arms.

"Here's the pilot's wallet." Yang produced a black leather wallet and handed it to Zindell. "I figured I should carry it separately."

"Fine." Zindell took the wallet and put it into his pocket. "I intend to transmit the identification data from the pilot's wallet first," he announced to everyone on the bridge, "then five or six of the others. I probably won't need any more. That should convince the Pentagon that we really have these people in custody."

"What about the explosives?" McClure leaned against the bridge rail in an exaggerated gesture of casualness. "Did you remember to take the explosives out of the box of gold?"

"Sure." Yang could see that the submarine captain was visibly relieved by his answer. "It took me awhile, but I found it. It was nearly the last box I opened."

"Naturally." Zindell nodded in sympathy, then looked toward the stern. He had emphatically told McClure that under no circumstances would he allow the crate with the radio-controlled explosives onboard the *Trout*. Zindell was glad to see that McClure had instructed Yang to comply. If things kept going this well, by dawn the operation would be history.

"I hid the explosives real well, just like you said." Yang was eager to show his cooperative attitude in whatever way he could. "It would take an army a week to find it." Yang gestured toward the *Yorktown*. The four of them on the bridge turned and looked at the giant ship for a few seconds.

"What about the man who helped take the ship out of Charleston—the man who isn't part of your group?" Having an outsider onboard was one part of the operation Zindell hadn't liked, but McClure had said that he could work it out. Apparently, he had.

"No problem." McClure glanced at Yang, then back at Zindell. "I've already given the orders. He'll be terminated."

"Terminated?"

"That's right. Once we put the gold on the boat, I sent my two best men to the *Yorktown*'s bridge." Yang reached up and readjusted the fit of his wire-rimmed glasses. "I expect that they've already disposed of the problem of Talbot."

Zindell stared at Yang for several seconds, then glanced around the bridge. Idle talk about cold-blooded murder wasn't the same as discussing casualties inflicted during the course of a battle, and he didn't want to be a participant in it. Zindell turned toward the stern of the *Trout*. "Your boat is unloaded."

"Okay." Yang turned around, stepped carefully down the ladder, then onto the main deck. He took a few more steps toward his boat before he turned around again. "I'll use the portable transmitter to stay in touch. I'm planning on getting my men off the *Yorktown* at four A.M. That gives us enough time to get here and into the sub before first light."

Zindell nodded. "Very well." He had raised his voice measurably so it would carry against the steady wind that blew toward him. "I've decided that five-thirty is the time we'll submerge. I don't want to be on the surface later than that."

"No problem." Yang turned and trotted down the submarine's deck, then climbed aboard his small boat. He waited until one of the men from the loading party tossed off the securing lines from the bow and stern. The skiff drifted away quickly in the current.

Zindell watched silently as Yang started the skiff's engine. The man then turned the tiller hard to port and the boat began to plow forward through the diminishing waves. Zindell turned back to McClure. "Since our diesel engines are still running, I'm going to reposition ourselves in reference to the carrier." Zindell pointed toward the warship, which had drifted to an unacceptable angle in reference to them. "I don't want to use our batteries to maneuver unless I absolutely need to."

McClure shrugged. "Suit yourself."

Zindell didn't reply. Instead, he reached for the communications headset that Harrison had left on the bridge. He put it on. "You two can go below," he said to Olga and McClure. "I'll take care of things from here."

"I've got one question," McClure said. He pointed to the *Yorktown*. "What time do you intend to shoot the torpedoes?"

"At five-twenty tomorrow morning."

"Before we submerge?" McClure looked puzzled.

"Yes. This isn't Hollywood. We're going to do it the easy way—which also happens to be the best way."

"How's that?" McClure leaned forward attentively. Battle plans and tactics always fascinated him, even if they involved a weapon as uninteresting as a submarine. "I thought that torpedoes were always shot while submerged. I thought you had to use the periscope to aim them."

"No." Zindell laughed. "That's John Wayne stuff. In reality, it's easier to point the boat directly at the target, then set the torpedoes to run straight. I'm planning to submerge again in a few minutes. Then we'll stay below the surface until nightfall, just in case the Navy decides to try a surprise airplane attack against us."

"Evening twilight will end at eight thirty-nine tonight," Olga volunteered.

"Thank you." Zindell peeked at his wristwatch. "That's a little less than six hours from now. After dark, we'll come to the surface again to charge our batteries. Being on the surface will also make it a great deal easier to remain in the proper relative position to the target."

"I see."

"At the first hint of dawn—five-twenty—we'll fire our torpedoes from our surfaced position."

"Regardless of whether or not the ransom money has been dropped, is that correct?" McClure had phrased it as a question, but there was little doubt from his tone that he intended it to be a statement of fact. That was one part of the plan he had been quite emphatic about.

"Correct." Zindell was not pleased with it—he would have preferred to leave the *Yorktown* alone if the ransom was paid in good faith—but he had to reluctantly admit that there were operational benefits to doing it McClure's way. "After the *Yorktown* begins to sink, we'll submerge and get the hell out of here."

"Very good." McClure nodded his approval.

"Another advantage with this plan, beyond what we've already discussed, is that the noise generated by the sinking of the *Yorktown* will effectively mask the noise we'll make in leaving the area. If the Navy does look for us, they'll have one hell of a job acquiring our sonar trail with the *Yorktown* going down."

"Great." Sonar trails meant nothing to McClure; watching the sinking of the *Yorktown* did. "What about the number of torpedoes?" McClure glanced at the huge gray hull a thousand yards in the distance. The thought of sending a tin fish crammed with explosives into its side caused a shiver of excitement to pass through him.

"Four torpedoes, at ten-second intervals. That should be more than enough to sink the *Yorktown*."

"Excellent." McClure rubbed his hands together, then turned and smiled at Olga. "Let's get below, so the captain can get on with his work."

"Certainly." Olga gave a half-salute to Zindell, then stepped toward the hatch. As she moved past McClure, she rubbed her body against his as she descended the steps of the ladder. A few seconds later she disappeared below. McClure followed her.

Jerome Zindell stood alone on the bridge. He fumbled with the communications headset to adjust it. "This is the captain," he finally announced into the boom microphone that hung in front of his mouth, his voice mingled with the incessant hum caused by the constant wind that blew across the open deck. "Engines ahead one-third. Steer twenty degrees to port." A tinny, disinterested voice acknowledged the order. A few moments later the boat tremored slightly from the increased pulses of engine power.

Zindell watched as the submarine began to inch forward. Curls of foaming white water began to roll across the rounded bow of the *Trout*, the water visibly churned for several yards on either side of the hull. But the agitated sea flattened itself quickly and was soon transformed into no more than a broad array of bubbles as it mixed in with the heaving dark swells of the ocean currents.

Zindell sighed, then turned to face aft. He rubbed the stump where his left arm used to be. He cursed the Naval accident that killed his father. He cursed the Navy lieutenant who seduced and ran off with his wife, Joan. But mostly he cursed the U.S. Navy for their treatment of him after he gave his arm in service to his country. *You bastards. My father and my wife weren't enough for you. You had to take my goddamn arm. You're all going to pay now*. The boat's twin screws continued to rapidly propel the submarine ahead, and they created another spray of white water to trail behind them. That white swath on the face of the dark sea quickly settled itself to a light green, then a dark green, then finally into the ink-blue color of the open ocean.

Jerome Zindell looked farther astern of their position. At a distance of no more than a few hundred yards behind his submarine, there was no visible evidence that the U.S.S. *Trout* had ever traveled across that section of the sea. Even at that short a distance behind them, the white wake they had created had been completely erased by the vastness and indifference of the treacherous ocean.

10

DREW O'BRIEN STOOD in the center of the hangar deck of the *Yorktown*. "We might as well relax, they've got us penned in." O'Brien gestured broadly, the sweep of his arm taking in the sealed hatchways that surrounded them. Those hatchways against the sidewalls of the cavernous hangar deck were, apparently, the only alternate ways to get out of the area they had been imprisoned in.

"I hate to give up so easily. It's not good for morale." Janet Holbrook allowed her eyes to wander across the group of passengers around her.

"I know." O'Brien shrugged, then joined her as the two of them looked at the faces of the people from Flight 255. Now that the excitement had died down—the close brush with death during the landing, the presence of armed terrorists with weapons pointed at them, the discovery that this ship was the *Yorktown* out of Charleston, a historic relic that had obviously somehow been stolen—most of the passengers now sat listlessly on the hangar floor. They had scattered themselves into groups of a dozen or so across the entire area, which was the size of a few tennis courts laid side to side. "This whole damn thing is unbelievable," O'Brien said as he looked around the section of the hangar deck they had been sequestered in.

"I read somewhere that hostages always say that."

"I'm glad that I'm predictable." O'Brien tried to smile, but found that he couldn't.

"I'm being serious," Janet answered. She edged slightly closer to O'Brien. "Think about most of the big hijackings. Think about the Entebbe rescue that the Israelis pulled off. It seemed unbelievable until someone managed to do it."

"I guess so." O'Brien nodded in agreement, then began to examine the hangar deck more carefully. This area of the *Yorktown* had been used as exhibition space for historic military displays. The well-preserved airframe of an old Grumman torpedo bomber occupied one corner of the area, the airplane's fresh coat of shiny blue paint making it appear lustrous in the reflected glow from the ceiling lights. The two-seat Grumman looked as if it were ready to fly, but O'Brien could tell from even this distance that the aircraft's engine was a fake. It was the bare skeleton of an airplane, no more.

O'Brien glanced down at the exhibition pieces that surrounded the old Grumman. Four bright-green torpedoes were lined end to end, the first torpedo with half its exterior skin cut away so that visitors could examine its insides. O'Brien let his eyes wander toward the forward end of the ship, where gangs of signs, plaques and mementos lined the walls. "They've stuck us away in a floating museum."

"What's that thing?" Janet asked. She gestured toward the turret-looking structure in the upper left-hand corner of the hangar deck. It stood approximately seven feet high and ten feet across, and it contained several small, thick windows. It appeared formidable and menacing. "Is it a gun emplacement?" she asked, but at the same time she wondered why anyone would design a warship with a gun emplacement facing the inside of the hangar.

"No." The faded lettering on the sides was visible enough for O'Brien to figure out what the structure actually was. "A conflagration station, see?"

"I see the lettering. What does it mean?"

"It's for fire watch." O'Brien remembered having once read something about the conflagration stations onboard aircraft carriers, probably from an old war novel. It was supposed to be the most boring shipboard duty an officer could pull. "Whenever there was work going on in the hangar bays, an officer would be stationed inside there. He would watch for accidental fire. If one began, the man would activate the overhead fire extinguishers from the control panel in there."

"I see." Janet looked up to where O'Brien pointed and she noticed for the first time the maze of crisscrossed pipes on the ceiling. There were fire-extinguishing nozzles every few feet along the piping. She motioned back toward the conflagration station. "Is there any way we can use that place to help our escape from here?"

"No. It's heavy gauge steel. Thick, shatterproof glass—built to withstand explosion and intense heat. The only access is from somewhere beyond the hangar wall."

"I understand." Janet allowed her eyes to wander around the solid lines of the steel structure before she looked back to O'Brien. "How could these people ever have gotten away with stealing this ship?"

"Your guess is as good as mine. I was the first who said it was unbelievable." O'Brien paused. "But I'm sorry to say that since they've gotten away with it this far, they might be able to get away with the rest of it, too."

"Do you think they'll leave us unharmed?" Janet had asked the question anxiously, not really wanting to hear what O'Brien might say.

O'Brien waited slightly too long before he answered. "Of course," he replied unconvincingly. He couldn't look her in the eye when he answered, so he turned away and pretended to examine the ceiling again. It was made up of plates of steel laid against corrugated metal ribwork and was at least forty feet above them. O'Brien knew that the outside of that roofline was what formed the flight deck that he had landed the airliner on, and that meant that the roof had been built too thick and strong to be tampered with. There was no way out that way, and ditto for the conflagration station. "I'm glad this part of the hangar is big enough for us." O'Brien said offhandedly in order to make conversation. "We've got enough room."

"Yes. A nice big space for pissing in our pants." Nat Grisby had joined in on the conversation without preamble as he stepped up to where O'Brien and Janet stood in the center of the hangar deck.

O'Brien frowned—he didn't need to be reminded of their problems, they were too numerous to be forgotten. "Our situation could be a great deal worse." When they had been forced at gunpoint to march down the stairs to the level beneath the flight deck, O'Brien had visions of them all being crammed inside a small compartment somewhere deep inside the bowels of the ship. That would have been even more of a nightmare for them. At least in this area—the rear third of the hangar, partitioned from the forward sections by a huge steel fire wall that he now faced—there was more than enough space to be comfortable.

"You're right. It could be worse. But that's not much consolation." Grisby stroked his full and bushy beard for a moment before he spoke again. "I've checked each of the sidewall doors carefully. Just like you figured, they're sealed tight. Welded shut, I think."

"Damn." O'Brien shook his head, then looked at the fire wall again. Effectively, they were sealed inside a big steel can without even a view of the outside world. "That exit seems like the only way out," O'Brien said as he pointed to the closed hatchway on the left side of the gray-painted steel wall. It was the entrance that they had been marched through when they entered.

"Sure is." Grisby frowned. "If they haven't welded that one shut yet, all we've got to worry about in order to escape from here is that maniac on the other side of the hatchway. You'll probably recall that he has a submachine gun."

"If we can distract him," Janet said, "that might be our chance."

"Which translates into no chance at all."

The three of them turned. James Westcott stood directly behind them. He had evidently been standing there long enough to overhear their conversation. "Should I take your remark as a legal interpretation, counselor?" Grisby asked sarcastically. He had already heard from Janet about the lawyer's cockpit tirades during the flight.

"Don't start playing hero with our lives," Westcott continued as he addressed his comment to O'Brien and ignored Grisby.

"Your airline is still legally responsible for us. I strongly suggest that you do something positive to control the impetuous and juvenile..." Westcott glanced at Grisby, then back at O'Brien, "... antics of a few of the members of this group. It still remains your job to protect us, captain."

O'Brien took a deep breath. As obnoxious as this man could be, he was right about the facts: it was still O'Brien's problem. O'Brien's responsibility. "Don't worry. I won't allow anything foolish to happen. No rash acts."

"Good. I'm certain that the passengers would appreciate it."

"Probably." O'Brien looked around at the group. There were nearly one hundred of them trapped on the hangar deck with him, and he could see that with a full hour having passed they had nearly all settled into the same sort of behavior pattern. They seemed drained of their energy, and what remained were stilted caricatures of people—as if a group of bad actors had been given the job of portraying zombies in a grade-B movie. Most of them sat silently and stared blankly ahead, hardly bothering to move a muscle. Those who spoke to the people beside them did so in low, choked-off voices. There was dread and fear etched deeply on most everyone's face. A paralyzing fear. A few of them wept softly, but most sat stoically without the slightest display of emotion. Without ever saying so, they had bought the attitude that the lawyer Westcott was selling— the attitude that there was nothing to do now but wait to see what the terrorists would do next, nothing to do but pray that the terrorists would be merciful.

But then O'Brien's attention was drawn further out, toward the corners of the area they were imprisoned in. There were a few people out there who milled around with a seeming purpose, who seemed to be probing and examining everything they could get their hands on. Three teenage boys poked around the old Grumman's airframe, and several others worked their way around the torpedoes or along the series of wall plaques and mementos. Even if their interest was no more than an idle curiosity, at least it was a positive sign. "I'm not so sure that we shouldn't try to do something. At least it would keep us occupied."

Westcott took a half a step backward, picked up his shoulders, and opened his mouth as if he were about to begin a long-

winded speech. But before the first words came out, Benny
Randolf ran up alongside, stepped in front of Westcott and
began to talk excitedly, his high-pitched voice taking a stab
into their pent-up tensions as if it were a sharp pin thrust into
a balloon. "I found something...no kidding, great
stuff...something we can really use."

"What is it?" O'Brien asked.

Benny did a slight dance step backward. He flung out his
arms and tilted his head. "F-o-o-d!" he shouted, the word dragged
out to several times its natural length. "Glorious food! There's
enough for everyone!" On that last word, most of the people
sitting rose and joined the mounting crowd that had begun to
swell toward him. "Drinks, too. Soft drinks." Benny produced
an exaggerated frown. "But we can pretend. We can make
believe it's Johnny Walker Scotch!"

"Where is it?" O'Brien shouted over the mounting chorus
of laughs and cheers. As immune to this sort of thing as he
thought he would be, O'Brien noticed that he, too, had begun
to smile like the others. He glanced quickly at Janet and noticed
that she also had a big grin on her face. This moment was
something they obviously needed. "Where is this food? Show
me." O'Brien physically turned Benny around to face in the
direction he had come from. A few seconds later the entire
crowd was following the two of them toward the rear of the
hangar deck.

"Here it is." Benny pried back the corner piece of sheet
metal that had covered an inconspicuous recessed compartment
in the rear wall. "A snack bar, for the tourists, I guess. I
squeezed in and found a refrigerator filled with hot dogs, hamburgers, ice cream and soda pop." Benny gestured repeatedly,
his arm stuck in the small opening in the sheet-metal covering
that he had managed to pry backward.

"Are there any other exits out of there?" O'Brien peered
anxiously over Benny's shoulder, but his heart sank as he
looked in. The snack bar was no more than a big metal closet
built against the carrier's rear bulkhead—there would be no
hatchway in there for them to use to sneak off the hangar deck.

"No. We're lucky as hell." Benny winked at O'Brien. "Now
we don't have to worry about those gun-toting bastards getting
in to steal our food."

"Right." O'Brien wondered if Benny were clowning mostly for the sake of everyone else, or mostly for himself. In any event, he seemed to be the only person who could whip up morale. "All we need is for someone to cook the food."

"I'll do it."

Everyone turned. A man in the rear—tall, slightly overweight, with big, muscular arms that protruded from beneath his rolled-up shirt-sleeves—stepped forward. "I can take care of this for you. I own a few fast-food places in Chicago. I can get this place shaped up in no time. My wife can help me."

"I'll help also."

"Me, too."

"Great." Benny slapped the backs of the two other volunteers as they stepped forward to join the man and his wife. With the help of several others, they had quickly dismantled the sheet-metal covering over the snack bar. "I'll have two hamburgers with ketchup," Benny shouted after the four of them had stepped behind the counter. "Hold the pickles." Others in the crowd began to shout food orders, until the boisterous, buoyant commotion was so great no one could be distinctly heard.

"Pipe down, for chrissake!"

The sudden shout had come from behind them, and it caused everyone to freeze instantly. O'Brien pivoted around and saw one of the young terrorists standing on the sill of the only working hatchway on their end of the hangar deck. He had long, unruly hair and wore black chino pants and a dark shirt. He held a submachine gun in his hands, the barrel of it pointed directly at them. "What do you want?" O'Brien asked quickly, his voice as firm and forceful as he could keep it.

The young man laughed. "My money, mostly. But I guess that ain't your problem. No matter, I got this delivery to make. Here." The young man stepped back through the hatchway for a moment, then reappeared. "I think this dog is thirsty as hell—give him something to drink." The young terrorist pulled a medium-sized golden retriever through the hatchway. He let the dog go.

"Aquarius!" A boy from the back of the crowd burst forward and ran toward the dog. When the golden retriever spotted the boy, she wagged her tail and darted ahead, the leash that trailed from her collar dragged noisily against the hangar deck.

"Just don't let her shit on the floor." The young terrorist followed his remark with a cackling laugh. He watched as the boy and dog met in the center of the hangar, then turned away and disappeared through the hatch.

The hatchway closed with a resounding bang. The noise echoed through the quiet hangar deck. O'Brien saw that the people around him had quickly lost what little positive attitude they had managed to develop. It was unquestionably the result of seeing once again the threat that they had nearly managed to forget. For several long moments the only sound in the hangar area came from the patterned breathing of the hundred hostages.

James Westcott was the first to speak. "Do you see what I mean?" He pointed to where the boy stood with his golden retriever. "They've lived up to their part of the deal. We'll be all right if we don't do anything to jeopardize ourselves."

"No. That is false." Takeo Kusaka walked slowly toward the core of the group from where he and his wife had been standing at the far hangar wall. "You must pardon me for saying this, but I must strongly disagree." As Kusaka stepped up to the center of the crowd he gave a slight bow in the direction of Westcott, but then turned to face O'Brien. "We make a grave error if we depend on the goodwill of men who have no goodness in them."

"Don't try to frighten people with generalities," Westcott said curtly as he wrinkled his nose. There was a rising level of anger in his voice. "You don't know what the hell you're talking about."

Kusaka wheeled around and faced Westcott directly. "I have just come back from that wall of photographs and historic data," the old Japanese man continued in a low, even-tempered voice. "It is very interesting that until just a brief moment ago I, too, was in favor of a plan much like yours."

"You've changed your mind?" Nat Grisby eagerly maneuvered himself between the Japanese man and the attorney. Anyone who would disagree with this Westcott guy was okay in his book. "Why did you change your mind?"

Kusaka gestured toward a series of bronzed plaques on the

hangar wall. "There is a remembrance on that wall to those who did not return to this ship during the closing days of World War II. One lieutenant, in particular, is noted as being lost in the battle of Otaru Harbor on July fifteenth, nineteen forty-five."

"For Christ's sake, let's get on with this." Westcott ignored the angry stares from some of the others in the crowd. "What difference could any of this make?"

"I was in the Imperial Japanese Air Force in nineteen forty-five. On that particular date in July, I was also shot down. At Otaru Harbor." There was an excited murmur of hushed voices from the assembled crowd. Kusaka waited for the undercurrent to die away.

"But how could that have changed your mind about our situation?" O'Brien asked the question to gently prod the Japanese man into being more direct. But even if it took time to get his story out—time was all they had at this point anyway—O'Brien had a gut feeling that this man's observations would be worth hearing. "Go ahead, please."

"The things I mention are a coincidence, nothing more. I quite well understand that as such. But that minor coincidence has caused me to focus my mind. It has made me remember what the years had allowed me to forget. It has reminded me that the character of the Americans was such that they could not be persuaded to be discouraged, no matter how hopeless that day's situation might seem. But it is more than that. There is something basic to the American mentality. It is very much a part of you, and very unique in the modern world." Kusaka spoke in halting yet deliberate tones. "You are a young nation compared to the remainder of the important nations of the world. We, in Japan, are an ancient people. We have long ago left behind the innocence of youth. We are very good at working within our system, our heritage. Your people are capable of . . ." Kusaka hesitated for a moment, deep in thought. Finally, he looked sheepishly to his wife. He spoke a few words of Japanese.

"My husband has asked for my assistance. We will attempt to translate a certain expression," Iva Kusaka explained to the group. "Excuse us for a moment." She spoke back and forth with her husband in clipped sentences of Japanese. Finally, she turned back to O'Brien. "I am so very sorry to be so slow with your language. But I believe that I now have the proper two words that my husband searches for in his desire to describe the American people."

"Yes?" O'Brien edged himself forward.

"Persistence and innovation. Those are the character traits my husband first observed at Otaru Harbor on that July day in nineteen forty-five."

A spontaneous outpouring of emotions began to flow from the hostages. It started with just a voice or two but, just like a surge of water flowing through an expanding crack in a giant dam, it picked up an incredible amount of volume and force with every passing moment. The people in the assembled crowd—nearly every one of them—were swept away by the sound of those two words, as if they had been keys to a lock that had kept them chained to their miseries. The sour expressions had instantly disappeared, replaced by looks of courage and determination. There was a renewed sparkle in nearly everyone's eyes. Persistence and innovation. Those words— words aimed at themselves, about themselves—had given them a reason to hope for a way out. Many of the passengers from Flight 255 began to speak loudly and forcefully to each other as they started, for the first time, to accept the idea that they must do something—anything—to get themselves out of their nightmarish situation.

"Then it's agreed." O'Brien shouted to get everyone's attention. The spontaneous outburst had shown him clearly that there was no need for a formal vote, that Westcott's proposal to do nothing further had been soundly overruled. "We'll work out an organized way to come up with ideas. Then we'll evaluate those ideas and decide which ones have the greatest merit."

"There will be a way. We can do it!" Grisby shouted. He turned to face the bulk of the crowd. "We can beat these bastards!" The crowd answered in a loud chorus of agreement.

"Okay. We'll break into groups based on individual knowledge and specialties. Try to sort yourselves into areas where you think you might make a positive contribution. Any of you with previous military experience—particularly Naval—get together near that Grumman airplane." O'Brien gave a few more orders to get the process started.

"Do you think this might work? Do you think we might come up with some angle that the terrorists haven't figured we could?" Janet was clearly in favor of this plan—being at the mercy of a group of madmen was something that had not sat well with her from the very beginning.

"I think that we might be able to do it." O'Brien smiled sincerely, but within a few seconds enough doubts had crept into his mind that he needed to work to keep the smile from fading.

"You're an ass. You'll be sorry you did this," Westcott snarled. He shook his head, then waved his finger threateningly at O'Brien. "You, of all people, should have known better. But you've been caught up in this. You're playing at being a general." Westcott pointed at the people around him. "All you've got is a rag-doll army, don't you forget it. You'll be sorry. You'll be sorry as hell that you didn't leave well enough alone." Westcott turned on his heels and stalked off toward a far corner of the hangar deck. A few of the others from the group took tentative steps in his direction, as if they intended to follow him. But none actually did.

"Should I try to talk to him?" Janet asked.

"No. Let him cool down first." But there was another reason Drew O'Brien didn't want to speak to Westcott just yet. A nagging voice in his own mind still had to be contended with. *We won't accomplish a damn thing. It might make the situation worse.* O'Brien swallowed hard, then turned and watched the faces of the people around him. They were certainly enthusiastic—but enthusiasm alone would be far from enough. They had to come up with some workable plan first, then somehow find the expertise, courage and discipline to pull it off. That would have been a formidable enough task for a well-trained squad of professional military men. To an assortment of airline passengers—many of them very young or very old—the job seemed beyond the impossible.

"I'll check on the groups that are forming. I'll let you know what sort of talent we've got," Janet volunteered.

"Yes. Okay." O'Brien had replied distractedly. No matter

how hard he tried to shake it, two other sentences—Westcott's final words, actually—kept playing over and over through his mind as if they were the lyrics on a broken record. O'Brien stood, his body tense and rigid, in the center of the hangar deck as the words flooded over him. *You'll be sorry. You'll be sorry as hell that you didn't leave well enough alone.*

11

IT WAS EXACTLY 3:45 P.M. when Secretary of the Navy Mitchell Schroeder walked into the Naval Command Center for the second time that afternoon. "Any new messages?" Schroeder asked as he stepped up to the command console in the center of the room, his gray suit appearing even more wrinkled and ill-fitting than it had when he first visited this room an hour before.

"No sir. No messages that you haven't already seen." Captain Dwight Martin pointed toward the stack of teletype papers he had put inside a manila envelope on the desk, then looked up at the puffy-faced, white-haired man who stood beside him. Martin wondered if Schroeder had indeed spoken to the President a few minutes before, as he had said that he intended to. For the first time since he had met the man, Martin understood why his job had made Schroeder appear at least ten years older than he actually was.

Schroeder pulled up a swivel chair, pushed it close to where the captain had positioned himself at the console, and sat down. He fiddled with a pack of cigarettes and finally managed to get a half-crushed cigarette out. He put the cigarette in his mouth, struck a match, and inhaled deeply. Schroeder then leaned forward, so he could speak in a voice even lower than his normal subdued tones. "The President is quite pleased with the way you've handled this," he began, passing along the only bit of good news that he had come back with.

"Thank you, sir," Martin squirmed at the compliment. It was more than he could have hoped for, but he knew that his career was not out of jeopardy yet. "Then, if I understand the implication, the President assumes that the teletype messages are valid?"

"Certainly." Schroeder laid the cigarette down on the corner of an ashtray and reached into his briefcase. He pulled out a pile of papers. "Here are the identifications that I've managed to have verified so far." Schroeder ran his finger along the printout sheet of names and numbers. "Everything matches perfectly—driver's licenses, Social Security numbers, the works."

"What about the pilot's identification?"

"Also correct." Schroeder pointed to where the name Drew O'Brien appeared on the sheet. "There's no question that the data was taken from official records of some sort. We'll just have to assume that the situation has come down precisely the way the teletype message has spelled it out."

"I see." Martin leaned forward, deep in thought. Out of habit he retrieved the orange golf ball from the corner of his desk and held it in the palm of his left hand. "Then the President feels that it's possible that these airline passengers are hostages on the *Yorktown?*"

"Yes." Schroeder reached across the desk, picked up the manila envelope and opened it. "According to my sources at the Federal Aviation Agency, a Trans-American flight—number 255—" Schroeder said as he tapped his finger against the last teletype message from the source known only as the U.S.S. *Trout,* "had crashed under mysterious circumstances. Supposedly, it was a collision with an unknown aircraft."

"When?"

"Approximately six hours ago."

"Where?"

"Eighty miles northwest of New York. But the kicker is

that, as of ten minutes ago, none of the wreckage had yet been found."

"Christ." Martin looked down at his hand and saw that he had absent-mindedly picked up the orange golf ball. He laid it back down. "What about the Coast Guard's search for the *Yorktown* wreckage? Have they found any more of it?"

"Not a damn bit. While I was on the telephone with the President, he had the commander of that Coast Guard search operation patched into the line. I don't recall the officer's name, but he was firmly of the opinion that there was something drastically wrong. He said that, in his experience, there should have been a great deal more wreckage than he had actually found—especially since the *Yorktown* has been turned into a tourist ship."

"What difference would that make?"

"Discounting the factors of age and maintenance, the *Yorktown* now has a great deal of floatable crap on it. Exhibits, signs, souvenirs, that sort of thing."

"I understand. That leaves only the *Trout* portion of the story still to be verified."

"Yes. I've made some confidential inquiries through the Department of State and the CIA. From what we can tell so far, that submarine is nowhere that we can locate. The Iranians have remained closed-mouthed as usual, but I understand that there are rumors coming out of Tehran that the *Sharaf*—that's their name for boat 566, the old *Trout*—is long overdue. It's presumed to have been lost at sea. No survivors." Schroeder reached for his cigarette and allowed himself to sit back in his swivel chair. He ran his fingers through the tufts of white hair that framed his temples. "From what I see so far, it looks to me as if we've got ourselves a full-scale hostage situation again."

"That's what I was afraid of." Dwight Martin had often congratulated himself for the good fortune of not having been in the Pentagon during the Iranian rescue attempt—that fiasco had torpedoed more than one officer's career. It now looked as if he were about to have his own opportunity for the whole world to watch him outwit the terrorists or, more than likely, make a giant ass out of himself. "Do you think that the Iranians are behind this?"

"I doubt it. They've already got more troubles over there than they can handle. Frankly, this entire affair is a little too sophisticated for their style of operation."

"I'd have to agree with that." Martin was about to ask another question when he realized Lieutenant Nash had stepped up to the desk. He looked up at Nash. "Has something come in?"

"Yessir." Ted Nash held two papers in his hands. "Here's the data you requested on the two radius-of-action problems." Nash laid the sheets of paper on the desk. He adjusted them carefully so that both men could read the papers. Nash began to point to the pertinent numbers. "Based on high-speed cruise conditions, and assuming that the *Yorktown* departed Charleston late last night, that ship could be anywhere within this range."

"That's a great deal farther out than where the Coast Guard is currently searching," Martin said as he examined the figures.

"Naturally." Schroeder slowly shook his head in disgust. "Someone has planned this thing very well. They've dumped enough debris close to the mouth of the harbor to throw the search off. That gave them the time they needed to accomplish the remainder of their plan undetected."

"We also did a radius-of-action computer printout on the airliner," Nash continued. "It showed quite clearly that the airliner could easily be down in the same area as the *Yorktown*, at least within the same time frame. The only thing I haven't put into this equation is the aircraft's fuel endurance. I didn't have that data."

"I'll get it for you." Schroeder took out a pencil and made a note to himself. "But don't be surprised when we find that it works, too. This entire affair has been very carefully planned so far. I doubt whether—ruse or not—the perpetrators have overlooked a factor as simple as fuel endurance."

"Then you believe what these people have said?" Nash's neutral expression slowly turned into a frown, as if his facial muscles were a block of butter laid in a hot skillet. "It still seems unbelievable to me."

"I'm afraid that it isn't." Schroeder waved his hand distractedly at the plotting board in front of them—he had already made up his own mind that the incident had actually taken place. It was now only a matter of time, a matter of finding out what would happen next. "I haven't gotten all the answers yet, but I do have a gnawing feeling that expecting any less than a full-blown problem would be wishful thinking on our part. The President feels the same."

"That was my reaction also," Martin added. There was no reason for him not to point out that he had thought along the same lines—the same lines as the Secretary of the Navy, the same as the President—from the very beginning.

"Lieutenant."

Nash stepped toward the technician at the teletype who had called out to him. "Something coming in?"

"Yessir."

Martin and Schroeder also walked across the room to join Nash. The three men stood in front of the teletype and watched as the words began to print.

TO THE SECRETARY OF THE NAVY; FROM THE U.S.S. *TROUT*. YOU HAVE HAD MORE THAN ENOUGH TIME TO VERIFY THE STATUS OF FACTORS INVOLVED. AS YOU NOW REALIZE, WE HAVE NEARLY 100 PEOPLE FROM TRANS-AMERICAN FLIGHT 255 NOW ONBOARD THE *YORKTOWN*. WE WILL TORPEDO AND SINK THE *YORKTOWN*, WITH ALL HOSTAGES ONBOARD, AT 0600 EASTERN STANDARD TIME TOMORROW MORNING UNLESS THE FOLLOWING DEMAND IS UNCONDITIONALLY MET:

TEN MILLION DOLLARS IN GOLD MUST BE PLACED IN A BUOYANT CONTAINER AND PARACHUTE-DROPPED—UTILIZING ONE TRANSPORT-CATEGORY AIRCRAFT WITH NO FIGHTER ESCORT—TO A POSITION ONE-QUARTER MILE ASTERN OF THE *YORKTOWN* BY 0430 HOURS, THE EXACT COORDINATES WILL BE TRANSMITTED TO YOU AT 0300 HOURS. IF YOU ATTEMPT TO OBSERVE OR INTERFERE WITH US IN ANY WAY, THE *YORKTOWN* WILL BE SUNK IMMEDIATELY. IF YOU DO NOT COMPLY WITH OUR DEMAND, ALL HOSTAGES WILL DIE.

"God Almighty." Dwight Martin could hardly believe what he had read. His eyes scanned the words a second time before he reached over and tore the paper off the teletype copy. "What now?"

"Come over here." Schroeder led the way toward the console in the center of the room. The two other men followed.

"This is incredible," Nash said in a numbed voice as he sat himself on the edge of the console. He pointed toward the teletype message in Martin's hand.

"It is, unfortunately, exactly what I expected." Schroeder sank heavily into his swivel chair, then gazed absently toward the plotting board at the front of the NCC. He held that pose for a full minute before he began to speak again. "I'll take this news directly to the President, although I can see already that we're going to have one hell of a problem. You know as well as I do what the new policy is in reference to dealing with terrorists."

"Yessir. I'm aware of it." Martin turned nervously in his chair. An outright refusal to negotiate was the cornerstone of the Administration's recent change in attitude in dealing with terrorists and hijackers. "Is there anything we can do? Anything else in the interim?" An odd calm had descended on the three of them, and Martin could see that it was a result of the frustration and impotence in this situation. "Basically, in the strictest sense, this isn't a military problem."

"That's true." Schroeder sat silently. "But I guess we should explore every option," he finally added. "Even evaluate the potential for a military solution."

Martin blanched. "Do you think that's a possibility?" With every passing moment the situation was becoming more and more like that imbecilic Iranian rescue attempt—only this time Captain Dwight Martin would be the official Navy scapegoat when things went sour.

"I doubt that the President will go for it, but we should keep him informed on that option." Schroeder glanced toward the plotting board where symbols laid against the plastic wall map indicated the locations and strengths of various Naval units in the area. "You might want to also begin to mobilize rescue vessels, in case the need arises."

"The message indicated that the terrorists wouldn't tolerate any ship or aircraft movements in their vicinity," Nash said.

"That's right." Schroeder bit into his lip. "But we do need more information. I'm certain that the President is going to ask for more hard data than we've gotten so far, although I don't have any idea what the hell he intends to do with it."

"I can send out an antisubmarine aircraft," Martin said reluctantly. He pointed to the plotting board. "I see that we've got a P-3 squadron conducting an exercise a few hundred miles north of the *Yorktown's* suspected position. I can instruct one of the aircraft to remain far enough out of the area to avoid detection by the *Trout*, but they'll still be able to get us new data."

"Can he do that?"

"Yes. I'm assuming, of course, that the *Trout* is still equipped with relatively old technology, in comparison to what we've got now."

"That's a valid assumption, I think."

"Okay. Then we should be able to get within thirty or forty miles without fear of detection. From that distance our P-3 aircraft can still get enough data to provide us with most everything we need."

"Make it fifty miles and you've got a deal."

"Whatever you say, Mr. Secretary."

"I'm not trying to second-guess you, captain. My concern is strictly with the risks to the hostages."

"Mine, also."

"Fine." Schroeder nodded his approval, then rose from his seat. "Don't take any chances."

"I won't."

"I'll get back here as soon as I can. I intend to meet with the President in person. This matter is far too sensitive, too important to attempt to handle on the telephone. Call my office and tell them to have my driver meet me at the south entrance." Schroeder crushed the stub of his cigarette into the ashtray.

"Yessir." Martin reached for the telephone.

"I'll get background material on the *Yorktown* and *Trout*," Nash volunteered. "I'm sure we've got things on file." He looked over to see if Martin had any objections. Apparently, he did not. "Are you leaving the building now, sir?" Nash added as he turned back to Schroeder.

"Yes."

"I'll walk you toward the exit."

The two men stepped toward the rear door of the NCC, then out into the hallway. Schroeder stayed half a step in front of the young lieutenant as they both walked rapidly down the long corridor lined with endless numbered offices. They stepped around the corner and toward the staircase that led to the lower level. "I hope you can find something in the files," Schroeder said as he paused at the top of the staircase. "We're sure as hell going to need something if we've got any chance against these bastards."

"I'll do my best, sir." Ted Nash watched as Schroeder turned and hustled down the long staircase. After a proper interval, Nash also began to descend that same staircase, although he was careful not to move too quickly. He didn't want to catch up with Schroeder because there was no way he could cover up his lie. The Navy files office was located on the fourth floor, but Ted Nash was obviously headed somewhere else.

They'd find out soon enough anyway. One of them would. There was no doubt in Nash's mind that this was the sort of information that Skip Locker had always wanted. It was sensational enough—yet it was also non-military. That was a perfect combination, a gift from heaven. As much as he tried to make himself go slow, Ted Nash found himself beginning to take the staircase two steps at a time. *If Locker isn't in the press office, he'll be in the cafeteria.* This story was worth a lot more than a free weekend at a fancy resort. Nash knew damn well that the inside story of Flight 255 could be a potential gold mine to whomever was the first to leak it to a grateful member of the press.

After he had observed the first few minutes of activity on the flight deck from his vantage point on the bridge of the *Yorktown*, Paul Talbot realized that he, too, would soon become a hostage—just like the passengers from the airliner had. Nothing that lying bastard McClure had said had been true, they were all pawns in McClure's macabre game. *They'll come for me soon. I've got to get the hell out of here.* But even with that thought running through his mind, Talbot was transfixed by the scene below. It was only when Richard Yang reappeared out from the tail door of the airliner—several of the passengers herded in front of his raised machine gun, a young boy being marched up to him at gunpoint by that crazy Solenko woman— that Talbot was able to break the spell long enough to turn and leave the bridge. *Get the hell out of here. You can't help them if you stay here.*

Talbot moved quickly from the bridge. He descended the stairway that led below and, as he approached the level of the flight deck where several corridors joined together, he heard the activity on the far side of the steel wall that separated him from the hostages. Footsteps, muffled voices, the sounds of crying and sobbing floated in toward Talbot. He stood his ground in the shadowy corridor for several seconds before he shook his head in disgust. *Nothing I can do now. Get away from here.*

Talbot turned and quietly stepped over a chain with a tourist sign that announced that the corridor was closed to the public. He moved down the little-used corridor toward the starboard exit that would lead to the gallery along the right side of the ship. Talbot soon reached the end of the short corridor. His perspiration-soaked hands fumbled several times with the latches on the seldom-used exit before he finally managed to release it. The rusty steel door swung inward, and Talbot cautiously stuck his head out to peek along the catwalk that ran along that side of the ship from bow to stern. Yang had not bothered to post any of his men along there, so Talbot decided to use that catwalk as his path of escape. He stepped outside and quietly reclosed the hatch behind him, then began to run forward— his body bent so low he would be certain to provide no visual clues of his presence to the armed madmen standing on the flight deck behind him.

The damp, brisk sea breeze pressed against Paul Talbot as he moved along the catwalk. The bite of that wind rubbed against his face and the sensation it produced caused him to realize that his cheeks were covered with tears. *My fault. I did it to them. McClure said it would be a single pilot and a gold shipment. He never mentioned hostages. Kids. Damn. Some of them are children. They could end up at the bottom of the ocean, just like my grandsons. My fault again. What have I done?* Talbot could hear the anguished voices from behind as stray words and clipped phrases from the passengers floated toward him. He worked hard at disregarding what he heard and concentrated instead on the quiet but rapid movements needed to step carefully along the catwalk, the deep-blue hues of the ocean clearly visible through the slats in the metal grating beneath his feet.

Bastards. Liars. Talbot knew what he really wanted to do, but he had to fight the impulse. Turning back now, charging across the flight deck in an irrational attempt to get Yang to release the prisoners—prisoners he had unknowingly allowed Yang and his gang to capture in the first place—would be pure suicide. Without even a weapon to fight with, Talbot had no chance against that arsenal of submachine guns. One unarmed man against six fully equipped maniacs. No chance at all, they had every advantage.

Every advantage except one. Talbot stopped near the end of the catwalk. He began to work the levers to open one of the hatches that would lead into the interior of the ship. *I know the* Yorktown. *I can stay away from them.* He didn't like the idea of running away and leaving the airline passengers helplessly behind, but it was his only advantage at the moment, so he had to use it. He was sure that Yang's madmen would soon come looking for him, so he had to find a spot where he wouldn't be trapped, where he could stay hidden until he found some way to help the hostages.

Talbot stepped inside the dark hull of the *Yorktown* and closed the hatch behind him. He stood quietly for a moment while his eyes adjusted to the low level of ambient light that came from around the curved corridor ahead. Talbot knew that the electrical and lighting circuits did not function on the forward end of the ship. He cursed himself for not having brought his flashlight down from the bridge, but he knew that the batteries in it were nearly dead anyway. He also remembered that none of Yang's men had thought to bring flashlights aboard with them, so Talbot's knowledge of where he was and where he was going would be something of an edge over those people who would be chasing him. He began to grope his way forward, slowly but steadily, the hint of light from around the corner of the corridor hardly bright enough to make his outstretched hand visible in front of him.

Talbot finally turned the corridor's corner. He stood at the source of light in a moderately sized room. There was a series of covered portholes along the front wall, and the glare from the sunlight outside squeezed around the edges of several of the porthole covers. This area was located at the bow of the *Yorktown* just beneath the lip of the flight deck and was known as the secondary con—the place where the ship would be steered and controlled during battle if the bridge's superstructure was too heavily damaged to be functional. Even in the faded light, Talbot could see the disarray that surrounded him—the flaking paint, the rusted, broken controls, the cabinets and charts and ship schematics that hung open with reams of papers from them scattered across the floor. Talbot walked to the center of the room and laid his hand on the master control pedestal. It was now obviously no more than a useless relic, a hunk of rusted metal whose wires and levers were dysfunctional from age and the constant erosion from the harsh sea air. Most of the other gauges in the secondary con were also broken, their strands of bundled wires rotted through, the various radar and display screens cracked and discolored.

But to Talbot, the real advantage of the secondary con came from its location. He could see outside the ship through the portholes on the forward wall. The other three walls of the room each had a hatchway access, which meant that there were three ways for Talbot to get himself out if he needed to. The hatch at the aft end opened up to a gallery that overlooked the forecastle—that huge area in the forward end of the ship that held the anchor chains and other heavy equipment. If Yang's men came looking for him that way, they'd be easy enough to spot in time for him to escape unnoticed. If they tried to come toward him through the corridors that led from either the port or starboard sides, Talbot knew that he would hear them stumble and grope through the darkness long before they would spot him. The secondary con was the place to be; he was safe for the moment.

Talbot sat himself down on the littered and filthy deck. His body was limp with exhaustion, but his mind whirled. *It's my fault. Everything is my fault. Keith and Thomas. Amy. Charlotte. Please forgive me. God, forgive me.* But even though he didn't have any idea how he would go about it, Paul Talbot now knew what he had to do next. *Do something to get the hostages free. Get control of the ship from Yang.* That was what he had to do, no matter what the cost.

12

THE VIEW OUT the windshield had turned milk-bottle white when they had entered the clouds an hour before. Now the choppy air came more often and it caused the large stubby-winged Navy airplane to bounce and jolt through the sky. Lieutenant Commander Nelson Nesbit sat in the cockpit's left seat and surveyed the indications on the green command scope mounted in the flight panel in front of him. The tactical co-ordinator had programmed in the new data as soon as they had received it from the Pentagon, and the aircraft's autopilot had already locked them on a direct course toward the initial search area. "How's the radio patch coming?" Nesbit asked as he slid his finger onto the intercom switch and spoke to the communications officer back at his station in the interior of the aircraft. "Are we ready to go with it?"

"Another minute, we're resetting the scrambler now."

"Okay." Nesbit shot a quick glance at his copilot. The lieutenant stared straight ahead into the opaque, vaporous sky that surrounded them, but Nesbit could tell that the young copilot was trying to figure out what would happen next. "We'll know more soon," Nesbit announced, just to show that he, too, had no real idea what this change in plans was all about.

The copilot turned in his flight chair and leaned a few inches closer to Nesbit. "It must be something big—they're sure as hell making a big enough deal over it."

Nesbit shrugged. "Maybe." But he knew from the way the communications were being handled that the copilot was probably right. They had been conducting a series of routine maneuvers less than thirty minutes earlier when the first top-secret teletype message had come through. It had instructed Nesbit to fly his antisubmarine aircraft toward a certain point several hundred miles off the Carolina coast. It also indicated that a follow-up message would be sent shortly. The second teletype signal—also top-secret—contained coordinates for conducting a patterned search, plus additional instructions on the codes for establishing a scrambled voice link direct with the Pentagon. It was highly unusual, to say the very least.

"I'm ready on the radio link, commander," the voice in the aircraft's intercom announced.

"Okay." Nesbit reached into a pocket of his green flight suit and pulled out a pencil, then punched several switches on his control panel. Finally, he reached for the microphone and pulled it out of the holder on his side panel. "This is Navy four-zero-four," he announced as he put the black plastic mouthpiece up to his lips. "Go ahead."

"Roger, Navy four-zero-four. This is the Naval Command Center. Do you read me?"

"Five square. Ready to copy." Nesbit looked over to the copilot, who had also taken out his pad and pencil.

"This is Captain Martin at the NCC. Am I talking with Commander Nesbit?" the metallic voice said.

"Yessir." Nesbit was taken back by the exchange of names, and it caused a cold chill to rise up his spine. *The brass only calls you by name when they've got bad news.* He felt his copilot's eyes being focused on him, but Nesbit did not look up. Instead, he pressed the radio transmit button again. "Go ahead, Washington."

"For security reasons, I must request that you be the only listening party on your end of the transmission. I have already taken the same precaution on my end."

Nesbit shook his head in disbelief. Something was so much of a secret that none of the other twelve officers and men in his crew could be a part of it. That was unusual, because they routinely handled top-secret data. *It might be something personal. Maybe Ginny's been in an accident.* Nesbit quickly tried to push that thought aside. "Stand by." He punched the intercom button and instructed the communications officer to route the incoming voice signal strictly to his radio set. He then punched the button to get back on the line with Washington. *God, please. Not Ginny.* His stomach began to churn and he could feel the penetrating looks he was getting from the copilot, but he ignored both distractions. *Calm down. Ginny is okay. This is something else. Strictly business.* When the panel lights showed that all the other commuications lines had been secured, Nesbit pressed his transmit button again. "I'm on the frequency alone, Washington. Go ahead."

"This is highly unusual," the tinny voice began, in a tone that seemed a blend of exasperation and disbelief. "Let me first give you a quick rundown."

Nesbit turned and faced his side window. The number-one propeller of their four-engine Lockheed P-3 spun contentedly out on the wing, and Nesbit watched as swirls of condensed moisture flew continuously off its tips. The wing itself tremored in irregular spasms as the aircraft continued to fly through the cobblestone air, the jolts of turbulence traveling visibly along its structure until they were absorbed by the aircraft's fuselage. As Nesbit listened to the incredible story being told to him by this unknown captain in the Pentagon, he kept his eyes fixed on the blur caused by the rapid swirling of the red-painted propeller tips.

When the captain from the Pentagon finished, Nesbit picked up his microphone again. "What you're looking for from us is surveillance, nothing more?" Nesbit asked. "Once we locate the target, we are to remain outside a fifty-mile radius—is that correct?"

"That's correct." There was a pause from Washington's end of the line before the electronically scrambled voice began to speak again. "But there might be more after that. There's a possibility that we might need you to pursue the *Trout*. Engage it, perhaps. That decision has yet to be made."

"Roger. I understand."

"I also need to ask you a couple of questions," the radio voice from Washington began again. "I need straight answers, not textbook stuff."

"Go ahead." Nesbit didn't know what to expect next.

"I know that hunting submarines is a difficult job. I know that the success of the search often depends on a great many variables. What I want to know is how conditions are today—what the actual chances for a successful chase will be, if we elect to attempt one."

"Conditions meet our allowable search profiles," Nesbit answered automatically. "Probabilities should remain within the normal range."

"Cut the bullshit, Commander." There was a pause in the voice transmission, but the man's labored breathing could be heard on the open microphone. "Let me rephrase that," he began again, his voice now much softer than it had been a moment before. "Between you and me, I need to know what it really looks like out there. I need the straight word—no exaggerations, no gold-plated bullshit—if we're not going to have a repeat of the Iranian rescue fiasco."

"Stand by." Nesbit looked around the familiar cockpit of his aircraft. The gray-painted panels were crowded with levers and switches. The endless rows of gauges and lights added measurably to the overabundance of things to watch. It was a crowded place, with too many warnings and signals for anyone to take in at once, and for the first time in his flying career, Nesbit began to feel hemmed in by it all.

"Navy four-zero-four, are you still there?"

"Yessir. Stand by. Just a few more seconds as we readjust our radio equipment." Nesbit allowed his thumb to slide off his transmit button, but he made no other move. He took a deep breath, then glanced outside at the veil of white they continued to fly through. *A Washington desk jockey. But he seems sharp. He deserves more.* Nesbit hit his thumb switch again. "Okay, Washington, I'm back with you. In reference to your question, if the data you've given me so far is correct, the chance of successfully tracking that sub won't be very good."

"Why?"

"Because it's not a nuclear sub, it's an old diesel-electric boat. You know as well as I do that when he's submerged and running on his batteries he puts out almost no discernible noise pattern."

"Give me an estimate for a successful search. A guess."

"I can't."

"You sure as hell can, Commander, and we both know that."

"You're asking too much from me, Captain." Nesbit wondered how far this conversation would go before the man in Washington began to pull rank, to threaten him for the information—the justifications—that he wanted. Nesbit had seen that happen too many times before, and it was a tactic he was prepared to stonewall against. But this guy seemed different. He was appealing to him on a different level.

"I'm well aware that I'm asking too much from you, Commander. It's no different from what they're asking from me." The radio link fell silent for a moment before the scrambled electronic voice began to speak again. "I'll give you my word that I'll take the blame if it goes sour, I won't make you a scapegoat no matter what. But for chrissake, give it to me the way it really is. You're the only man at the scene—which means that you're the only man I can get a realistic guess from as to what our actual chances will be."

No scapegoats. He's being honest. "Okay, I'm with you." Nesbit squirmed in his flight chair—he had just accepted a verbal promise from a superior officer he had never met, a verbal promise that would be as insubstantial as the white vapor they flew through if everything went to hell and there was an inquiry over why he had made operational statements contrary to official policy. Nesbit swallowed hard, then put that distinct, unpleasant possibility out of his mind. "I'd say that successfully tracking that sub comes down to one chance out of ten, at the most."

"Shit."

"Finding a submarine is like looking for your keys in the dark," Nesbit volunteered. He had said so many negative things already that a few more wouldn't make any difference. "High technology isn't everything, although that's what most of the brass begins to think after they've spent too long at a desk. Crew experience means a lot, but just as important are the water conditions. They'll play one hell of a role. Our boy in that sub either lucked out or knew damn well what he was doing."

"Why?"

"Because he picked a transitional time of the year to pull it off. September is one of the worst months for conducting antisubmarine warfare."

"Because of the weather?"

"Not the weather, although it's crappy enough out here— low clouds, reduced visibility—to stack the odds a little more in his favor. Like I said before, the real problem will be water temperatures. Random currents of cold mingled in with the warm. It plays havoc with the sonar gear."

"And the fact that he's got a diesel boat will make it even worse?"

"Exactly. If you've got any doubt about how tough finding a diesel can be, think back to what happened in Sweden in the fall of eighty-one, and again in eighty-two."

"The Russian submarines that snuck into Karlskrona Harbor?"

"Right. The first one was a whiskey-class diesel boat— approximately the same size and capabilities of the *Trout*. That's why the Kremlin picked that boat over one of their nuclear ships to penetrate the Swedish coastal defense line. If that moron of a Soviet captain hadn't gotten his ass hung up on a sandbar, no one would've ever known that he had managed to slip in and out of the most heavily guarded military zone on the Baltic. As far as the second incident went, no one ever got close enough to find out what kind of sub it was."

"I remember the incidents very well. I see what you mean."

"If the Russians could pull that off in those close, shallow quarters, what kind of chance do you think I've got out here in the open ocean?"

The man on the radio sighed audibly. "I get your point, Commander. I appreciate the straight word."

"Fine. Just remember that I'm the messenger, not the message. It's not my fault that it's bad news. We'll do our best out here, but it's an odds-on bet that we won't be able to follow the *Trout* once he begins to leave the area."

"If he doesn't actually sink the *Yorktown*, will tracking the *Trout* become any easier?"

"Not much. Without the conflicting noises from a sinking ship, our odds go up slightly. Maybe two chances out of ten."

"Roger. Understand." The radio link from the Pentagon stayed open while the man on the other end mulled over his options. "We'll update your orders via teletype. Send the target data to me as soon as you get it. Be certain to remain at least fifty miles from the vessels."

"Will do." Nesbit glanced up at his copilot. The young lieutenant was turned slightly away in his flight chair as he worked hard at making himself appear disinterested in what he was officially not allowed to be a part of. Nesbit shook his head in disgust—the situation, the secrecy, their own lack of ability to guarantee positive results—then pressed the microphone button again. "Should I prepare our torpedoes for possible use against the *Trout?*" he finally asked. "Do you think we'll be attempting a search-and-destroy mission?"

"You should get ready," Washington answered. Some static had begun to fill the line, and it covered the deadpan voice being transmitted to the aircraft. Even with that interference on the frequency, the meaning of the next transmission came across loud and clear. "But from what you've told me so far, Commander, most anything we do is a waste of time. It sounds like the people aboard the *Trout* have already got us beat hands-down."

"He's the one," James Westcott said in a low, threatening voice as he pointed across the hangar bay. "Our pilot could do away with this insanity by giving one order. Sit tight, that's all he's got to say. But the way it's going now, when the shit hits the fan it'll be his fault."

"Maybe...I'm not so sure." Roy Bishop shook his head in an agitated, perplexed motion, then ran his fingers through the loose strands of hair that framed his taut, angular face. He glanced one more time at the exhibit aircraft a dozen feet to his left, where he could nearly see his own reflection in the highly polished deep-blue paint of the fuselage. Bishop looked below the old warplane's wing, toward the landing gear, where three of the teenage boys continued to examine the tires and struts with great interest. Enough of their conversation floated across the short distance to make it obvious to Bishop that they were trying to figure out some way to make those components into makeshift weapons. "Everyone seems to be a part of this idea."

"It's a mass hallucination, nothing more. That pilot has managed to parlay our fears into senseless bravado and irrational acts."

Bishop glanced around the hangar bay. From what he could see, everyone—the young and the old, the men, women and children—were involved in this attempt to turn their meager resources into weapons of defense. Bishop pointed to where several of them stood. "What about that Japanese man over there—the one who spoke to you earlier. What he said made sense. Everyone agreed."

"Don't be ridiculous." Westcott frowned, then wrinkled his nose. "Nobody in this group has the right to jeopardize our well-being by potentially angering these terrorists. That old Jap is living in the past—he's admitted as much himself."

"I guess."

"Legally, we're simply victims. We are supposed to be afforded maximum protection by our *de facto* grantors—which remains the airline."

"Oh." Bishop had understood Westcott's words, but had no idea about their meaning or substance. He decided that the man must be on the right track because he was, after all, an educated attorney.

"It's also obvious that this pilot," Westcott continued, his voice laced with the same manufactured anger his many years in the courtroom had honed to a fine cutting edge, "is interested only in his own self-glorification."

Bishop appeared bewildered for a moment, but then began to slowly shake his head in disagreement. "The pilot doesn't seem that way to me. I thought he was . . . ."

Westcott cut him off with a wave of his hand. "I'll agree that the pilot—what's his name again?"

"O'Brien."

"Right. Well, he *thinks* that he's doing the proper thing by getting us worked up, by getting everyone carried away with delusions of grandeur." Westcott allowed his voice to mellow in order to keep himself from frightening away his intended accomplice by saying too much too soon. If his plan to keep his legal case intact were to work—there was no sense in not taking advantage of this unfortunate situation as best he could—then Roy Bishop would be the man to carry out the actual legwork. "This situation is the ultimate example of *decipimur specie recti.*"

"What?"

"The road to hell is paved with good intentions." Westcott paused long enough to allow his words to sink in. "Unfortunately—both for us and for him—Captain O'Brien is dead wrong."

"You think so?" Bishop looked across to where O'Brien and a few of the others stood in the center of the sealed-off hangar bay. He then turned back to the attorney who stood beside him. "But so many of them seem to agree. The man with the beard does. So does the lady pilot."

"The hell with what she thinks," Westcott answered flippantly. He had allowed himself to point directly toward her, but he stopped himself in time and put his hand down before anyone in the hangar bay had noticed. The last thing he wanted now was a direct confrontation. "Just because she sat in the cockpit, that doesn't give her any extra authority."

"I only meant that what she had said made sense."

"Only on the surface." As far as Westcott was concerned, that smart-ass lady pilot had been too snippy to him once too often—and that made her the last person in this group that he intended to deal with from this point on. "You can't trust her opinion. She's doing backflips over the pilot."

"Really?"

"Look for yourself." She stood near O'Brien, the two of them in an animated conversation about some point or another. The way she stood, the way she looked at him was *prima facie* evidence that she was acting out some fantasy of love. Westcott had learned many years before that fear, love and hate were all the same—different names for the same bubbling fountain of emotions that sent otherwise rational adults into spasms of nonsensical behavior. They were useless burdens to carry.

"I see what you mean," Bishop agreed as he watched the

woman pilot. He hadn't noticed it before, but now that the attorney had pointed it out it was obvious that she—Janet Holbrook was her name, as he recalled—was in awe of O'Brien. She stood very close to him and seemed to hang on his every word.

"We can't trust her. She's a rubber stamp for him." Westcott made a gesture of dismissal with his hand. "As far as the guy with the beard is concerned, he's nothing but a backwoods bimbo who thinks he's on a deer-hunting expedition in the mountains. He'll get one hell of a surprise when he finds out that today's prey has the ability to shoot back."

"Then what do you think will happen?"

Westcott sidled up closer to Bishop. "That's an interesting question." He knew that working with this dumb rube of a real estate salesman from Chicago would be no different than steering another blue-collar jury into seeing a touchy case his way. "If I had to guess, I'd say that we are apt to put ourselves in great peril."

"How?"

"If the terrorists figure out that O'Brien and his amateur army are attempting to find some way to overthrow them, our status will change from being a benign problem to an overt one."

"I don't follow you."

Westcott smiled. *Of course you don't. You're an asshole.* "Listen, my friend," he said as he laid his arm on Bishop's shoulder, "at the moment we're just bargaining chips, like so many gold nuggets. It'll stay that way as long as we don't try anything stupid. They have no reason to harm us—in fact, just the opposite. But once we show these people that we might strike back, no matter how ineffectual that strike might be, we then become the enemy."

"I see." Bishop shifted his weight nervously. "But if there's no chance, why is this O'Brien trying so hard? He seems like a smart enough guy. He sure did a great job landing the airplane."

"He's a high-paid bus driver," Westcott snarled, although as soon as the words had come out he instantly regretted them. *Remember the code of behavior.* "No, that's not what I meant."

Westcott chided himself for forgetting to follow one of the oldest adages of trial law—that first and foremost a good lawyer never insults a sacred cow. Airline pilots were held too highly in the public's opinion for him to allow a derogatory comment to slip out. "What I meant is that perhaps he sees the bigger picture even more clearly than we do. It's possible that O'Brien's actual concern is strictly for his company's welfare."

"That doesn't make any sense."

"You'll have to trust me on this point of law, my friend, but it's the absolute truth." Westcott wondered for a moment if what he was about to say had any real basis in law. Probably not. He took half a step forward, then paused to make certain that Bishop was following. He was. "If O'Brien can get us to do something overt against these people—people who have us as prisoners—then our actions will make us responsible for our own fate. In other words, if we get hurt trying to overpower these terrorists, it'll be our fault and not the airline's."

"Really?"

"No question about it." Westcott watched Bishop's eyes. At first he appeared genuinely surprised, but slowly the idea began to make more sense to him. "By cooperating with our captors," Westcott began again as he moved in with his closing statements, "we keep ourselves neutral. That way, the airline will be liable for our pain and suffering—mental, as well as physical—when we eventually get back. If we participate in some foolhardy attempt to free ourselves, our entire case for damages against the airline will be thrown into a muddle."

"Okay . . . I see . . . right." Bishop nodded his enthusiastic approval several times before he spoke again. "But what should we do? How can we stop O'Brien? How can we stop the others?"

"Simple." Westcott leaned close to Bishop. "You and I can mingle. Watch and listen. We should be able to figure out what sort of harebrained scheme these clowns have come up with." Westcott gestured toward a knot of passengers at the far wall. Several of them were huddled over the display of exhibit torpedoes. "When we figure their plan out, we can then act on their behalf."

"On their behalf?"

"Certainly. They'll thank us later—once we've been released and they see that we've done nothing to complicate our case against the obvious negligence of the airline."

"What do we do?"

Westcott took a deep breath, wrinkled his nose and leaned even closer. He knew that the next line he spoke was important, but he could tell from his years of persuasive arguments in the courtroom that Bishop would be completely in his corner on this issue. The matter was as good as closed, now that Westcott had found the man who would do the actual legwork for him. "Once we know what their plan is, we can save everyone's life. All we have to do is tip the terrorists off."

It was contrary to his normal cautious judgment, but Paul Talbot had maneuvered himself slowly and carefully from the bow section of the *Yorktown* to the forward part of the hangar bay. His footsteps fell silently as he walked across the shadowy deck, but in his own mind those same footsteps sounded like loud and patterned drumbeats. Talbot's face was soaked with perspiration, and it trickled down his neck and transformed the front of his white shirt into splotchy patterns of dampness. After several more steps across the deserted forward end of the hangar bay, Talbot stopped dead in his tracks to listen again.

His own heart was pounding loud enough to make it seem as if it could mask any other noise, but after a short while Talbot decided that there was no one around. From where he stood, he could barely make out the top of the steel firewall that had been pulled across the aft portion of the hangar. *Another hundred feet.* That would be, he imagined, where Yang and his men had imprisoned the people from the airliner. *Go slowly. Be careful. If they spot me, I'm a dead man.* Talbot stood his ground for a few more seconds, to allow his eyes to adjust to the even dimmer light that worked itself across the unlit end of the hangar bay where he stood.

A dozen feet in front of him were the wing tips of two of the *Yorktown*'s display aircraft. The white wing tip of a Korean-vintage Navy jet sat a few feet below the dark-brown paint of the World War II B-25 bomber. Talbot took a step toward the B-25's fuselage, to remain well in the shadows in case Yang or his men suddenly walked across the hangar deck from the other side. *Work your way toward the prisoners. See what their situation is. See if you can help.*

Suddenly, Talbot heard a noise from ahead. He froze in position and held his breath. Another noise—a creaking followed by a loud bang—filled the cavernous hangar bay. There was no question that a hatch had been opened. Before he could get his thoughts focused, Talbot heard the sounds of several footsteps moving in his direction. Then he heard voices.

"You two stay along the starboard side of the ship. The three of us will stay to port."

"What if we see him?"

"Call out to him. Try to sound friendly. Don't take a shot at him until you're sure of a kill."

"Right."

The footsteps and voices continued to grow louder as Talbot stood as silently as he could in the darkness beneath the wing of the B-25. Yang's voice—cold, abrupt, abrasive—was the measuring gauge that showed Talbot that the group was approaching rapidly. Talbot knew he couldn't stay where he was, but there was also no place else to go. If he attempted to make a dash for any of the hatchways that led from the hangar deck, they would spot him long before he got out. *You stupid bastard, they've got you now.*

Talbot looked at the B-25 to his right. That was his only chance. He took the remaining steps toward it as quickly and quietly as he could. When he reached the airplane he kneeled down beneath its fuselage. With sweat-soaked hands he began to turn the lever on the aircraft's belly hatch while he prayed that the mounting hinges had been greased recently enough that they wouldn't make noise.

They had been. Talbot swung the short metal hatchway down. *No false moves. No noise.* He reached in and grabbed the B-25's interior ledge with both his hands, then began to swing himself forward and upward as if he were a trapeze artist mounting a high ledge. Within a few seconds his entire body had been pulled up and into the old World War II bomber.

"Where do you think he can be?"

"Somewhere forward, as far away from us as possible."

"How much time we gonna spend looking for him?"

"You in some sort of rush? Got a heavy date?"

"It's a waste of time, that's all. He'll go down with the ship, just like the rest of them."

"Maybe, but I hate loose ends. If he isn't locked in the hangar bay with them, then there's still a chance that he'd survive."

"I doubt it."

"Me, too. But there's no sense taking chances. That's why I want to find him."

"Okay. Sounds like a good idea."

"Your vote of confidence in my methods of operation have become a real inspiration to me."

"What?"

"Never mind."

Stay quiet. They'll kill me if they find me. Talbot allowed himself to breathe again, but only in shallow, irregular gulps. His hand nearly slipped off the perspiration-drenched aluminum rail once, but he somehow managed to get his nails dug into the metal facing well enough to hold on. He had reached down and grabbed hold of the hatchway door, and he had slowly pulled it toward him until it was positioned nearly flush with the bottom of the fuselage again. From outside, everything about the B-25 would appear normal—or at least Talbot hoped so. Even through the aluminum skin of the airplane Talbot could clearly make out the individual sounds—the conversations, the banter, the multiple sets of footsteps—of Yang and his men.

Talbot lay awkwardly against one of the sets of ribwork that made up the lower section of the interior of the aircraft's fuselage. A cross-member had begun to press uncomfortably hard against his lower back and it caused him great pain. He ignored the pain as best he could.

"When we gonna weld that hangar bay hatchway shut? It makes me nervous having those people still able to get out."

"We'll weld the hatch closed soon, when we get the word from the submarine that there's no chance they'll need anything else from those people. If we weld it shut too soon and we have to get back to them, we'd have one hell of a job."

To Talbot, Yang's voice had reached its peak volume and had already begun to fade. All he had to do was wait it out until they had left the hangar deck, then get out of the airplane and work his way aft. Talbot took a deep breath to relax himself. The air in the old airplane was musty and foul. Talbot's eyes wandered around the interior of the old B-25 as he waited for the last sound of Yang and his search party to fade in the distance.

Talbot saw that he was in a small area in the midsection of the aircraft, an area approximately six feet square. He remembered now that he had once stuck his head into this area when the B-25 had first been donated to the *Yorktown* two years before. There were a few foldable jump seats extended from the sidewalls, and they were all covered with a visible layer of dirt and dust. Several feet above Talbot's head was a Plexiglas bubble, no longer transparent because of the accumulated grime, that had once been used for navigational purposes.

The cockpit itself was accessible by going forward through a three-foot opening, and Talbot could make out the silhouette of the cockpit windshield by leaning slightly forward. Likewise, there was a narrow exit to the rear that led to the bomb bay. Talbot was thankful that this particular B-25 had been an operational aircraft just before its donation to the *Yorktown* as an exhibit, because that meant that its interior was cleaner than a great many of the relics onboard the historic ship. Talbot knew damn well that if the dust had been any heavier, it might have caused him to sneeze or cough—and that would've been the end of it for him.

Talbot took one more deep breath to steady himself, his hand over his nose and mouth to keep out the dust. He then opened the hatchway of the B-25. After waiting a few more seconds, he lowered himself slowly out the opening. When he attempted to stand on the hangar deck, Talbot was momentarily amazed at how rubbery his legs felt—until he looked down and saw that they had begun to shake quite visibly.

I've got to calm down. I'm the only chance those people have. Talbot braced himself against the side of the fuselage and allowed himself a brief moment of rest. But he knew now that his options from this point on would be measured in minutes. Maybe less. *Weld the hatch closed soon. They'll all go down with the ship.* Whatever he was about to do, Paul Talbot realized that he had to begin to act right now.

13

THE CAPTAIN HAD evidently given the order to once again change the interior lighting of the submarine from white to red, and that had bathed the control room in an eerie, somber glow. As far as Ed McClure was concerned, the decreased lighting in no way adversely affected what he was now looking at.

"My mother volunteered to be one of the first to go to Cuba, as part of that East German hospital group." Olga Rodriguez leaned farther back against the cornerpost of the navigator's table as she continued her conversation with McClure. She had made her voice as soft and compelling as she could, and she could sense that her efforts were not wasted. "My father had been a very important man in the revolution. He had been part of Che Guevara's group. My mother and father were married very soon after she arrived. They are still in Cuba today, although my father spends much time with the military detachment in Africa."

"Is that so?" McClure edged himself closer. Another button of Olga's jungle camouflage blouse had opened, and it exposed even more of her suntanned flesh. "I can see that you've inherited a great deal from your parents. That endowment right there, for example." McClure allowed his outstretched hand to move slowly toward her chest.

"I have one brother," Olga said as she intercepted McClure's hand before it reached her. She held it tightly in hers. Her eyes looked to the left and right just long enough to search the corridors for any sign of Harrison. He had evidently remained in the rear of the boat where the captain had sent him a short while before. That was fortunate. Other than the two crewmen at the bow and stern planes a dozen feet away—their backs to where she and McClure stood—the two of them were alone in the control room. "In reality he is my half-brother. His name is Diego. He, too, is still in Cuba. He works in the transport ministry. He is in charge of the railroads." Olga had allowed her voice to trail off. She stood in the ensuing silence with her eyes locked on McClure's face. She caressed him in her mind, from the raised left eyebrow to the trim mustache. His face was almost gentle until he smiled. His smile was cold, almost frightening. It was the smile of a man who was capable of great extremes. She supposed what they were all doing on this mission was considered an atrocity by most of the world. She remembered hearing that during the war Ed McClure had locked a group of young Vietnamese boys inside a hut, then burned it to the ground as an example to the other boys in the village who might also try to lie to him. A drug deal, she had heard. Olga wondered if this was true. She saw only a strong man, a leader. *Weaker men will say many lies about men they fear.* She wanted this man. *Please do not smile, Ed McClure. Do not ruin what I have planned.* Olga took McClure's hand to her lips and began to gently kiss the tips of his fingers.

"Not here. This is not the place," McClure whispered. He nodded over his shoulder toward the two men at the diving controls, their backs still turned. "We've got to go somewhere else."

"Certainly." Olga looked up and down the corridor again. "I think it would be best if we go forward."

"Suit yourself."

Olga allowed McClure's hand to slip from hers. She stepped past him and began to head down the narrow corridor. "Follow me."

"Sure thing." McClure followed closely, his eyes fixed on

the silhouette of the woman in front of him. It had been more than two weeks since he had taken that cheap whore in New York, and McClure was now more than ready for what lay ahead. Better yet, this particular woman was obviously no twenty-dollar hooker. She would not be satisfied in doing only what she had been paid for. The way she walked, the way she moved, the way she touched him told McClure that the next hour would be time well spent.

They walked quietly past the captain's cabin. The door remained closed with, presumably, Captain Zindell on the inside. Neither of them made the slightest sound as they stepped farther along, past the empty wardroom. They stepped across the raised ledge that separated the forward torpedo room from the remainder of the boat. As they maneuvered themselves inside, McClure was happy to see that the torpedo room was empty. The rows of neat bunks lined the walls on both sides. Clusters of valves and pipes were jammed in every corner, and chains and loading tackle dangled down from the ceiling above. Two of the twenty-foot-long torpedoes were still positioned in their racks between the bunks. McClure closed the hatchway behind him.

"Use the locking lever." Olga pointed to where the secondary latch could be thrown. "Then no one from the outside can open the hatch to gain access."

"You afraid of Harrison?"

"I only want privacy."

"Bullshit. You're afraid of Harrison."

"There is no sense in not keeping this to ourselves." Olga took a step toward McClure—she realized now that she could hardly wait any longer to have him. "It is a simple precaution, no more."

McClure let out a short laugh. "Sure, lady. There's no sense burning your bridges." He suspected that her real reason in hiding from Harrison was that she didn't want to alienate him— that she might want more of him later. If McClure wasn't so worked up himself, he knew that he might not let her get away with that kind of crap. "You're right, we can keep this to ourselves," he said. *I'll fix you later, you bitch.* McClure began to unbutton his shirt, his eyes locked on her expression. From where he stood, it appeared that she had begun to tremble in anticipation. "You look like you're in heat," he said coldly, as if he were commenting on a penned animal.

Olga ignored his intent. "Your words are a very poor substitute for what I need." Her tongue ran across her upper lip. "Hurry. We do not have much time."

"This isn't going to take a lot of time."

"Yes it will." She stepped forward and laid her hands, palms open, on McClure's bare chest. Carefully, as if she were running her fingers across a delicate sculpture, she allowed her fingers to travel downward until they were resting near the top of his belt. She was nearly ready to move her hands even lower when she spotted the glass-covered viewing port in the hatchway. "Damn," she swore softly as she pointed to the small porthole. "We must do something to cover that."

"No peep show, huh?" McClure laughed again as he finished unbuttoning his shirt. He took the shirt off. "I'll use my shirt, like that knight guy. How's that for my being a gentleman?" McClure hung his shirt on the hatchway bolt and draped the cloth carefully across the porthole. "Satisfied?"

"Not as yet." There was a grin on Olga's face as she placed her hands on McClure's pants leg. "But perhaps I might be satisfied very soon."

"I'm willing to bet on it." McClure took her arm. He pulled her toward him. With his other hand placed behind her head, McClure maneuvered her mouth to his. Their lips—both very wet, tense, full of energy and aggression—locked together. A considerable amount of time passed before McClure finally forced himself to back away from her.

"Where shall we do this?"

McClure's grin broadened. "In the center of the room."

Olga looked puzzled. She gestured toward the middle of the torpedo room. "There is nothing there. Nothing to lie on, nothing to lean against. On both sidewalls we have bunks." She pointed to the series of mattresses lined against the walls, one strung above the other. "They are small, but they will do."

"Too early for that." McClure took her arm again. This time he led her to the center of the room. Without waiting for another word, he began to undress her.

Olga stood as quietly as she could, her eyes locked on McClure's fast-moving hands. The firm, cold touch of his fingers against her breasts caused her to shiver and catch her breath. As her pants were removed and laid to the side, she watched as the bolas and pearl-handled knife fell to the decking plate with them. Olga tilted back her head and half closed her eyes as McClure continued to work with his hands.

It was something in the far corner that first caught her attention, something partially hidden by one of the torpedoes. Olga opened her eyes wider. It took her several seconds to finally realize what she was seeing. A wool blanket. Erratic motion. An arm, a shoulder. Olga took a startled half-step backward when it dawned on her that the moving hulk in the shadowy corner in the front of the torpedo room was one of the crewmen.

"This is very interesting." Ned Pierce swung his legs out of the bunk, his hand against the nose of the torpedo that had hidden him. He yawned conspicuously, slid the rest of his body out of the bunk, then stood up. "This is one hell of a show. Better than the sex dream I was having." Pierce's face filled with its hideous smile while the gold fillings in his teeth gleamed. His eyes roved up and down Olga's tense, naked body. "You've got your shit together, lady—I'll say that much."

"Close your eyes, nigger. This is out of your league." McClure took a step toward him.

"Sure thing, boss-man," Pierce answered in a trumped-up Southern drawl. "I'll just go on back to playin' in the cotton fields while the white folks is playin' in the poontang."

"Watch your mouth, you son-of-a-bitch." McClure stood between Pierce and Olga. She had come up close to him and he could feel the warmth of her naked body against his own bare back. "You better get the hell out of here as quick as you can."

"No question about it." Pierce strode toward the sealed hatchway at the aft end of the torpedo room. "I've got lots of things to do. My report to Mr. Harrison, for example." Pierce spun around and glowered at the two of them. "I'm sure he's gonna find this news interesting as all hell."

"Don't let him tell anyone," Olga whispered in a frantic voice. "Harrison is a crazy man. He will kill me, just as he had killed his first wife. She had done even less with another man."

"Is that so?" McClure was slightly surprised to hear that Harrison was capable of that sort of thing. "Are you sure he wasn't bullshitting when he told you?"

"The information came from Captain Zindell. It is the truth. He killed his wife when he discovered that she had flirted with another man." There was unmistakable anguish in Olga's voice.

"This business is gettin' more interesting with every passin' minute." Pierce gave a wave with his free hand as he reached for the hatchway locking lever. "I'd sure as hell like to hear more, but I've got this important business elsewhere in the boat."

"Wait."

Pierce glanced disinterestedly over his shoulder, but what he saw immediately received his fullest attention. McClure, who was still standing in the center of the torpedo room, had produced some sort of small weapon out of his pants pocket. It was aimed directly toward Pierce. "Put that thing down." Pierce had tried to sound angry, but his words had come out too nervously to appear as anything other than pure fear. Pierce slowly turned himself around to face McClure fully. "If you fire that gun in here, you'll put a hole in the boat."

"You're right. No gun-firings are allowed." McClure had the smallest smile at the corner of his mouth, as if he were privy to a secret that no one else shared.

"Do not fire the pistol." Olga took her hands away from where she was covering her bare breasts and put them on McClure's shoulder. "It is too much of a risk. Reason with him, that will be enough. I am sure I can find something to satisfy him enough to keep his silence."

"Shut up, you goddamned whore." The thought of sharing the woman behind him with a man like Pierce was enough to turn his stomach. "I'll take care of you later," McClure said as he turned his head slightly to glance at her.

"Look out!"

McClure jerked his head around and saw that Pierce had begun to lunge toward him. Without another conscious thought, McClure pressed down on the weapon's trigger.

The forward torpedo room instantly filled with a strange noise that sounded more like a suddenly flattened tire than the explosion of a bullet. A blur of darkness propelled itself from the front of the small weapon and toward the black man who lunged at McClure. For an instant all action froze as the three of them stood their ground, the black man stopped in mid-flight by some mysterious force that had caused him to grab for his arm. Pierce's eyes widened and his mouth dropped open. He emitted one short gasp before he tumbled forward and fell heavily to the floor.

"What happened? What was it?" Olga stared down at Pierce's body. It had begun to twitch obscenely. The man's head and neck trembled from a series of continuous muscle spasms. First one leg and then another began to convulse wildly.

McClure put the weapon back in his pocket, then kneeled beside Pierce's body. "Shit." He rolled the man over and looked into his eyes, then at his arm. "It's right here. This is where I nicked him."

"With what?"

"A poisoned dart." McClure patted his side pocket. "It's a great weapon in a confined area. Normally, it would kill a guy instantly. I guess he didn't get much of a dose."

"Will he live?" As Olga continued to look down at the black man's body—several of his muscles still twitched, but the general convulsions seemed to be lessening—she suddenly became aware that she was still naked. "What should we do?" she asked as she again put her hands up to cover her breasts.

McClure stood up. "I don't know. There was a frown on his face. "His heart is beating. It shouldn't be. That probably means that he'll live."

"Oh." Olga was at a loss for words.

"When Zindell finds out that I've got a weapon, I'm going to get that I'm-the-captain crap from him all over again."

"It will be difficult to cover the facts." Olga pointed down to the body on the floor. The black man had already begun to look better: his muscle spasms had stopped and his eyes were partly opened. "He is beginning to revive. When he tells Zindell what has happened, there will be much trouble between the two of you."

"Maybe." McClure allowed himself to scan slowly around the torpedo room, as if he were looking for something specific. His eyes locked onto an area toward the forward end of the room. He began to smile again. "But Zindell's first got to figure

out what I did before he can cause me a problem over it."
McClure bent down and started to pull Pierce's inert body
toward him.

Olga stepped toward the sidewall, grabbed a blanket off one
of the bunks to wrap her naked body in, then turned back to
McClure. "You cannot be serious," she said in a low voice as
she watched McClure drag the semiconscious black man across
the floor. "If you kill him, we gain nothing but his own silence.
It will be more than obvious from his wound that a weapon of
some sort was used. The captain will most certainly figure out
that much."

"That's where you're wrong." McClure reached the forward
end of the torpedo room and allowed Pierce's body to slump
back to the floor. "But I don't have time to debate it with you,
he's starting to come around already." McClure glanced again
at Pierce, who had found enough strength to open his eyes and
raise his head up off the cold decking plates. "In another few
minutes he'll begin to shout his goddamned head off. That'll
bring Zindell in here—and trouble for both of us. Come over
here and give me a hand."

"How?"

"You'll see." McClure stepped around Pierce's body, grabbed
him by the ankles and spun him around. In a few seconds he
had the man facing feet first toward the front of the submarine.
McClure leaned forward and took hold of the brass locking
handle on the number-five torpedo tube. He spun the lever
several times, then swung the heavy metal door open. "Get
behind him. Shove."

"Okay." Olga followed the order without question.

The pressure from the woman's hands on his shoulder caused
Ned Pierce to waken even more from his drugged stupor. By
the time his legs had been guided into the dark and gaping
mouth of the torpedo tube he had regained enough of his senses
to know for certain what would happen next. Pierce attempted
to squirm sideways, but he had nowhere near enough energy
to do it. He tried to shout, but all he could force up through
his throat was an odd and curdled squeal. By the time his entire
body had been shoved inside the opened torpedo tube, Pierce
was able to control his muscles long enough to turn slightly

around to face McClure. Other than that move, he could accomplish no more.

McClure looked down at the frightened, pleading eyes that faced him. "Glad to see that you're feeling better," he said passively. McClure knelt closer to where Pierce's head rested inside the rim of the long and polished-steel cylinder. "But I think I know what will make you feel really great. It's something that you've been asking for." McClure stepped aside. He pushed closed the heavy brass-plated door and spun the locking levers shut. "Pleasant dreams."

"This is no good," Olga said. She readjusted the blanket she had wrapped herself in. "It will take only a short time before someone finds him inside there. Even if he has already suffocated—the volume of air in the torpedo tube is large, it would take some time to suffocate—his wounds would still be obvious."

"You're batting a thousand today, lady." McClure stepped around her to position himself next to the control panel for the torpedo tube. "Except that you're wrong again." In rapid sequence he began to throw the necessary valves and levers as he had learned how to do just a few hours before from one of the other crew members. "Watch this."

As Olga stood, incredulous, McClure tripped the last lever in the sequence. A charge of compressed air was suddenly released into torpedo tube number five. It caused the room to fill with a near-deafening roar. McClure laughed loudly, but his voice was buried beneath the sudden wall of sound from the torpedo tube firing.

Inside the torpedo tube, the first impact of the high-pressure compressed air forced out both the cold water that had poured into the tube moments before and Ned Pierce's limp body. Pierce was still conscious at that point, still holding his breath against the force of the incoming water that soon would have drowned him.

But as the compressed air propelled Pierce's body through the torpedo tube, the rapid motions against his neck and shoulders caused Pierce to bang his head hard against the metal lip of the tube as he was pushed out. Involuntarily, the impact caused Pierce to take a deep breath, which caused the salty ocean water to pass through his nose and mouth and down his throat. The last sensation that Ned Pierce experienced before he finally lost consciousness for the last time was the aching pain and rapid swelling of his chest as the cold seawater filled his insides and pushed away what little life-giving air he had managed to hold in his lungs.

"God Almighty!" Olga grabbed McClure by the shoulder and shook him. "What will I say to the control room? How will I explain this torpedo-tube firing to the captain?"

"Simple. Tell them that you've fired a water slug."

"Water slug?"

"Yes. Tell them that some asshole must have left tube number five flooded down. You fired a water slug to clear it."

"Are you sure?"

"I'm a fast learner. I've got a good memory. Trust me."

"Okay. If you're sure."

"I am."

Olga reached for the telephone handset that hung on the bulkhead partition. Within a moment she had both the control room and the captain on the line. Within a few moments after that, she hung the handset back into its cradle again. "They were satisfied," she said, amazed herself at how easily her lie had been accepted. "The captain thanked me for taking care of the matter. In fact," she continued, "he said that he felt that Pierce was probably the man responsible."

"Then it serves him right for being turned into shark bait, doesn't it?" McClure grinned, then reached up and slowly but forcibly pulled away the wool blanket that Olga had wrapped herself in. With one more powerful motion, he spun her around. He leaned Olga's body against the rounded nose section of the torpedo that lay on the port rack.

"Hurry. We have little time left," Olga said in a hoarse whisper as she closed her eyes and pressed her body against the metal of the torpedo's warhead. The cold, sterile sensation caused by her bare stomach and chest being laid against the smooth metal sent a shiver through her.

"Take it easy. We've got enough time." Ed McClure then began to complete the task that he had started more than a half hour before.

14

"OFFICIALLY, THEN, THIS is not a military matter," Captain Dwight Martin said, his words coming out slowly and distinctly. He wanted to verify the underlying intent of what the Secretary of the Navy had just told him.

"Exactly." Mitchell Schroeder nodded in agreement. "Although the President has personally requested your help. A sort of temporary duty."

"I'm pleased to be as much help as I can." Martin began to frown. With the prospects that lay ahead, he knew damn well that even the unofficial involvement would be too thin a shield if the crap started to fly. "I assume there's an operational reason that the President wants to keep the mission on a non-military basis."

"Naturally." Schroeder reached for his cigarettes and took one out. He stood silently while he fumbled for a match, lit the cigarette, then inhaled deeply. He finally turned back to Martin. "If we go the official military route, the operation would of necessity be transferred to the military command center." Schroeder slowly blew out a long plume of gray smoke.

"Then we'd be ass-deep in jurisdictional arguments with the top brass. Everyone would want a slice of the pie."

"Probably."

"Unquestionably." Schroeder decided to omit the fact that the President didn't think much of the particular military commanders he had been saddled with in this administration. Instead, the interservice rivalry angle would be as good an excuse as any for explaining his actions. Fortunately, he and the President had been friends during college, so working this problem out solely through the Navy had been the President's natural choice. "The Air Force would insist on high-saturation bombing, while the Marines would probably want to attempt an assault on the *Yorktown*. God knows what the Army would request." Schroeder smiled, but he had only been half joking. "At least the way it is now, we can avoid that sort of problem." Schroeder looked across the room, toward where Lieutenant Nash and the technician hovered over the channel-01 teletype machine. From where he stood, the machine appeared ominously silent and inert. "We want to avoid too much input from the top brass, especially if things come down as I assume they will."

"How's that?"

"That we won't have any options. In comparison, this situation is far worse than the Iranian hostage affair. At least back then, we had a group of sympathetic Iranians lurking around Tehran on our behalf. The CIA spooks were getting hard data back to us. The Iranians themselves didn't know what they were doing or what they wanted next."

"I see your point. These terrorists we're dealing with have managed to thoroughly isolate the hostages. Worse than that, they're obviously professionals." Martin tapped his finger against the stack of teletype messages from the *Trout* that lay on his desk.

"Yes. Professionals. They've got total control of the situation. They staged the event in a place where we can't hope to even approach them without grave risk to the hostages. In other words, they've got us by the balls."

"Then what do we do?"

"We wait." Schroeder was about to add more when he noticed that Lieutenant Nash had begun to lean over the teletype machine. A few moments later he reached up and ripped a piece of newly printed paper off the scrawl, then turned toward them.

"Here it is," Nash announced as he rushed up. He held the paper out so that either of the men could take it.

Schroeder took the paper, laid it on the desk and began to read.

TO SECRETARY OF THE NAVY, FROM U.S.S. *TROUT*. IN REFERENCE TO YOUR PREVIOUS MESSAGE, THERE ARE ADDITIONAL FACTORS YOU ARE OBVIOUSLY NOT YET AWARE OF. SHIPMENT OF GOLD VALUED AT 25 MILLION DOLLARS WAS ONBOARD TRANS-AMERICAN AIRCRAFT—IT IS NOW SAFELY ABOARD THE *TROUT*. WE HAVE ALREADY ACCOMPLISHED THE MAJOR PORTION OF OUR MISSION. WHAT WE OFFER NOW IS A SIMPLE EXCHANGE: THE NET WORTH OF THE TRANS-AMERICAN AIR-LINER, PLUS THE *YORKTOWN*, ARE FAR IN EX-CESS OF THE TEN MILLION DOLLARS WE REQUIRE IN ORDER TO LEAVE THEM INTACT FOR YOUR RETRIEVAL. IN ADDITION, OF COURSE, ARE THE LIVES OF THE NEARLY ONE HUNDRED PASSENGERS AND CREW.

WE RECOGNIZE THAT THE PREVIOUS PUBLIC STATEMENTS MADE BY THE GOVERNMENT IN REFERENCE TO THE MORATORIUM ON FUTURE DEALS WITH TERRORISTS AND HIJACKERS COULD EASILY PROVE TO BE AN EMBARRASS-MENT TO YOU. THERE IS AN EASY WAY OUT OF THIS DILEMMA. THE ADDITIONAL MONEY FOR THE SAFETY OF THE LIVES AND PROPERTY CAN BE PAID SECRETLY SO THE PUBLIC NEED NOT KNOW. AS FAR AS THE PUBLIC WOULD BE CON-CERNED, THE STOLEN GOLD SHIPMENT WOULD HAVE BEEN THE ONLY REASON BEHIND THE HIJACKING OF TRANS-AMERICAN FLIGHT 255. IF YOU DO NOT PUBLICIZE THE RANSOM PAY-MENT, NEITHER WILL WE. LOGIC DICTATES

THAT YOU COMPLY WITH OUR REQUEST FOR
THE ADDITIONAL TEN MILLION DOLLARS. IT IS
A REASONABLE FEE FOR WHAT IS BEING OF-
FERED. SIGNAL YOUR ACCEPTANCE VIA TE-
LETYPE MESSAGE ON THIS CHANNEL NO LATER
THAN 0100 HOURS. IF YOU DO NOT, THE *YORK-
TOWN* WILL BE SUNK.

The three men stood silently for a short while after they had
finished reading. Schroeder reached over for the swivel chair,
spun it around and sat himself down.

"Bastards," Martin said in a low whisper.

"At the very least." Schroeder rubbed his eyes, then glanced
back at the teletype message. "The words are bad enough," he
said as he tapped the paper with his fingers, "but their arrogance
is incredible. It's more the tone of this thing than the actual
content that tells me how insane the person who sent this message must be."

"I'd agree with that." Martin sat himself down on the edge
of his desk. Out of nervous energy he looked around and quickly
spotted his orange golf ball where it sat on the corner of the
desk. For one irrational moment Martin had the overwhelming
urge to pick up the golf ball, walk out of the NCC and head
straight for the golf course. There, at least, none of this cra-
ziness would exist—his biggest problem would be in keeping
his hook out of the lake on the fourth hole. Martin found himself
almost rising to his feet several times before his self-control
overpowered him enough to keep him firmly where he was.
He turned his head and began to scan the teletype document
once again. "What do we do now?"

"There's not much choice, either way."

"That's true." Martin nodded reluctantly in agreement. "But
at least these bastards are promising to stay quiet about the
ransom. I guess that's something. Will the President buy that
sort of deal?"

"Yes." Schroeder sighed, then reached for the telephone.
"The President knew about the gold shipment. The airline people already told us. I didn't mention that fact in the last message
I sent to the *Trout*, I wanted to see what their response would
be."

"Now we've got it."

"We sure as hell do." Schroeder shook his head sorrowfully. "Both the President and I suspected that this would be the course they would take." Without waiting for either of the Navy officers to speak, Schroeder picked up the red command telephone in front of him. He uttered a coded phrase to the military operator, and within a few seconds the President of the United States was on the line.

Captain Dwight Martin found himself stiffening to attention while he watched the Secretary of the Navy explain the situation to the President. "I wouldn't want to be in his place," Martin whispered to Nash across the desk. "It's a hell of a rotten choice to make."

"Sure is." Ted Nash squirmed, but more out of what was in his own mind than what Martin had said. *I'll meet you in an hour. I'll have everything you'll need by then.* Nash wondered for an instant if he had gotten himself in too deep with Skip Locker, but then he dismissed the idea. *Don't get chicken shit. It's a non-military matter, they've said so themselves.* He thanked God that he had overheard that part of the conversation about it being non-military, because that made his involvement with Locker less of a problem. Before Nash could convince himself of that point any further, Schroeder had hung up the command telephone and had turned directly to him.

"Have your technician get ready, I'll need to send another message. We have authority from the President to accept their terms."

"Really?" For some reason, Nash found that concept discomforting. He could feel the ring of perspiration as it began to gather around the collar of his uniform shirt. "We're going to go along with everything they've asked? All their demands?" He couldn't pin down the feeling, but for some reason the President's acceptance of the terrorists' terms had pulled this whole incident in a direction other than the one he would have preferred.

"Yes." Schroeder nodded his head in the manner of a man who had agreed with the decision on a moral level, but not on a practical one. Still, he had little choice. "The only non-negotiable condition we have is that absolute secrecy must be maintained. We are to proceed according to their terms, but only so long as the public is not made aware of the actual conditions that we are being forced into meeting. According to the President, if the word of the ransom payment somehow leaks out, we are to go immediately to plan number two."

"Number two?" Nash worked hard at keeping his expression neutral, but he sensed correctly that his muscles had grown too taut, his eyes too wide. "If I may ask, sir, what exactly is plan number two?"

Schroeder swept his hand through the air as he gestured toward the plotting board's map at the front of the room. "If the public finds out that we intend to pay a ransom to terrorists, we must deny that allegation emphatically."

"What will happen then?" Nash asked. He had become almost too frightened to listen to the answer.

"Simple." Schroeder rose from the swivel chair and leaned against the desk. He looked more hangdog now than he had at any other time since the incident had begun, as if the last ten minutes had managed to visibly age him. "If we go with plan number two, we need to prepare ourselves to lose a few things."

"Lose a few things?"

"Yes. A relic of an aircraft carrier, a commercial jetliner and the lives of approximately one hundred innocent men, women and children are the price we'll be paying for sticking to our principles if the truth leaks out."

The pavilion in the center of the courtyard sat in the deep shadow cast by the Pentagon's towering brown walls, the late afternoon sun sitting too low against the western horizon to be seen. Even though the pavilion itself had closed a few hours earlier, several people lingered on the benches and in the grassy areas of the expansive courtyard. Lieutenant Ted Nash hurried past them, careful to avoid any glances that might have invited a casual conversation. His mind was too intent on the problem that he wrestled with to deal with vacuous chitchat and, besides, Skip Locker was due to meet him at the Ground Zero hamburger stand in just a few minutes.

When Nash reached the wooden structure in the center of the courtyard, he walked around it once to be certain that Locker had not already arrived. Satisfied that he had gotten to their rendezvous spot first, he leaned up against the wall where the wooden shutters had been pulled down and locked after the lunchtime crowd had come and gone. Nash worked hard at not appearing overly anxious to any of the bystanders in the courtyard who might notice him—mostly military personnel who worked at sectors that continued to function beyond the normal bureaucrat's hours. Several times Nash forced himself to breathe deeply to steady his nerves. *I've done it now. What the hell was I thinking of?* What started out as a silly, harmless tip to a reporter who could do him some good had somehow mushroomed into a life-and-death situation. *Innocent people will die if this story leaks out.*

Several minutes passed with no signs of Locker. It was nearly 6:30. Nash shook his head in disgust at the situation, then reached into his pocket and took out a handkerchief. *I've given him too much already. He's already left to print what he's got.* Nash wiped the growing line of perspiration off his forehead.

"A little too warm for you today?" Skip Locker said as he walked briskly around the corner of the small wooden building and into Nash's view. "You should be enjoying the heat more, it's the last we'll see of it until next spring."

"You're late." Out of habit Nash glanced at his wristwatch, then back at the man who stood a few feet to his left.

"I didn't know that our schedule had become critical." Locker grinned, enjoying whatever was the cause behind Nash's obvious discomfort. "What's the news?"

"We've got to kill the story."

"What?"

"There's more to this than we first thought."

"I don't understand." Locker carefully maneuvered himself to a position where the microphone of the hidden miniature tape recorder in his coat pocket would be most effective in picking up the lieutenant's voice. He had already taken the precaution of checking over the device and turning it on before he walked into the courtyard, and now he was damn glad that he had brought it along. Whatever Nash was going to add to the incredible story of an aerial hijacking and a ransom demand, would certainly be worth hearing and recording. "Don't be silly. I've spent the last two hours working out the background details on the *Yorktown* and *Trout*. Everything's set to go, it'll make one hell of a scoop."

"We can't do it." Nash glanced from side to side to be certain that no one else was close enough to overhear. "This hasn't turned out like I thought it would."

"What does that mean?"

Nash bit into his lower lip. It was obvious that he had said far too much already, but there was no other way out except to give Locker a complete explanation in order to convince him not to go ahead with the story. "It's more complicated than we thought."

"Go ahead, I'm listening," Locker said skeptically.

"The hijackers sent another teletype message a short while ago. They've already got twenty-five million in gold." As he continued with his explanation of the incredible series of events that had occurred in the last two hours—the general text of the last teletype message, the President's decision—Nash watched the young reporter's eyes for some signs of sympathy, some indication that he, too, was shocked by the turn of events. All Nash could see on Locker's face was an alert but neutral expression, as if he were hearing nothing beyond a recitation of bland but pertinent facts on a technical subject. "Do you see what I mean? There's no way we can release a story like this."

"That's an interesting point." Locker allowed the penetrating silence to hang between the two of them for several seconds. After a short while he turned away and faced the closed and locked door of the hamburger stand a few feet to his left. "This is an odd place, don't you think?" Locker volunteered in a casual voice, as if the earlier conversation had not taken place.

"I don't follow you." Nash didn't know what Locker's point would be, but something inside him told him that it wouldn't be something he wanted to hear. "What are you talking about?"

"I'm talking about inappropriate behavior." Locker waved his hand in a broad motion that took in the courtyard and the high brown walls of the interior of the enormous five-sided building that surrounded them. "We frivolously label the center courtyard of the Pentagon—the world's most sought-after military target—as ground zero. Then we build an outdoor café on the same spot and give it the same name. The Ground Zero

Café. Very cute. This way, we can chew hamburgers and drink milkshakes on the tranquil spot that most people agree will someday become a nonexistent molten hole, thanks to the dozens of Soviet missiles that are programmed for the peak of this very building." Locker pointed toward the neat wooden cupola that sat above the center of the roofline of the hamburger stand. "Ironic, isn't it, how a place this peaceful can be the number-one military target in the Western world. It's inappropriate, to say the very least."

"I don't follow your point." Nash didn't know what to say. He didn't want to press Locker too quickly, but on the other hand he had to get back to the NCC as soon as he could. He didn't have time for nonsensical conversations. Nash peeked at his wristwatch, then glanced up toward the countless windows that lined the brown walls that surrounded him on all sides. He felt as if there were officers at each of the windows watching him, each of them writing down exactly what time and what place he was having this conversation with this civilian reporter. *I never should have dealt with him. I must have been crazy.* "I've got to get back. What I need from you right now is your assurance that we can forget everything. You can understand why we can't risk releasing a story like this."

"Not really." Locker stood silently while the expression of horror and revulsion slowly spread across Nash's face. "Don't take this personal, but what you're asking is too much. This is the story of the century."

"There are lives at stake, for chrissake!" Nash had raised his voice too loud, and several of the people on the park benches within a few dozen feet had turned toward him. Nash stepped closer to Locker and dropped his voice to a whisper. "If the story gets out, the President won't go ahead with the ransom payment. Those people will die."

"There are lives at stake here, too," Locker answered quickly, his words tumbling out as if they had been rehearsed. "Everyone in the country has their neck on the chopping block, but that doesn't seem to bother the military mind."

"What in God's name are you leading up to?"

"It's not me, it's what you and your friends are leading up to. It's the promise of a push-button nuclear nightmare that you and your friends in this building are responsible for." It was the first time Locker had used that phrase since he had picked it up during his coverage of the antinuclear peace march on the Pentagon earlier that summer. The phrase had such a good sound to it that he decided to continue with that line of banter—it was as good a way as any to distract Nash and confuse the real issue. "You people have built a hamburger stand on ground zero, then you have the audacity to overtly call it by that very name. Nuclear war isn't a joking matter, or aren't you aware of that? I suppose what you really want is for us to get used to the idea of being vaporized into dust whenever the mood strikes you."

"Wait a minute . . ."

"No. You've had your say too often in the past." Locker searched his mind for a few other of the key phrases he had heard. The only additional ones he could recall seemed even less applicable than the ones he'd used already. It was, like they had taught him on the debating team at Yale, now time to wrap it up. "Don't tell me that I'm jeopardizing lives. All I'm doing is informing the public. If there's any inappropriate behavior here, it's yours."

"That's pure bullshit and you know it." Nash was angry, but he knew that he couldn't afford to say what he wanted to. "We've got to be reasonable," he pleaded, his voice more controlled. "The terrorists are going to kill those people."

"Maybe the terrorists are bluffing."

"Don't be a damn fool, why should they be?" Nash's face flushed with anger. He had a feeling that Locker was toying with him, that his decision had already been reached.

"I guess you're right. If the gold shipment has been verified . . ."

"It has."

". . . then there's no reason why the terrorists won't go ahead as they've threatened. They're winners already—from here on it's just a matter of how big they win, that's all."

"Exactly." Nash wondered if he were getting through to Locker. He glanced at his wristwatch again. "Can I depend on you? I'm asking you not for my sake but for the sake of the hostages." Nash knew that what he had just said seemed incredibly self-serving, but he had been sincere. The thought of those innocent people being murdered by a gang of madmen had shocked him back to his senses, back to his responsibilities.

"I'll tell you what," Locker said in a conciliatory tone, "I'll meet you halfway."

"There is no halfway."

"Sure there is." Locker stood with his hands in his pockets and rocked gently back and forth, as if he were a used-car salesman about to close a deal for a car selling for twice what it should. "I'll hold this story until everyone is safe. At that point, I'll print it. That'll give me the scoop I need over the other news services."

"Are you going to print the part about the ransom payment?" Nash watched Locker carefully as he asked the question.

"No. Of course not," Locker said. *It'll be a cold day in hell when I leave out the best part of the story. This is more valuable than your tin-soldier career—this will get me to the top.* "You have my word. Nothing about the ransom payment. No news releases until after those people are safely back."

"Okay. Good." Nash nodded his head slowly; something was obviously on his mind. He turned and took one step away, then stopped. He stood his ground for several seconds.

"Something wrong?" Locker asked.

"No." Nash turned back toward Locker. "But there is one more thing."

"What?" Locker had already taken a few steps away from the pavilion in the opposite direction—he was anxious as hell to get going, anxious to get in his car and personally dump this story on the editor-in-chief's desk. It was, he knew, far too important and complex a story to be sent in on the telephone.

"I appreciate your cooperation."

"That's all right," Locker answered as he waved his hand in a gesture of dismissal. If the bureau chief rushed the story onto the wire, it would go out in time for the evening TV newscasts in the East.

"I'm serious," Nash said. "I really do appreciate how you're taking this. To show you what I mean, I'm going to get more hard data for you. That'll give you something of a scoop when you finally do release the story."

"Like what?"

"How about an exact copy of the terrorists' last teletype message—the one that told about the gold heist and the ransom demand?"

"That would be great." Locker could hardly believe his ears, it was an offering from heaven. He, alone, would be the only newsman to have the exact wording of the ransom demand, the exact copy of what had come across the Pentagon's teletype. That sheet of paper would make a great TV display, if the TV crews weren't fortunate enough to get on location fast enough to film the sinking of the *Yorktown*. "When can you get it to me?"

"Meet me back here in twenty minutes. No, better yet, meet me inside the building," Nash said as he pointed to the Pentagon's nearest entrance off the courtyard. "On the second floor, ring C, corridor three."

"Second floor, ring C, corridor three. Twenty minutes," Locker repeated. He watched as Nash turned and strode away. *I'll be glad to wait twenty more minutes. This story will take me to the top.* Locker leaned back against the Ground Zero hamburger stand and began to grin ear-to-ear. *When this story hits the wire services in an hour or so, you and your military buddies are going to take a lot more notice of me.* Locker leaned farther back and began to snicker. *By this time tomorrow, that big-shot Lieutenant Nash is going to think I'm a lot taller than five feet ten.*

15

MARION MILLER TOSSED her long blond hair back and forced herself to smile. She took a small mirror out of her pocketbook and looked at her expression. It was, she could see, too contrived, too phony. *Damn. Play it like any other role. Don't try too hard or he'll never believe it.* Marion continued to try on facial expressions, a craft she learned in one of her college drama classes, until she found one she thought might work. She put her mirror away and began to walk toward the sealed hatchway door on the hangar bay wall.

"Be careful, Miss Miller," Emma Adams said. She stepped up to her teacher as she walked past on her way to the hangar door.

"Of course I'll be careful." Marion reached out and touched Emma's arm. "He's just another audience."

"I saw him before. He looked like he could be real trouble."

"I've faced tougher audiences." A few strands of wispy hair dangled across Marion's cheek and she brushed them back with a slow, casual motion. "All I intend to do is keep his attention."

"Okay." Emma glanced up at the hatchway. It remained closed.

"If he sticks to his past schedule, he should open the door very soon to check on us. That's where I want to be when he makes his next rounds," Marion said as she pointed to a spot near the closed hatchway. "Then it shouldn't be too hard to strike up a conversation with him."

"Right." Emma looked at her drama teacher for several seconds, as if she wanted to say more. Instead Emma leaned forward, embraced her quickly, then pushed herself back. "Do you want me to hold your pocketbook?"

"Yes. Thank you." Marion handed the pocketbook over to her student. She smiled at Emma, then turned around and began to walk rapidly toward the opposite corner of the hangar bay. Marion could feel Emma's eyes on her, but she did not look back.

When Marion Miller reached the hangar bay partition she leaned against it and took a deep breath. She then glanced at her tiny gold wristwatch. The young terrorist on the other side of the locked hangar bay hatchway was due to open that door at any moment to check on them, if his past performance held true. *You can do it. Break a leg.* As Marion stepped nearer to the door, she saw that its big steel locking bolts had begun to spin themselves out. *Get ready. You're almost on.* She took another step toward the door with the same sort of unhesitant flourish she would have used had she been entering a dramatic scene from the wings, stage left. This was, in her mind, business as usual—except that for this performance she had the worst case of first-night jitters since her high-school stage debut. The gray-painted steel hatchway door creaked as it continued to be opened slowly by the unseen terrorist on the other side.

"What the hell are you doin' here?" The young man in the black jacket and dirty turtleneck poked his head through the opened hatchway. The barrel of his submachine gun stuck out a few inches ahead of him. "I thought I told you people not to be gettin' too damn near this doorway."

"I'm sorry." Marion continued to stand where she was. She worked hard at trying to appear to be what she guessed this fellow might be interested in. He was her age, or maybe a year or two younger. He was no more than a few inches taller than she, but he was solid and muscular. From the way his long black hair was slicked back, she thought he was probably vain about his appearance. His eyes were alert, but somehow blank— he was a purely physical person. "I guess I forgot. I was just standing here, that's all." Marion ran her tongue lightly across her lips. She tossed back her long hair again. "I'm just tired of talking to those people. I don't know any of them, I don't have anything to talk to them about."

"That so?" Jeff Eddings took a careful step across the hatch-way sill and into the hangar bay. He lowered the barrel a fraction of an inch from where it had been pointed, dead center, at the blonde's chest. Eddings had been bored to death by his assignment from Yang to stand guard at the hangar bay hatch-way and, every half hour, to check up on the hostages. Eddings was itching for contact of some kind, something to take his mind off the endless, monotonous job that he had been given. "You can stay here. For a little while."

"Thanks."

Eddings stepped up closer to her, then gazed over the rest of the crowd in the hangar bay. None of those hostages had come close enough to do any harm, which showed a great amount of good sense on their part. In some ways Eddings had been deeply disappointed that, so far at least, he hadn't found a reason to fire the submachine gun for real. "They seem peace-ful enough. That's smart, if they don't want no trouble."

"They don't."

"Good." As he continued to watch the hostages, Eddings thought that once or twice he caught the eye of people as they glanced up toward where he stood. They seemed to have a new and strange look on their faces, something like an angry scowl. After a short while Eddings thought that he had figured out why. "I think you ain't gonna be so popular. Not if you stand here with me."

"The hell with them." Marion gestured toward the crowd in the center of the hangar floor with her thumb. She allowed a small frown to play at the corners of her mouth. "I don't owe them nothin'. Like I said, I don't know none of them. They don't mean nothing to me. Jerks, mostly."

"That so?"

"Yes."

"You traveling by yourself?" Eddings had turned his body

more toward her. He leaned his back against the hatchway ledge, the barrel of his submachine gun dropped toward the floor, but it was still held in such a way that it could be raised in an instant. Eddings let his eyes rove freely up and down her compact body and made no secret of what he was looking at. "You've got it together pretty good," he said as he took in the curves of her upper body.

"You probably always say that." Marion could see that her act was working, that the audience had been hooked. She was glad that she had removed her bra and slip as part of her costume. She usually was self-conscious of her large breasts, but she knew that they were great props for this performance.

"Hell no, I don't say nothin' like that. Only when it's true." Eddings nodded in agreement with his own remark, then began to look her over again more conspicuously than he had the first time. The red sweater she wore rode tightly across her breasts and inward again at her narrow waistline. She was one hell of a sexy number. "I got a few minutes if you wanna talk. I don't need to check in on the walky-talky for another twenty minutes," Eddings said as he tapped his finger against the small black transmitter that hung from his belt.

"Sure thing." Marion forced a broader smile on her face. *Keep it going, don't let down. He's a tough audience, he could turn.* Her stomach churned from tension. She stuck her chest out slightly farther and moved imperceptibly nearer to him. As she had explained earlier to Captain O'Brien and the others, she didn't know what she might accomplish by coming on strong to this young homicidal maniac. Maybe nothing at all. But if she got his attention, that might be a beginning. Maybe there would be more. She was ready to give it everything she had, everything she could—even if it meant more than she would publicly want to admit to, more than she could stomach to think about. But even making love to an animal like him would be worth it if there was a slight chance that he might be distracted. He was no more than nineteen or twenty years old, which meant that maybe he could be conned by her into dropping his guard long enough for Marion to grab his gun.

"You're the kind of lady I was always interested in."

"Really?" There was something behind where the young terrorist stood in front of the hatchway. It caught Marion's attention. It was something in the shadows of the dark area on the far side of the wall—a movement of some sort. A man. He was moving slowly and silently toward the hatchway, his arms out in front of him. Something in his manner told Marion not to say anything or give any indication of her having seen him. "I had a boyfriend who looked just like you. We lived together for a few months."

"Yeah?" Eddings leaned slightly forward, as if he were about to take a step toward the girl. But as he did, he heard a faint sound—a single footstep—behind him. He lurched around, the barrel of the submachine gun being raised up and outward toward whatever might be the threat from behind.

But it was too late. Paul Talbot had already reached the threshold of the hatchway when the young terrorist began to turn around. Without the slightest hesitation he took a hefty swing with the short section of welding rod he had picked up off the hangar workshop floor a few minutes before. The heavy rod caught the boy squarely across the middle of his face just as his eyes met with Talbot's. The short, startled sound he emitted was cut short by the sickening thud of the metal rod as it broke the young man's nose and cheekbone. An instant eruption of blood squirted out of the elongated gash that ran from his left ear to his right cheek. The terrorist fell heavily to the floor, the submachine gun crashing loudly against the steel decking.

There were a few seconds of silence, followed by a burst of startled sounds from the crowd in the hangar bay as most everyone swelled forward. One of the male hostages scooped up the submachine gun from the deck and pointed it, more or less, at the unknown stranger who had overpowered the young terrorist. Jeff Eddings lay bleeding on the hangar bay floor. "Who are you?" the man asked in a quivering voice, his hand shaking visibly as he held the submachine gun.

"Paul Talbot." The old man leaned against the bulkhead, closed his eyes and took several quick, deep breaths. "I'm not with them," he finally said when he opened his eyes again. "I was . . . tricked." Paul Talbot shook his head at the feeble sound of his own words, his inane excuse. But he knew enough to not make a full confession right now; it would only complicate matters for no reason. "I want to help you. We need to do something. Fast. There's not much time left for you, not for any of us."

"What do you mean?" Drew O'Brien pushed his way through the crowd and toward the old man who stood trembling in the archway. "Are you all right?" he asked as he saw how ghostly white his thin face was.

"Yes... I'm okay... there's no time... we've got to hurry ... I need to..." Talbot's feet began to buckle under him. He grabbed at the hatchway door ledge to steady himself.

"You men grab him. Help him to the corner. I'll talk to him there." O'Brien pointed to an empty corner of the hangar bay. "Janet, you take charge of the terrorist. Get someone to help you stop the bleeding, then tie him up. Put a gag on him, too— I don't want to take any chance that he'll start to yell for his friends if he comes to."

"Right." Janet Holbrook nodded her understanding, then motioned for a few of the others to help her as she knelt down beside the unconscious, bleeding young terrorist.

"Nat, you take the submachine gun. Station yourself at the door." O'Brien gestured for the man who had first picked the weapon up off the floor to hand it over to Grisby. "But use good sense. They've still got us outnumbered—we can't afford a pitched battle."

"What am I supposed to do if they start to come for us?" Grisby asked as he took the weapon from the man and cradled it in his arm. "It's got a full clip, but you're damn right about being outnumbered. The odds are pretty heavy in their favor because they've got an arsenal to use against us."

"Right." O'Brien frowned at the obvious truth in Grisby's statement. "That's why we've got to come up with something to give us an edge." The airline captain turned away and took a step toward the corner of the hangar bay where the old man who had overpowered the terrorist was seated. The man's limp body rested awkwardly against the hard steel plating of the hangar cornerpost. Several of the passengers milled around him, some talking, some giving him food and water. Someone had lit a cigarette and passed it to him, and the old man inhaled deeply on it, the expelled gray smoke circling around his head. He wasn't answering any of their questions, but at least he physically appeared to be a little better than he had a few minutes before.

"Wait," Nat Grisby called out. He stood at the entrance of the hatchway and glanced nervously out into the darkness on the far side, then back at O'Brien. "What do I do if they start to come? Should I fire if I have to?"

"I don't know. You're supposed to be the backwoods expert, use your own judgment." O'Brien didn't like giving that sort of answer, but he didn't know what else to say. Unless they came up with a rational plan for overpowering the terrorists, he knew that they didn't stand a damn chance with one solitary weapon against five or six. He took one more step forward before he was stopped again, this time by a woman's hand on his shoulder.

"There's one more thing," Marion Miller said when O'Brien turned around. She pointed to where Janet and the others hovered over the inert body of the young terrorist. "One of the last things he said to me before the old man hit him was that he had to check in on his walky-talky in twenty minutes."

"Christ." O'Brien nervously ran his hand across his chin. "That doesn't give us any time at all."

"I know."

O'Brien stood his ground for several seconds as he glanced around the hangar bay. One automatic weapon, with no spare ammunition to speak of, to defend nearly one hundred men, women and children against half a dozen crazies armed to the teeth. Worse yet, they had—at the most—another fifteen minutes to come up with some way to turn the tide, some way to gain the advantage against those overwhelming odds. "Grab that walky-talky and bring it to me."

"Okay."

"By the way, that was one hell of a fine job you did," O'Brien said before she could turn away. "That took a lot of courage."

"Thanks. You can applaud later." Marion smiled warmly, obviously proud that her talent had been of some use. She then trotted toward where Janet and the others continued to hover over the unconscious young terrorist.

O'Brien cleared his throat. "Everyone, listen to me," he

said loudly as he raised his hands to get attention. The noise of the crowd quickly fell to a hush. "Everyone's got to pitch in. We need ideas. Talk among yourselves. Try to come up with some way we can gain a bigger advantage over these people." O'Brien noticed that the attorney Westcott was standing to one side of the crowd, an exaggerated grimace on his face, his lips moving in animation. He was saying something—something unquestionably negative—to the people beside him. O'Brien tried to ignore Westcott as best he could. He cleared his throat, then continued. "We've had a good break so far, but we still need a great deal more if we're going to get out of this without a major problem." O'Brien omitted any mention of what that problem might be. A complete bloodbath, more than likely. "We don't have much time." He paused again, unsure of how much more he should say.

"How much time *do* we have?" a man in the back shouted to break the silence.

O'Brien waited several seconds to answer as he wrestled with the alternatives of what he might say. The group of passengers from Flight 255 had done pretty well so far at meeting this situation head-on, so he decided that they deserved the whole truth. O'Brien glanced at his wristwatch. "The information we have is that thirteen minutes from now the terrorist is supposed to check in on his walky-talky. If we don't have any new ideas by then, it would be my guess that the other terrorists will figure out what happened."

"Then what do we do?" the same man asked.

"Your guess is as good as mine." O'Brien took a tentative step toward where the old man sat in the corner of the hangar bay. He was glad that he had told them the truth, but that he had still left out some of the more explicit details. O'Brien knew damn well that if the group didn't come up with a definite plan within thirteen minutes, it was an odds-on favorite that the terrorists would come in shooting. That gave the people from Flight 255 less than a quarter hour to live.

16

THE CENTER OF the hangar deck was comparatively dark, and Steven Harris was glad for at least that much. He continued to march stiffly through the shadows just outside the opened hatchway that led back into the bay where he and the other hostages had been imprisoned until just a short while before. Steven cradled the fake submachine gun in his hands—a crude, makeshift design constructed out of a welding rod and a few scraps of wood—as he worked hard at not glancing too noticeably toward where Mr. Grisby stood. Steven knew that Mr. Grisby had the real submachine gun in his hands, aimed carefully toward where the terrorists would be coming from. At the moment, that seemed like very little protection.

Get yourself into the role. Don't look at the audience. Miss Miller's words ran through his mind as Steven tugged nervously at the itchy, uncomfortable collar of the dirty black turtleneck, the one they had taken off the unconscious terrorist. *Relax. Become the character you're playing.* Steven tried very hard to concentrate on his assignment. He was a terrorist now, guarding the entrance to the hangar bay where the hostages were being held. He didn't give a damn about their lives, all he cared about was keeping those people caged. Steven knew that he had to keep up that façade until the rest of the gang stepped into sight. That moment would be his cue to launch into the act that Captain O'Brien had rehearsed with him.

A loud but slow creaking sound began to float across the darkness from the other side of the hangar bay. Steven tugged at the waist of his pants to pull them up, then continued to march back and forth across the front of the open hatchway. *I should have rolled up the cuffs, that guy's legs are longer than mine. Don't trip, it'll look too phony.* Steven heard footsteps and muffled voices, apparently coming toward him from the darkness beyond the display aircraft. *If they didn't buy that radio message, I'm dead.* Streams of perspiration rolled down his neck and gathered up in a puddle where the black turtleneck rubbed against his skin. Steven resisted the temptation to glance toward the sounds that came toward him while he prayed that the cut-off radio message they had sent a few minutes before— clipped phrases of words sliced into unintelligible gibberish by the tinkering one of the passengers had done with the wires inside the walky-talky—had sounded like trouble with the radio, not anything more.

"Eddings! Is that radio broken? Did you drop the damn thing again?"

Steven spun himself around. He held his body in such a way that, with the light from the open hatchway behind him, only his silhouette would be visible to the people who came toward him. "Yeah," he shouted tersely, his voice as near to what Miss Miller had said the unconscious terrorist's voice had sounded like as he could imitate. Since they were nearly the same height and build, if he didn't say too much, Steven felt he could get away with this impersonation for the few brief seconds that were required. At least he hoped so. "Over here," he shouted, this time his arm raised in an open gesture, the imitation submachine gun held with its tip pointed slightly upward to make it even more visible from across the hangar bay. Having a stage prop was a waste of time if the audience couldn't see it.

"What is it, for chrissake? I gave you one damn simple job, but you don't seem able to follow instructions." Richard Yang strode purposefully toward where his man guarded the hangar hatchway, his own weapon held casually in his arms. Behind him several of the others—all armed with the same type of weapons—followed him. "Didn't I tell you to keep that god-damn hatch closed? What the hell's wrong with you?"

Steven grunted an unintelligible response, something he hoped would pass for an expression of regret. The man in the front of the group marching toward him had stepped out of the deep shadows beneath the wing of the B-25 in the center of the hangar floor and into the half-light that poured through the opened hatchway. Steven desperately wanted to glance toward where Mr. Grisby was, hidden in the corner of the other side, because he needed that reassurance. *Play the role, forget the audience.* Somehow, he managed to control himself enough to prevent his head from turning. Instead, he concentrated on watching the leader of the terrorists as he walked toward him. *Five more steps, that's the cue. Four. Three. Two.*

"Did you have any problems? Any problems with them?" Yang took another step toward where Eddings guarded the hatchway. He was beginning to get an impression that something was wrong, but he didn't know what. "I hope to hell you haven't been telling them anything." Yang was no more than a dozen steps away when Eddings suddenly twirled around. He faced the hatchway as if he had heard something, his sub-machine gun pointed toward the opening. "What is it, Eddings? What's happening?"

"Quick!" Steven had shouted the word as gutturally as he could, but he didn't wait around long enough to see if that last imitation of the unconscious terrorist's voice was as convincing as the first ones had been. Steven had his excuse now, one that would allow him to take the few steps between him and the open hatchway door without the risk of the madmen behind him becoming wise, without the risk of them beginning to shoot. In nearly one motion, Steven Harris had vaulted over the threshold of the hatchway and into the hangar bay, then turned abruptly to his left and disappeared to safety behind the steel plating of the bay wall.

"Wait!" Yang took one more step toward the entrance before he realized that something had gone wrong. But it was already too late. Yang froze in his tracks. He now knew that it hadn't been Eddings at the entrance to the hatchway, that he had somehow been tricked.

"Don't move!" Nat Grisby shouted, his voice echoing in the stillness of the hangar. He stayed crouched behind the wall of metal drums he and the others had erected near the far wall. "Drop your guns! Drop them right now, or I'll shoot!"

"Christ!" Yang pulled up his weapon and squeezed the trigger as he dove toward the wheel of a nearby display aircraft. "Fire! Fire at them!" he shouted, his words drowned out by the enormous racket of his own submachine gun and—in answer to it—the sound of the weapon that fired toward them. "Keep firing! They've only got one clip—make them use it!"

From where he was behind the strut of the hollowed-out hull of some World War II relic of an airplane, Yang could easily see the first results of the battle between them and the hostages. Frank Davis and Mary Solenko had been hit. They both lay motionless on the hangar floor, Davis far to the rear, Mary Solenko nearer to the center. Yang was too far away to tell for sure if either of them were still alive. He looked toward the barricade of steel drums near the far wall. He could make out enough movement behind the drums to tell that there was more than one person back there, although he was certain that they had only one weapon between them—the one submachine gun that imbecile Eddings had somehow let them have. "Listen to me," Yang shouted, now that the firing had momentarily ceased. "You don't have a chance. You don't have much ammunition left. We've got you surrounded. Outnumbered. Give up now and we'll just lock you back in the hangar bay." Yang waited with his submachine gun raised, hoping to be able to blow off the head of the first person who showed himself—regardless of whether or not they might be surrendering. After a few seconds it was more than obvious from their silence that they weren't going to take the bait. "Okay, you've asked for it," Yang said in a loud, firm voice. Yet even as the words came out, he wondered what the hell he would be able to do next.

"What should I do?" a voice not far from Yang whispered. It was Bill Kurtz, the youngest of the terrorists. "There's only three of us now. Maybe we should run for it. Maybe we should give up."

"Stay cool." Yang knew that Kurtz would be the first to break if things got rough. "Where's John—do you see him?"

"Yes. He's by the nose of that next airplane, behind the tire." Kurtz leaned out far enough from his hiding place behind the brightly colored cutaway display of an aerial bomb to make himself visible to Yang. "Over there, see him?"

"Right." Yang could make out the side of John's face in the vague, diffuse light that reached far into the darkened center of the hangar deck. "You keep me covered, I'm gonna go 'round the back to get him."

"Okay." Kurtz stuck the barrel of his submachine gun around the edge of the hunk of metal he lay behind. "Go ahead."

"Not yet, I need more cover. Count to five, then give me a two-second burst." Yang didn't intend to take any chances, even if it meant having Kurtz waste ammunition. His own ammunition clip was nearly full, and that was all that mattered to him.

"Count to five. A two-second burst," Kurtz repeated in a flat, drained voice.

"Right." Yang took one more breath, then crouched down, his submachine gun held rigidly to his chest so he wouldn't drop it when he began to run. He had just positioned himself properly when the sound of Kurtz's firing began. Yang pushed himself off without hesitation and bolted toward where John Solenko was.

Yang was nearly all the way across the open span when the first of the hostage's shots—single shots, not a burst from the captured submachine gun's automatic firing position—kicked up chunks of metal shards from the decking plates near his feet. Yang dove heavily onto the floor near Solenko's position.

"Pretty close," Solenko whispered hoarsely. He looked down at where Yang lay prostrate on the hangar deck a few feet from him.

"It sure as hell was pretty close. That guy's a good shot. He didn't have much trouble putting half a clip into Mary." At the mention of Solenko's wife's name, Yang could see the expression on Solenko's face begin to change.

"I was thinkin' that she's just faking." Solenko peered out from around the side of the tire he had hidden himself behind. "She could be . . . just waitin' for a better shot . . . at them . . ." His voice, which had started at a whisper, had trailed off to nothing.

"Don't be an ass." Yang picked himself up on one leg and looked squarely at Solenko. "They did a good job on her—although she's probably not dead," he added quickly. "They'll finish her off in a few minutes, as soon as they get a chance."

"What can we do?" Solenko leaned back against the tire and shook his head slowly from side to side, as if he were in deep thought. "If she's hit, we've got to get to her."

"Sure. That's my plan." Yang crawled over to where Solenko was, lifted himself up and looked the man squarely in the eye. "We can save her, but only if you follow my instructions to the letter. Are you ready?"

"Yeah." Solenko nodded enthusiastically, then glanced out toward his wife's body. She lay at a grotesque angle on the cold hangar floor, her legs tucked up and her arms trailed behind her.

"Okay. Listen to me." Yang grabbed Solenko's shoulder and forced him to turn away from his wife—he knew damn well that no matter how stupid the man might be, he would soon see the growing puddle of blood beneath her head, the growing puddle that showed that she had unquestionably already been killed. "There's time to save her, if we hurry. I figure they've only got a few shots left, that's why they've gone from automatic to single shot." Yang motioned toward the line of steel drums against the far wall.

"But we're too far in the open. They'll get me for sure if I try to reach her."

"Not necessarily. Not if I get them first." Yang surveyed the battle scene in front of him. As reluctant as he was to admit it, he and his men had been set up marvelously. The only thing that stopped the ambush from getting all of them at once was the hostages' lack of weapons. Even now, because the hostages had set themselves at such a good spot on the hangar floor, there was no way that Yang could make a break for the single exit at the far corner without exposing himself to their gunfire. He could either wait out the hostages in hopes that they would waste their ammunition soon—a chance that seemed unlikely, the way they were handling themselves at the moment—or else he could use someone else as a decoy. Since Yang knew that McClure was determined to stick to the original schedule for sinking the *Yorktown,* only option number two seemed workable. What Yang needed in order to implement his new idea was an unknowing volunteer—and for that job, John Solenko would do just fine.

"I wanna get Mary out of there," Solenko said.

"We both do." Yang edged nearer to Solenko. He could tell from the man's emotional state that he would buy most any plan, as long as it had Yang's assurance of success. "We can pull this off, trust me."

"What do we do?"

"Easy. You give me one minute to position myself further to the left," Yang began as he pointed toward the edge of the deepest shadow from the B-25's overhanging wing. "Then you come around this way." He motioned with his arm to show Solenko what he meant.

Solenko blinked. "What happens then?"

"Once you're in position, you'll have a clear path to get to Mary. When the man with the submachine gun raises himself up in order to follow you—you see how they've got to come around the other end of their barricade in order to follow you toward where Mary is . . ."

"Yes, I see."

". . . then I'll have a perfect shot at them from my position in the rear. Even if I miss, which I don't think I will, my shots will drive them back far enough for you to have a clear run to pull Mary back to this spot."

"Okay. Good." Solenko glanced out at his wife's body, back at Yang, then down at his wristwatch. "One minute?"

"From right now." Without waiting for another word, Yang began to maneuver himself rearward, careful to keep himself hidden in the deep shadows and out of line of any potential gunfire from the barricades. When he reached the point beneath the center section of the B-25, he turned toward the left wing, his body still crouched low, his own weapon held close to his chest. Yang knew that from the end of that overlapping shadow from the wing he had no more than a three- or four-second dash to reach the dark corner on the far side—a run he could make in complete safety while the hostages aimed and fired at Solenko. Once he reached that exit on the far wall, Yang would go below to radio the submarine in order to have them ready to pick him up, then leave the *Yorktown* as quickly as he could.

From his position beneath the end of the wing, Yang could see Solenko quite clearly. The man had maneuvered himself to the proper side of the tire and was crouched down in preparation to spring out toward the body of his dead wife. Yang got himself onto his haunches in order to be ready for the quick spring across the open space. When he did, he saw something out of the corner of his eye. It was a figure—a solitary man— at the closest end of the line of barrels. He was approximately forty feet away, but even at that distance Yang could easily see what his intentions were. Yang had hardly enough time to make up his own mind about his change in plans when he saw Solenko jump out from behind the tire and run toward the body of his wife.

"Stop!" The hostage with the submachine gun moved quickly to the farthest end of the barrels and rose up slightly to take aim at the incredible fool who was now in the center of the open hangar floor. "Drop the gun or I'll shoot!"

"Yang! Now, for God's sake!" Solenko had already realized that he was far more exposed than he thought he would be. He looked around at the shadows that surrounded him for a brief instant before he faced forward again. More out of instinct than any rational attempt to save his own life, he pressed the trigger of his own weapon. The burst from his submachine gun cut diagonally across the row of steel barrels, the bullets ricocheting off in every direction, splinters of torn metal following them. The shots from the hostage's weapon came a few seconds later, and the bullets immediately found their mark. Solenko let out a loud scream as the short burst caught him dead-center, picked him up slightly, then dropped him heavily on the hangar floor.

Yang had already moved out from under the shadows, but instead of heading for the exit he had shifted his attention to the newest target of opportunity. The solitary man at the near end of the barricade had used that very moment to lunge out himself, toward where the body of Frank Davis lay sprawled across the submachine gun that he had carried. Although it only took a few seconds for the entire sequence to be completed, Richard Yang found himself gazing down at Paul Talbot as the old man attempted to snatch the heavy submachine gun from where it lay beneath Davis' massive and inert body. "Okay, pops. Leave it. Get up quickly. If you don't, I'll blow your goddamn face off."

Talbot looked up, startled. He hadn't expected anyone from that corner of the room, so he had disobeyed O'Brien's direct order about staying behind the barrels and rushed out to get another weapon for them to use before their one gun had run out of ammunition. When the one terrorist made his suicidal run toward the center of the hangar floor a few moments before, Talbot decided that he could use that distraction to safely capture another gun for them. He had been wrong. "You son-of-a-bitch," Talbot said as he rose slowly to his feet, his arms raised above his head. "But they don't know me well enough. They won't trade my life for that gun they've got."

"I wouldn't think of asking." Yang grabbed Talbot, spun him around, then stuck the barrel of his submachine gun into the old man's ribs. "Listen to me, all of you," Yang announced in a loud voice. "I'm walking out of here with this gentleman in front of me. He'll make a nice shield for your bullets, so I'd advise you not to waste them." Yang began to back away carefully toward the exit at the far end, his attention on the men in front of him. "This couldn't have worked out better for me. I know for a fact that this man knows every corner of this tub, so I'd much rather have him with me than with you."

"Let him go. We'll let you out of here." Drew O'Brien stood up from behind the barricade, but he gestured for Grisby to stay low, the barrel of his gun aimed toward Talbot and the terrorist.

"Sure, you'll leave me alone," Yang said. He laughed. "Tell me another one about Santa Claus and the Easter bunny." Yang had nearly reached the exit when he stopped again. "Kurtz? Can you still hear me?"

"Yeah. I was getting worried. I thought you forgot me, that you were gonna leave me." Bill Kurtz rose up from where he had remained hidden the entire time behind the strut of the display aircraft at the other end of the hangar bay. "I'm coming."

"Good. I don't want loose ends." Yang watched as the young

man threaded his way carefully toward him, the barrel of his weapon pointed at the men at the barricade.

"Here I come."

"Don't bet on it." Without a word of warning Yang squeezed the trigger of his submachine gun and sent a short burst into Kurtz. The young man sagged to the floor immediately, the gun in his hands clanking loudly as it crashed to the steel decking.

"For God's sake, that's your own man," O'Brien shouted incredulously. "What the hell did you kill him for?"

"Because he's a coward. He's useless. That's one less distraction for me to cope with." Yang backed another step, opened the hatchway slowly, then began to retreat into the dark corridor behind. "I'll keep pops with me as insurance, but I'm certain you're not so foolish as to try to follow me. You've got control of the *Yorktown,* that should be enough for you."

"What are you going to do with him?" O'Brien shouted as Yang and the old man disappeared into the corridor that led somewhere into the bowels of the ship. But there was no answer from them, except the sound of their fading footsteps as the two of them hurried down the corridor to someplace unknown.

It had taken several minutes for the two of them to wind their way around the narrow corridors that led deeper and deeper to the interior of the *Yorktown.* With Richard Yang shoving from behind, Paul Talbot stumbled and fell twice—one of the times cutting his arm slightly on a jagged piece of metal on a narrow catwalk.

"Where are you taking me?" Talbot asked as he continued ahead because of the prodding of the muzzle at his back.

"Don't play stupid with me, pops. You know as well as I do where we're going."

"The engine room?"

"Good guess, you win the prize." Yang pushed the barrel of the submachine gun a little farther into Talbot's spine. "You're gonna get your prize soon, too, so don't you worry."

Talbot didn't answer. Instead, he concentrated on trying to find something or some way to overpower Yang, to get that gun pointed away for just a moment. Even though Yang was less than half his age, Talbot felt that if he could get the gun away from him he would take the chance, no matter how desperate it might be.

"To the left. Open the hatchway."

Talbot complied. He stepped over the sill and into the mustiness of the aft engine room. "I thought you already destroyed the engines," Talbot said as he gestured toward the array of boiler pipes and turbine components below. The odor of diesel fuel hung heavily in the air, and it coated everything with a fine, slippery film. The two men began to move even lower on the catwalk, toward the base of the control panel for the number-two engine.

"You're right about the engines, pops, although it won't make a damn bit of difference to you in the long run." Yang balanced the submachine gun carefully in one arm while he used the other to keep a firm hold on the handrail in order to keep himself from slipping on the slick deck plates. "Go down the ladder. Sit on the floor with your back to the panel. Keep your hands where I can see them. Don't try anything stupid, because if you do, all you'll be accomplishing is a shortening of your life."

"Cut the bullshit. I know that you're going to kill me." Talbot allowed himself to stare at Yang with undisguised hatred for a few seconds before he began to maneuver himself carefully down the metal ladder that led to the lowest level of the engine room. He glanced to both sides as he descended the ladder, in a desperate search for something that he might use as a weapon. There was nothing there, not a scrap of iron, not a spare tool, a section of rail, a coil of wire. "What do you need me here for?" Talbot asked as he reached the base of the control panel. Talbot sat himself down slowly, his legs curled under his body in such a way that he would be able to spring out toward Yang if the opportunity somehow presented itself.

"That's something I don't mind telling you, pops." Yang grinned. "What I said before was true, that if I left you up there you might be leading a search party for me right this minute. I knew that I needed to come down here once more, and I didn't need your knowledge of the ship as leverage against me."

"What do you need to be down here for?" Talbot asked in a conversational tone. He knew that as long as Yang continued to talk, there was still hope. The clock had not run out yet.

"For a simple reason, although one you weren't aware of. In addition to the transmitter on the bridge—one that I've already destroyed, so don't get any bright ideas about that one—I had another radio down here, my emergency method of contacting the submarine. I'm gonna use it right now to let them know that I'm on my way. After that, I'll destroy this radio too."

"Then what?"

"Then I'm going to kill you."

"Why?"

"Why not?" Yang adjusted his wire-rimmed glasses, then took another step to his left. "Besides the fact that you know me too well—a fact that won't be pertinent anyway, since everyone on this ship will die at dawn when the torpedoes hit—there's also the additional risk that your knowledge might represent. As unlikely as I can imagine it will be, the fact remains that you do know a great deal about this old tub of shit. If I eliminate you, I eliminate the last chance that the hostages can come up with some way to fight back, some way to use this ship against us. With control of the *Yorktown* in their hands, I need to make certain that everyone stays put and that the ship stays disabled." Yang waved the barrel of his submachine gun toward the machinery to his left. "As you can see, pops, I think we've done an admirable job at making this engine into nothing more than a hunk of scrap iron."

Talbot's eyes ran up and down the banks of valves, piping, gears and shafts that comprised the running gear of engine number two. Even from a few dozen feet away, Talbot could easily see that several critical components had been destroyed beyond repair, that it would take teams of experienced technicians several days to put this engine room back into working order.

"I can see that you appreciate our handiwork," Yang said as he watched Talbot's eyes. "I'll spare you the agony of asking by informing you that the number-one engine room has also been equally disabled."

"You're a real son-of-a-bitch."

Yang shrugged, then grinned. "I guess I'll have to consider the source. If I were in your position, I wouldn't think much of me, either." Yang took two steps to his left and reached behind a sheetmetal panel. "If you'll excuse me, pops, I've got a call to make."

Talbot watched as Yang turned the radio on and made a few adjustments to the controls on the set. *No time left. Try anything.* Talbot was just about to leap forward—an act of desperation that he knew had just about a zero chance of success because of the way Yang had the submachine gun pointed—when he noticed a slight quiver in one of the needles on the control panel. *Steam pressure in manifold three.* The buildup from the boilers hadn't been bled off yet. *Manifold three.* Talbot's eyes ran up and down the rows of pipes on the ceiling until he found the one he was looking for. *Manifold three, overpressure relief. The one we hadn't repaired.*

"Hello, *Trout,* this is the *Yorktown.*" Yang said into the microphone. "We've had a problem."

"Go ahead, *Yorktown.*"

Talbot turned his body slightly as he visually followed the maze of pipes that led from manifold three. *The crossover duct is still disconnected. The exposed pipe is only a few feet above his head.* Talbot tried not to look too pointedly at the spot near Yang where the pipe ended abruptly, the new section not yet attached. *Manifold three has pressure. It can be vented through the overpressure line.* Without pausing for a second so that any one of the thousand reasons against it would register in his brain, Paul Talbot suddenly dove away from Yang and toward the gang of levers on the left side of the control panel.

Before Richard Yang could twist to his right and raise his submachine gun, the old man had scrambled across the oil-soaked floor fast enough to already have his hand on the lever that controlled the emergency steam release for manifold number three. In less than an instant the old man had released the safety chain and had yanked the handle fully back. An enormous, billowy flow of hot frothy steam flooded out of the exposed end of the opened pipe as it spit itself into the aft engine room.

Richard Yang was less than four feet from the exposed end of the pipe, facing it, when the boiling swirl of steam began. Before he had even sensed what had happened, his hair and eyes had been boiled beyond recognition. Most of the skin on his face was turned into a mushy-soft layer of paste—a layer which was then peeled back by the enormous force from the hot air and boiling liquid. The plastic inserts on Yang's wire-rimmed glasses melted instantly, then began to adhere to the now-exposed bones across the bridge of his nose. Yang's neck and shoulders—slightly farther away from the effects of the direct blast of super-heated steam—turned lobster-red as the blood vessels in them ruptured.

Yang's hideous scream was completely smothered by the roar of the escaping steam. His body—the muscles convulsing wildly—pitched forward, the weight of the submachine gun he held in his arms helping to steer him in that direction. The plastic microphone and the rubber microphone cord melted and stuck to what was left of his arm. As he pitched forward, the stretched cord yanked the radio from its rack, tumbled it over and smashed it on the floor. Just a short moment before Yang's body would have hit the floor his hand and finger muscles began to contract involuntarily because of the myriad of con-flicting signals caused by the roasting that his brain had taken. The submachine gun, which was unaffected by the cascading bath of boiling steam, responded in the fashion in which it had been designed.

A short burst of bullets spit themselves out the barrel of the submachine gun before Yang's finger finally slipped off the trigger. The bullets hurled themselves in the direction that they had previously been aimed—toward the floor at the base of the control panel.

Paul Talbot, who had stayed on the floor to be as far beneath the flow of steam as possible, had been only marginally affected by the hot mist. But Talbot was repeatedly struck by the bullets. By the time the firing had ended and the noise from the steam had died away, Paul Talbot lay sprawled across the deck plates, unconscious, with one bullet in the leg, one in his hip and three in his stomach.

17

THIRTY MINUTES HAD gone past since Skip Locker had last seen Lieutenant Ted Nash. That meant that their planned rendezvous on the second floor of the Pentagon was already ten minutes behind schedule. Locker paced back and forth nervously, unsure of what to do next. *Screw him, I've got enough to blow half the people in this building into new careers. I'm not waiting any longer.* But in spite of his own words, Skip Locker continued to wait in the hallway of the second floor of ring C, corridor 3, as he had been instructed. While the information he had gotten so far was great, a copy of the terrorist's last teletype message would be a fabulous addition. It would be an extra rocket he could use to guarantee that his career would be launched into the stratosphere.

"Skip—over here!"

"Where the hell have you been?" Locker rushed down the corridor toward where Nash had suddenly appeared out of a doorway. "I thought you said twenty minutes." Locker was out of breath as much from nervousness as from the small amount of running he had just done down the corridor. "I thought maybe I had gone to the wrong place or something."

"No, this is the right place." Without preamble Nash turned and began to walk rapidly down the empty corridor. He glanced over his shoulder and saw that Locker was half a step behind. "It took me a few minutes more than I thought it would to get this," he continued as he waved the sheaf of papers in his hand.

"Is that the teletype message?"

"Yes. That, plus a few other things. I'm keeping my end of the bargain, just like you're keeping yours."

"Let me see them." Locker picked up his stride to try to match Nash's pace, but the man's longer legs were too much for him. "Christ, slow down," Locker panted as he broke into a slow trot in order to keep up with the larger man in front of him. "Let me see the messages," he repeated as he reached out to take them.

"No, not here." Nash yanked the sheaf of papers away and held them closer to his chest. "Too much of a risk. There are too many people still in the building."

Locker looked over his shoulder, then back up the corridor. "The place is empty, for chrissake. You could post them on the wall and no one would notice." Locker pointed to a bulletin board as they scurried past, the entire surface plastered with dozens of government notices.

"I'm not taking any chances. I've already taken considerable chances so far."

"Suit yourself." Locker shrugged, more out of resignation than understanding.

"I will." Nash then came to a stop so suddenly that Locker nearly collided with him. "But I intend to live up to my end of our bargain, just like you'll live up to yours. I've got us a place where we can speak freely. A place where you can make copies of whatever documents you need. After that, I've got to return the originals to where they came from before anyone gets wise."

"Naturally." Locker nodded in agreement. He used their brief stop to catch his breath. "But where the hell is this road race taking us? Have you got some specific place in mind?" Locker gestured along an endless row of closed doors that lined the corridor on both sides. "Most of these offices are empty, any one of them would do."

"What I have in mind is better than an office," Nash whispered as he leaned closer to Locker. "A place with a copy machine. A paper shredder. A place where we're guaranteed that no one will bother us. Is that okay?"

"Sure." Locker decided to play along with Nash's nonsense, at least for the few minutes more it would take to get the material he wanted. After that, Nash would become *persona non grata* in these corridors anyway, so it wouldn't hurt if the lieutenant got one last look at them. "Where is this spot you've picked out?"

"One of the sub-basement briefing rooms."

"The vaults?"

"Yes."

"Lead the way." Locker had heard about the super-secret rooms in the sub-basement of the building—an area that wasn't even listed in the public documents about the Pentagon. Some of the briefing rooms, it was rumored, were vaultlike enclosures with elaborate security locks. They each contained electronic counter-measures designed to prevent anyone outside from penetrating the secret discussions that were conducted inside the room no matter how sophisticated their electronic eavesdropping might be. Locker smiled. That location would add another nice element to his story, an element about how he had to gather information utilizing the very safeguards designed specifically to prevent secret information from getting out of the Pentagon. A bit of irony was always a good counterpoint for any story.

"Follow me." Nash began to move ahead rapidly again. When he reached the staircase he took the steps two at a time, then had to wait at the bottom for Locker to catch up. The two of them started walking again. After they had traveled through a few more corridors and staircases, they were face to face with a steel door that had an electronic locking device on the outside.

"Do you know the code?" Locker pointed to the dozens of buttons on the face of the lock.

"I hope so. If you punch in the wrong code two times in a row, the master siren goes off."

"Christ Almighty." Locker fidgeted—the last thing he needed now was an alarm that brought out the guards. "This isn't necessary, just hand me the papers."

Nash ignored him. He reached forward and began to punch a code into the machine. After a few seconds Nash realized that Locker had been watching over his shoulder too intently. "Don't strain your eyes trying to see these numbers. The code is changed twice a day."

"Oh." Locker smiled sheepishly; he had been caught doing something silly. It had been an especially stupid stunt on his part since he knew damn well that in a few hours he'd never be permitted inside the Pentagon again—not even as a tourist, probably. But that was an insignificant price to pay for a scoop like this. "Just curiosity, nothing more," Locker added in the way of explanation.

"Don't worry about it." Nash punched in the last few numbers, then grabbed the lock and turned it. The silver steel handle spun effortlessly. A few moments later the door itself began to swing inward. "We're almost there."

"Good." Locker glanced at his wristwatch. Five minutes past eight, they had wasted a great deal of valuable time with this unnecessary display of secrecy. Still, if this sort of charade was what it took to pry top-secret information out of Nash, Locker was more than happy to go through with it. "Is this the vault?" he asked as he followed Nash down the new corridor that led farther into the bowels of the building.

"No." The two men turned another corner, then entered a staircase. They hustled down first one, then another flight of narrow stairs. Once again they entered another nameless corridor, also lined with closed and locked doors on both sides.

"Here we are." Nash stopped in front of a gray hinged-steel plate that looked more like the internal partition from a warship than anything that belonged inside a building. "This lock has a different code," Nash volunteered as he stooped over the electronic device and began to play with its buttons. After a few seconds a low-toned buzzer sounded briefly, then an amber light above the door flashed on.

"What does that mean?" Locker pointed to the long row of colored lights, although only the amber one was lit.

"It means that the room is ours." Before Nash could add anything else to his explanation the door's buzzer beeped twice and the red signal light above the doorframe flashed on and began to pulsate. "That," Nash said as he pointed toward it, "tells us that the room can't be tampered with from the outside. It's totally ours."

"Wonderful." Locker stepped across the doorsill and he followed Nash in. For some reason he felt particularly uncomfortable in this place, although he had no idea why. The room itself was fifteen feet square, with a wooden conference table in the center surrounded by upholstered chairs. Two rows of overhead fluorescent lights provided the illumination. In the corner were a copy machine and what Locker took to be the paper shredder. "What's behind the partition?" he asked as he pointed to the fiber glass divider that covered part of the adjacant wall.

"Two separate areas. Toilet to the right, kitchen to the left."

"They've got you covered on both ends, huh?" Locker smiled at his own joke.

Nash didn't respond. Instead, he stepped quickly across the room and began to lean his body against the bulk of the heavy metal door. In a few seconds he had pushed it closed. A red light above the interior of the door continued to blink, just like the red light above the outside of the door had. Nash reached for the interior handle and spun it until it locked with an audible click. At that moment, the red light above his head turned from blinking to steady.

"What's the light mean?" Locker asked. He was beginning to enjoy himself, beginning to plan out how this experience would make wonderful material for the inevitable follow-up sidebars that his story on the hijacking would promote.

"It means that the time sequence lock has engaged." Nash leaned back casually against the heavy metal door and folded his arms. "That means that no one can get in—and we can't get out—until the time I've programmed into the machine has elapsed."

"Very good." But there was something in Nash's eyes that told Locker this news was anything but good. "How much time did you set it for?" Locker asked tentatively, his words coming out with far more anxiety than he had intended.

"Sixteen hours from now."

Skip Locker stumbled backward. *Sixteen hours!* "What the hell . . . are you . . . crazy or something?"

"No. Just the opposite." Ted Nash began to smile, for what

would be the first time for him that day. "I'm keeping my end of the bargain, just like you intended to keep yours." Nash allowed the deepening grin to play across his face before he continued. "Your problem is that you've got a big mouth, that you've said too much. The major prerequisite for being a good liar is that you need a good memory to pull it off. Quite obviously, it's a requirement you don't meet."

"I don't understand." Locker leaned back against the conference table, still in shock. Snips of scattered thoughts whirled through his mind.

"At the Ground Zero hamburger stand, just before I left you, the last thing I asked was if you wanted a copy of that message from the terrorists. I asked because I wanted to see if you intended to use it—to show it on television, to print it."

"So what?"

"Nothing, except that I'd already told you that the terrorist's message contained their demand for the ransom payment. In your greed you forgot that just one minute before you had given your word that you would never say anything about that aspect of the situation—about the President's decision to pay the ransom. You promised me that you would never print any of that."

"I . . . I was just . . ."

"But I could tell what you were really thinking when I offered you that little bit more. A smell of cheese always brings out the rat." Ted Nash shook his head in disgust as he glared down at the man who stood in front of him. "That was a terrific plan you had to get yourself a hot story. I bet you would have gotten a nice promotion out of it, too. The fact that it would have meant the deaths of those hostages meant nothing to you," Nash added with contempt.

Locker stood silently for half a minute. Finally, he began to nod his head in a gesture of acceptance. "I've got to hand it to you," he responded, his voice surprisingly cheerful. He had obviously totally regained his composure. Locker stood upright and waved his hand at Nash. "But I'm afraid I'm still going to get my story. You think you've covered all the angles, but I'm happy to say that I've outsmarted you. I would have preferred to give this story to my editor in person, but that small point doesn't matter now. I've already made provisions for the possibility of a foul-up of some sort. The major point is that, at this very moment," Locker said as he tapped his wristwatch, "one of the people from my office will be picking up a copy of a tape from my locked desk in the reporter's office on the first floor. What it contains," Locker continued, his voice gloating with pride, "is an exact copy of this tape." He reached into his jacket pocket and pulled out the miniature tape recorder he had hidden in there.

"A copy of the tape you made of me? A copy of the explanation of everything that occurred to the hostages, including the business about the ransom demands?"

"Exactly." But as much as he tried to keep the psychological upper hand between them, Locker could tell from the casual way that Nash had figured out what was on the miniature tape recorder that he had already figured that fact out much earlier. Locker shifted his weight nervously as he looked up at the lieutenant's eyes.

"When your man picks up that tape and plays it," Nash began nonchalantly, "I think he'll be sorely disappointed." Nash rubbed his hands together before he spoke again—the next line was the one he had been looking forward to for the past half hour. "During the time you were waiting for me on the second floor, ring C, corridor three, I was busy elsewhere. Down on the first floor."

"First floor?" Locker winced, although he had no idea what Nash was leading up to.

"Yes. In the reporter's office. Naturally, I couldn't tamper with your desk—a fact I'm sure you were aware of. With the other reporters sitting in the office working on the Air Force budget story, it would have been too much of a risk for me to take. But the one thing I could accomplish inconspicuously was to lay two briefcases at opposite corners of your desk."

"Briefcases?" Locker was perplexed, none of it made sense to him. He had already figured that no one could break into his desk with the reporters working in the room. But Nash had done something else. "What the hell are you talking about?"

"About technology, my friend." Ted Nash took one step toward the center of the room where Locker stood. "About modern solid state circuits. About two powerful electromagnets that, in the span of just a few seconds, can completely erase everything recorded on a tape. Your tape. In case you're not aware of it, erasing a tape is done magnetically. If a magnet is strong enough, it can erase a recorded tape from several feet away." Nash paused long enough to allow Locker to finish with the low groan that had begun when the facts about erasing tapes were being explained to him.

"Damn it, but I know the truth!" Locker suddenly shouted. "You can't keep us here forever! When the door opens, I'll march out of here and tell the world what happened!" Locker gestured toward the steady red light above the steel door with a trembling hand. "You haven't outsmarted me, you've just delayed me!"

"Don't bet on it," Nash answered calmly. "Because it will be your word against mine. It'll be your word against everyone's—the President, the Pentagon staff, the hostages. You've got zero proof. If you stop and think about it for a minute, that means that you've effectively got no story. Add that to one other factor—that you can't get any story into print until long after all the other news services have already covered it. If you say anything about a ransom payment, I'm willing to bet that it'll look like pure fiction—some calculated invention on your part to cover your own lack of a scoop." Nash smiled broadly, then rubbed his hands together once again. "By the way, there is one additional thing."

"What?"

Nash pointed a few feet away, to the miniature tape player that Locker had laid on the conference table moments before. "I'm going to take the tape out of that cute little machine of yours. Then I'm going to feed that tape into the shredder. But before I do, I think I should advise you," Nash continued, his words slowing down so their meaning would be totally clear, "that when I'm finished shredding that tape I'm going to spend a little extra time on you."

"Keep your hands off me." Locker backed a few feet away from the conference table, until the back of his legs bumped into one of the upholstered chairs. "I'm warning you, you'd better leave me alone." Locker had tried to sound forceful, but instead the result came out more as a plea than a threat.

"I'm going to go over you carefully, to be certain that you

don't have another copy of that unfortunate tape stuck away somewhere on your person," Nash said, as if Locker had just said nothing. He knew there was probably no other copy of the tape, but the opportunity to harass Locker—even slightly—was too nice an option to pass up.

"There isn't any other tape. I swear it."

"Like you told me that you wouldn't let out the facts about the ransom payment? No, I'm afraid you're out of chances to tell the truth." Nash took half a step toward where Locker was standing. "I don't think you have any idea how much trouble you've caused. I had to explain everything to Captain Martin. He was nice enough to give me a chance to try to get out of this situation on my own. He said that would be the only way I would stand half a chance of saving my ass, since there could obviously never be a public court martial for me to defend myself at."

"No court martial? What does that mean?"

"If they court-martialed me, the Navy would be admitting that I had been involved in something highly secret. Since none of this ransom business officially occurred, it stands to reason that I couldn't have told anyone about it."

"They sure are treating you rotten." Locker had spoken the line with feigned empathy, in the hopes that he could get Nash to nibble at the bait, to get Nash to feel that this event had turned into a battle of the two of them against the Navy.

"For ten cents I'd put your face through that steel wall," Nash answered through clenched teeth, even though he made no overt move toward Locker. "Don't try that psychological crap on me, I've already made up my mind." Nash exhaled slowly, then began to shake his head. "How do you think I got this briefing room, by telling the brass that I wanted to picnic down here? Martin authorized this room for me so I could try to paddle upstream. The way it stands right now, I think I stand a slight chance that I won't be busted out of the Navy." Nash shrugged in despair. "When this door opens in sixteen hours, my problems are just going to begin. It serves me right for dealing with someone like you. But at least I managed to prevent you from endangering the lives of those innocent hostages."

"Listen, I can help you out of this," Locker blurted out. "I'll tell them . . ."

"You're a son-of-a-bitch." Nash took another step forward. "You don't understand how damn little you're going to be able to help anyone, at least around here. I'm only sorry that you haven't broken any actual laws so we could string you up."

"That's right, I haven't broken any laws. Just remember that." Locker looked across the conference table defiantly.

"That's true. When this door opens, you're a free man. You can walk out. But until then, I think that I can convince you to cooperate with me to the fullest." Nash smiled broadly, then flexed the tensed muscles in his arms. *Rough him up, just a little. Like Captain Martin said, then maybe he wouldn't be so quick to pull this kind of crap in the future.*

"I haven't broken any laws!"

"That's true, very true." Ted Nash took slow and deliberate strides toward where Skip Locker had begun to cower in the far corner of the locked conference room.

"It is now nine-thirty," Olga Rodriguez said as she held up her wristwatch for the others to see.

"Let's get on with it. We can't wait forever."

"I'll be the judge of that." Jerome Zindell looked across the submarine's small wardroom table toward where Ed McClure sat. On top of everything else, the man had taken what was customarily the captain's chair, the one with the high upholstered seatback. It was a fact that Zindell had decided to ignore, but he certainly didn't intend to ignore any more of McClure's challenges to his authority. "With the current situation on the *Yorktown,* we'll have to remain flexible. I'm not certain that we should surface quite yet."

"I agree with the captain," Clifton Harrison said. He ran his hand across his bushy beard, then began to speak again in cool and measured tones. "We have to assume that Yang's last transmission was cut off because he was somehow overpowered by the hostages. Remember that the message he got out just before the transmission ended was that he was experiencing some sort of problem." Harrison leaned forward and placed his elbows on the green plastic tablecloth. "Since he hasn't transmitted again during the last hour—and, from what we can tell, he hasn't left the *Yorktown*—then there's no other logical explanation for what happened."

"What the hell difference does it make?" McClure sat farther back, in an exaggerated display of casualness. He took another toothpick out of his shirt pocket and popped it into his mouth. "When you think about it, it only means that there's more gold for each of us. From now on, control of the *Yorktown* is no more than an academic point."

"How can you be so sure?" Zindell didn't want to be in a position of needing to ask for McClure's opinion, but this unexpected change in plans had rattled him and he knew it. *Don't play supercommander. Ask your officers for help whenever you need it.* As always, his father's words made a great deal of sense to him, although Zindell knew damn well that his father would never have asked a man like McClure for so much as the time of day.

"The problems aboard the *Yorktown* are unfortunate, but I agree that they are really of no consequence." As Olga spoke she looked across the table at Harrison, then allowed her eyes to scan either side toward both McClure and Zindell. "It was hours earlier when we received the message from Yang that both the ship's engines had been permanently disabled."

"That's right," McClure nodded. "Yang also confirmed that he had destroyed the radios inside the airliner, and also the small transmitter on the ship's bridge. His emergency radio works on only one frequency—which means that if the hostages use it, they can only contact us." McClure smiled broadly. "So what if they've managed to string up Yang and his friends by their balls? By now the hostages must realize that all they've managed to do is give themselves a bigger area to roam in. Instead of being locked inside the hangar bay, they're now trapped onboard a ship that's lying dead in the water—and with no way of communicating with the outside world."

"What about the skiff? Do you think they might try to use that small boat to escape?" Zindell turned his body so that he could rest the stump of his left arm against the sidewall. He then looked around the table as he waited for an answer.

Harrison was the first to speak. "Even if they tried, that one small boat won't hold more than a couple dozen of them. There are no other serviceable skiffs on the *Yorktown,* Yang had already taken care of that. If they do launch that skiff, we'd probably hear its engine on our sonar. Then we could ram and sink it, if we wanted to."

"Or even let them go, for all the difference it would make."

"That's no good," McClure interrupted. He glared at Olga, to show her that her last comment about letting some of the hostages escape did not sit well with him. "They should go down with that ship, every one of them. That's the only way to tell for sure that none of them know anything about who we are or what we intend to do. Yang might've figured out more than we told him and—take it from me—he wouldn't be much of a tough nut to crack." McClure's cold, intimidating smirk played across his lips. "Speaking of nuts, if they put Yang's nuts in a vise he'd sing like a choir boy."

"Okay." Zindell rocked forward in his seat and strummed his fingers nervously against the wardroom table. "I see your point." He knew it was time for a decision, that he had put off making one for as long as he could. "We've waited long enough. I've got to get the *Trout* on the surface very soon in order to charge the batteries or we're going to have an electrical problem during our submerged portion of the escape run." Zindell stood up, then turned around in the narrow confines of the wardroom. "I'm going to check with Moss one more time, to be certain that there's no sign of activity from the *Yorktown*. When he convinces me that the ship is still dead in the water and that there's no one else out there, I'll come back for you. At that time, we'll surface the boat." Without waiting for a reply from them, Zindell stepped into the corridor that led from the wardroom, then turned aft toward the control room of the *Trout*.

"We're a full hour behind our planned schedule, and our fearless leader still wants to wait longer." But McClure had waited until the sound of Zindell's footsteps had faded down the corridor before he had said anything. He took the chewed-over toothpick out of the corner of his mouth and flung it toward the rear wall of the wardroom. It landed on the shelf where the coffeepot sat. "I'm getting damned tired of this bullshit."

"So am I—except that I think that most of the bullshit is coming from you."

"Is that so?" McClure sat expressionless, as if Harrison's comment had not been directed solely at him.

"Yes." Harrison sat a few inches farther forward on his chair. "Take your recommendations about the disposal of the explosives, for example. That's one line of bullshit that might come back to haunt us."

"How?"

"We should have had Yang dump those explosives he took from the airliner overboard, rather than hiding them on the ship."

"It's not a good policy to get rid of munitions. You never know when you might need them."

"That's asinine. All you've done is given the hostages a chance to find them."

"No chance at all. I personally told Yang where to hide the explosives."

"Based on what I've seen of your planning so far, that news doesn't thrill me."

"Please," Olga interrupted before McClure could respond. "Let us not get into this. It is already done, finished. It is pointless to talk about." But even as she watched Harrison, she could see that his words were actually more about something other than what he was saying. This was the first time that the three of them had been alone together, and it was evidently creating a bad effect on Harrison. Whether he knew for certain what had gone on between her and McClure or had only guessed at it, it made no matter, because the results were the same. "Perhaps we should go to the control room to see how the captain is doing," Olga said nervously.

"No." Harrison gestured for her to stay where she was. "We're going to follow the captain's orders. He told us to stay here."

"Very well." Olga wanted to look toward McClure, but she was afraid of doing something even as innocent as turning her head. *He is insanely jealous. He is also afraid of McClure. Those factors together will make him irrational.* Olga could read Harrison's fear of McClure as easily as if it were in letters on a billboard. "Let us not bicker over small points, the major job goes well. It is something we can be proud of."

"Sure. Proud as hell." Harrison had answered tersely, his angry words aimed at Olga. "But some of the things we've done lately aren't worth being proud of. Do you agree?"

"It is pointless to talk this way," Olga repeated, her voice as calm and as soothing as she could make it. *This man is too jealous, yet also too afraid. He is irrational. He is violent.* With the hand that was beneath the table, Olga carefully unbuttoned the fastener around the top of her pearl-handled knife. She drew the knife out of its sheath, careful to keep her actions slow enough so as not to draw notice to any movement.

"Don't tell me what the hell a pointless act is and what isn't!" Harrison's voice was nearly shrill. He began to hunch his body farther forward in his seat and he ran his trembling fingers back and forth through his beard. "I don't need any lectures! Not from a whore like you!"

"Then what sort of whore would you like to hear a lecture from?" Those were the first words McClure had spoken since he had answered Harrison's question about the explosives. McClure turned his body slightly so he faced Harrison fully, then slowly slid both his hands to the top of the wardroom table. "Maybe you'd rather hear it from someone else. Maybe you'd like to hear a lecture from a whore like your mother."

Clifton Harrison leaped across the table like an overwound spring, his body nearly on top of McClure before the other man had so much as raised his hands in defense. "You bastard! I'll kill you!" he shouted at the top of his lungs, the pent-up emotions of jealousy and hatred triggered by an insult that actually meant very little to him. Coffee cups and ashtrays flew off the table in all directions and crashed loudly against the metal walls and flooring. "I'll kill you!" Harrison shouted again, this time his words partially choked by the wild gyrations that he and McClure had locked themselves into.

"Stop! Both of you!" Olga staggered to her feet, then backward against the wall as she watched in horror as the two men continued their violent struggle. Their arms and legs kicked and flew in all directions and their bodies rolled back and forth several times across the small wardroom table before they finally fell, locked together, heavily to the floor. But somehow Harrison had gotten the advantage and had pushed his body on top of McClure's. Harrison then began to pound his fist senselessly into McClure's face, shoulders and chest, although the blows were partially deflected because of the awkward angle he was at.

He is a murderer. Without realizing what she was about to do, Olga rushed forward. She held the pearl-handled knife in her extended hand.

The stainless-steel blade of the knife caught Harrison squarely in the back, less than an inch to the left of his spine. The long blade buried itself quickly through his flesh and, before Olga became aware of what she had done, it had sliced the man's heart nearly in two. Harrison went limp instantly, his arms and legs sprawling out across McClure's body.

"God Almighty! What happened?!" Zindell stood at the entrance to the wardroom. He looked down at the two bodies on the floor. Even as he watched, a torrent of blood began to flow from the hole around the imbedded blade of the pearl-handled knife stuck in the middle of Harrison's back. "What happened, for God's sake?"

"Nothing." McClure shoved the inert body off him and rolled to his feet. He took a few deep breaths, then turned to face Zindell again. "A difference of opinion."

"What?" Zindell looked at McClure incredulously, then back at the body sprawled on the floor.

"A difference of opinion, that's all." McClure also glanced down at Harrison's body. He then looked up at Olga. She stood a few feet away, her mouth still open, her arms hanging slack at her sides. "Your executive officer here," McClure said as he gestured toward Harrison's body, "had decided that he wanted me to die." McClure began to rebutton his shirt and to brush the dirt off his pants. "But I'm happy to report that your third in command wanted me to live." McClure flashed a big smile at Olga, then stepped over Harrison's body as if it weren't even there. "The only thing I can figure," McClure said as he stepped out of the wardroom and turned to walk down the stretch of corridor that led to the center of the submarine, "is that she figures that I'll be a good man to have around."

_18_

THEY MOVED CAREFULLY up the winding passageways with Paul Talbot securely strapped to the stretcher. He had opened his eyes a few times and had moaned once or twice, but other than those few indications his body appeared ominously lifeless.

"Do you think he'll make it?" Janet Holbrook asked after she had let the men carrying the stretcher get far enough ahead to guarantee that Talbot would be out of earshot.

"Can't say. Not for sure." The ever-present smile on Benny Randolf's round and puffy face had faded. He fidgeted with his bow tie, then looked back to where Janet stood. "I know a little first aid, that's all. His injuries are way out of my league."

"Take a guess." Drew O'Brien put his hand on Benny's shoulder. "I heard you say that you've seen wounds like that during the war."

"That was forty years ago." Benny shrugged. He knew that he was evading the issue because he didn't want to say what he already suspected. "Not good," he finally added after a long silence. "The fact of the matter is that everyone I saw with wounds like that eventually died."

"Damn." O'Brien began to walk up the corridor slowly. The others followed. He had nearly reached the base of the next set of steps when James Westcott rushed down the steps toward him.

"I told you this would happen," Westcott said, out of breath. "We were lucky as hell that no one else got hurt."

"Yes, we were. Lucky as hell." O'Brien tried to turn away and climb the stairs, but Westcott stepped in front of him.

"That answer is not good enough. You've got to do something to prevent anything else from happening." Westcott swept his arm around him in a gesture meant to point at the knot of passengers who milled around the *Yorktown*'s corridors. They were working their way back to the hangar deck, as O'Brien had instructed them to. "I hear them talking. They don't know when they're well off. They want to try to start the ship's engines again in a half-baked idea of trying to ram the submarine. Some of them want to try to launch an attack on that submarine with a small boat. It's all crazy." Westcott wrinkled his nose in a gesture of deep disapproval. "We've got control of the ship, that should be enough." *If we launch an attack, the defense attorneys will call it an act of provocation and recklessness. Then I'll have an uphill battle in court.* "You've got to stop that sort of talk."

"If we left it up to you, we'd still be locked in the hangar bay and be at the mercy of that gang of madmen. Is that what you want?" Janet surprised herself by coming forward and speaking before O'Brien had answered, but she couldn't help herself from doing it. For the first time in her life she felt an urge that translated to mean that, if she were bigger and stronger, she would have taken a swing at the obnoxious man in front of her. "Is that what you want?" Janet repeated scornfully.

"Don't get flippant with me, young lady." Westcott turned from her and faced O'Brien again. "The point is, if you had followed my advice that old man would still be unharmed."

"But not for long." Nat Grisby walked slowly down the stairway to join the other three at the base of the corridor. When he reached the spot where they were, Grisby turned and glared openly at Westcott. "I thought attorneys knew enough to wait until all the evidence was in before they came to a verdict."

"Now wait a damned . . ."

"What's up?" O'Brien asked as he interrupted Westcott's objection. He pointed up the stairwell where the group carrying the stretcher had disappeared.

"A great deal." Grisby edged forward, then positioned his body in such a way that he spoke with his back facing Westcott. "The old man came around long enough to tell me a few things. Before he released the boiler steam to do away with that fellow he called Yang, he had evidently confirmed again the fact that the terrorists intend to kill us at dawn whether or not they received the ransom payment."

"You can't believe what the old man says, he's delirious." Westcott rocked back and forth on his heels, as if he were standing in front of a courtroom bench addressing a judge and a jury.

"The old man was perfectly rational." Grisby ran his fingers through his bushy beard, then turned back away from the attorney again. "As we already knew, the airliner was carrying a great deal of gold in its cargo compartment. The terrorists have that gold onboard their submarine, which is sitting several hundred yards to our left." Grisby gestured toward the blank gray steel wall of the ship's corridor, as if the submarine would be plainly visible in that direction. "At dawn, they intend to sink the *Yorktown* as they begin their escape, just like the old man told us when he first came to us."

"Yes." O'Brien rubbed his hand nervously along the edge of the stair handrail. "I've been thinking about that. At first, I didn't believe him either—but now I do. We have to assume that the terrorists are serious about sinking us at dawn because, either way, they would win."

"Why do you say that?" Janet asked.

"Because it makes sense, in a perverted sort of way. They come out of this with either twenty-five million or thirty-five million, depending on whether or not the ransom is paid. The twenty-five million is probably enough to satisfy them, so the extra ten million is overtime pay. Besides, for all they know of the current situation, some of the men we overpowered might still be alive. If they left us free and those men were turned over to the authorities, they would probably know a great deal about the people onboard the submarine—more than the people on the submarine want anyone to know."

"I told you we shouldn't do this!" Westcott kicked his foot loudly against the side of the staircase. "We've captured their people, so now they'll need to kill us!" He didn't believe that line of reasoning for a minute since his own courtroom experiences had convinced him that criminals were big talkers and little else—nothing but brainless buffoons with big mouths.

"Shut up, for Christ's sake." Grisby shook his hand threateningly at the attorney. "You don't know what you're talking about. According to the old man, the terrorists were going to kill us anyway."

"They wouldn't," Westcott retorted.

Grisby frowned at the attorney, then turned away. "But the big news," he began again as he faced O'Brien, "is that the old man . . ."

"Talbot."

". . . yes, Talbot, he says that he's got an idea for our escape. It's our only chance, he says."

"What is it?" O'Brien stepped toward Grisby. He could feel the press of Janet's body behind him as she, too, moved closer.

"He's very weak. I told him to wait, to save his strength until I got you over to listen."

"Let's go." O'Brien led the procession by taking the steps ahead of him two at a time. He turned quickly down the new corridor, just in time to see the men carrying the stretcher work their way through the hatchway that led to the hangar deck. In just a few seconds more O'Brien had joined up with them. He motioned for the men carrying it to put the stretcher down on the hangar deck floor. He knelt beside Paul Talbot. "Can you hear me?" O'Brien asked in a low, steady voice as he placed his hand gently against the old man's arm.

Talbot slowly opened his eyes. For several seconds he looked up at the man who hovered over him before he began to speak. "Yes," he finally said in a low, thin voice. "I hear you—we have almost no time left."

"I know. What's your plan?"

"There." Talbot picked his arm off the stretcher and, with a trembling hand, pointed toward the rear of the hangar bay toward the B-25. "That's a real airplane . . . not an exhibit. It was donated two years ago. They flew it into Charleston. We hoisted it on a barge to bring it to the *Yorktown*." Talbot laid his arm back down. He coughed once, the sound of the fluid in his lungs now unmistakable. "Engines are real . . . all we did was drain the fluids." Talbot closed his eyes for a few seconds, then opened them up again. "We have gasoline and oil in the storage tanks beneath the workshop . . . you can clean the plugs . . . put in a battery from the tractor . . . it should be able to fly."

"We'll never get everyone into that thing!" Westcott had shouted out his interruption so quickly that most of the crowd had missed the old man's last few words. "I, for one, do not want to entertain any idea that benefits only a handful of us," Westcott added as he addressed the crowd that had circled around where the old man lay on the stretcher. "It's crazy. Totally crazy." Westcott turned away, as if his words had been the closing argument on the discussion. Several of the passengers began to agree with Westcott as they looked first at the old man on the stretcher, then across the hangar bay toward the World War II twin-engine bomber.

"Too small to carry us," the man next to Westcott said. "No good."

"It's also too big to get off the carrier. It's a land-based bomber," another man from the group chimed in.

"Wait." O'Brien held up his hand for silence. The murmur of the crowd died away. "He's trying to say something else." Except for the sounds of the old man's labored breathing, the entire hangar bay had become silent again.

"Not true . . . it can fly . . . from the *Yorktown*." A sudden attack of coughing seized Talbot and it caused him to rock his head back and forth.

"Lie back. We'll talk later." O'Brien shook his head in sympathy as he tried to soothe Talbot. He reached down to readjust the blanket that lay across him.

"Is there any chance that it might work?" Even as he asked, Grisby looked skeptical.

"No," O'Brien said.

"That's what I figured."

"You figured right." O'Brien sighed with resignation, he had hoped that something in the old man's idea would be useful. "Even if we managed to get the B-25 to be flyable again—a job that, in itself, might be possible—we couldn't get more than a dozen people into it." O'Brien scanned the faces of those who stood around him. "We've either got to do something as a group or not at all. We can't spend time on a plan to get only a small percentage of the people to safety. It stands to reason that as soon as we flew off the deck, that would be the submarine's signal to sink the *Yorktown* and begin its escape. That would mean certain death to everyone we left behind." O'Brien heard the startled murmurs from the assembled group, but he had no intention of lying to them. They had gone too far together to be given anything but the hard truth.

"Don't forget that it's a land-based bomber," Westcott announced to seal the vote against the old man's plan. "I know for a fact that it wasn't meant to operate off an aircraft carrier."

"That's typical of what you know," Nat Grisby said curtly. "You're wrong again."

"What?"

"One of the most famous attacks of World War II was flown with B-25's—and off an aircraft carrier of the same class and size as this ship."

"I find that difficult to believe."

"The Doolittle raid on Japan. *Thirty Seconds Over Tokyo,* or haven't you heard of it? They launched from the carrier *Hornet*—which happened to be the *Yorktown*'s sister-ship." Grisby waved his hand toward the B-25. "Anyone who's old enough would remember that, or at least they should." Grisby watched as the older people in the crowd began to slowly murmur their recognition of the truth in what he had said. "If we got that airplane to run, we could get it off this ship. At least I think so. What do you say, Captain?"

O'Brien rose to his feet. He turned and looked at the B-25. "Probably." He knew that two years of dry storage would do nothing harmful to an airplane, that the machine should still be flyable. "We'd need to push the airliner overboard first to clear the deck, but that wouldn't be too much of a problem if we use the onboard tractor." Yet even while he spoke, O'Brien had begun to shake his head negatively. "But like I said before, the B-25 does us no good. We can't escape in an airplane far too small to do the job."

"What about the airliner—any chance of using it again?"

"Absolutely impossible." O'Brien looked up at the over-weight, middle-aged man at the rear of the group who had asked the question. "For several reasons. The landing gear is broken away and, from what I recall, I think the left wing is cracked at the root. Even if the airliner weren't severely damaged, a jet that size couldn't get half of its required takeoff speed before running off the deck."

"Oh." The man who had asked the question looked down at the decking plates, embarrassed.

"But it was a good question," O'Brien added. He didn't want them to hold back ideas, no matter how silly they might sound. "Keep trying, maybe there will be something else we'll come up with."

"Listen to me . . . please . . ." Talbot had forced himself to open his eyes and focus on the pilot. He gestured weakly for the man to come nearer to him. When he had, Talbot raised himself slightly on one arm and, after coughing once to clear the mounting taste of bile from his throat, attempted to muster enough to say what was on his mind. "Not for flying people off . . . to attack . . . everything in here is real." Talbot gestured feebly around the hangar bay, toward the exhibit of torpedoes. "Build one torpedo from parts of the others . . . attack the submarine . . . before they shoot."

"But we have no explosives. None of these torpedoes have any live explosives in their warheads." O'Brien kept his ear close to the old man's lips so he could hear his way out of that unsolvable dilemma, even though he knew there wouldn't be one. Putting together one usable torpedo from all the old relics on the hangar floor might be possible, but it wouldn't mean a damn thing without an explosive tip on it—something that an exhibit ship obviously wouldn't have onboard. Launching a non-explosive torpedo at the submarine would be the equivalent of throwing a pebble at an elephant.

Paul Talbot lay perfectly still for what seemed an eternity. Twice he opened his eyes slightly, but the pain and the fatigue from his wounds caused him both times to close his eyes again before he could speak. His head seemed to swim in giant, lopsided circles. The burning in his stomach was almost more than he could bear. But finally the sensations backed away long enough for him to open his eyes again. "Explosives." He had said that one word clearly. "You had them... Yang put them... somewhere..." Talbot's head fell back to the stretcher before he could add any more.

"We had them?" O'Brien stood up, puzzled. He turned to the others. "Does anyone know what he means?"

"I think he's delirious," Westcott hurried to add.

"I hate to admit it, but I think that for the first time I have to agree with the attorney." Nat Grisby glanced over his shoulder at the gloating smirk on Westcott's face, then back at O'Brien. "The old man isn't making sense anymore."

"You're wrong—he's making a great deal of sense." Janet Holbrook stepped up to where O'Brien hovered over Talbot. "Don't you see what he's saying?" She had begun to talk excitedly. "The explosives that the terrorists had planted on the airliner—they must have taken them off and hidden them somewhere on this ship!" Janet waved her hands in a widening circle. "Somewhere onboard the *Yorktown* is that last ingredient we need! We've got a bomber that flew as recently as two years ago, a stack of old torpedoes that we can combine to make one functional torpedo—and now some explosives to put inside!"

"But if they hid the explosives, we'll never find them. This is an enormous ship, and we've only got until dawn."

"That should be more than enough time." The man who spoke the line was one of the passengers. He stepped into the center of the group. Trailing a few feet behind him was his ten-year-old son—and the boy's dog. "Aquarius is a retriever. A damned good one." The man pointed to where the golden-colored dog sat on the floor at the boy's feet, her tail wagging slowly back and forth in a steady, rhythmic beat. "Michael and I trained her to do just the kinda' thing you're talkin' about."

"The dog can find the explosives?" Janet asked.

"Right." The man motioned for the dog, and it obediently rose to its feet and walked slowly toward him. "All we need is a sample of what we're huntin' for. Aquarius can sniff it out easy."

"I'm not so sure," Westcott said in a loud voice from the far side of the group he had moved to. "This isn't a duck hunt. A dog might not be any good at it."

"That's not true." O'Brien faced Westcott directly. "You're

probably not aware of this, but security people at most airports use trained dogs for precisely that purpose—to comb a bomb-threat area for explosives."

"Great. Then the odor of the explosives should be strong enough for Aquarius. She'll be able to tell if there's any in a room as soon as she goes in." The man reached down and patted the dog on the head, an act which caused her tail to begin to slowly wag again.

"We can take her to the airliner. We can let her smell the galley area where the first explosion occurred. That should give her the scent," Nat Grisby added.

"It sure would." The man turned to O'Brien. "What do you say, give it a try?"

"Absolutely." O'Brien rubbed his hands together enthusiastically. At long last they seemed to be getting somewhere. "Take half a dozen people with you. Do a patterned search, beginning at the forward end of the ship. It stands to reason that they'd put the explosives up forward to keep them as far from us as possible."

"Will do." The man snapped his fingers and the dog rose to its feet again, then began to follow him and the young boy as they walked rapidly across the hangar bay. On the way, the man picked several others from the dozens of volunteers that he passed.

"The rest of you, give me your attention," O'Brien announced after he was satisfied that the explosives-hunting group was headed in the right direction. "Let's get a few more assignments out. These are the working groups we'll need, so I want you people to decide for yourselves which ones you're best suited for." O'Brien scanned the faces of the men, women and children around him. For the first time in a long while he thought he could see a spark of genuine hope in their eyes. "To work on the B-25, we'll need people who know mechanics. If you're good with your hands and understand machines, gather over by the airplane." O'Brien watched as, one by one, twenty or so of the people on the floor hurried over to where the historic bomber sat in the hangar bay.

"Looks like we got a good number of mechanics," Grisby said with a relieved smile.

"Yes. That should be enough, as long as nothing is broken

beyond repair." O'Brien hated himself for bringing up a negative factor, but he was trying to cover all bases. "Now, what else do we need?"

"Volunteers to get the airliner off the flight deck." Grisby looked around the group. He nodded toward the people who raised their hands. "That should be enough. Meet up on the flight deck above us—I'll be there in a minute."

Benny Randolf stepped into the inner circle and walked up to O'Brien. "I think the hardest job is going to be the assembling of the torpedo." Benny turned half-around to face the crowd. "I've got a little background with torpedoes from World War II, but I'm sure going to need help from knowledgeable people." Benny waited several seconds, but none of the remaining passengers raised their hands to volunteer to join him. "Come on, let's go, I need straight men for this act," he said in a singsong voice as he shuffled his feet in the opening steps of a comic dance. "Who wants to participate in our version of the torpedo follies?" Several people began to laugh. "This is no time for stage fright," Benny added with a smile. "If you've got mechanical knowledge, come over to my group—we'll be gathering together near that collection of torpedoes at the far end of the hangar."

"Please excuse me, but your torpedoes were very much different than ours," Takeo Kusaka said as he stepped up from the pack of passengers still left in the center of the hangar bay. The elderly Japanese man bowed slightly toward Benny. "If you will be kind enough to indulge my ignorance, I would be most pleased to assist in whatever way I might."

"Great." Benny put his arm on Kusaka's shoulder. The two of them began to head for the group of display torpedoes on the far end of the hangar. By the time they had gone no more than thirty feet, a couple of dozen other men and women had decided to join them.

"What about him?" Janet asked O'Brien in a low voice. She pointed to Talbot, his body motionless on the stretcher, his eyes tightly shut.

"We should get him out of here." O'Brien could easily read the pained expression on the old man's face. "Too noisy, too much activity around him."

"I'll pick a group to take care of it." Janet gestured toward several women who were standing close by. "Where do you want him?" she asked as the women came up to take charge of the critically wounded man on the stretcher.

"It doesn't make any difference. Someplace quiet. Out of the way—but someplace where the people with him can see what's going on." O'Brien thought it over for a few seconds. "Bring him up to the ship's bridge," he said to the group of women who had gathered around the stretcher. "He said earlier that he had been on the bridge when we landed. It should be relatively comfortable up there—and you'll be able to see what's happening." O'Brien knew that when the action began there would be no time left to retrieve anyone from the bowels of the ship. But he decided to cut his remarks off at that point since there was no need to get too graphic about the horrible possibilities that could lay ahead for them. "Any questions?" They had none, and he and Janet stood silently as the women picked up the stretcher and took Paul Talbot off in the direction that would lead to the *Yorktown*'s bridge.

"Wait." James Westcott stepped out from behind the few people who still remained in the center of the hangar bay. "I have one question."

"What?" O'Brien waited patiently for the question, knowing full well it would be something he didn't want to hear.

"My question is, who, exactly, has designated you as our sole boss?"

"The airline." O'Brien looked Westcott squarely in the eye. "The flight you purchased a ticket on was under my command. By extension, the problems that have come from that flight are still my responsibility."

"I'm glad that you see it that way." Westcott took a pad out of his coat pocket and scribbled a quick note. "Your admission to responsibility—liability, actually—is a point worth making a note of. I'm only sorry that you didn't use more prudence in allowing those passengers," Westcott continued as he waved toward where Benny and the others hovered over the display torpedoes across the room, "to talk you into a senseless, dangerous course of action."

"I'm sorry you feel that way," O'Brien answered coldly.

"I do." As he spoke, Westcott noticed that the young Japanese man who stood on the periphery of the group a few dozen feet away was motioning discreetly to catch his attention. That young fellow was, as Westcott recalled, the assistant to the older Japanese man who had made that silly speech about perseverance a few hours before. Westcott turned back to O'Brien. "But I can see that nothing I say makes a damned bit of difference to you."

"I'm taking all factors into account before I make any decisions," O'Brien replied.

"Clever of you to say that, but we both know that it isn't true." Westcott continued to drone on to O'Brien, but his real attention was now focused on the young Japanese assistant. He hoped that this man wasn't foolish enough to ask him to help with their ridiculous torpedo project. The man gestured once more, then began to walk toward a hatchway on the other side of the hangar bay. "From this point on, I'll simply stand aside and watch you as you continue to jeopardize our hard-won safety." Without waiting for a reply, Westcott marched away from O'Brien and directly toward where the young Japanese man stood, alone, by the far hatchway.

"I bet he's a very successful lawyer," Janet said after the attorney had walked away. The tone of her voice left no doubt that she wasn't paying him a compliment.

"Forget him." O'Brien looked up at the B-25. "I'm going to climb inside the cockpit. I want to see if I can figure out how to fly it."

"Do you think it'll be very difficult?" The two of them began to walk toward the nose of the World War II bomber. "It looks like a vicious sort of airplane," Janet said. "Especially when I compare it to the little Pipers I usually fly."

"I hear that a B-25 can be a real tiger," O'Brien answered. "But I've flown a number of similar-sized airplanes in my career. I imagine I'll be able to keep it in tow."

"I look forward to watching you do it." Janet eyed him carefully, to see if he had picked up on her meaning. Obviously, he had not. "You'll need a copilot. I'm going with you," she blurted out after she could figure out no other way to approach the subject.

"No."

"Yes."

"It's too dangerous."

"Then it's too dangerous for you." Janet stopped beside him. "It's not any less dangerous being aboard the *Yorktown*— not if they torpedo it."

"They might not. You never can tell." O'Brien shuffled his feet nervously.

"Cut out that line of garbage. You and I both know that you're lying."

"Yes, I am." O'Brien ran his tongue across his dry lips. If this were any other time and place, he would have sorely wanted her company. In the short time he had known her, Janet seemed to be everything that most of the women he had met in his life had not been. But now was not the time—and this was certainly not the place. "I can fly it by myself. There's no need to have you with me." Against his better judgment, O'Brien found himself reaching out and placing his hand on her arm.

"That's where you're wrong." Janet motioned to the B-25, its flat-sided nose section only a few feet from where the two of them stood. "Except for our attorney friend, we all seem to agree that this torpedo attack might be our last chance. Our only chance."

"Yes, but . . ."

"So if it's our only chance, we've got to make it as complete a chance as we can." Janet took O'Brien's hand off her arm, but she continued to hold his fingers in hers. "Anything could happen. A stray bullet." She squeezed his fingers as she spoke. "But if you . . . fell unconscious," she said, half-choking on the words, unable to phrase it any other way, "then there would be no one left to fly the airplane, no one left to finish the attack. I might be able to do it—at least I'd have a chance."

"Are you sure?" O'Brien stepped closer to her, even more aware now of the tiny freckles on her cheeks, the richness of her smile, the gentle lines of her neck. "It's not going to be pleasant."

"Believe me, I know that." Janet laughed once, then looked back at his eyes. "I'm scared to death. That probably means that I realize how dangerous this really is. I can hardly keep my stomach down. But the bottom line is that if some-thing . . . happened to you . . . then I might be able to finish the job. Everyone else in the group is doing what they can. I'm the only other pilot, even if I am a rank amateur. But my qualifications to be your copilot are far better than anyone else's in the group. I need to do my share."

O'Brien stood silently for several long seconds, his eyes roving over the drab fuselage of the old B-25. Finally, he turned back to Janet. "Okay," he said in a flat, emotionless voice. His forced tone was an effort to obscure how very much concerned he was over this decision, no matter how logical and inescapable it might have been. "Okay," Drew O'Brien said again. "You and I will fly the attack together."

Shojiro Ichiki was not certain that the thing he was about to do was correct, but he was certain that it did indeed need to be done. As the American attorney walked up to him from across the hangar bay floor, Ichiki motioned to indicate that the man must remain silent but that he should follow. Ichiki turned and led the way into the interior of the *Yorktown*. In less than a minute they had reached a passageway that led below, and Ichiki began to descend the staircase.

"Wait." Westcott had called out in something between a whisper and a shout. "Where are you taking me? What's this all about?"

"Very soon. My English much limited. I must show you."

"Tell me first, there's no one around." Westcott scanned the gray, shadowy corridor that they stood in just to be sure. It remained empty.

"Too complex. But I agree, you are right. I will show you." Ichiki did not wait for the American's reply, but instead began to march down one passageway and then another, until they were on a lower deck three levels below the hangar bay.

"This has gone far enough. I'm not moving another damn inch until you give me an idea what this is about." Westcott stood his ground at the base of the stairs that they had just descended, even though the young Japanese man had continued to move quickly down the corridor ahead.

"Almost there." Ichiki waved his hand in rapid motions. "Much worth the walk."

"Where are we going, for chrissake!"

"To print shop. Very interesting information, you will enjoy very much." Ichiki turned and began to walk again, although he took the precaution to peek over his shoulder a few seconds later to verify that the American had followed. He had. After they had gone another hundred feet down the dimly lit corridor that led toward the *Yorktown*'s bow, Ichiki stepped across the sill of the hatchway he had been looking for. "We are here."

"It's about damned time, I'll tell you that." Westcott stepped into the room quickly. "Now, what's this all about?"

"Do not move. I have gun."

It took Westcott a few seconds before he realized what the young Japanese man had said, and a few more seconds to verify the fact by looking down at the man's hand. Even in the low level of light that came from the single lightbulb in the corridor, the outline of the dark-metal pistol could be seen in the man's grip. "What's the meaning of this? Put that damned thing down. Where did you get it?" Westcott took one step forward, as if he intended to take the weapon from the Japanese man.

Ichiki raised the pistol. "I do not want to kill you, but I will if the need arises. Stand quietly."

Westcott froze in position. Blood began to rush to his stomach and for an instant he felt as if he might faint. In all his years of dealing with and defending criminals, he had never been on this end of a weapon. "What do you want from me? They've already taken my money." Westcott made a tentative motion toward where his wallet had been before the terrorists had robbed him, but a slight movement from the barrel of the pistol stopped him.

"I will answer your question," Ichiki said. "I found this weapon on the dead body of the one terrorist I was instructed to search. I kept the weapon for myself, for solely this purpose."

"But what do you want from me?" Westcott repeated, his voice now pleading.

"You are a poison to the group. I have watched and listened while you have nearly changed the minds of too many of our good people. It is dangerous to leave you up there," Ichiki said as he gestured to the corridor down which they had come from the hangar bay.

"Don't be ridiculous."

"It is you who takes the meanings of things until they have become ridiculous. When my company's president, Mr. Kusaka, spoke against you hours before, what he had said was much true, yet you gave him no acknowledgment of that. It was then that I understood how dangerous you might become to our group."

"This is nonsense. I've done nothing except point out the facts." While he spoke, Westcott continued to watch the barrel of the pistol. A few times the idea of rushing the young Japanese man crossed his mind, but his own deep-seated fear allowed that impulse to slide away before it had developed into a conscious plan.

"The courage of the group of passengers from our airline flight is no more than a thin covering over the raw element of our own fear." Ichiki spoke clearly and distinctly, his words reverberating off the enclosed space they stood in. "You can, with the sharp tool of your words learned for that purpose in your American law schools, scratch too deeply our covering of courage. That will leave us exposed. I cannot allow that."

"You're going to kill me?" Westcott could hardly believe that those words had come out of his own mouth, yet the evidence of the pistol aimed at him was more than enough to show their validity. "Don't do it. Please."

"I will not kill you—unless you are foolish enough to attempt to overpower me." Ichiki wondered for a moment what he would do if the man lunged toward him, since he had already emptied the bullets from the gun and left them hidden in the far corner of the hangar bay. Ichiki had done that to prevent any accidents, to prevent an accidental killing of either himself or the American attorney if there would have been a struggle between them. So far, his plan to remove this man from the hangar bay had worked very well, the bluff had worked. "Behind you is the room that we have been in search for."

"What room?" Westcott spun around and read the stenciled labeling above the hatchway. His heart sank.

"Yes. The jail of the ship, which is marked as *brig*. There are five individual cells inside. Please step into one of them." Ichiki motioned with the unloaded pistol and was pleased to see that the American attorney had begun to step forward in compliance. "I will lock you in. Then I will sit out here with the key. If we are struck by a torpedo, I will immediately unlock you."

"Why are you doing this to me?" Westcott's voice was

quivering. He stepped inside the barred door of the first cell and watched as the Japanese man swung the lock shut.

"I know nothing of torpedoes or airplanes," Ichiki answered as he pulled up a chair and sat himself down across from the prison cell, the key to the cell in his hand. "But I do know of people and of courage. At this moment the people in our group are working very hard to complete their plan. This will be my contribution in the hope that our group will be successful in the fight for our lives."

19

FROM WHERE HE lay on the bunk in the captain's sea cabin of the bridge of the *Yorktown*, Paul Talbot could see the helmsman's steering controls. The brass wheel rocked gently back and forth in random motions, which signified that the power for the ship's steering had earlier been shut off. Without engine power to propel them through the water, there was no need for them to steer the ship. Talbot kept his eyes on that wheel for as long as he could, until the pain from his wounds became so severe that he had no choice but to close his eyes again.

"Are you all right?"

Talbot forced open his eyes. He looked up at the woman who hovered over him—one of the group of passengers who had brought him up to the bridge and now attempted to nurse him. "Yes," Talbot said in a weak voice. He attempted to smile, but that was too much of an effort for him.

"Lie quietly. I've sent someone down to the airliner to get more first-aid kits. We should be able to find more medication to ease your pain."

Talbot nodded his appreciation. Although she was far younger, she had the same kind, generous face as Charlotte.

It was that same benevolent expression that their daughter Amy had inherited from her mother. Talbot gestured for the woman to lean closer to him. "Please . . . promise me . . . you'll leave the bridge . . . if there's trouble. All of you."

"Don't worry. We know what we're doing." The woman carefully adjusted the blanket around the old man's body. "Just lie quietly."

Talbot began to pick his body up slightly, as if he were about to get up from the bed. But before he had raised himself more than a few inches, he began to cough. The deep sound from his fluid-filled lungs echoed through the small space of the *Yorktown's* bridge.

"Lie down. Try to relax." The woman, who had been joined by two others from the rear of the bridge, gently maneuvered Talbot back onto the captain's bunk.

"No. Wait." Talbot coughed again, the pain from his movements causing him to close his eyes in agony. After a few seconds, he managed to open his eyes again. "Can't lie. No more. Hard to breathe. Need to sit up . . ." Talbot ended his short sentence with another fit of coughing, this one louder and longer than the last.

"No." The woman tried to lay him back down again.

"Maybe we should let him sit up." The second woman looked down at Talbot's pain-wracked face. "I think I read somewhere that it's better to sit upright. To drain the fluids from the lungs."

"Are you sure?"

"No." The first woman looked down at Talbot, then shook her head. "I'm guessing. I wish I knew more than elementary first aid."

"Please. Let me sit up. In there." Talbot pointed feebly toward the corner of the bridge, the area surrounded by rows of black windows that displayed the impenetrable darkness outside.

"He means that chair in the corner." Both women looked out to where the upholstered captain's swivel chair sat on the left side of the ship's bridge. "We should let him do what he wants," the first woman finally said.

"You're right. Maybe he knows what's best. It might help."

"It might. Let me get the others." The second woman stepped

out of the captain's sea cabin and came back quickly with several of the other women from their group. "Gently, now. Everyone grab hold—we're going to move him to the chair so he can sit upright." Without another word the woman picked Talbot up and carried him to the captain's chair on the bridge as carefully as they could.

The pain from the movement was so severe that several times Talbot thought he might black out. *Hold on, stay conscious. I've got to see this through.* Although he did think that it might help his breathing somewhat to sit upright, Talbot's actual reason for wanting to be moved was to make it possible for him to see the flight deck, to see if the plan he had given the hostages stood any chance of success. *My fault, all of this. Please, God, let them get out of this alive.*

"Careful. Use the blanket to keep him upright." The woman placed Talbot on the captain's chair of the *Yorktown*, then tucked the blanket around him so he would be in no danger of falling off.

Talbot, who had kept his eyes closed as they maneuvered him to the chair, began to listen to the sounds of his own heartbeat. His heartbeat had grown louder for awhile, but soon it had quieted down. Now, it seemed faint, irregular. Talbot opened his eyes. "What time is it?" he asked the woman who stood closest to him.

"Quarter after four. It'll be dawn in less than an hour."

Talbot nodded, then glanced at the sterile blackness out the window. After a few seconds of looking blankly straight ahead, Talbot turned his attention below, to the scene on the *Yorktown*'s flight deck.

Faint outlines of the airliner's wings and fuselage were barely visible from the small amount of light that poured out of several of the opened hatchways. Dozens of people swarmed everywhere on the deck, and the chugging noises of a tractor floated up through a mix of voices. Everyone sounded calm, professional, matter-of-fact. Beyond the far edge of the deck, nothing at all—not the submarine, not even the surface of the ocean itself—was visible, and that added ominously to its menacing feeling. Still, the activity on the flight deck was reassuring. From what Talbot could tell, the effort to clear the disabled airliner off the *Yorktown* was going very well.

"We've just received word from below that the B-25 appears to be in flyable condition," the first woman said as she leaned closer to Talbot. She spoke in a soothing, hushed voice. "The torpedoes, too, are proving to be less trouble than they first thought. The man in charge said he expected to have one ready to use by dawn." The woman could easily see from the old man's expression that these were the subjects his thoughts were on.

"Explosives." The word had come across Talbot's dry lips with an awkward sound to it because of the bile lodged in his throat. "The dog."

"Yes. You were asleep at the time. Aquarius found the hidden explosives that had been taken off the airliner. They were in a room in the forward part of the ship."

This time, Talbot managed a small smile before he began to cough again. There was, he could taste, something else in his throat now—blood, perhaps. He tried to put that thought out of his mind—except that this time he began to experience some difficulty in keeping his thoughts from becoming muddled. *Dog. My blood.* "They're out there—I know it," Talbot suddenly said, the outstretched finger of one hand pointed at the black void to the port side of the ship.

"Yes. We know."

"Bastards." Out of exhaustion, Talbot's head fell back against the chair. "They're still out there." *Yang and McClure.* "Got to stop them."

"We will," the woman answered in a calm, neutral voice. She knew that the old man had begun to hallucinate again— as he had so often during the last few hours.

"Bastards." *They lied to me.* Talbot coughed once, then his body trembled with a spasm. "We've got to stop them," he muttered, his voice now unintelligible. *Stop them. They lied to me. Got to. Before they kill. Killed. Keith and Thomas.* At the thought of his grandson's names Talbot felt his chest begin to constrict. His eyes, even though they had already been shut, had begun to ache from deep inside.

"Just relax," the woman who hovered over him said in a voice nearly too low to be heard. "We'll be very quiet now. You should sleep." The woman motioned to the others who stood on the *Yorktown*'s bridge. One by one, the assembled group began to walk toward the hatchway that led to the gallery ledge outside. As they passed Talbot, a few of them reached up and touched him gently on the shoulder or arm, as a gesture meant to indicate that they would be nearby. But every one of them knew that there was nothing they could do for this gravely injured old man—nothing anyone could do.

Keith. Thomas. Amy. Paul Talbot opened his eyes slowly. He faced the black window glass of the bridge for a full minute before he found the energy to speak. "Amy . . . on my birthday," Talbot rambled, ". . . last year . . . Keith and Thomas . . ." Talbot sat himself further upright, using what little strength he still possessed. "Amy . . . gave that to me . . ." Talbot pointed toward the tape player that he had put on the ledge near the captain's chair.

The woman who stood nearest to Talbot wiped away the flood of tears that crossed down her cheek. She looked at Talbot's face—it was covered with perspiration. His thinning gray hair was also laced with rivulets of moisture. That moisture ran down the deep crevices of his neck and disappeared behind his shirt collar. The woman cleared her throat, then spoke. "Do you want me to play it? To turn the tape player on for you?" she asked, her lips close to the old man's ear, her hand resting on his shoulder. She didn't know what else to do. She could see the sudden change in his appearance the last few minutes— the drawn-down and glassy look to his eyes, the increasingly yellowish-white cast to his skin.

"Yes. Birthday. My Amy . . . turn it on."

The woman leaned forward and pressed the button. She then turned and walked a few steps away before the first sounds of the music began to come out of the tape player on the shelf next to Paul Talbot; she could not bear watching him any longer.

The cold blackness of the windows that surrounded the bridge somehow caused the sound of the melancholy piano to resonate even more sharply and hauntingly than it had the first time Talbot had heard it. When Willie Nelson's voice began, the notes that he sang were both thin and, at the same time, extremely rich. The words and the sounds flowed out of him as effortlessly as water being poured from a pitcher. It was the push of every note and phrase from that Willie Nelson recording that caused the old man to go back in time to that one moment he could not get himself past. *Keith. Thomas. God help them. I've killed them.*

Paul Talbot somehow found the strength to sit himself up even higher in the captain's chair on the bridge of the *Yorktown*. He focused as best he could at where the horizon line would meet the surface of the ocean to the east of the ship. Indistinctly, as if it were no more than a black-on-black canvas, he thought he could see the first hints of the early morning gray as it crept slowly up from its hiding-place like some timid animal crawling cautiously out of a dark cave. "Dawn," Talbot mumbled. But his voice was far too weak to be understood.

The music of Willie Nelson continued, its melody lying over Talbot. "September." Talbot's vision was blurred from the pain, from the fatigue, and from the swelling of tears that covered his eyes. *Keith. Thomas. God, please, forgive me. Let them live. Let them all live.*

> *The days dwindle down*
> *To a precious few*
> *September*
> *November*
> *And these few precious days*
> *I'll spend with you*
> *These precious days*
> *I'll spend with you.*

Talbot's hand, which had been raised a few inches off the woolen blanket that he had been carefully wrapped in, dropped down. The beating of his heart, which had become even more irregular during the last few minutes, beat only once more before it stopped completely. The final image that registered in the recesses of his mind was of that last day, more than one year before, when he had walked the deck of the *Yorktown* with his daughter, Amy, and his wife, Charlotte. Holding hands with him—their small fingers wrapped tightly into his, their faces turned attentively and glowingly upward as he pointed out the sights to them—were Paul Talbot's grandsons, Keith and Thomas. The boys' faces appeared the way Talbot would remember them last. The way he would remember them always.

• • •

Jerome Zindell stood on the dark bridge of the U.S.S. *Trout*. The submarine rocked gently on the surface in the diminishing swells of the sea that they rode on. Zindell could see that, as forecast, the weather had improved rapidly. By mid-morning, at the very latest, the skies would be clear. Then the warm sun would give them yet another advantage. "The weather is in our favor. By noon, it'll be even harder to find us," Zindell said to make conversation with the two others who stood on the cool, damp submarine's bridge with him.

"That so?" Ed McClure leaned against the flat metal sidewall while he continued to stare straight ahead through the blackness. Tiny pinpoints of light several hundred yards away were the most obvious indications of the presence of the *Yorktown,* the light evidently coming through opened hatchways that led onto the ship's flight deck. "Why will it be harder to find us?" McClure finally asked with little interest. He did not bother to turn toward Zindell because he did not look forward to another dissertation on submarines. As far as McClure was concerned, if he never saw another of these foul, claustrophobic sewer pipes, that would still be too soon.

"Because the sun will warm the uppermost layer of ocean water. That cap of heat will make anti-submarine sonar gear even less reliable." Zindell forced himself to smile. The fact about the benefits from warming water was a big ace up his sleeve—it was something he had looked forward to telling McClure about. But, curiously, Zindell found no enjoyment in passing on the news. He guessed that it was because he had become too anxious, too nervous to feel anything other than the tensions of the last few hours. "Remember how long the Swedes hunted their own harbor for that mysterious submarine a few years back?" Zindell said, to get back to his point. "It was the varying water temperature that made the difference. That's why the Swedes couldn't find it."

"Exactly. We will get the same help from the water temperature. We will also get help from the noises that come from the sinking of the *Yorktown,*" Olga volunteered as she peered toward the nearly invisible silhouette of the ship. "Because of that combination, the people who hunt for us will never find us."

"Right." Zindell glanced at the woman. She had taken another step to be closer to McClure—the man she had committed murder for a little more than an hour earlier. *Lunatics. They deserve each other*. Zindell would have attempted to add more, to say something placating to both of them—except that at that very moment he had become aware of the growing sound that they had all been waiting for.

"Look." McClure pointed toward the sky. Above the submarine was a single light, far in the distance. McClure grinned, ear to ear. "An airplane. Sounds like a turboprop. A Navy Hercules, I'd guess." He glanced down at his wristwatch. "They're a little late," McClure added nonchalantly, as if he were commenting on the late departure of a commuter train.

"Only five minutes late," Zindell answered automatically. He didn't need to look at his own wristwatch, he had counted each of the passing moments carefully enough to know exactly how late that airplane was. "Here comes the parachute," he said. The second chute that they had insisted on in their last teletype message to the Pentagon—the parachute with the flare hung beneath it—had been dropped a few seconds after the main one. The eerie phosphorous light that came from it lit up the area well enough to make the progress of the main chute plainly visible. That had been their intention.

"They seem to have complied." Olga put her hand on McClure's shoulder. "It is almost over, we have beaten them. All that is left now is for us to pick up the ransom money. Then we can submerge. Disappear."

"Don't forget one thing." McClure pointed straight across the submarine's bow. The outline of the *Yorktown* had become increasingly visible, a combination of the phosphorous glow from the flare as it parachuted down to a point some distance astern of the ship, plus the increasing dull-gray light of the approaching dawn. "First we need to sink the ship. After that, we can pick up the ransom."

"The sinking of the *Yorktown* seems more important to you than the money." Zindell worked hard at trying to keep his comment neutral, but it still came out as too brash, too much of a challenge.

"Maybe it is." McClure scowled. "That factor shouldn't

make a damned difference. My deal with you was that we were going to sink that ship. That's what we're going to do." McClure took his eyes off Zindell just long enough to glance at the enormous shadowy outline of the old warship that rode on the waves. It sat in full broadside view, no more than a few hundred yards away. The thought of sending that giant ship to the bottom was nearly enough to send a shiver of delight through him. It was something that the combined enemy forces of three wars hadn't been able to do—yet Ed McClure was going to accomplish it on his own. It would be the ultimate display of his superior military tactics, if he did say so himself.

"Don't get yourself worked up—I fully intend to sink that ship. Like I said before, we need the acoustical cover to guarantee our escape."

"When in hell are we going to do it?" McClure did not want his own involvement diminished in the eyes of the crew members.

"In a few more minutes. As soon as we get enough daylight to find the ransom buoy without too much hunting." Zindell waved his hand toward the dark sea astern of the giant ship, toward the spot where the parachuted ransom container had splashed into the sea. The second parachute with the flare had dropped near it, but it had already extinguished itself in the water. "Once we send our torpedoes into the *Yorktown*, we'll have only a few more minutes before this place is swarming with antisub aircraft. The noise from the ship as it sinks, plus the warming water, will provide enough cover for us to safely get our asses out of here. But we can't afford to float around the area on a pleasure cruise, we've got to make quick tracks."

"I understand." McClure was about to add something else when a sudden noise in the distance startled him. "What the hell was that?" He wheeled around.

"Look!" Olga stood with her mouth open. She pointed at the sight in front of them. Even in the half-light of pre-dawn, it was obvious that the Trans-American airliner had slid off the flight deck of the *Yorktown* and had fallen to the sea. At that moment only the aircraft's red tail still stuck up out of the water as it continued to sink quickly beneath the waves.

"How could that happen?" Zindell asked. He watched until

the airliner had completely disappeared into the ocean before he turned to McClure. "I don't understand. How could that happen?"

"It must've been closer to the edge than we thought. Maybe Yang is still alive. Maybe the people on the ship strapped his ass in the airliner and sent him deep-six." McClure laughed loudly. "What the hell damned difference does it make? The airliner was going into the water in just a few minutes anyway."

"Yes, but..." Zindell nervously rubbed his hand against the stub of his left arm. He glanced first at the ship, then back at McClure. "It's not right. Something is wrong."

McClure opened his mouth to answer, but before his first words could come out, another new sound drifted across the open water toward them. It was a raspy, grating noise. "Give me the binoculars!" McClure ripped the binoculars out of Olga's hands before she had a chance to hand them over.

McClure focused the binoculars quickly. As he did, he was astonished by what he saw. "This is incredible! How the hell could they manage that!"

"What is it?!" Zindell snatched the binoculars away from McClure. He focused on the aft end of the *Yorktown*. "Damn it!" The grating, gnarling noises were engines. It was an airplane. It was sitting on the aft service elevator. "A medium-sized airplane. Both engines roaring." It was being raised up from the hangar bay to the flight deck on the hydraulically powered elevator. "This is impossible!"

"Wait..." McClure, who had found a second pair of binoculars on the submarine's bridge, focused in again on the aft deck of the *Yorktown*. "It's a B-25, a World War II medium bomber. It's that old display airplane they had onboard. They somehow got it to run."

"Yang must have helped them. He might even be with them. We must stop them." Without binoculars, Olga could not clearly see the aircraft on the *Yorktown*'s deck—but she could easily hear the B-25's engines. They were being revved up. "The airplane sounds ready for takeoff! Do something! Quickly!"

"Fire our goddamned torpedoes, you moron!" McClure flung his binoculars down against the steel deck of the bridge. They shattered into a thousand pieces. "Fire our torpedoes!" he yelled again.

"Yes. I will, yes . . ." Zindell spun himself around. He grabbed for the communications headset that lay on the ledge in front of him and strapped it on. "Control room!" he shouted, far louder than was necessary. "This is the captain—prepare to fire all torpedoes!" Zindell glanced over his shoulder at the ship. The B-25 continued to sit on the aft end of the now-cleared flight deck, its engines running, its nose pointed straight down the deck's centerline.

"Do we need to prepare the torpedoes—is there anything we need to do first?" Olga asked. Her eyes locked onto the scene across the water.

"No. Nothing. Everything is ready." Zindell was thankful that he had the forethought to long ago prepare the torpedoes for firing. All four torpedoes had been adjusted and aimed hours before—all that was necessary now was to have the man in the control room push the master control firing buttons. "Fire the torpedoes!" Zindell shouted into the mouthpiece of the communications headset that hung around his neck. "Numbers one through four! Fire them all. Now!"

20

THE NOISE INSIDE the old war plane was incredibly loud, and several times Janet Holbrook found herself about to take her hands out of her lap and put them up against her ears. What stopped her was the need to be instantly ready to take over the copilot's controls once they were airborne, something that would occur very shortly.

Janet ran her eyes quickly across the flight panel in front of her. The instruments—the ones that were left, there were a number of dishearteningly empty holes in the panel—made sense in a vague sort of way. Once again she tried to convince herself that the B-25 was nothing more than a big and angry version of the small Pipers that she normally flew. Up until this moment, she had talked herself into it. But faced with the archaic and half-scavenged instrument panel of the old military airplane—an aircraft that was nearly fifteen years older than she was—it was hard to keep even the simplest piloting principles in her mind. *Don't worry about anything except the flight controls. They'll be heavy as hell, but they'll work. They'll work just the same as what you're used to.* The thorough preflight briefing that Drew had given her had done a great deal to boost her confidence. But now, with the engines running and revved up to full power, the vibrations and noise had blown her carefully constructed shell of confidence aside as if it had been made out of nothing more than gossamer.

"Ready!" Drew O'Brien had to shout at full voice in order to be heard. He glanced to his right at the young woman who sat in the copilot's seat. She looked bewildered, even frightened. But there was something about the way she held her head, the way she continued to look around the cockpit, that told O'Brien that she would hold on. He was glad as hell that Janet had volunteered to come along with him.

"I'm ready." Janet gestured with her hand as she pointed down the *Yorktown's* empty flight deck. All the people from the handling crew—the men and women who had helped to get the B-25 into its takeoff position—stood to one side, safely out of the way. From that point on, the fate of everyone depended on how well Drew O'Brien could handle the old World War II bomber.

Without another word, O'Brien released the aircraft's brakes. The B-25 lurched forward, its acceleration rapid and reassuring. But the end of the short flight deck loomed not very far ahead, the sudden dropoff to the sea even more alarming because of the height that the carrier's deck rode above the waves. If the airplane didn't have sufficient takeoff speed by the time it reached the edge of the deck, it would fall off nose-first and churn itself into the water. It would then dive beneath the waves very quickly—even quicker than a submarine could. If the B-25 did fall of the edge of the deck, there would be no escaping from the cockpit. In all probability, neither of the people in the cockpit would even know what hit them.

The *Yorktown's* flight deck had already been two-thirds used up by the accelerating B-25 when O'Brien felt the initial beginnings of a positive response from the flight controls he held in his hands. Three-fourths of the way down the deck and he suddenly sensed that the B-25 was nearly ready to fly. With less than twenty-five feet to spare, O'Brien yanked back hard on the flight controls. The aircraft staggered off the *Yorktown*, the far edge of the deck sailing beneath them with just a few inches of clearance for the still-spinning wheels. "Gear up!"

"Gear coming up!" Janet yanked on the lever to retract the wheels.

"Give me a report!"

Janet turned her head sharply left and craned to watch the submarine—it was a routine they had practiced a dozen times while they sat in the hangar bay waiting to be hoisted to the flight deck. Fortunately for them, the dull gray light of pre-dawn had given way to the first clear rays from the sun as it poked itself to within a few degrees of the horizon. "The sub is maintaining position. No sign of movement," she shouted into O'Brien's ear. As the aircraft was wheeled into a tighter turn to make its approach toward the submarine, the steep angle of bank gave Janet an even better look at the long, menacing silhouette that was their target. "No torpedo wakes!"

"Are you sure?"

"Yes!" Janet scanned the front of the submarine again, but she was certain that there was no sign of any bubbles, no visible trail of wake. According to what Drew had told her earlier, a long and frothy wake would be the indication that meant that torpedoes had been released toward the *Yorktown*. "No torpedoes. There are people on the sub's bridge, it looks like three of them. Wait. They're going below."

"No time left." O'Brien snapped the airplane's flight controls hard left. There was an instant response from the old B-25. As it wheeled around in a nightmarishly tight turn, the airframe began to vibrate in the beginning throes of a pre-stall buffet. Fighting his natural piloting instincts, O'Brien disregarded the signal and kept the airplane in as tight a circle as he dared. "Bomb bay open! Get ready!"

"Open!" Janet pushed down the next lever in the sequence as she had been taught. A sudden rush of noise and air added to the already high volume that filled the cockpit of the old airplane. She looked over her shoulder to verify that the big doors in the center of the belly had opened. They had. Looking past the long and bright-green body of the lone torpedo that sat in the bomb bay, Janet could see the waves and whitecaps that visibly lapped over one another only a few hundred feet below. The long white cord that trailed from the cockpit to the makeshift torpedo release clips dangled loosely. "Bomb bay open! The torpedo is ready!"

"Stand by . . . stand by . . ." O'Brien's words, still shouted, were mostly lost to the slipstream and the engine noises that nearly deafened them both. But even if he couldn't be heard, it was now more obvious what the plan was, more than obvious when the torpedo would need to be released. The submarine—sitting low but motionless in the water—began to rapidly grow in size as it framed itself, dead center, in the windshield of the B-25. The old airplane continued to dive toward the submarine. "Stand by . . ." O'Brien pushed farther down on the flight controls to get even closer to the top of the ocean. He picked his right hand up off the aircraft's throttles and held it conspicuously in front of Janet. "Now!" he shouted, as soon as the proper moment had arrived. His hand dropped down to confirm his verbal signal, just in case she couldn't hear his words.

But Janet had heard him clearly. She tugged hard on the long cord that, moments before, she had wrapped around her hands. The arrangement that the people from the torpedo assembly group had come up with to release the old torpedo from the bomb bay seemed a simple one—and one that everyone thought would be more dependable than the airplane's rusted-out bomb release system. But even before the cord had reached its full travel, Janet could tell from the sickening feeling in the pit of her stomach that something had gone wrong.

"What happened?" O'Brien shouted. He was unable to take his eyes off the flight instruments, unable to look away from the view out the windshield in order to turn around to look for himself. The black hull of the submarine flashed beneath the blunt nose of the B-25 as O'Brien waited to hear what Janet would tell him.

Janet looked over her shoulder. The bright-green torpedo was still in the bomb bay, although it now hung at an odd angle. The makeshift nose clip had released as it should have, but the tail cord had not. The torpedo was now stuck, half in and half out, its explosive nose section jammed hard against the forward edge of the bomb bay of the old B-25.

After he had given the order, it took Jerome Zindell several seconds to realize that the torpedoes from the *Trout*, for some unknown reason, had failed to fire.

Edward McClure, who had positioned himself at the far

edge of the submarine's bridge in order to have the best view of the sinking of the *Yorktown*, whirled around and faced Zindell. "What the hell have you done? Where are the goddamn torpedoes?"

"Christ Almighty." Zindell stood where he was, his gaze locked straight ahead. He ignored McClure and concentrated instead on the voice that poured into his earphones, the voice from the control room that explained that nothing at all had happened after the firing buttons had been pressed.

"Do something, hurry, quickly." Olga pointed frantically to the airplane on the *Yorktown*'s flight deck, which had just begun its takeoff roll a few seconds before.

"He'll never get it off in time." But while McClure watched, the old B-25 managed to lift off the flight deck and begin its climb. "He's coming this way," McClure said as the three of them watched the bomber start a tight turn that would eventually bring it around and headed toward them. "Get those damn torpedoes launched. We've got to get the hell out of here!"

Zindell ripped the communications headset off his head and flung it on the deck. "I don't know what happened, it was all set up!" Without waiting for either of them to comment, he stepped into the opened hatchway in the floor of the submarine's bridge and scrambled down the ladder as rapidly as he could, his one hand lurching from rung to rung. "Batten down the hatches, we're going to dive," he called up to Olga who was the last person to leave the *Trout*'s bridge.

"No we're not. Not until we fire those torpedoes." McClure had caught up to Zindell, and the two men stood face to face in the small conning tower above the control room.

"We can fire torpedoes after we submerge."

"You told me that it's easier to fire from the surface. I don't want to take any chances of missing."

"As long as we stay close to the *Yorktown* and pointed straight toward it, the torpedo shot is still relatively easy—at least it will be if we can get the goddamned torpedoes to work." Zindell, who looked perplexed, started to turn away.

McClure grabbed him by the shoulder. "Listen to me. Carefully. I don't care if we're on the surface or submerged, but if there's any goddamn way on earth you can fire those torpedoes, you sure as hell better do it. That was our deal."

McClure looked coldly at Zindell. "You'll be sorry if you don't, I promise you."

"But what about the airplane?" Zindell said. "What's he trying to do?" He looked up at the hatchway above his head, which Olga had already sealed shut. For all his years of submarine experience, Zindell had never been under an actual attack before, it was a new and frightening experience for him.

"Relax, it doesn't mean a thing." McClure leaned back against the periscope housing in a deliberate attempt to appear casual. "They've probably got a dozen people crammed inside that old wreck of an airplane—it wouldn't hold any more than that." An odd smirk played at the corners of McClure's mouth. "The women and children bullshit, more than likely."

"How do you know that the pilot isn't up there alone? How do you know that he doesn't intend to crash into us?"

"Don't be ridiculous." McClure waved his hand at where the hull's roofline curved above his head. "If that was his intention, we wouldn't be standing here right now. He would've accomplished his goal already." At that very moment, a low roar from the airplane came close enough to be heard, even inside the sealed submarine. The noise passed as suddenly as it had begun. "See what I mean? He's trying to scare us, that's all. There's nothing else he can do. It's a pure bluff."

"You're guessing." But Zindell had to admit that what McClure said made sense. After a few seconds he nodded reluctantly in agreement. "Okay. We'll submerge first, then I'll work on the torpedoes. We'll have Olga stay at the periscope, to keep us aligned on the target." Zindell nodded toward the woman, then turned back to McClure. "But if we haven't found the problem in the next ten minutes or so, we're going to forget the ship and the ransom money and get the hell out of here."

"Fine." McClure knew that he had no intention of letting the *Yorktown* and that money go—not in ten minutes, not in ten hours—but there was no need to argue that point just yet. In ten more minutes the torpedoes from the *Trout* might well be headed toward the *Yorktown*.

"Submerge the boat," Zindell ordered as he descended the ladder that led from the conning tower to the control room below. "To periscope depth. Maintain our position and bearing on the target."

"Yessir." The men in the control room responded quickly to the order, and soon the U.S.S. *Trout* was on its way down to a depth of fifty feet where only its periscope would stick above the waves.

"What do you think?" McClure finally asked after he had watched Zindell hover over the master firing board for a short while. "Can you fix it?"

"I don't know yet, it seems so . . ." Zindell's eyes, which had roamed continuously up and down the electronic board, suddenly found the answer he was looking for. "Son-of-a-bitch!" He spun around, his face contorted with anger. "The firing board has been *manually overridden!*"

"What does that mean?" McClure took an involuntary step backward, away from Zindell.

"The water slug, you idiot! Didn't you and Olga reposition the override controls after you had manually fired that water slug from the forward torpedo room!"

"No . . . I didn't know we were supposed to."

Zindell didn't wait for the rest of McClure's explanation, he turned and began to run as fast as he could through the narrow confines of the submarine toward the forward torpedo room. *I can fire the torpedoes manually.* He knew now that he could get the torpedoes away by individually activating the manual firing levers on each of the tubes, that it would be faster to do it that way than to try to reconnect the master firing board and put the electronic data back into sequence.

"Wait, I'm coming!"

Zindell ignored McClure's shout, although he could hear the man's footsteps only a short distance behind him as the two of them began to sprint down the narrow corridor that led past the captain's stateroom and the wardroom. *Another minute at the most, then we can get the hell out of here.* Zindell didn't bother to look back over his shoulder to check if McClure was still there because he now knew that he didn't need any help from anyone. After he repositioned a few valves and levers, he would be able to manually launch the torpedoes at the *Yorktown*. Jerome Zindell stepped across the hatchway sill and headed straight for the torpedo tubes. *Fucking McClure. He's a goddamned madman. He'll get us killed if I let him.*

Once he had flown over the submarine, Drew O'Brien started the B-25 into a shallow right bank. "Take the controls—I'm going back."

"What should I do?" Her request had been more a plea than a question, but Janet did not hesitate to take the controls as she had been instructed.

"They'll feel very heavy. Keep the airspeed where it is." O'Brien pointed to the appropriate gauge on the copilot's panel as he began to get up from the pilot's chair. "A shallow turn, then straight and level to give yourself some room to maneuver. Once you've gone out far enough, turn back and line up on the sub like I did before."

"Wait!" Janet wrestled with the airplane's flight controls for another few seconds before she could divide her attention enough to finish what she was about to say. "Look out the side window—the submarine is beginning to dive!"

O'Brien leaned over Janet and watched out the side window. There was no doubt about it, the long black hull was settling slowly into the water. "But there's no forward movement, see?"

"What does that mean?"

"That he's staying in position. To fire torpedoes." Without waiting for her to answer, O'Brien jumped down the small step at the rear of the cockpit and moved farther back, the blast of swirling air and the roar from the incessant wind increased markedly. By the time he stood near the explosive nose cap of the bright-green torpedo, his eyes had begun to water from the bite of the cool, damp, erratic breeze that whirled around him. O'Brien turned toward the cockpit and cupped his hands around his mouth. "Head for the sub," he shouted as loud as he possibly could. "I'll push the torpedo out!"

Janet glanced over her shoulder toward him, a puzzled look on her face. She finally shook her head negatively to show that she could not hear what Drew had said, even though he was no more than fifteen feet away.

O'Brien turned toward the torpedo again. While he sat himself down on the crossbrace at the forward edge of the bomb bay, he prayed that she would figure out what he had meant. *I'll need to guess at our position, that's all I can do.* O'Brien began to try to concentrate on the airplane's motions, so he'd have some idea—no matter how approximate—of when they were near enough to the submarine again to attempt to drop their torpedo. *Be careful, this is our only chance.*

O'Brien grabbed a metal stanchion with his left hand in order to keep himself in position, then took hold of the dangling rope from the torpedo's aft release clip with his right. He looked down at the nose cap of the torpedo. The people on the *Yorktown* had wired the explosives to make the weapon as foolproof as possible, so they simply mounted a firing pin into the center of the nose cap. Whenever that pin was forced inward, it would trigger a blasting cap, which in turn would set off the high explosives. O'Brien placed his feet carefully to either side of the protruding pin, in order to keep himself from inadvertently pushing against it.

Suddenly, the B-25's wings began to rock vigorously from side to side. O'Brien grabbed hold of the metal stanchion to his left even tighter, to prevent himself from being tossed out the opened bomb bay a few feet beyond where he sat on the crossbeam. *What the hell is happening?* He shot a quick glance over his shoulder to try to determine if the violent motions were turbulence or a control problem, but from where he sat he could not tell. The rocking motion stopped for an instant, but then began even harder the second time. *Intentional.* The rolling motions were too positive, deliberate and rapid to be outside a pilot's control. *A signal. Janet is signaling me to release the torpedo!* O'Brien responded by immediately yanking on the cord with his one hand while he pushed against the nose of the torpedo with every ounce of energy that he could force into his legs.

"Let me help."

"Leave me alone, you've done enough already—you damn madman!" With his one arm, Zindell pushed McClure away. He then turned back to the number-one torpedo tube. All the other valves and levers had already been positioned, all that was necessary now was for him to press the manual firing pin.

Jerome Zindell reached up toward the last switch in the sequence needed to manually fire the number-one torpedo at the *Yorktown*.

As she had been ordered, Olga Rodriguez had remained in the conning tower of the *Trout*. She had raised and focused the periscope, and had spent the first few seconds determining that the submarine's position in relation to the *Yorktown* had remained stable. Then she began to scan the sky for sight of the airplane that had taken off from the carrier's flight deck a few minutes before.

The first sight of the airplane came when the periscope was being swung through its port quarter. At first Olga thought that the airplane was going away from her, but within a few seconds she realized that it was growing in size—growing quickly, coming head-on, barreling down low and straight. *Our periscope is sticking ten feet above the waterline. That is what they are aiming toward!* The frightening sight of that warplane as it hurtled directly toward her caused Olga to freeze in position, her hands wrapped tightly in a death grip on the periscope's focus knobs, her eyes glued to the viewing lens.

Under the pressure of the force being applied to it, the nose cap of the bright-green Mark 14 torpedo was finally set free from where it had been jammed against the forward crossbrace of the aircraft bomb bay. The torpedo tumbled out into the slipstream, then fell quickly into the water a few hundred feet below. The propulsion gear inside the torpedo, which had been previously adjusted to run upon release from the aircraft, began to operate on schedule. The twin tail-mounted propellers on the torpedo were already rotating when the bright-green body disappeared beneath the surface of the sea. The depth guidance system inside the Mark 14 had been set to keep the torpedo at a depth of twenty feet, but because of the torpedo's weight and its release angle from the aircraft, it had dove down too far to begin with. The Mark 14 torpedo was in the process of realigning itself toward its proper depth setting when its nose cap impacted firmly against the flat metal side of the conning tower of the U.S.S. Trout.

• • •

Olga Rodriguez had not noticed the bright-green projectile as it fell from beneath the airplane and landed in the water not far from the submarine. Instead, she had kept her total attention riveted on the airplane itself. Olga yanked on the knob and rotated the lens of the periscope rapidly upward so she could visually follow the two-engine airplane as it passed harmlessly overhead. *They are trying to frighten us, it is all a bluff.* That was the final conscious thought that registered in Olga's mind.

The bright-green torpedo from the B-25 hit squarely against the flat side of the conning tower of the submarine, less than six feet from where Olga stood as she looked through the periscope. At impact, the high explosive in the nose cap detonated. The steel plates of the sidewall crushed inward as if they were no more than a stretched piece of thin plastic. Olga's body was pulverized into unrecognizable chunks of bloody flesh and smashed bone within an instant of the initial impact.

As the force of the sudden explosion continued and expanded, it began to act like a giant can opener. It slit the midsection of the submarine nearly in half, as if it were no more than a toy model being opened by a hacksaw. Inside the framework of the sub, every cross-member within twenty feet of the impact point snapped or buckled. What the carnage of the explosion itself did not do to the crew members and the equipment near to it, the on-rushing seawater did. As if an enormous dam had burst, a massive wall of water swept through the insides of what remained of the midsection of the submarine within a handful of seconds after the explosion. The individual crew members were battered unmercifully and then drowned, the sub's equipment torn from its mountings and swept away. The water spread quickly fore and aft into the remaining sections of the submarine that had not been initially damaged by the torpedo's explosive force. As the seawater spread through its hull, the U.S.S. *Trout* began to rapidly sink.

Jerome Zindell was thrown heavily to the deck when the torpedo exploded, his fingers being wrenched away from the manual firing pin of the number-one torpedo tube just before he could press it.

"What happened?!" Edward McClure picked himself off the

steel floor plates where he had been thrown near to Zindell. "What happened?!" he repeated. For the first time in his life he sounded, even to himself, uncontrollably frightened.

"We must've been hit." Zindell shook his dazed head to clear it from when the impact against the floor had nearly knocked him unconscious. "We've got to get out of here." But before he could do much more than stand up, Zindell saw the forward edge of the cascading water as it churned into the companionway of the adjacent compartment and toward the forward torpedo room where they stood. "The hatchway—hurry!" Zindell stumbled forward as the submarine lurched awkwardly beneath his feet. He struggled toward the doorway, the irregular movements of the sub as it wallowed from side to side making it even harder for him to keep his balance. "Close the hatch! Help me!"

The first of the water had already splashed across the steel threshold and into the forward torpedo room by the time McClure had arrived at the hatchway. Without a word, the two of them struggled to seal the door against the increasing force of the mounting water on the other side that rose higher and higher with every passing moment. Just before it would have been physically impossible for them to do it, the two men somehow managed to get the watertight door closed and its locking lever spun shut.

"Now what do we do?" McClure's eyes were wide, his heart pounded, his face was drenched with a combination of seawater and sweat.

Zindell took one quick breath to steady himself, then stumbled to his feet. "The emergency hatch in the ceiling." He pointed toward it. "It's the only way out."

The submarine suddenly began to lurch again. A loud and horrible creaking—the noise of grinding, twisting metal—came from somewhere behind them. "Hold on!" Zindell had shouted, but mostly for his own benefit. In spite of his tightened grip on the handle of the hatchway door, he was thrown to the floor again as the random, spastic motions of the submarine increased.

"We're going down, we're sinking—I'm getting the hell out of here!" McClure had not taken more than two steps in his panicked rush toward the escape hatch at the center of the room when all the interior lights suddenly went out. "Help me, God help me!" McClure continued to shout irrationally as he stumbled and fell to the floor again. The inside of the torpedo room was absolutely, impenetrably black.

Zindell ignored McClure's hysterical shouts. He groped his way forward, the familiar sections of the room falling into hand despite the nightmarish darkness that completely enveloped them. At one point he bumped into McClure's leg, but he said nothing. *Nuclear submarine* Thresher *sinks, 129 die*. As those old newspaper headlines flashed through his mind, Zindell continued to search for the ladder that would lead to the escape hatch. *One hundred twenty-nine, plus my father. My father.*

The noise of the first hull rivet as it exploded inward into the torpedo compartment was startlingly loud—as loud as a high-powered rifle being shot in the confines of a small room. "What was that—what's happening?" McClure was shouting again and thrashing around wildly at the aft section of the torpedo room, totally disoriented and in a full, uncontrolled panic. "Where the hell are you, goddamnit! Help me!"

But Zindell did not answer. *Rivets are blowing in. We're too deep. There's no escape*. He had just found the base of the ladder that led to the escape hatch, but instead of climbing upward he allowed his body to sink slowly down onto the floor. Several inches of water inside the torpedo room lapped over him as he sat stunned by what he now knew. *Too deep. Almost crush depth*. The escape hatch was useless because the submarine had already gone too deep, sunk too far toward the bottom of the ocean for anyone to live outside the boat for even a brief moment.

One hundred twenty-nine die as U.S.S. Thresher *sinks*. Zindell began to sob audibly and hysterically as more and more of the rivets from the overstressed hull continued to ricochet randomly across the insides of the doomed submarine. The rivets bounced noisily off the very steel plates that would soon collapse inward like eggshells. Zindell sat in the unnatural darkness the same way he knew that his father must have as he waited endlessly for that inescapable moment that was now nearly at hand. In a matter of another few seconds or few minutes at most, Jerome Zindell's life would be ended by the enormous pressure of the same sea that had crushed his father to death more than twenty years before.

Drew O'Brien moved forward from the bomb bay area of the old B-25 and stood behind the copilot's seat. "There's no doubt that we've sunk it," O'Brien said in a moderate voice as he pointed over Janet's shoulder and toward the sections of wreckage that floated on the waves. The airplane's engine power had been pulled back far enough to a lower setting to make their cockpit conversation less of a strain. "There's an oil slick, too," O'Brien added as an expanding black smear bubbled up from the depths below. "The sub has gone down for sure."

"Thank God." Janet Holbrook banked the warplane into another circle of the area, this one wide enough to allow them to pass overhead the *Yorktown*. "Look—everyone's on the deck." She nodded toward the front windshield. Ahead of them, the flight deck of the huge gray aircraft carrier was lined with the hostages from Flight 255. "They're waving at us."

"Yes." O'Brien laid his hand on Janet's shoulder. "Go ahead and rock the wings again, just like you did before."

"Okay."

As she rocked the aircraft's wings vigorously from side to side in answer to the people who waved at them from below, O'Brien watched her. *She's an incredible woman. We couldn't have done this without her.* O'Brien opened his mouth to tell Janet how courageous and competent she had been, how indispensable. But before the first words had come out, he changed his mind and decided not to say anything, not just yet.

Janet pushed slightly forward on the control wheel and pitched the airplane even lower. She flew the old B-25 perpendicular to the broad deck of the *Yorktown,* no more than fifty feet above the heads of the people who owed their lives to this old relic of a warplane. Once the carrier's flight deck had flashed by beneath them, Janet glanced over her shoulder toward Drew. "Which way should we head?"

"Straight west, until we see the coast. We've got more than enough fuel to get to dry land. We should be able to find a suitable airport as soon as we get to the coast."

"What about the people on the *Yorktown?*"

"I'm sure that the Navy will pick them up shortly. There's no doubt that they've been watching every move out here, at least from a distance."

"That makes sense." Janet lapsed into silence for a few seconds. She then looked back at the man who stood behind her. "Do you want to fly now?" She gestured toward the flight controls that she held in her hands.

"Absolutely not. We've seen enough of your flying technique to know that you don't need anyone to bail you out." O'Brien allowed his fingers to gently massage her shoulder. "I'll give you some help with the landing, but other than that, this is your flight. You've certainly more than proven that already."

"Thanks." Janet smiled gently and sincerely, then turned back to the flight controls.

"Just hold this heading. We should be able to see the coast shortly."

"Right."

O'Brien moved from behind Janet's seat and climbed into the pilot's chair. Once he had buckled his seat belt, he glanced toward her again. Janet Holbrook was, he was certain, the most beautiful, competent and courageous woman he had ever met. Once they were on the ground, Drew O'Brien intended to spend considerable time telling her so. When he was finished telling her that, he intended to tell her much, much more.